DAYLIGHT COMES

JUDITH
MILLER

FREEDOM'S PATH · *book 3*

DAYLIGHT
COMES

BETHANYHOUSE
MINNEAPOLIS, MINNESOTA

Published by Bethany House Publishers
11400 Hampshire Avenue South
Bloomington, Minnesota 55438

Bethany House Publishers is a division of
Baker Publishing Group, Grand Rapids, Michigan.

Printed in the United States of America

ISBN-13: 978-0-7642-0000-7
ISBN-10: 0-7642-0000-3

Library of Congress Cataloging-in-Publication Data

McCoy-Miller, Judith.
    Daylight comes / Judith Miller.
        p.   cm. — (Freedom's path ; bk. 3)
    ISBN-13: 978-0-7642-0000-7 (pbk.)
    ISBN-10: 0-7642-0000-3 (pbk.)
    1. Nicodemus (Kan.)—Fiction. I. Title.
    PS3613.C3858D39   2006
    813'.54—dc22   2006019416

To
Ellen Irwin,
with thanks for your
steadfast friendship
and encouragement

*The path of the righteous is like the first gleam of dawn,
shining ever brighter till the full light of day.*

—PROVERBS 4:18 NIV

CHAPTER

— 1 —

Nicodemus, Kansas • August 1882

W*hat have you done? What have you done?* The horse's hooves pounded out the words in an unrelenting cadence that constricted Moses Wyman's throat as tightly as a hangman's noose.

He strained in the saddle and bowed his shoulders against the ache that had plagued him for the last five miles. The train ride from Topeka had been tiresome, but the final miles atop his sturdy horse had proved the most grueling leg of the journey. His time away from home had lasted longer than anticipated. And though Moses hungered to once again embrace his wife, he feared his news would dampen the sweetness of their reunion.

The horse snorted and pranced, wanting his head as they approached this more familiar territory. They'd both been gone far too long—Moses in Topeka, where he'd served as the elected representative of Graham County at the statewide Republican convention, and his horse at the livery in Ellis with Chester Goddard. With only a nudge, the horse galloped northward until they were a short distance from town.

With a tug on the reins, Moses slowed the animal to a trot and entered the outskirts of Nicodemus. Since the day he'd arrived in Nicodemus, he'd loved this town and its people. Even though he'd not been one of the original settlers, Moses delighted in telling others their story. He swelled with pride whenever given the opportunity to relate how the small band of ill-prepared African Americans, who had arrived in Kansas with little more than their dreams and expectations, had successfully established a town for themselves. Believing the promises of the men representing the company that had plotted the town, they'd come west expecting what they'd been promised: an established community of businesses, churches, homes, and a school. Instead they'd been greeted by nothing but the empty Kansas prairie. In spite of the unfulfilled promises, most of those first pioneers had remained. With an indefatigable determination and an unflagging faith in God, they'd built homes, churches, a school, and businesses. Now Moses, too, hungered to contribute something more to the community. Editing and printing the newspaper provided a measure of fulfillment, but not enough to smother the burning fire in his belly. He wanted to see Nicodemus spread her wings and soar, and grow as abundantly as did the fields of wheat and corn that dotted the township's acreage.

New residents often arrived in Nicodemus—folks who opened a business in the heart of their little town, or purchased a farm on its outskirts, or sought employment among other people of color. But for each one that came, another departed. This was a grueling place, with its ongoing plagues of harsh weather and hard times. One thing Moses knew for certain: for a town to grow, it needed the railroad.

Urging his horse onward, he caught sight of the home he shared with his wife. Truth stood on the porch as if she'd known the exact moment he would arrive. His heart swelled as he waved and called her name. Without a doubt, she had been God's greatest blessing in his life. He prayed she would accept his unexpected news with enthusiasm. However, his heart told him otherwise. He would tell her first thing. Then again, perhaps he should wait until the entire family was gathered together before breaking the news. . . .

"Moses! I've missed you so. It seems as though you've been gone for months." Truth raised up on tiptoe to meet his lips, her kiss filled with longing. "I'm never going to agree to such a separation again. I want you right here in Nicodemus with me. One of the other men can represent Graham County at those conventions in Topeka."

"Indeed, they *may* need to elect someone else as their representative in the future. However, I believe you would enjoy Topeka. I'm only sorry you weren't feeling well enough to go along with me this time. I must say you're fairly glowing right now. The doctor has pronounced you well?"

With an enthusiastic nod, she confirmed he had declared her fit as a fiddle. Gently tugging on his hand, Truth led him into the house and to the parlor. Moses dropped down beside her on the brocade divan.

Truth was nibbling her lower lip—a sure sign she had something important to tell him. "I want to hear all that occurred at the convention," she said. "But first I have a special surprise to share with you."

His wife enjoyed a surprise more than anyone he knew, and he wondered what she had come up with while he was gone. Perhaps she had planned a special meal with the entire family. He hoped so, for he was hungry. He leaned forward.

Truth's eyes sparkled as they met his. "We're going to have a baby, Moses. Can you believe it?" She stroked her hand down his cheek. "That's why I wasn't feeling well." She clasped his fingers. "Isn't this wonderful? Aren't you thrilled? You're going to be a father. Imagine! We're going to have our very own child."

His stomach lurched and he swallowed hard. A tumult of emotions assaulted him. He jumped to his feet and pulled Truth into an embrace, fearful she would detect the panic in his eyes. "I'm delighted, my dear." He sounded like a croaking bullfrog and gulped a lungful of air, praying that he would quickly regain his composure.

"I can hear the emotion in your voice. I know you had given up hope."

Moses clung to her. How could he possibly reveal his news now? They would celebrate this moment with unbridled joy. He would tell her later.

She wiggled from his embrace and graced him with a look of pure adoration. "I'm so happy, Moses. I've invited the family to supper tonight so that we can make the announcement together. I've not told anyone because I wanted you to be the first to know, but this has been the most difficult secret I've ever been required to keep."

Leaning forward, he kissed her forehead. "Thank you, my dear. Keeping such news to yourself must have been extremely difficult." He chuckled, hoping to mask his apprehension.

She watched him carefully as he sat down. "You don't appear quite as excited as I expected. Although I must admit I didn't know *how* you would react." Her brows furrowed. "Was there some sort of difficulty in Topeka?"

He could easily clear the air by revealing exactly what had occurred in Topeka. But he wouldn't spoil this moment in their lives. "You know that I have always prayed for children, Truth. Still, I must admit I am more than a little surprised. Please try to understand—I had no idea . . ."

She smiled broadly before kissing his cheek. "Of course you didn't—nor did I. Let me fix you a cup of coffee and then you can tell me about the convention. I'm anxious to hear how you were received and how the voting went."

Moses didn't attempt to stop her. He needed a few moments to gather his wits about him. The news of the child made him question whether he'd made a mistake. Perhaps he should have prayed more. Had his decision been one of pride rather than God's urging? He rubbed his forehead and longed for a solution to this dilemma.

More than anything, he wanted to be alone and think. He stood and massaged the back of his neck with one hand. "I'm going to take my bag upstairs and unpack," he called. "There's no hurry for the coffee, Truth. If you don't mind, I may take a short nap."

Truth peeked into the hallway. "In that case, I'll go ahead with my supper preparations while you rest. I'm sure you're tired. I can hear about the convention along with the rest of the family at supper."

She retreated into the kitchen and Moses trudged up the stairs, feeling the weight of his recent decision. He opened his bag and carefully separated the clean clothes from the dirty, the slow, methodical process somehow calming his nerves. After removing his shoes and jacket, he lay down on the bed to pray. He had uttered only a few words to God when his eyelids began to droop.

Moses was uncertain how much time had passed when he awoke to the sound of voices. Jerking into an upright position, he yanked his shoes onto his feet and grabbed his jacket. Anxious to greet their guests, he rushed down the staircase while shoving his arms into the sleeves of his waistcoat. A shrug of his broad shoulders forced the coat upward, and the wool fabric settled evenly across his back. Stopping in front of the hallway mirror, he straightened his tie and wondered why his wife hadn't awakened him before their guests arrived. Surely she realized he would have preferred a few moments to formulate his thoughts.

"There he is!" His father-in-law's voice boomed throughout the house when he caught sight of Moses in the hall. "We're all anxious to hear 'bout what went on in Topeka." Ezekiel patted the seat beside him as the rest of the family offered their greetings. "Sit down and tell us."

Truth wagged her index finger back and forth. "Not now, Pappy. Supper is ready, and I know how you men are—you'll start talking and I'll never get you around the table."

Moses pulled Truth into a gentle hug. "Your daughter's correct, Mr. Harban. We don't want this fine meal to grow cold."

With a sigh of resignation, Ezekiel sat down at the table and the rest of the family followed. Moses sat at one end and Ezekiel at the other. Truth's sister and brother-in-law, Jarena and Thomas Grayson, were seated on one side, with Silas and Grace on the other. Silas Morgan was their only guest who wasn't a relative; however, if he had his way, he and Truth's twin sister would soon be wed. Refusing to remain in the high chair, Thomas and Jarena's little daughter, Jennie, rested comfortably on her mother's lap. The little girl wiggled her tiny fingers toward the bowl of mashed potatoes near her mother's plate.

Moses eyed the child, who had turned one several months ago. Little Jennie had been named after Ezekiel's deceased wife, and the entire family doted upon her. Somehow it was difficult to imagine he and Truth would have a child of their own at this time next year. The mere thought of his wife's condition caused his worries to rise anew.

After Ezekiel had offered a prayer of thanks for their meal, he turned his attention to Moses. "Now, then, pass dat platter of chicken down the table and start to talkin'. I wanna know ever'thing that happened from the minute you get off the train in Topeka 'til you get back home."

Truth patted Moses's hand. "No politics at the table, please. The medical community agrees that food is best digested when table conversation is pleasant rather than conflict-ridden and divisive."

Ezekiel stared at his daughter as though her hair had turned green. "You sound like Dr. Boyle's daughter 'stead of mine. When'd you take up usin' all that highfalutin' talk 'bout medicine and the like?"

"There's no need to make fun just because I'm attempting to use proper grammar. In fact, when we were growing up, Jarena constantly insisted that Grace and I speak properly. Isn't that right, Jarena?"

Her older sister nodded while attempting to curtail little Jennie's antics and a possible catastrophe with the platter of chicken.

The dinner conversation turned to the usual topics of weather, crops, the Sunday morning sermon, and little Jennie's latest accomplishments. Moses had hoped to mention his news during their meal, but Truth's remonstration against political discussions had quashed that possibility.

"I prepared a lemon cake for dessert. Moses's favorite," Truth announced. "After we've finished our cake, Moses and I have an announcement to make."

Ezekiel's eyebrows arched as he looked down the table at his son-in-law. Moses gave a slight shrug of his shoulders and turned his attention back to his dinner plate. The sooner they finished eating, the sooner the entire ordeal would be over. Once Truth announced the baby, and congratulations were extended, Ezekiel would turn the conversation back toward the Republican convention. That's when Moses would make *his* announcement. With any luck, the family would embrace the news and Truth would be caught up in their excitement. He hoped God had looked with favor upon the brief prayer request he'd uttered before falling asleep earlier today.

With the family gathered in the parlor a short time later, Truth nudged Moses. "Go ahead and tell them."

He tugged at his jacket and cleared his throat. Before he could speak, his father-in-law grinned broadly and pointed at them. "You two's gonna have a young'un, ain't ya?"

Truth folded her arms across her waist and frowned. "Pappy! You spoiled our surprise."

Ezekiel laughed and shook his head. "Don' take no big education to figure out what kinda surprise you was gonna tell. You was feelin' poorly every mornin' fer two months afore Moses left fer Topeka."

Moses scratched beneath the edge of his starched shirt collar. "Maybe it didn't surprise any of the rest of you, but it certainly astonished me. I'm feeling rather foolish that it didn't occur to me before I left for Topeka."

"Ain't no need fer you to feel foolish. With all her medical talk 'bout digestion and the like, I reckon Truth is the one who shoulda figured out what was ailin' her." He guffawed and slapped his knee.

Moses clasped her hand and gave his wife an encouraging smile. "This is an important event for us, and Truth wanted us to be together when we shared it with all of you. I'm pleased she waited until I came home from Topeka. She wanted to give me the good news first."

Truth brightened, and Moses clasped her hand while she accepted congratulations from her family.

As the women continued to chatter, Ezekiel clapped Moses on the shoulder. "Let's pray fer a boy. We could use some more men in this here fambly. Now if my daughter ain't got no more objections, I'd like to hear 'bout the convention."

Thomas pulled his chair closer. "I'm wantin' to hear, too. How did they treat you in the capital city, Moses?"

Suddenly the room became quiet. Everyone was looking at him— all of them anxious to hear the details of his representation as a delegate to the convention. There was no holding back now. He carefully related the events, answering each of their questions in detail, all the while attempting to gather his faltering courage.

"I's mighty glad you was there, Moses. Makes me plumb proud

that my son-in-law represented Graham County. Course, I was proud of ya anyway. Did them fellas know Governor St. John appointed you to serve as county clerk fer Graham County last year?"

The question provided the opening he needed. "As a matter of fact, they did. What's more, the day I arrived in Topeka, members of the Republican Party approached me and asked if I'd consider running for state auditor."

For a moment everyone was silent, but then their voices exploded into an onslaught of questions, each one attempting to be heard above the other. Moses finally signaled for quiet. "I can't make out any of your questions with everyone talking at once."

Truth's lower lip trembled. "You didn't agree, did you?" Her eyes shone with fear—or was that anger?

"Course he did, gal. Why, jest being asked to serve is a genuine honor." Ezekiel leaned forward and rested his long arms across his thighs.

Moses avoided his wife's piercing gaze. "You're correct, Ezekiel, I did agree. They were pleased by my acceptance. In fact, I was on the ballot with the final contender."

"A white fella?" Ezekiel rubbed his large hands together and leaned even closer.

"Yes."

"Now ain' that somethin' to be proud of! Did ya make a decent showin' when the votin' was all said and done?"

Moses nodded. "I won the bid."

CHAPTER

— 2 —

I *won the bid.* Nothing had been the same since Moses had uttered those four words. Truth pulled the bedcovers over her head, wanting to remain buried in the darkness just a while longer. *Just a while longer and then I'll get up. Just a while longer and everything will be fine. Just a while longer and I can accept Moses's decision. Just a while longer and then I can breathe. Really breathe.*

The air had rushed from her lungs in one giant whoosh the night he'd announced his candidacy, and she hadn't been able to inhale a deep breath since. The unexpected pronouncement continued to swirl in her head by day and visit her dreams by night. Not only had his revelation surprised her, it had rendered her powerless. She'd taken to her bed and remained there.

While she'd been devastated by the news, her family had been euphoric, thrilled for what his election to office would mean to their people and to the entire town of Nicodemus. She, too, understood the honor and the possible benefits—but not now, and not Moses. Let someone else go.

Cold fear gripped her heart with each thought of moving to Topeka and being separated from her family. How could she possibly give birth to her first child surrounded by total strangers? *Please don't let Moses win the election.* A tear slipped down her cheek as she whispered her prayer into the layers of blankets that covered her head. She tried to lift the sheet from her face but couldn't find the strength for even that simple task.

Moses had promised a visit from the doctor if she wasn't up and about by the time he returned at noon. Yet with each attempt to push away the covers, her hands froze in place and a tiny voice said: *Just a little while longer.* And each time, she complied. As the morning sun spilled into the room and threatened to erase her cocoon of darkness, Truth nosed deeper into the covers and spread her fingers across her stomach. Their baby rested somewhere deep beneath her outstretched hand. Already, she wanted to offer protection—keep him safe at home surrounded by family who would love and safeguard him. *This is a time to be filled with joy—not fear and foreboding.* She repeated those words over and over until she could finally peek out from beneath the covers.

Blinking against the sunlight, Truth sat up slowly and then wiggled her feet into the slippers beside the bed. Bracing her knuckles against the mattress, she pushed herself upright. *There!* She'd managed to uncover her head and stand up. Surely, the rest should prove easier. At least she hoped so.

Very slowly, she made her way down the hall. Light filtered

through the nursery window and scribbled spiny designs across the floor. With each gust of wind through the branches, the jagged pattern twisted and curled as it beckoned Truth forward. Her slippers whispered across the wood as she walked into the tiny room she'd sketched into their house drawings less than two years ago. Even though she and Moses had accepted their childless state, they'd agreed a nursery shouldn't be dismissed. Just in case.

However, she hadn't objected when Moses had made the tiny room into a small library and sitting room shortly after they'd moved into the house. He would often get up during the night and sit in the room, reflecting upon ideas for the next edition of the newspaper. Nevertheless, the day after her doctor's visit, she'd packed many of his books into wooden crates. The room would need different wallpaper—something in pale yellow and white would be nice. If Moses won the election, new wallpaper wouldn't matter. They'd be living in Topeka, and her baby wouldn't sleep in this little nursery adjacent to their bedroom. Once again, she sent a prayer winging toward heaven. *Please don't let him win the election.*

Now that she was up, she should finish packing the books. The bookshelves must be emptied regardless of whether Moses won or lost the election. She had removed only a few volumes when a loud knock sounded at the front door. Truth peeked out the nursery window, but the porch roof blocked her view. She could see nothing below. If she checked the window in her bedroom she might be able to glimpse a carriage on the street.

She stopped short as she neared her dresser. The mirror image staring back at her was proof enough she couldn't—no, she *wouldn't*—

answer the door. Dark circles underscored each of her dark brown eyes, and her hair stood on end. She wasn't even dressed. However, the familiar click and groan of the front door proved a remarkable incentive. With lightning speed, she ran to her room, grabbed her pale blue chambray wrapper from the foot of the bed, and shoved her arms into the sleeves.

She was tying the belt when her older sister called out. "Truth? Are you home? It's me—Jarena."

For a moment she considered tiptoeing down the hallway to hide in the linen closet. *Silly thought.* There was no need for such antics. Jarena wouldn't rebuke her for remaining abed so late in the day—or for her unkempt appearance.

Truth had nearly calmed her frayed nerves when the sound of murmuring voices drifted up the stairs. *Someone was with Jarena!* Bad enough Jarena should find her in this disheveled state so late in the morning, but she couldn't bear for one of the neighbors to see her. Perhaps it was merely her other sister, Grace, with Jarena.

I'd best find out who's with her. "I'm not dressed, Jarena. Are you alone?"

"You ain' dressed? What's got into you, gal? We's comin' upstairs right now."

Miss Hattie! Truth knew the older woman's announcement wasn't open for discussion. She needed to waylay them for at least a few minutes. "Is that you, Miss Hattie?"

"You knows it's me, Truth."

The tip of Miss Hattie's parasol clicked a rhythmic pace as she ascended the steps. Truth made a hurried return to the mirror and grimaced at the sight. Not much she could do in thirty seconds except brace herself for Miss Hattie's appearance.

Miss Hattie had been a friend of the Harban family long before they departed Kentucky, and the old woman brooked no nonsense— from anyone. She had crowned herself matriarch of Nicodemus and all its inhabitants soon after the first group of settlers had arrived in Kansas. Since those early days, Miss Hattie had ruled with an iron hand. No doubt she had come to Truth's house today to offer an opinion and issue advice.

The old woman's form soon filled the doorway. She pointed her ancient umbrella at Truth. "Land alive, jest look at you! How long since you been outta that bed?"

Truth bowed her head. "Only a couple of days. I wasn't expecting visitors."

Miss Hattie shuffled across the room and plopped down on the edge of the bed. "Now that there goes without sayin'." She turned her attention to Truth's sister, standing in the doorway. "You comin' in here, Jarena?"

Jarena came inside the bedroom, cradling little Jennie in her arms. "Sorry to get you out of bed, Truth. We stopped by the newspaper office before coming to the house. Miss Hattie wanted to offer her congratulations, and Moses said he was sure you'd be pleased to see us. He said to let myself in if you didn't answer."

Truth raked her fingers through her hair. "I am pleased to see you. I was in the midst of packing some books when you arrived."

Miss Hattie frowned and wagged her head back and forth. "That there how you dress to do your housework nowadays? In your night-clothes?"

Truth ignored the question and opened the doors of her wardrobe. "If you'll give me a few minutes, I'll join you downstairs. Perhaps you and Miss Hattie could make some coffee." Truth cast a pleading look at her sister.

Miss Hattie thumped the tip of her umbrella on the wood floor. "You ain' even made no coffee yet? You done got you a severe case of the lazies since you moved to town." The elderly woman used one of the bedposts to steady herself as she stood up. "See that you's down them stairs in ten minutes. I ain' gonna spend all my visitin' time sittin' and waitin' fer you to decide to get yerself dressed." She shook her head as she lumbered toward the door. "Um, um, what would your pappy say 'bout such goings-on."

Once again, Truth knew the old woman didn't expect a response. She'd learned long ago that it was usually best to remain silent where Miss Hattie was concerned. The woman had an opinion about every-thing from raising children to planting corn, and no one was ever allowed to disagree, especially if you were younger than she was—and there was nobody in Nicodemus any older than Miss Hattie!

Truth pulled a dress from the wardrobe and tossed it across the bed. Though she longed for a confidante—someone who might listen and understand, someone who could explain away her fearsome thoughts and dreams—Truth knew that person would not be Miss Hattie.

Moses had likely decided the two women would prove more effec-tive in getting her up and moving than his threat to bring the doctor home with him. Nevertheless, Truth would have preferred the doctor's ministrations to Miss Hattie's critical looks and sharp tongue. Unfortunately, she'd had no say in the matter.

Moving quickly, Truth washed her face, donned the dress, and patted her unruly hair into place. Her appearance remained far from respectable, but there was little more she could do in the brief time allotted by Miss Hattie. The rasping noise of the coffee grinder muffled her visitors' chatter, but their animated banter suggested they were in the midst of a weighty discussion. *Probably about me.* The room fell silent when she walked into the kitchen. Proof enough that she'd been their topic of their conversation. Not that she was surprised—or even cared all that much. She'd be the first to admit her behavior had been far from normal for the past several days.

"Don't let me interrupt your conversation, ladies."

"Oh, I's not gonna quit talkin'. I done come here for a visit. Now set yourself down." Miss Hattie pointed at one of the chairs.

Truth did as she was told but truly wished Miss Hattie would quit issuing orders. After all, this wasn't the woman's home. "What brings the two of you visiting today?"

Miss Hattie shifted little Jennie in her arms. "When Jarena tol' me the doctor give you good news, I was hankering to offer my best wishes. I know you and Moses is pleased. To tell you the truth, I was beginning to wonder if the two of you was ever gonna have a young'un. You's as slow 'bout starting a family as you was 'bout gettin' married."

Truth bristled at the remark. As usual, Miss Hattie had overstepped her bounds. "I'm *delighted* we were able to set your mind at ease, Miss Hattie."

Before the old woman could rebuke her for the mocking response, Truth jumped up, removed coffee cups from the cupboard, then set out the sugar and cream. Perhaps Jarena would take pity on her and urge Miss Hattie toward home once they had finished their coffee. Using an old apron to protect her hand, Truth lifted the coffeepot from the stove.

"I'm not certain the coffee has boiled long enough," Jarena said.

Ignoring her sister's warning, Truth filled the cups. "I like my coffee weak. It upsets my stomach when it's too strong." She placed a cup in front of Miss Hattie and another one before her sister.

Miss Hattie stared into the cup. "This here looks more like dishwater than coffee, but I won't complain since I'm your guest."

Truth stifled a laugh. Guest or not, the statement *was* a complaint, and all of them knew it. Rather than exchange barbs with Miss Hattie, Truth engaged Jarena in conversation. "Are you planning on visiting the dry goods store and returning home in time to prepare the noonday meal?"

Her sister shook her head. "Thomas is working in the fields with Pappy and Silas today. I packed dinner pails for all three of them so I wouldn't have to worry about hurrying back to the farm."

Truth's shoulders sagged. Her visitors might be here for the duration of the morning! She knew Miss Hattie didn't have to hurry home. The older woman lived with her granddaughter's family, and Nellie would be at home preparing the noonday meal. Truth secretly wished Nellie had come along instead of Miss Hattie. She wanted to ask Nellie about young Nathan's birth. Although the boy was nearly five now, the memory of his birth still haunted Truth. Nellie's son had arrived that first winter in Nicodemus, and both Nellie and the baby had nearly died in the process. Pappy had sent Jarena to lend aid to Nellie, but he'd instructed his two younger daughters to return to their bed. Truth had tried to sleep, but the screams had made it impossible. When she couldn't bear to listen any longer, Truth had buried her head under a cornhusk pillow. Each time Nellie had screamed, Truth had rustled the cornhusks, hoping to drown out the shrill cries. Her attempts hadn't worked, for in the quiet of a winter night, nothing covered the sound of Nellie's screams.

Miss Hattie clanked her cup back onto the saucer and startled Truth from her thoughts. "Let's get to the business at hand."

Truth's stomach lurched. Business at hand? "Whatever are you talking about, Miss Hattie?"

"'T's talkin' 'bout your attitude, young lady. I done heard how you been actin' since Moses got back from the capital city." She leaned forward, shifting Jennie in her arms, and pointed a crooked finger at Truth. "You ain' conducting yerself like a godly woman, Truth. You should be pleased as punch that them folks in the Republican Party wanted a colored man on the ballot. Why, that there is some fine news fer our people. What's wrong with you, gal? Instead of encouraging Moses, you take to yer bed to show him you's unhappy."

Truth bit her lip to hold back the tears that threatened to overflow. Hadn't she already said all of those things to herself? She didn't need Miss Hattie shaking a finger under her nose to remind her how she should act. She took a sip of coffee and calmed herself. Miss Hattie wouldn't understand her fears—she'd tell her to trust the Lord. Oh, she wanted to cast her cares before the Lord and forget they existed. But so far, her attempts had proved futile.

"I've *tried* to overcome my reluctant feelings about his candidacy." Those few words were as much as she could manage for the moment.

Jennie's eyes fluttered open. She whimpered for her mother and Miss Hattie handed the child over to Jarena's care. "I s'pose most of the time tryin' would be enough. But this here is different—it's important that one of us is runnin' fer office. 'Sides, I don't think none of us believe folks is gonna elect a colored man to such a high office as state auditor."

"You don't know that for certain. In fact, he won the nomination by a landslide with only six coloreds voting at the convention. There must be *some* white folks willing to elect a colored man. And we all know Moses is so light-skinned he can pass for white." Truth's hands trembled as she leaned back to rest her shoulders against the cool oak of the kitchen chair. The fact that she'd been able to counter Miss Hattie's statement only served to bolster her own fears.

Miss Hattie rubbed her hands together as though the words had been a balm to her weary soul. "Maybe we *will* get us a colored man elected. Praise the Lord!"

Struggling to maintain her composure, Truth walked to the stove to retrieve the coffeepot. "If that happens, I'll be forced to leave Nicodemus and move to Topeka, Miss Hattie."

"Is that what this here takin' to your bed is all about? Land alive, chil', if that's the worst thing that happens, you should be running up and down the streets shoutin' hallelujah."

Jarena grinned as Miss Hattie waved her arms overhead.

Truth swallowed back her tears. "This isn't funny, Jarena. If you had to pack up and leave all of us behind, you wouldn't take the matter so lightly. How would you have felt if none of your family had been around to lend support when Thomas was missing in Indian Territory? Or if no one you love had been there when Jennie was born?"

With a look of concern, Jarena patted Truth's hand. "But the one who loves you the very most *will* be there. You know Moses wouldn't miss the birth of his firstborn, and no matter where you go, you'll have Jesus with you."

Her sister's words were true enough, but they weren't the sympathy Truth longed to hear. "I know Moses loves me, Jarena. But the last thing I want to do when I'm expecting my first baby is to leave my home."

"You's jest scared, but having a baby ain' nothing to be afeard of. You's gonna have the good Lord to look after ya." Miss Hattie gazed heavenward and then nodded. "Yes indeed. I do believe the Lord is givin' you a blessed opportunity to rely on Him. You know the Bible says our God's jealous. He wants us to look to Him first when we's havin' difficult times 'stead of lookin' to each other for help. Maybe the Lord's wantin' you to trust Him to carry you through. Get out your Bible and read 'bout Sarai and Abram—you remember that story?" The old woman didn't wait for a reply. "God tol' Abram to go and Sarai followed with him. You think she was complainin' and layin' in the bed like you?"

Truth shuddered. "As I recall, Abram let his wife end up with the

Pharaoh down in Egypt for quite a while. You think that's supposed to encourage me?"

Miss Hattie sighed as she lifted her ample body from the chair. "God delivered both Abram and Sarai, and He blessed them in a mighty way. You think 'bout trustin' God and see if that story don't apply to you." She patted Truth's shoulder and picked up her parasol. "Now, I think it's time I get myself over to the store and give Miz Wilson my order."

Jarena stood up and hoisted Jennie to her hip. "I love you," she whispered as she placed a kiss on Truth's cheek. "Pappy said we'd come over after church on Sunday if you wanted some company. I'd be pleased to bring along some pies for dessert."

Truth followed her guests to the front door. "That would be nice. Maybe you and Grace and I can spend some time alone."

Miss Hattie turned after stepping onto the front porch. "While you's thinkin' 'bout what I said, you might consider doin' somethin' with that hair of yours." With a wink and a grin, she waved her parasol in the air and headed off with Jarena alongside her.

CHAPTER

— 3 —

Though her stubborn nature argued against it, Truth followed Miss Hattie's final instructions. After all, she *did* look disheveled. Peering into the dresser mirror, she tamed her hair into a presentable style before hastening back downstairs.

There would be little time to prepare the noonday meal, but she would do her best before Moses arrived home. Deciding to heat thick slices of ham and fry up a skillet of potatoes and onions, she set to work. While she peeled and sliced, an unbidden remembrance of her aunt Lilly and one of the predictions she had made came to mind— words of warning that Moses and Truth weren't well suited and a declaration that her sister, Jarena, was the better choice for a man of obvious power, distinction, and money. Most importantly, the money! Aunt Lilly could sniff out a wealthy man like a bee drawn to a nectar-filled bloom. And she had been correct in her assessment of Moses.

Truth's husband had been reared by a wealthy white family in

31

Massachusetts and educated far beyond the likes of most coloreds—at least any of the coloreds Truth had ever known. Prior to his arrival in Kansas, Moses had succeeded in all of his business ventures. And shortly after an article had appeared in the newspaper regarding Nicodemus, he'd decided to personally investigate the town. In less than five years, he'd set up newspaper offices in both Hill City and Nicodemus, married Truth, and constructed their new home. Now he'd likely be adding *state auditor* to his list of accomplishments.

The knife nicked Truth's finger as she recalled Aunt Lilly's exact words. *"What if Moses has political aspirations, Truth? What if he chooses to move from Nicodemus? Are you willing to leave this town and help him aspire to something greater if that should be his choice?"* Truth rinsed a trickle of blood from her finger and wrapped it with a strip of cloth as the question continued to replay in her mind. Thinking such a day would never come, she'd been nonchalant with her response. Flippantly, she'd told her aunt that Moses would never make such a decision without first consulting her. Truth had disregarded her aunt's warning. Unfortunately, Moses *hadn't* first considered her feelings—nor had he consulted her. His recent behavior had served to compound her mounting fears about their future. What other decisions might he make without her?

"Do I smell ham and fried potatoes?" Her husband's words preceded him down the hall.

"You have a good nose." She turned her cheek to accept his kiss. "Dinner will be ready in a few more minutes."

Moses's eyes shone with delight as he surveyed her appearance.

"You look lovely today. I'm pleased it won't be necessary to have the doctor come calling."

Ignoring the remark, she stirred the potatoes. "Why don't you set the table for me?"

He gingerly removed two table settings from the shelf and arranged them on the table. "If we move to Topeka, I'm going to hire someone to help you with the housework and cooking. Maybe your friend Dovie would be interested. You could write to her."

Dovie. Truth hadn't heard from her old friend in well over a year. In her final letter, Dovie had mentioned she'd soon be without a housekeeping position if the congressman who employed her lost his bid for reelection. Shortly thereafter, Truth had written to inquire, but she'd never received a reply. Perhaps Dovie had taken a job elsewhere, married, or even moved to another town.

For now, Truth didn't want to talk about Dovie or Topeka. She placed their meal on the table while Moses arranged the silverware. Changing the subject, she inquired if his work had gone well throughout the morning.

Moses forked a piece of ham and dropped it onto his plate. "It did. I managed to accomplish more than expected. However, I'm certain you have more news to report than I. Miss Hattie and Jarena stopped by the office and said they were coming to pay you a visit. Did you enjoy their company?"

How could she truthfully respond to that question without saying she'd found Miss Hattie's interference overwhelming? She picked up the bowl of potatoes and passed them to her husband. "I must admit I'm not fond of unexpected company. I'd rather be prepared when I receive guests." At least she'd managed to avoid a lie.

Moses gave her an appreciative look. "Well, your present appearance is stunning. Besides, Jarena isn't a guest—she's family. And Miss Hattie's considered a part of nearly every family in Nicodemus."

That much was true. And whether sought after or not, Miss Hattie's opinions were freely given. "Speaking of guests, Pappy and the rest of the family are joining us for dinner after church on Sunday."

Moses scooped a helping of potatoes onto his plate and nodded. "We should spend as much time as possible with family between now and the election. That way, we won't have any regrets should I be elected."

Not have any regrets? She inhaled a deep breath and forced herself to remain calm. Best to shift the conversation to a more neutral topic. "I believe I'll do some shopping this afternoon. Is there anything I might purchase for you?" Instantly, she knew her question sounded foolish, for the newspaper office was only a short distance from the general store, where Moses could easily purchase anything he needed without difficulty. All other topics of conversation eluded her at the moment.

Moses reached across the table and cupped her hand beneath his own as he thanked her for the kind offer. "Tell me, what did Miss Hattie have to say about our news?"

Not knowing whether he meant news of his bid for state auditor or news of the baby, Truth decided to assume the latter. "She was most pleased for us." Truth picked up her plate. If she began to clear away the dishes, she'd not be required to elaborate.

"If I didn't know better, I'd think you were attempting to rush me out of the house. I haven't even had a second cup of coffee."

"I'm sorry. I'll get the pot when I take the dishes to the kitchen. I had hoped to complete my shopping as early as possible. I may need to take a brief nap before starting supper this evening." Though she doubted she'd actually require a nap, Truth wanted Moses to depart before they exchanged words that might lead to an argument.

"No need for more coffee, then. The sooner I complete my work at the office, the sooner I'll be back home this evening." He carried his plate into the kitchen and then kissed her on the cheek. "I look forward to spending a leisurely evening with you. I missed our evening chats while I was in Topeka."

Why must he continue to talk about Topeka? Every time he mentioned the place, a new wave of fear washed over her, mingling with an increasing dismay over his actions. How had Moses so easily decided about their future without giving any thought to her wishes?

Truth walked alongside her husband until they reached the front door. Rising up on tiptoe, she accepted his kiss and waited until he was out of sight before returning to the kitchen. Yes, they would talk tonight, though she doubted either of them would be completely satisfied with the outcome. He would likely think her fears and worries over the baby foolish, and any request to withdraw his name from the ballot would surely be ineffective.

———

Moses looked through the stack of paperwork on his desk before glancing at the clock. He shook his head. Although there was much work requiring his attention, he shouldn't be late for supper this evening. A late appearance might set Truth on edge and make the evening's discussion all the more difficult.

There had been little doubt the announcement of his candidacy had displeased and upset Truth. And although the news of an expected child had delighted him, he'd been caught unawares. They had both longed for a child, but he'd given up hope when month after month they'd been disappointed. Why, he'd not even considered her illness might be related to such a condition when he departed for Topeka. However, he needed to assure her of his love and support—and his pleasure that they would soon welcome a son or daughter into their home.

He placed a glass paperweight atop the sheaf of papers, locked his office, and headed off toward home. As he bounded up the front steps, he uttered a quick prayer that the evening would go well. More than anything, he wanted a return to peace within the confines of his home.

Do you?

The questioning inner voice startled him. *Of course I want peace.*

How much?

Moses hastily went inside the house and banged the door behind him. He hoped to distance himself from the stinging question as easily as he shut out the hot August wind. Right now he wasn't certain he did want peace more than he wanted to serve as state auditor.

The waning sunlight splashed through the kitchen window and framed Truth in a luminescent halo as she turned to greet him. The sight of her beguiling smile assaulted him with an even heavier burden of guilt. Perhaps he should withdraw his candidacy. No doubt the other Republican candidate would be pleased to step in and fill the slot. Yet he didn't want to give up this opportunity—not for himself and not for their people. Surely Truth would understand that Nicodemus needed to be on the route for one of the railroad lines being planned across the northern half of the state. His presence in Topeka might bolster the town's chances of being chosen as one of the train stops. After he explained these reasons in more detail, Truth might more readily accept his decision and support his nomination.

He inhaled the aroma of the simmering chicken stew. "Smells good." He rubbed his hand in a circular motion over his stomach. "And I'm hungry enough to eat all you've cooked."

Truth giggled as she stirred the kettle. "I doubt you could eat even half of this. In addition, I've prepared biscuits and then there's chocolate cake for dessert. You'll want to save a little room for those."

When the dishes had been cleared away, they sat down in the parlor, Moses balancing a coffee cup on his knee and Truth perched on the edge of the same settee, facing him. Anxiety overpowered him as he struggled to find the proper words to begin their conversation. He lifted his cup and took a sip of coffee.

"I don't want to leave Nicodemus."

He peered over the lip of the angled cup and met his wife's unwavering gaze. He need not flounder any longer. The discussion had begun. He placed his cup on the saucer on the side table and took Truth's hands in his own. "I do understand how you feel, Truth."

She shook her head, looking sad. "No, you don't understand. If you did, you wouldn't ask me to leave Nicodemus and everyone I love."

Her words pierced Moses like lightning splitting a cottonwood tree. "Am *I* not counted among those you love, Truth?"

"You're twisting my words, Moses. You know I love you, but you're asking me to give up everything else and follow you. It's not as though we've ever actually talked about leaving Nicodemus." She shifted and pulled her hands free. "Before we married, you led me to believe you'd be content in Nicodemus. Would you feel betrayed if *I* made plans to leave Nicodemus without your consent?"

Moses accepted her argument as valid, yet he had to make her understand his decision had been much more than a whim. "It would depend upon the circumstances. If your plan was merely for selfish purposes, I would be upset and angry. If the decision was based upon an important cause, on the other hand, I'd make every attempt to support your choice."

She dropped her weight against the back of the sofa and stared at the fireplace. "And because you consider this an important cause, you believe I should cheerfully pack my bags and close up the house."

Hoping to lighten the mood, he gave her a playful wink. "Well, I'll not ask that you do so *cheerfully*. But I would ask that you give thoughtful consideration to the importance of winning this election— both for us and for our people. Will you agree to give this issue your thought and prayer?"

She gave him a sidelong glance. "I've done nothing else since your announcement. I'll continue, but that doesn't mean I've agreed."

He moved closer and embraced her. "I understand. I won't ask for anything more right now. At any rate, I may not even win the election." He cupped her face between his palms. "I'm delighted you're going to be the mother of my child. I love you very much. You know that, don't you?"

"And I love you." She brushed his lips with a feathery kiss. "As you said, you've not yet won the election. All my worry may be for naught."

He wondered if she'd been listening to him when he'd pled his case. Did she truly not grasp the importance of having one of their people win a statewide elected office? If he was elected, he would be the first Negro ever to hold statewide office in Kansas—and most other states, for that matter!

He hoped she would do as she'd said and continue to pray and think about the issue. He would ask nothing more of her for now. After all, he didn't want her to begin praying for a loss at the polls.

CHAPTER

— 4 —

After a final prayer, Pastor Mason dismissed the congregation and then waved his arms overhead. "Wait! We need to offer Moses our congratulations," he shouted over the murmurs of the crowd. "And don't forget the elections will be held in less than three months. All you men need to get out and cast your votes."

The preacher's final remark was followed by a loud chorus of amens from most of the congregants, but Truth said nothing. In fact, she decided her husband should be thankful women didn't have the right to cast a ballot in this election because she would vote for the opposition!

Before Truth and Moses, along with Grace, could exit their pew, three people had clasped Moses's right hand and promised him their votes. One by one, the men greeted him with the same refrain: "You got my vote, Moses." She wanted to tell them to vote for the

Democrat instead, but she dared not say such a thing aloud.

"I's glad to see you up and about, Truth. You's lookin' much better than the last time I saw you," Miss Hattie commented as she walked by, never missing a step as she continued on her way.

Truth sighed. The woman did have a way about her! She felt Moses's hand on her elbow as he guided her forward a few more paces. At this rate they wouldn't make it out of the church for several hours. Before another well-wisher could stop him, she said, "I believe I'll go on ahead with Grace and Jarena. We can get the meal set out, and you men can follow along later."

Pleased when Moses nodded his agreement, Truth took Grace's hand. "Let's find Jarena and go on home. The men are going to follow after a bit."

A short time later, the three women were walking toward Truth's home, all of them anxious to visit without the fear of others over-hearing their conversation. Little Jennie giggled as a breeze caught her baby bonnet and blew it off her head. Much to Jennie's amusement, Grace vaulted upward and grasped the hat with one hand and then plopped it on the baby's head, saying she was going to double knot it this time. The baby bounced and giggled in reply while Grace secured the hat in place.

As they walked up the front steps of the house, Grace took hold of Truth's hand. "I hear Miss Hattie gave you one of her famous speeches earlier in the week."

"She surely did." Truth frowned at her sister. "It's no fun being the object of Miss Hattie's attention!"

Grace nudged Truth playfully. "But she leaves the rest of us alone when she's quibbling with you. She's been busy embarrassing the day-lights out of me for the past six months. Every time she sees me with Silas, she hollers to ask when we're gonna jump the broom."

Oh yes, Miss Hattie had done the very same thing to her after she and Moses announced they would wed. The old woman acted as though her very life depended upon marrying off every single young woman in Nicodemus Township.

While the three sisters busied themselves in the kitchen, Jarena stopped long enough to tap Truth on the shoulder. "I know this election is going to bring wide acclaim to Nicodemus for years to come. We're all very proud, Truth."

Truth marveled at her sister's remark. Why did they all think she was pleased by Moses's decision—especially now, when she was expecting a child? The entire town, including the members of her family, viewed Moses's bid for election as a matter of community pride. As far as Truth was concerned, the depth of her family's pride would be measured by their willingness to help should Moses be elected. Since they freely expressed that his position as state auditor would prove a wondrous thing for the entire community, she had decided to test the depth of their good wishes.

Once everyone had been seated around the table, with plates filled and thanks given for their meal, the conversation turned to the upcoming election. Thomas offered to help if there was anything he could do to assist Moses with his campaign.

Before her husband could reply, Truth scooted to the edge of her chair and leaned forward. She wanted to make eye contact with her brother-in-law when she told him exactly how he could help. By the time Truth had articulated her plan, both Thomas and Jarena were visibly bewildered. They looked, in fact, utterly astonished that Truth had asked them to leave their own home and move to town—into her house.

She could not understand their reluctance. The home she and Moses had built was nearly new, and it simply should not sit empty and deteriorate while they were gone. To have some unknown family move in was out of the question. Thomas would still be able to maintain his farm; his acreage wasn't far from town.

Jarena clamped an unrelenting gaze upon Truth. "I see. If you must endure a scrap of unhappiness in your life, you want to be certain we all suffer with you."

How could Jarena say such a thing? Truth was offering a very nice home! Much nicer than the soddy Jarena and Thomas lived in on their land. She couldn't let her sister's remark go unchallenged. With the confidence of a skilled debater, she reminded her that they had all expressed their desire for Moses to serve as a state official and had avowed the importance of his election. If they had been declaring the truth, surely they should be willing—even want—to sacrifice on his behalf.

Though she'd expected them to intervene, her father and Moses remained surprisingly silent throughout her exchange with Thomas and Jarena. She could only assume they agreed with her stance. Empowered by that belief, Truth continued. Perhaps knowing Jarena was caring for her house would dispel her fears over being uprooted.

As her argument drew to a close, she focused on Grace. "Also, I want Grace to accompany us to Topeka and stay with me until after the baby is born."

Her second appeal was met with immediate arguments from both Silas and her father. Once again, Truth waged a remarkable debate against her family. Grace remained silent, seemingly thunderstruck by her sister's request. Finally, Moses clanged his spoon on the table and pointed out that Grace might wish to offer an opinion in the matter.

Grace's big eyes flitted from Silas to Truth to her father. "Unless you divide me in thirds, I don't see how I can make all of you happy. How am I supposed to decide? If I make one person happy, the other two will be unhappy."

Ezekiel leaned forward, obviously prepared to take command. "T's gonna be lots happier if you stays in Nicodemus."

Truth frowned at her father. Hadn't he been one of Moses's strongest advocates, pushing her husband to accept Governor St. John's appointment as the Graham County clerk, encouraging him to represent the Republican Party at the state convention, lauding the fact that his name would be on the ballot for state auditor? Was it truly so difficult for all of them to understand Truth's concerns, her desperate need to have family around her if she had to move to Topeka?

My father is willing to see others take a risk or change their lives in order to serve a noble cause, but only if such change comes at no expense to him. And as her fears continued to escalate, she politely pointed out that fact. Her comment only served to escalate the argument to another level until Moses reminded them that the family might not be together for Sunday dinners much longer. He suggested they enjoy their coffee and dessert in a more peaceable fashion.

Though all of them complied, the remainder of the meal was strained. Truth was glad when the meal ended and the women retreated to the kitchen by themselves. There was little doubt she needed to reinforce her arguments to Jarena and Grace in private. While they cleared and washed the dishes, Truth quietly explained the fears and worries that plagued her, though neither of them appeared to completely understand. Jarena avowed Truth would have excellent medical care in Topeka, while Grace pointed out that most babies were born without a lick of difficulty. Those things might be true, but they did little to assuage the nagging trepidation that had taken up residence within Truth's heart.

By the time they'd completed their tasks in the kitchen, she had received an agreement from both of her sisters. Jarena was certain she'd have little difficulty convincing Thomas they should lend their support by moving to town. And though Grace remained doubtful whether Silas would understand, she had acquiesced when Truth had pointed out she wasn't yet officially engaged.

After she'd finally elicited agreement from her sisters, Truth gestured toward the parlor. "You two go and join the others. I'll take care of the rest."

After returning the serving bowls to the proper shelves, Truth removed her apron and hung it on the peg. She absently decided to cut through the dining room, but she stopped midstride at the sounds of a heated exchange. Silas and Grace! She flattened herself against the wall and remained perfectly still. She hoped the floorboards wouldn't creak.

"Truth is bein' downright selfish and you knows it, Grace. Sounds to me like she done learnt too many lessons from yo' aunt Lilly 'bout how to control folks. I knowed from the first time I met her back in New York that she was headstrong, but I never did realize how far she'd go to git her own way. She don' care 'bout nobody but herself."

Heat rose in her cheeks. How could Silas say such things about her? She wanted to swing around the doorway and tell him how wrong he was. She cared about others. Wasn't she the one who'd brought him back from New York with a promise of a good life on the Kansas plains and his very own farm? And hadn't she kept her promises to him? Hadn't she cared about him?

"Please don't be angry, Silas," Grace said. "I do understand your objections. But Truth is frightened and we're twins. I need to help her. I promise I'll come home once the baby's born."

He mumbled a reply that Truth couldn't make out.

"No, I give you my word. I'll be back before the child is two weeks old."

Two weeks? Truth hoped Grace would remain far more than two weeks after the baby's birth. However, there was no need to argue that point now. There would be plenty of time to discuss Grace's return date.

Maybe Moses will lose the election. That would be the best solution of all.

CHAPTER

— 5 —

Macia Boyle remained silent during the evening meal, much the same as she had ever since her return from Europe in September. Though her overseas journey with Mrs. Donlevy had been scheduled to last only six months—eight at the very most—Macia had been away from home nearly two years, due primarily to Mrs. Donlevy's physical complaints throughout their travels in Europe. Much like Macia's own mother's sickness, Mrs. Donlevy's bouts of illness appeared to come and go at will.

On several occasions Macia had threatened to leave the woman in Europe and journey home by herself. But Mrs. Donlevy would plead her case and promise to book passage the moment she was well enough to travel. At one point in their travels, Macia even accused the woman of being an imposter. However, Macia's doubts were proved inaccurate when Mrs. Donlevy died at a villa in Italy only a few days after Macia had made the unfortunate remark.

That entire episode was almost more than Macia could bear. She was ill prepared to make the proper arrangements. Had it not been for the assistance of a kindly priest, she wouldn't have been able to carry the heavy burdens placed on her shoulders.

Father Viccaro took charge and completed all of the necessary preparations. Though not normally a proponent of the practice, he suggested Mrs. Donlevy's body be cremated for ease in transporting it back to the United States. Macia had no idea what the woman's relatives might think, but she agreed. In fact, she would have agreed to almost anything in order to return home in a timely fashion. So she boarded the ship carrying Mrs. Donlevy's ashes in a bronze urn. When the ship was beset by stormy seas, Macia nearly came undone at the thought of poor Mrs. Donlevy's ashes spilling about her cabin. She was most relieved when she delivered the container to Mrs. Donlevy's second cousin, Myrtle, at the pier in Norfolk. In fact, handing over the ashes was nearly as gratifying as seeing her brother Carlisle waiting for her on the dock.

She completely lost her composure when her older brother drew her into a consoling embrace and expressed his sorrow that her travels had gone awry. And though Carlisle hadn't planned to accompany her back to Kansas, after he observed Macia's fragile state, he managed to gain a special leave from his job to travel with her. The courage and strength she'd exhibited throughout her travels in Europe completely dissolved once she set foot in the United States. Carlisle assured her she'd be her old self when she was back among friends and family in Hill City. However, nothing could have proved further from the truth.

If anything, she became even more despondent, for shortly after her departure for Europe, her parents had hired a young woman, Fern Kingston, to replace Truth Harban as their cook and housekeeper. Supposedly, Fern had been traveling in a wagon train with her brother and his wife when an argument ensued. Unhappy with her situation, Fern decided to leave the wagon train when they neared Hill City. Apparently, Macia's mother viewed the girl's arrival as a godsend. She could cook and keep house to perfection, and her disposition was pleasant.

When Macia discovered Jeb Malone was courting Fern, and Fern discovered Jeb had once had romantic inclinations toward Macia, life in the Boyle household took a downward turn. It was obvious to Macia that her mother was delighted with Fern—both as a house-keeper and as a prospective bride for Jeb Malone. And Macia knew she had no right to complain. When she'd departed for Europe, Jeb had clearly stated that he wouldn't wait for her. Even so, Macia had been certain he would. Had it not been for Fern Kingston, he surely would have welcomed her back home with open arms. Instead, she received no more than a nod and a quick "Welcome home" when he came calling on Fern.

Macia's father turned to her when the evening meal was complete. "I think we should all attend the Fall Festival on Saturday night. I hear there are going to be folks from all the nearby communities in attendance."

Attend the Fall Festival? The acclaimed Dr. Boyle might be qualified to set a broken bone or stitch a wound, but attending a dance wasn't going to heal what ailed his daughter. She didn't want to leave the house, much less attend the festival and the harvest dance that followed. Jeb would surely be escorting Fern.

Fern lifted several plates from the table. "You should get out and have an evening of fun, Miss Boyle. Jeb invited me to attend several weeks ago, and I can scarcely wait for Saturday to arrive."

Though Macia immediately thought of several unkind retorts, she merely acknowledged Fern's suggestion with a nod and excused herself from the table. Of course Fern was anxious to attend the party. *She* would have an escort: Jeb Malone, Macia's beau.

Before she could escape the room, her father clasped her hand. "Why don't we take a walk? It's a lovely evening, and you need some fresh air. You've remained cooped up in this house far too much these past couple of weeks." Pulling her along by the hand, her father led her out of the house and down the front steps. When they'd reached the street, he gently tucked her hand through the crook of his arm. "Hiding in the house is not going to change your circumstances, my dear." His smile was tender, and he gently patted her hand as she held onto his arm. "The only way to overcome this setback is to accept the fact that you played a role in what has happened. Jeb was prepared to marry you, but you chose to accompany Mrs. Donlevy."

"At Mother's insistence," Macia argued.

"That may be true, but you could have denied her request. That fact aside, it's too late to cry over what's in the past. While you were enjoying the fine museums and touring exciting locales in Europe, Jeb moved on with his life. You can't blame him—or Fern."

How could she explain to her father that she did indeed blame Jeb—and Fern—and everyone else who had continued to move ahead and enjoy life during her absence? If she voiced her feelings, she would be judged selfish, though she ought not care. She wished someone would understand *her* feelings. Perhaps her father was correct. Rather than taking to her room, she should get out. How else could she make folks understand that she'd been wronged?

Her father appeared delighted when they returned home and she announced she would attend the festivities Saturday evening after all.

Macia rotated to one side and then the other in front of her mirror, wanting to observe the full effect of her dress. It was one of the latest fashions from Europe, even boasting the shorter sleeves that likely wouldn't be seen in this country for at least another year or two. The gown, specially fashioned by a Paris designer, was made of three differing stripes: an open-mesh fawn silk, dark blue velvet, and shimmering navy satin. Custom-stitched needlepoint lace decorated the bodice. The gown had been a gift from Mrs. Donlevy—fitted and sewn by the designer's own staff while Macia and Mrs. Donlevy toured the celebrated city. There was no doubt Macia would outshine everyone else at the gathering. She tucked two jeweled combs into her hair and nodded with satisfaction.

Not surprisingly, Macia's mother had taken to her bed with a headache and declared she'd not attend the festival. However, Macia's father was waiting in the foyer with an appreciative gleam in his eye when Macia descended the stairs.

"You look absolutely stunning, my dear."

She whirled around to show her new gown to full advantage. "A gift from Mrs. Donlevy."

Her father gave an appreciative nod as she completed her pirouette. "It is a lovely gown, but not nearly so lovely as the young lady who wears it."

After draping her shoulders with a shawl that matched the beige silk insets of her dress, Macia grasped her father's arm. Perhaps the evening wouldn't be so terrible. Fern had taken the afternoon off work and departed the house earlier in the day. Jeb had probably invited her to supper; at least he wouldn't be calling for her at the front door. Her father assisted Macia into the carriage, and soon they were on their way. Though the festival was but a short distance away, she was pleased for the carriage. She didn't want the hem of her new gown dusting the ground.

The Brotherhood Hall had been festively decorated for the occasion, and the music and revelry were in full swing when they arrived. Even though the party had been slated for eight o'clock, it appeared that many folks had arrived much earlier. Macia spotted Jeb and Fern the moment she and her father walked through the door. Jeb, his hair slicked down and wearing a navy jacket that complemented his blue eyes, was leaning close and handing Fern a cup of punch. He met Macia's stare when she entered the room but quickly averted his eyes when Fern looked up to follow his gaze. Fern moved closer to Jeb's side and slipped a possessive hold on his arm. Macia turned away, angered by Fern's self-satisfied look.

Careful to keep her back toward Jeb and Fern, Macia surveyed the room. Her father had been correct. There were many folks she'd never seen before, and she wondered where they'd come from. The musicians took up their instruments and the attendees began to pair off.

Her father was about to escort her onto the floor when a handsome stranger approached and introduced himself. "I hope you won't think me forward, Miss Boyle, but I had hoped you might agree to dance with me."

Macia narrowed her eyes. How did this man know her name? "And you are?"

"Garrett Johnson. Walt and Ada Johnson's nephew. My aunt pointed you out the moment you arrived. You are by far the loveliest woman in attendance." He grinned and came closer. "Mrs. Kramer is green with envy. She was telling my aunt that she hopes to imitate the pattern of your gown for her customers."

Macia assessed the newcomer. He was certainly attractive and well-spoken. She glanced at her father, who immediately stepped aside as he obligingly handed her over to Mr. Johnson. "How long have you been in Hill City, Mr. Johnson?" Macia asked.

"I arrived two weeks ago—and please call me Garrett," he said as they started dancing. "Otherwise, I'll think you're speaking to my uncle."

Macia laughed and nodded her agreement before inquiring about his visit to Hill City. He revealed that he had studied business in college and had also developed an interest in photography while attending school. Now, with funds from his father's estate, he planned to establish a business that would yield a good return. And though

Macia didn't say so, she was surprised he'd chosen Hill City as the site for his entrepreneurial venture.

As they continued to circle the room, he squeezed Macia's hand. "And now that I've met you, I don't believe I'll ever want to leave."

Before she could respond, the leader of the musicians held up his hand and called for the dancers to exchange partners with the couple to their immediate right. Macia froze as Garrett released her. Oblivious to her awkward predicament, Garrett danced off with Fern in his arms. While the other couples moved around them, Jeb and Macia remained fixed in place. Finally gathering his wits, Jeb held Macia at a distance and woodenly led her across the dance floor. A cool breeze filled the room, but Macia could barely breathe. Her hand was perspiring, or was it Jeb's?

Jeb's little sister, Lucy, beamed and waved from her position along the edge of the dance floor. When Macia smiled back, Jeb's shoulders relaxed and he finally spoke. "You look lovely this evening . . . not that you don't always . . . look lovely, that is."

She should respond in kind, but a fleeting remembrance of Fern's smug look wiped away all thoughts of decorum. Macia wanted nothing more than to inflict pain. "This is the gown Mrs. Donlevy had specially made for me to wear to our engagement party. Silly me, I didn't realize you would take up with the first eligible woman who set foot in Hill City."

Jeb's eyes widened, and he reeled as though she'd delivered a blow to his stomach. "If memory serves me, I never promised to wait for you. Did you truly expect me to greet you with open arms? You were gone nearly *two years*, Macia."

She hastened to mention it was Mrs. Donlevy's illness that had prolonged her stay. Jeb shook his head. He obviously preferred to believe she'd remained abroad of her own choosing. Angered by his behavior, she determined to make a stand. Without thought of the consequences, she leveled a steely glare upon him. "If you continue to see Fern, there will be no hope of any reconciliation between us."

In response, Jeb tilted his head back and laughed. Not a quiet chuckle or a guffaw but a loud belly laugh that captured the attention of the couples dancing nearby.

Hurt and embarrassed, Macia jerked free of his arms and hastened across the dance floor. She'd made a fool of herself. Likely Jeb would tell Fern of her ultimatum. Life had been difficult enough living in the same house with Fern. After this episode, how could she possibly endure the woman's presence each day? Perhaps she could convince her father to dismiss Fern and find someone else.

She rushed through the doorway and nearly knocked her younger brother, Harvey, to the ground. He chuckled as he took hold of her upper arms. "I didn't realize you would be so anxious to see me arrive."

Harvey cut a dashing figure. Her brother's years away from home had matured him. Although Macia hadn't believed he would come back to Hill City, he'd been good to his word and had assumed ownership of the local newspaper. It seemed he'd given up his lazy habits and become a conscientious businessman.

Harvey peered over her head and waved at Garrett, grinning as the man drew near. The two men greeted each other in a familiar manner. When Harvey attempted to introduce Macia, Garrett quickly interrupted. "If you had arrived on time, you'd know I've had the pleasure of dancing with your sister—and I hope to enjoy her company for the remainder of the evening." Garrett lightly touched Macia's elbow. "I was afraid you were attempting to escape my company when you left Jeb standing in the middle of the dance floor and hurried toward the door. And Fern expressed her concern, also."

Heat rose in her cheeks as the two men awaited a response. Though she'd like to know exactly what Fern had said, Macia dared not inquire. Instead, she said she needed a breath of fresh air and hoped they wouldn't question her further.

"Have you told my sister of our plans?" Harvey asked Garrett. Macia looked back and forth between the two men. Harvey laughed and slapped Garrett on the shoulder. "You should tell her. She's quite intelligent and might even have some ideas for us." With that, Harvey strode off and approached a lovely young lady standing across the room.

Macia hadn't seen the girl before—though there were any number of strangers in the crowd. She nodded toward the girl and asked Garrett, "Do you know that young lady?"

"Mattie Lawson. Her folks own a spread about ten miles north. Harvey tells me they came here from Iowa about a year ago. I believe Harvey's taken an interest in her, but he has competition from several others." Garrett chuckled. "With the long hours he works, I fear Harvey finds himself at a disadvantage."

There was little doubt Garrett had properly analyzed Harvey's feelings. Her brother held the girl closely while the two of them circled the dance floor. Harvey seemed to have eyes for no other. Perhaps her little brother would be making marriage plans before she did.

Garrett softly touched her shoulder and offered his arm. "Why don't we move away from the doorway and enjoy a breath of air?"

Garrett led her to one of the benches that had been arranged just outside the hall's entrance. A harvest moon shone overhead, and the crisp smell of autumn hinted at the change of season. Once they were settled outdoors, Macia pressed for details. She wanted to hear about the business venture Harvey had mentioned. Other than farming, she could think of no investment opportunities in this desolate country. Her own father had invested in farmland before they arrived in Hill City. Back then, her father had thought that Harvey would become a farmer. The very idea still remained a family joke.

"I think this would make an excellent place for a cannery," he explained. With the vast surrounding farmland, he thought a person could turn a good profit if the railroad laid tracks nearby. "The railroad is the key to making this work. There are plenty of farmers who will sell us beans, tomatoes, and corn, but once the goods are canned, we need the railroad."

Macia was thunderstruck by the idea. She knew there were large canneries in Chicago and she'd heard folks mention some in Iowa, but a cannery out on the western plains sounded ludicrous to her. However, Garrett spoke with assurance, convinced the plan could work. He wasn't concerned about workers, either. He figured there were plenty of folks who'd be willing to work for him. But the entire concept depended upon the railroad.

"Shall we stroll for a bit?" Garrett asked.

She rose in response. "And where does Harvey fit into this plan?"

Garrett laughed. "He certainly won't be working in the cannery."

She took his elbow and they walked along the road. "Nor will he be investing a vast amount of money. Instead, Harvey will lobby the railroad tycoons when the proper time arises."

The comment surprised Macia. Her brother had developed into quite the businessman since his return from college. A far cry from the laissez-faire way of life he'd embraced back in Kentucky years ago.

Though she had hoped to ask a few additional questions, Garrett pleasantly called a halt to further business talk and insisted they rejoin the festivities inside. Gathering her skirts in one hand, Macia moved alongside him. She would have much preferred to remain outdoors, distanced from Jeb and Fern, but raising an objection would require far too much explanation. For now, she would attempt to avoid the couple. Tomorrow she would speak to her father about Fern.

CHAPTER

— 6 —

There was a crispness to the October morning that warned of winter's impending arrival. Macia bent forward against a surge of chilly wind and tugged her cloak tight about her neck. She should have waited until after the noonday meal to visit with her father. At least the sun would have warmed the blustery air by early afternoon. However, her father had warned of his busy schedule, and this might be her only opportunity for a few moments alone with him. And this discussion must take place away from the house—where Fern wouldn't be privy to her request.

She shivered as she entered the office. Her father had arrived nearly an hour earlier, and she was pleased for the warmth of the fire he'd started. When he reached for her cloak, she shook her head and then took a seat opposite his desk. "I promise I won't keep you from your work for long."

She knew from the tilt of her father's head that he was pleased to hear that bit of information. He probably had much to accomplish before his first patient arrived. After settling into his chair, he gave Macia his full attention. As she spoke, her father smiled and nodded at the appropriate moments. And by the time she had concluded her entreaty, she believed he understood her plight and would grant her request.

Her confidence began to wane, though, as he stroked his chin and focused on a spot a few inches above her head. When he finally cleared his throat, Macia leaned forward, anxious to hear what he would say. "I know it is humiliating and somewhat difficult to have Fern living under the same roof." He tapped his pen on the desk. "But I can hardly dismiss her. The young woman is in need of her wages, and we have need of a housekeeper."

Tears stung Macia's eyes, and she swallowed hard. He was more concerned over Fern's welfare than her own!

She kept her gaze fixed upon her tightly clenched hands. "If she had the assurance of employment elsewhere and another housekeeper could be found to replace her, would you then agree?"

"Possibly. But I doubt whether such arrangements could be made, my dear. Difficult as it is, I believe you must endure this situation for the present." Her father glanced at the clock. "I do apologize, Macia. I wish I had more time, but Mrs. Wilton will be arriving soon for her appointment."

She rose and silently walked toward the door. Suddenly, unwilling to accept the full measure of her father's edict, she turned. "But if I could make the arrangements?"

Her father peered at her over the top of his reading glasses. "I do want you to feel comfortable in our home, Macia. If suitable provision can be made, I won't object." He pointed his pen in her direction. "But don't get your hopes up. I don't want you to be disappointed."

She agreed and hurried from her father's office before he could change his mind. A visit to the general store was in order. Mrs. Johnson would know of anyone seeking employment as a housekeeper. The mercantile was the place where folks stopped to purchase their goods, but they also stopped by to catch up on the latest news. Mr. and Mrs. Johnson were always among the first to know the comings and goings in Hill City. In fact, Mrs. Johnson made it her business to elicit tidbits of news from the store's visitors. And she also made it her business to pass along the scraps of gossip to any listening ear.

Mrs. Johnson was near the front door, arranging a new shipment of fabric when Macia entered. She glanced at Macia's arm and her smile faded slightly: she was obviously unhappy Macia wasn't carrying a basket. And she knew Macia wasn't one to share gossip. The woman was astute when it came to business, but she enjoyed hearing the latest rumors even more. If another customer entered carrying a basket and list, Macia would quickly lose the older woman's interest. She surveyed the fabrics and commented on the quality of several pieces. If she mentioned her need for several new winter dresses, maybe Mrs. Johnson would warm to her.

One comment proved to be all that was required. Immediately, Mrs. Johnson started pulling out various bolts of fabric, commenting on each one as she placed them before Macia. Knowing what was expected, Macia responded favorably as she surveyed the plethora of choices. She rubbed each piece of cloth between her fingers, careful to intersperse her personal questions with inquiries regarding the fabrics. Surprisingly, Mrs. Johnson remained by her side even though several of her favorite customers entered the store.

Unwinding a piece of dark blue print, Mrs. Johnson draped the fabric across Macia's shoulder. "That color is good with your complexion." She nudged Macia's arm. "Garrett mentioned how much he enjoyed your company at the Fall Festival." She tucked her chin close to her chest and drew nearer. "He also said the dark blue shade of your gown was quite becoming on you." She lifted the fabric from Macia's shoulder and slowly began to wind it onto the bolt.

"I'll consider this piece. My father seems to think shades of green are better suited to my blond hair and pale skin."

Mrs. Johnson returned the bolt of blue fabric to the table with a hefty thud. "Did you enjoy Garrett's company? He's a fine-looking man—an excellent catch. An intelligent, hardworking man who is going to go far in this world. You should give him strong consideration, Macia."

She nodded, but she knew Garrett would purchase a ticket for the next train out of Kansas if he heard his aunt attempting to sell him like a barrel of goods.

"All of us are pleased when new folks move to the area, Mrs. Johnson. In fact, I wondered if you'd recently met any newcomer who might be interested in a housekeeping position."

The older woman hesitated for a moment, and then mentioned the recent arrival of German immigrants—a family that had purchased acreage several miles outside of town. Macia perked to attention. Mrs. Johnson's penchant for gossip might prove helpful after all.

The older woman ran her fingers along the rows of fabric and finally pulled a bolt of green fabric from the pile. She offered it to Macia. "They have a daughter who was asking if I needed help in the store. She speaks English, but I don't know if her parents understand the language. She appeared eager to find employment, so she'd likely be a hard worker. Maybe she'd be interested in a housekeeping position. Has Fern talked Jeb into setting a wedding date?"

Macia bristled. The question caused her physical pain. Fortunately, Garrett walked into the store, tapped his finger on the piece of deep green silk fabric, and recommended it as the perfect selection for her.

Macia looked at Mrs. Johnson and shrugged. "You see? Green!" Macia grinned at Garrett. "My father also believes green is the perfect color for me. With both you and my father in agreement, I suppose I'll have no choice but to select this piece."

Garrett's eyes sparkled. He took her by the arm as his aunt moved to assist another customer. "I was hoping you'd also agree to have supper with me this evening. I know I'm breaching proper etiquette, but I hope you'll forgive me and agree."

Macia laughed. "Since you've discovered the perfect piece of fabric for a new gown, I believe I'll be able to overlook your impropriety this one time." The grandfather clock in the corner of the store chimed the hour. "I had best be getting home lest Mother worry. I'll expect you at . . . say seven o'clock?"

Garrett nodded. "Until then."

Macia had gone only a short distance when the sound of Lucy's voice caused her to stop and turn. The girl raced at full tilt, her braids blowing behind her like tails on a kite. Though nearing fifteen, Lucy neither appeared nor acted much older than an eleven- or twelve-year-old. Conceivably it was the lack of a woman's influence in her life, or perhaps she merely wanted to remain a little girl for a while longer. In any case, during Macia's absence, it seemed as if the clock had ceased ticking for Lucy.

Macia waved. "Slow down, Lucy!" She could envision the girl flying headlong onto the hard dirt-packed street.

When she finally reached Macia's side, Lucy leaned forward and gulped in deep breaths of air. Her braids fell across her shoulders, and her cheeks resembled two ripe tomatoes. When she'd finally recovered, she grasped Macia's arm. "Thank you for waiting. I've wanted to come and visit, but Jeb said it wouldn't be seemly. Then when I heard you talking in the store . . ."

Macia's mind reeled as Lucy's lips continue to move. She didn't hear the girl's words. Instead, her thoughts were consumed by how much Lucy might have overheard. Would Lucy tell Jeb or Fern that she'd been inquiring about a housekeeper? If Fern discovered the news, there was no telling what repercussions might follow. And if Lucy told Jeb, he'd surely think Macia was behaving in a contemptuous manner.

Lucy tugged on Macia's hand. "Well, what do you think?"

"A-a-about what?"

An exasperated sigh escaped Lucy's lips. "You haven't been listening, have you?" An indulgent smile crossed the girl's lips when Macia shook her head. "I've been wanting to come and visit and wondered if now might be a good time. We don't have to tell Jeb that we plan to remain friends."

A peddler's wagon approached, and Macia pulled Lucy aside. Macia gathered her wits about her and quickly agreed. "I'm pleased you stopped me. If you'd like to accompany me back to the house, I have several gifts for you. One from each of the large cities I visited in Europe. We can have a cup of tea, and I'll tell you a little about all of those places."

"Oh yes!" The girl's braids bounced up and down.

Too late, Macia remembered Fern would be at the house. She hesitated, unsure what to do. If she withdrew her invitation, Lucy's feelings would be injured. Furthermore, what difference could it make to Fern if Lucy came for a visit?

Lucy's gentle tug pulled Macia from her thoughts. "Is Fern leaving town? Is that why you asked Mrs. Johnson about a new housekeeper?"

Macia swallowed hard. Her conversation with Mrs. Johnson had likely caused Lucy concern that yet another person she'd grown to love was going to slip away. No matter the repercussions, Macia knew she must set the girl's mind at rest. More than anything, Lucy needed to hear the truth.

Giving the girl's hand a gentle squeeze, Macia explained Fern was not planning to leave Hill City. "But I think both Fern and I would be happier if she worked for someone else."

"Because of Jeb?"

"Yes, Lucy, because of Jeb." She struggled to find the proper explanation. "It's uncomfortable for Fern and me to be around each other since we both . . ."

Joy sparkled in the girl's eyes as she peeked up at Macia. "Love him?"

Oh no! How was she going to tactfully answer *that* question? They continued down the street, her mind racing to find the proper response. "We have both *cared* for Jeb, so that makes the situation somewhat difficult—for both of us."

"So Fern wants to quit working at your house?"

"I don't really know, Lucy. I haven't spoken to her just yet, and I'd appreciate it if you didn't, either. I must make sure there is another position available for her and that we can find someone to replace her. Do you understand?"

Lucy looked sad but agreed. "I won't say anything—to anyone."

Relief flooded over Macia as they walked up the front steps and entered the house. She wasn't certain where Fern would be, but the gifts were in her bedroom. Perhaps that would be a good out-of-the-way place for her to visit with Lucy. Macia led Lucy upstairs, hopeful they would avoid Fern. She knew Lucy wouldn't mind doing without tea once she began opening her gifts. While Macia gathered the presents from the bottom drawer of her chest, Lucy hung up their cloaks and sat down in one of the chairs overlooking the small flower garden at the rear of the house. In short order, Macia placed the gifts before Lucy and told her she could begin.

Her pleasure was evident as she exclaimed in delight after opening each package. She giggled at the smiling hand-carved donkey and delicately traced her finger around the small cameo necklace Macia had discovered in Italy. A joyful squeal escaped her lips as she opened first the exquisite piece of lace and then a miniature porcelain figurine of a young girl with braids. But it was a leather-bound journal that truly captured Lucy's heart. She jumped from her chair, accidentally knocking it to the floor as she rushed around the small table to embrace Macia.

Without warning, the bedroom door opened. Macia and Lucy startled and stared wide-eyed as Fern glared back at them. "It would appear the two of you are having a gay time." Her gaze dropped to the unwrapped gifts lying on the table. She squared her shoulders. "I see you're trying to win Jeb back by using your wealth to impress Lucy."

Lucy placed a protective hold on Macia's shoulder. "She is not! You're just jealous because she cared enough to bring me presents."

Fern pushed the door closed behind her and stepped closer. Her eyes narrowed into two thin slits as she grasped Lucy's wrist and pulled her away from Macia. Lucy winced as Fern's hold tightened. "Don't you *ever* speak to me in that manner again, young lady." She swung her arm toward the table. "All of this is nothing but Macia's attempt to worm her way back into your brother's good graces. Well, it isn't going to work." She moved forward, and before Macia realized what was happening, Fern swept the gifts off the table and sent them crashing to the floor.

Macia couldn't believe what had happened. She jumped to her feet and retrieved the broken pieces of porcelain, for the rug had done little to protect the fine piece of glassware. Thankfully none of the other gifts had been damaged.

As quickly as she'd committed the deed, Fern's demeanor changed. She hastened to request forgiveness from both of them, and although

Lucy hesitated, she finally acquiesced. There was little doubt Fern wanted the matter concealed from Jeb and forgotten. And though Macia quickly decided she wouldn't speak to him regarding the incident, Fern's behavior had been disconcerting. Lucy's wrist still bore a red circle where Fern had grabbed her.

Before exiting the room, Fern forced Lucy to agree to come and talk before the girl departed for home. Likely she wanted assurance nothing would be reported to Jeb.

When they heard Fern's footsteps retreating down the back stairs, Lucy carefully fingered the pieces of broken porcelain. Tears glistened in her eyes and then slowly trailed down her cheeks. "Why does she have to be so mean?" The words were a mere whisper.

Macia opened her arms and Lucy leaned into her embrace. "Don't you worry, dear. I can find you another piece of chinaware every bit as pretty as that one."

Lucy sniffed. "She doesn't like me, Macia. She wants Jeb, but she doesn't want me. After they're married, I'm afraid she'll be unkind to me all the time. *Then* what shall I do?"

Lucy once again rested her head against Macia's shoulder, her thin frame wracked with hiccoughs as she wept. The girl's fresh tears dampened the shoulder of Macia's shirtwaist, and she pulled Lucy closer. She longed to say or do something to relieve the girl's pain and fear. But for the moment, it seemed what Lucy needed most was the warmth of an embrace and the knowledge that someone truly cared about her.

Reaching up, Macia stroked Lucy's flaxen hair. "You will always be welcome wherever I am, Lucy, and you know that Jeb loves you more than anyone in the world. He would never let anybody hurt you." It was true. Jeb had cared for Lucy ever since their parents had died. He would do anything to protect his little sister.

Lucy drew in a shaky breath and released Macia from her hold. Pulling a handkerchief from her pocket, Macia tenderly wiped Lucy's face and then tucked an errant strand of hair behind one ear.

"I'd best get home before Jeb begins to worry."

Lucy's voice warbled as she spoke, and Macia hastened to lighten the mood before fresh tears began to flow. "Let me gather your gifts together. I believe I have a small basket you can borrow to carry them." Macia patted the girl's shoulder. "It will give you an excuse to return for another visit."

Lucy's lower lip trembled. "I'll try to come back when Fern isn't here."

Macia placed a light kiss on the girl's cheek and reminded her of Fern's earlier admonition. "Best you stop by the kitchen on your way out of the house. Fern's expecting you. It will only make matters more difficult if you slight her."

A short time later, she heard the familiar bang and click of the front door as it closed. Her thoughts wandered back to her earlier discussion with Mrs. Johnson. Even if the German girl wanted to accept a position as their housekeeper, she must still locate work for Fern. This could prove nearly impossible, yet she wouldn't give up hope. She opened the door of her bedroom closet, one of the delightful concessions her father had granted when they'd built their new house. Macia hadn't wanted her gowns stuffed into wardrobes or hanging on pegs gathering dust. Her fingers trailed across the various fabrics until she reached the pale green silk dress. Pushing aside the gown on either side, she removed it from the closet, gave it a vigorous shake, and spread it upon her bed. Velvet tucks covered with beige lace lined the bodice and gave the dress a special look that she particularly liked. Just today Garrett had selected the dark green silk fabric at his aunt's store, so perhaps he would think this gown comely. She would wear it for their supper engagement this evening.

After giving the gown one final look of approval, Macia peeked in on her mother. The older woman's soft snores were evidence Macia would not be taking tea with her mother this afternoon. Careful to avoid the squeaky floorboard outside her parents' bedroom, she softly closed the door. It might be a good idea to pay a visit to her brother at the newspaper office. Harvey might know someone who had need of a housekeeper. Fern was a good worker, even if she was no longer a good choice for their household—at least not so far as Macia was concerned.

Stopping by her room, she picked up her cloak and spotted Fern walking up the back stairway with a tea tray. "Mother is sleeping and I'm going to the newspaper office. No need to set a place for me at supper as I'll be dining out this evening."

Fern gave a curt nod and retreated back down the stairs without comment. No wonder poor Lucy had been reduced to tears. Fern's icy stare would wound even the hardest heart.

Sashaying toward the newspaper office, Macia loosened the top button of her cloak. The sun now shone brightly, and all evidence of the earlier chill had vanished from the air. Sunlight dappled the windows of Harvey's office and formed tiny prisms that danced like colorful rainbows across the glass. The unexpected beauty caused her to smile as she entered the office.

When the bell over the door jingled merrily, Harvey looked up from his work. "Don't you look happy."

His pronouncement reminded Macia why she'd come. Her smile faded. "Happier than I truly feel. I've come to see if you can help me solve a problem."

He tilted his wooden chair back on two legs and laughed aloud. "Now there's a request I never thought I'd live to hear—my sister actually seeking my advice."

Macia waved the comment away and launched into a full recital of the recent events involving Fern and Lucy. She remained forthright and honest as she explained her anxiety regarding Fern. "Though my initial reservations about Fern were due to my own embarrassment, I am truly worried that she may be cruel to Lucy. Yet if any of us say anything to Jeb, I'm afraid he will go directly to Fern with his questions."

"And Fern will blame Lucy and make her life miserable."

"Exactly. Even knowing all of this, my impression is that Father will not dismiss Fern unless she has the promise of employment elsewhere."

The front legs of Harvey's chair banged onto the wood floor as he dropped forward and stared out the front window. When Macia could bear the silence no longer, she waved her handkerchief in front of his face.

He frowned. "There's no easy solution. Even if Fern leaves Father's employ, it doesn't resolve Lucy's issue. This matter needs more thought than I can give it at the moment." He waved his arm at the printing press. "I must get back to work, but I'll try to come up with something."

She thanked him and headed back outdoors. When she arrived home a short time later, her mother called her into the parlor. Though she had planned to go upstairs and read, Macia joined the older woman. "You're looking well this afternoon, Mother."

Mrs. Boyle thanked her and motioned for Macia to sit down and pour the tea. "Where have you been? I've been wondering."

Macia frowned as Fern walked into the room. "Why didn't you tell Mother I had gone to the newspaper office?"

"How could I? You didn't tell me you were leaving the house."

Macia gasped. The woman was boldly lying over an inconsequential matter. Did she hope to cause Macia difficulties with her own family members?

Taking up one of the china teacups, her mother bobbed her head in a placating manner. "We all forget things from time to time, my dear."

Macia gritted her teeth. She quickly downed her tea and excused herself to dress for her evening supper with Garrett.

The day had been nothing short of disastrous. She hoped this evening would be the opposite. A quick glance at the clock revealed she had sufficient time to relax a bit before dressing. She lifted her Bible from the chest and opened the book. An audible sigh slipped from between her lips as her eyes settled upon a passage in Romans. *"Bless them which persecute you: bless, and curse not."* A twinge of guilt pricked her heart. Perhaps if she reacted with kindness, Fern would see the error of her ways and treat Lucy with fondness. Macia closed her eyes and uttered a prayer for God's help, for she would surely need it. She closed the Bible, and as she considered the ways in which she might show Christ's love to Fern, she looked at her dress lying on her bed.

From her vantage point, the lace-covered bodice appeared to ripple in an unusual manner, and Macia moved closer to examine the gown. She gasped at the sight: the lace had been shredded and the velvet inserts slashed. Instead of the soft lace overlay and velvet tucks, gaping holes now decorated the bodice. Macia clenched her hands into tight fists. "Fern!" Her scream echoed off the walls. Grabbing the dress from her bed, Macia stomped out of the room and down the hallway. That evil woman had ruined her dress!

When she marched into the kitchen, Fern was complacently peeling potatoes as though she'd not heard a thing. Macia shoved the dress at her. "Why did you do this?"

Fern arched her eyebrows. "I don't know what you're talking about. Is there something amiss with your gown?"

Macia ranted and raved until her mother entered the kitchen to investigate the fracas. Still, Fern continued to deny any knowledge of the misdeed.

"Maybe Lucy had something to do with this," Fern told Mrs. Boyle. "She's the only other person who's been in the house today."

"The gown was perfectly fine when I placed it on my bed, and Lucy had already departed," Macia argued.

Fern shrugged as she picked up another potato. "She might have come back later. Girls can be very sneaky when things don't go their way."

Macia seethed. "I know you did this, Fern, and you may be certain that the cost of this gown will be withheld from your wages."

Turning away, Macia hurried back upstairs. So much for showing God's love. So much for blessing those who persecuted her. Tears welled in her eyes. She had failed the first test.

CHAPTER

— 7 —

Nicodemus, Kansas • November 1882

The crisp day dawned bright without a hint of snow or sleet on the horizon. While Moses voiced his elation that the day had finally arrived, Truth privately nursed her fears. Election day! By this time tomorrow, the votes would be tallied and winning candidates announced. Though a final count of all the votes wouldn't be received in Nicodemus until a later date, Truth's ultimate fate would be sealed. She had lived in dread of this day since Moses's return from Topeka and the announcement of his candidacy. Since that day, she had been praying. Soon she would have God's answer.

Truth was probably the only soul in Nicodemus who hoped her husband would lose the election. The entire town wanted nothing more than to have one of their own hold statewide office. Particularly Miss Hattie. The woman had become an avid campaigner, brandishing her umbrella as she made her way through groups in the churchyard on Sundays or during her visits to the general store. There was no hesitation when she spoke of who should be elected state auditor—and no one dared contradict her.

Though Miss Hattie's words weren't eloquent, when she mentioned the railroad, everyone sat up and took heed. Of course, whether Moses could truly help bring the railroad to Nicodemus was highly questionable. However, the old woman's rhetoric made it sound as though his election would make the railroad a shoo-in, as if the two went hand in hand. Truth didn't understand why folks thought the state auditor position could help bring the railroad to Nicodemus, but she didn't argue.

In addition to their move, Truth worried Moses's new position would keep him away from home frequently. Although he'd assured her the assistant auditor would travel to the various county seats to examine any accounting irregularities or to investigate payment of arrearages for school lands, Truth remained unconvinced. Moses wasn't a man who easily assigned such duties to others. After he was sworn into office, Truth envisioned the assistant auditor sitting in the Topeka office while Moses traveled the state resolving disputes. Moses wouldn't find satisfaction sitting in a stuffy office registering patents or compounding interest payments owed to the state. Truth didn't doubt the sincerity of her husband's promise, but she did doubt his ability to keep it. And that was cause for yet another worry.

Cast your cares on me.

She ignored the soft command. Instead, she repeated her continuing prayer. *Please don't let him win the election.*

———————

Folks in Nicodemus Township had decided early on that if Moses carried the vote in the western counties, he would ultimately carry the state. And the residents of Nicodemus didn't plan to wait for the final results before holding their celebration. Though Truth had proposed they wait for the final outcome of the election before hosting the party, her suggestion had been immediately vetoed after church last Sunday. In fact, the congregation had acted as though she'd suggested a traitorous act. Rather than argue, she'd agreed the party would proceed as planned.

Truth tugged on the skirt of her ill-fitting dress. Although she'd let out the seams, it wouldn't be long before she'd be relegated to less fashionable dresses that would accommodate her increasing figure. Hopefully, she would still be living in Nicodemus, where she could freely discuss her changing shape and the impending birth with her older sister. Having Jarena nearby would serve to lessen her fears. She slid her hand across the front of the wool skirt and attempted to imagine how she would look in January. If elected, Moses would be sworn into office on January 8. She uttered one final prayer before descending the stairs. There was much to prepare for this evening's party.

She'd been in the kitchen only a short time when a knock sounded at the front door and was quickly followed by Miss Hattie's unmistakable voice. Truth wilted as the older woman announced her presence.

Why had she come calling at this hour of the day? The gathering wasn't to begin until early evening.

Swiping her hands down her apron, Truth headed across the kitchen. She could hear the distinctive clomp of Miss Hattie's heavy steps. Truth greeted the older woman and offered her a chair in the kitchen.

Miss Hattie dropped a food-laden basket atop the worktable and announced she was ready to do whatever she could to make the evening's celebration a success. Truth groaned inwardly. Miss Hattie would be ordering her around for at least the next ten hours.

Before she could offer an objection to Miss Hattie's early arrival, the older woman headed for the front door. "Calvin's bringin' in more food. I gotta go and make sure he don't squash them pies."

Truth shook her head. Miss Hattie's son-in-law, Calvin, was no doubt pleased to be depositing the old woman on her doorstep for the remainder of the day. Once again, she wished Nellie had come calling instead of Miss Hattie. Calvin grinned as he entered the kitchen carrying the parcels of food. In a hushed voice, he warned Truth she'd best be careful not to squash Miss Hattie's pies. Truth giggled.

When Calvin had completed his tasks, he kissed Miss Hattie's weathered cheek and bid the duo farewell. "He's off to cast his vote fer Moses." Miss Hattie's chest swelled as she made the announcement. "Now, les get busy. Don't look like you got much food ready for all them people that's gonna be coming to offer congratulations."

Truth sucked in a deep breath. "Or their condolences. We can't be certain just yet."

Miss Hattie glowered as she extended her neck. She resembled an angry rooster primed for a fight. "You sho' do bend with the wind, gal. When Moses come home from Topeka, I recall you sayin' he was gonna win the election what with all them white fellas votin' for him at the convention."

No need to argue. At this point it would serve no purpose. Truth handed Miss Hattie an apron. "Why don't we get started on this food?"

Miss Hattie nodded. "That's fine. 'Sides, ain't nothin' more to say 'bout the election since we all know Moses is gonna win."

Truth sighed. Miss Hattie always had to have the last word.

As the day wore on, folks continued to gather, the guests becoming more boisterous as Truth's energy waned. When Jarena arrived, she insisted Truth rest for the remainder of the day. Normally Truth wouldn't agree to such a suggestion, but by midafternoon, her nerves were worn as thin as a threadbare dish towel. Being around Miss Hattie all day had taken its toll. She trudged upstairs and fell upon the bed.

Daylight had faded when Truth awoke with a start. The sound of laughter and loud voices drifted into the bedroom. Disoriented, she shifted her legs and sat on the edge of the bed. What time was it and who was causing the uproar downstairs? As soon as she asked herself the question, she remembered the party. Taking only a moment to arrange her hair, she walked to the top of the stairs and was greeted by a throng of visitors. She searched the crowd for Moses and then spotted him across the parlor. After waving him toward her, she started down the steps.

When she had nearly reached the bottom of the stairway, some-one shouted, "Your husband has won the election, Truth! He left his opposition in the dust!"

Her knees buckled and she grabbed the handrail, thankful for the support. Moses reached her side and held her by the waist as she lowered herself onto the tread.

She looked up at him through a murky fog. "Is it true? Have they already announced your victory?"

Before Moses could respond, Miss Hattie waved her parasol in the air and ordered the guests to move back and give Truth room to breathe. Truth wished Miss Hattie would heed her own advice and join the crowd. Instead, she hovered nearby, fanning the air while issuing instructions to breathe in and out. Did the old woman truly think she'd forgotten how to breathe? How else did one breathe except in and out? Truth leaned close to Moses and suggested they go upstairs.

Miss Hattie gave the couple her unsolicited permission and advised she'd check on progress in the kitchen. "But don' be up there too long. You's the one folks is wanting to see, Moses."

Moses laughed and agreed, but Truth shuddered at the remark. "I do wish she'd quit interfering. You'd think she was a member of the family."

As they walked down the hallway and entered their bedroom, Moses stroked Truth's hair as though she were a small child. "She means well."

Truth frowned as she settled into the rocking chair that over-looked the rear yard. "I know you're anxious to get back to the guests.

But I need to know . . . is it true that you've been declared the winner?"

"It's still unknown. The folks here in Nicodemus are speculating I've won because I've been declared a clear frontrunner in this part of the state."

Truth met his unwavering gaze. "But you believe you've won, don't you?"

"I do, but what I think doesn't matter. It's the votes that will elect me." He traced his finger down her cheek. "You need not begin fretting just yet."

She enveloped his hand with hers and held it tightly. She wanted to tell him of her fears, but now was not the time. She could hear folks downstairs chanting his name. "We had best return downstairs before Miss Hattie comes up to fetch you."

When they reached the parlor, Moses embraced Truth's waist and signaled for the throng to quiet. Much to Truth's surprise, he explained he was delighted they had all come to join in the festivities, but since there would be no definite word until later in the week, he suggested they call a halt to the celebration at midnight. Though there were a few groans and exclamations of disappointment, their guests were mostly in agreement.

However, Miss Hattie commandeered the group's attention. "We's all gonna come back here on Friday night. All you ladies bring some food so's Truth don't have to do no cookin'."

Before the invitation could be withdrawn, shouts of jubilation erupted. Hoping Moses would do something to put Miss Hattie in her place, Truth squeezed his hand. Unfortunately, he was already nodding his agreement.

Truth wandered through the parlor and dining room, straightening furniture and checking tabletops for dust. She wanted to feel assured the house was in order for tonight's celebration party. Though she longed to take a brief nap, she wouldn't want their visitors to think her a poor housekeeper. Accordingly, she circled the rooms several times before giving her final approval.

Although Moses had privately voiced his displeasure over Miss Hattie's invitation to the community, he was clearly thrilled the gathering would reconvene this evening. Tonight the town would truly celebrate his election. The votes had all been counted, and the telegram from Topeka had declared Moses the winner by a landslide. Erik Peterson had ridden like the wind to bring the message from the telegraph office. The voting citizens of Kansas had spoken, and so had God. Truth would not have her way in this matter.

A knock sounded at the front door and Truth checked the mantel clock. Just before four. She'd specifically sent word that Miss Hattie need not arrive until after supper. Truth trudged toward the front door and exhaled a sigh before she yanked it open.

Her jaw went slack and she simply stared, momentarily rendered speechless.

"Aren't you going to invite me in?"

Truth moved to the side. The scent of floral perfume filled her nostrils as the woman came into the foyer. Her fashionable gown gently rustled as she brushed past Truth. "I wasn't expecting . . . I mean, I'm surprised . . . I expected Miss Hattie to be standing on the porch."

Aunt Lilly's familiar laughter filled the foyer. "Don't you love a surprise?"

Truth shook her head. She'd had enough surprises to last her a lifetime, and the last thing she wanted was yet one more—particularly the arrival of Aunt Lilly at her door.

Though Pappy and Lilly had made amends before Lilly departed Nicodemus, Truth wondered if he would be displeased to see her. More importantly, why was Lilly at her place rather than Jarena's? Jarena and Lilly were more than aunt and niece; they were mother and daughter—by blood, if not by any other bond. She peeked out the front door. Two large trunks and a large leather bag sat nearby.

Lilly followed her gaze. "I'm having the remainder of my things shipped."

"Remainder?"

Stopping in front of the mirror, Lilly rearranged the lacy jabot that topped her wine-colored wool traveling dress. "Yes. I'm relocating. But we can leave those outside until I've decided where I'll be staying."

Truth swallowed hard as she followed her aunt into the parlor. *Where she'll be staying?* If Lilly planned to remain in Nicodemus for an extended visit, surely she would move in with Jarena—or even Pappy. Truth was afraid to pursue the topic, for there was no telling what answer she might receive. Moreover, there were chores that needed to be completed before her guests arrived. She'd not had time to explain the celebratory party when she heard Miss Hattie's familiar voice.

The old woman pushed open the front door and charged forward. "Who's that there baggage on your porch—" She stopped mid-sentence and frowned at Lilly. The old woman squinted and took a step closer. "Is my eyes deceiving me, or is that Lilly Verdue?"

Truth smiled at Miss Hattie's little game of cat and mouse. "You know it is, Miss Hattie."

A throaty *harrumph* erupted before Miss Hattie made her way into the parlor. "I'm guessing you's back here to stir up some more of that trouble you's so good at brewing."

Lilly's soft laugh rippled through the room. "The only thing I've continued to stir up is my own perfume, Miss Hattie." She leaned down and placed a kiss on the old woman's wrinkled brow.

The surprising gesture nearly caused Miss Hattie to topple over backward. Touching her index fingertip to her temple, she narrowed her eyes. "What's come over you? You lost your mind since you ske-daddled out of Nicodemus?"

Lilly tilted her head to one side and gave Miss Hattie an exag-gerated wink while Truth wondered what she'd done to deserve the presence of these two women in her parlor only hours before a large group of guests was due to arrive. Even though neighbors were bring-ing food, there were many tasks to complete before the house would be ready for visitors. As the two women continued their sparring, Truth edged her way toward the hallway. At least she could take charge of the kitchen without Miss Hattie's interference. She'd nearly made it through the dining room doorway when Miss Hattie brandished her parasol and waved Lilly aside. Before Truth had time to catch her breath, Miss Hattie had regained control of the party preparations.

With each new arrival, Truth endured a similar ritual: a polite inquiry about the baggage, a surprised exclamation, and a barrage of questions for Aunt Lilly. No one, though, appeared more surprised than Jarena. After delivering only a perfunctory kiss to Truth's cheek, she'd made an immediate beeline to Lilly's side, and the two of them now engaged in a whispered exchange. While Truth observed the twosome from across the room, she remembered she'd not mentioned Moses's victory to her aunt. Likely Jarena had already told her.

Truth sauntered across the room and joined the two women. "I suddenly realized I hadn't mentioned why we're hosting this evening's party, Aunt Lilly."

Lilly arched her perfectly shaped brows and shrugged. "Is a *reason* required for entertaining friends and family?"

Truth was uncertain whether her aunt intended the remark as a question or insult. "Of course not," she replied demurely. "But in this case we are celebrating Moses's recent victory. He's been elected state auditor." When Lilly didn't comment, Truth glanced at her sister and then turned back to Lilly. "You already knew, didn't you?"

"I received a letter from Jarena shortly after Moses was nominated. Though I hadn't seen formal notice of his victory, I never doubted he would win." She moved closer. "You *do* recall I told you this would happen, don't you?"

Her aunt continued talking, but Truth heard no more of Lilly's comments. She directed a questioning look at her sister. Not once had

Jarena mentioned corresponding with Lilly. The idea that the two of them had been exchanging letters was not as disconcerting as realizing Jarena had kept a secret from the family. Or had she? Perhaps Jarena had told the others. Was Truth the only one who'd been in the dark? Grasping her skirts in one hand, Truth excused herself and hurried to the kitchen.

Passing through the dining room, she took hold of Grace's arm and tugged her along through the kitchen and then outdoors into the bracing autumn air.

"What's gotten into you, Truth? It's cold out here." Grace folded her arms across her chest and briskly rubbed her upper arms.

Light filtered out through the kitchen window to reveal her sister's frowning face, but Truth paid no heed to the cold or her sister's puckered brow. "Did you know Jarena's been corresponding with Aunt Lilly?"

Grace stared at her in surprise. "You brought me out here in the cold to ask *that*? What's gotten into you, Truth?" She yanked her sister by the hand. "Come on! Let's get inside."

Truth clasped her fingers tightly around Grace's hand and refused to budge.

"I believe she mentioned writing a letter to Aunt Lilly." Grace shrugged. "Don't know what difference it makes. Now can we go back inside?"

"Did Pappy know?"

Grace yanked loose. "I s'pose. We never talked about it. Do you need to rest for a while? What's wrong with you?"

Truth shook her head. From the strange look on her sister's face,

Grace thought she'd become mentally unstable. Best she not dig any further or Grace would mention her questions to Jarena.

The remainder of the evening passed in a blur. The guests came and went, the food trays were continuously filled and emptied, well-wishers offered their congratulations, and laughter filled the house. Late in the evening, Truth surveyed the roomful of remaining guests. From outward appearances, all seemed well. She doubted anyone could surmise that a thorn of betrayal had lodged in her heart.

Though Truth had privately protested, Moses insisted the family remain for the night. The hour had been late when the final guests departed, and he'd pointed out there were ample accommodations for everyone—including Lilly. Truth had shivered at the prospect of having her aunt's belongings moved into the house. Truth was sure Lilly would view that act as an invitation to remain as their houseguest.

The following morning the entire family gathered in the dining room for breakfast, thanks to Jarena's efforts. Exhausted by the previous day's activities, Truth had remained abed as long as possible. In fact, had Moses not awakened her, she would have slept through breakfast. She truly wanted sleep more than food—or company.

Once seated at the dining table, Truth settled into her role of hostess and casually inquired into her aunt's future plans. Lilly helped herself to a spoonful of scrambled eggs and explained she'd made no definite plans other than to get out of Colorado before the winter snows set in.

Ezekiel speared a piece of ham and dropped it onto his plate. "Where you two gonna live when you's in Topeka, Moses?"

Moses wiped his mouth with the linen napkin. "That's still to be decided. I thought we'd travel to Topeka sometime in the next week or two and see about finding a place. If I can arrange to have Harvey Boyle take over the newspaper here, I'd like to get settled in Topeka as soon as possible. I'm planning to go to Hill City today and visit with Harvey."

His response came so quickly Truth wondered if her father and husband had prearranged the question. Likely they wanted to prepare her for the inevitable. Besides, she had come to realize that discussing their departure from Nicodemus was easier for Moses when others were present.

Truth wanted to visit the doctor before setting their timeline for departure. She'd experienced a small amount of bleeding over the past week, but she didn't want to blurt out such personal information in front of the entire family. How could she fashion a reply without appearing obstinate? "If you want to travel to Topeka and secure a house for us, I won't object, my dear. However, I wouldn't wish to depart before Christmas. I don't know when we'll be able to return home for a visit; besides, Grace couldn't depart now, either."

"Uh-huh, she's right about that," Grace affirmed. "I already promised Silas I'd wait until after the holidays to leave."

Lilly tapped a finger to her lips. "I'd be pleased to go along, Moses. I can assist you in finding a suitable house. And if I like the town, I may decide to settle there in the capital city."

A deafening silence followed the revelation. Lilly's surprising announcement could mean only one thing—trouble.

CHAPTER

— 8 —

Hill City, Kansas

Macia had been waiting at the newspaper office for at least an hour. Though she'd told her brother she needed to speak with him, she knew he would continue with his printing until the job was completed. Thankfully, it appeared he would soon finish.

Outside, the wind tumbled loose brush and debris down the street while gray clouds hung heavy in the sky. Macia wondered if Hill City would soon be covered in a blanket of snow. Even though a warm fire blazed nearby, she shivered at the thought of the approaching winter. November was much too early for snow—at least as far as she was concerned. However, snow arrived in western Kansas any time from

October to May. Once the farmers planted their winter wheat, they were pleased to have the snow providing moisture and acting as a winter blanket for their crops. At the moment, Macia wasn't interested in crops or weather.

When the din of the press finally ceased, Macia stepped to her brother's side and began to question him. She had hoped to hear that he'd been successful in locating a housekeeping position for Fern. Unfortunately, that wasn't the case. Harvey hadn't found a thing.

"I wish Father would heed my request and withhold Fern's pay for ruining my dress. If he'd comply, I believe Fern would immediately begin to seek employment elsewhere."

Harvey brushed a lock of chestnut brown hair from his forehead and started to replace the type in the proper compartments of the type case. He waved her forward and pointed at the chase that held columns of type. "I doubt you'll gain Father's agreement, so you'd best practice your patience. You know how he dislikes confrontation."

As she removed type from the chase's iron frame, Macia peered out the front window. "Have you seen those folks before?"

Harvey followed her gaze and then shook his head. A buggy with four occupants slowly rolled down the street. Macia watched as the conveyance stopped in front of the newspaper office. A couple that appeared to be about the age of Macia's parents stepped out of the buggy, soon followed by a boy of approximately twelve years and a pretty daughter that seemed to capture Harvey's interest.

Macia poked him in the side. "I thought you were interested in Mattie Lawson."

Harvey laughed. "I hardly know her, although Garrett tells everyone I've all but placed an engagement ring on her finger."

Before they could discuss Harvey's romantic relationships, the front door opened and the foursome entered. The man stepped forward and offered his hand to Harvey. "Vernon Faraday. My wife, Lula, and my children, Camille and Jonas."

Harvey shook the man's hand, but the sparkle in her brother's eyes was clearly intended for Camille. "Harvey and Macia Boyle. Pleased to make your acquaintance—all of you."

Camille's smile faded, but she nodded at Macia. "Pleased to meet you, Mrs. Boyle."

Macia giggled at the greeting. "I do apologize for my laughter, but I'm Harvey's *sister*, not his wife."

Camille's enchanting smile promptly returned at the pronouncement.

"It's a pleasure to meet all of you. What brings you to Hill City?"

Though Mr. Faraday stepped forward, his wife offered the response—one that seemed stilted and rehearsed—albeit interesting. Macia questioned the validity of the woman's reply. Why would a successful pharmacist leave his business, his home, friends, and extended family to move west? She bit her lip at the thought. Likely for many of the same reasons her own father had decided to leave Kentucky several years ago.

From all appearances, the Faraday family had much in common with her own. Though they weren't Southerners, they were educated and had an air of refinement. Macia's mother would be delighted: finally someone she could relate to might be settling in the community. The very thought made Macia anxious to have the Faradays call

Hill City their new home. It had become painfully clear that her mother needed someone or something to keep her mind occupied. Otherwise, the long hours closeted in her bedroom would only continue. Possibly Mrs. Faraday would provide her mother with an added incentive to enjoy life.

As for the other members of the family, Camille was friendly enough and close to her own age—she might even be someone with whom Macia could form a friendship. And it certainly appeared Harvey would soon be vying for Camille's attentions. Her brother looked quite smitten with the new arrival. Young Jonas might prove an excellent intermediary for Harvey's cause, since the boy seemed fascinated by the printing press.

However, Mr. and Mrs. Faraday expressed no definite commitment to Hill City. Rather, they were searching for a town in need of a pharmacy. When they'd noticed the doctor's office was closed, Mrs. Faraday had decided the next best place to procure an answer to their question would be the newspaper office.

Harvey's chest swelled with pride. "You're absolutely correct. A good newspaper is the pulse of a community."

Mrs. Faraday screwed her lips into a tight knot. "I'm not sure if it's the pulse, but it's usually where you can find the folks who know everyone else's business."

Macia noticed her brother's chest deflate a bit as he hastened to explain his newspaper provided a valuable service by keeping the community informed.

The woman shrugged. "Newspapers provide exactly what folks want—gossip."

Obviously, Harvey's profession would garner no accolades from the matriarch of the Faraday family. Without further ado, Mrs. Faraday launched into a litany of questions regarding the size of the community, number of physicians, nearest pharmacy, and whether Harvey thought the doctor would be amenable to a pharmacy in town. "You know how doctors can be. Many of them prefer to dispense their own drugs—more money lining their own pockets." A hint of anger edged her words.

Macia retrieved her cape from a hook on the wall. "I believe you'll find my father more than welcoming. He's been anxious to see a pharmacy in Hill City. In fact, why don't I accompany you and you can ask him for yourself? He should still be at home. My mother's health has suffered of late, and he usually spends time at home with her after the noonday meal."

A deep blush tinged Mrs. Faraday's cheeks, and Macia suspected the woman hadn't made the familial connection. Mr. Faraday's smug grin, on the other hand, seemed to indicate he had known all along. In all likelihood, Mr. Faraday had observed the signage on the office door while his wife had not. He gave his wife a condescending look.

Harvey pointed to his buggy. "Just follow us. The house isn't far." While the Faradays clambered into their carriage, Harvey assisted Macia into his and then settled in the seat and took up the reins. He glanced at his sister and gave a slight shake of his head. "There's something strange about Mr. and Mrs. Faraday. I can't put my finger on it."

Macia patted her brother's arm. "I trust you'll soon know. After all, you newspaper people are nothing but gossips." She sputtered the final words and then burst into a fit of giggles. "You're right, though. They act as if they're not very fond of each other, but remember how Mother and Father were when Father decided we would move west? A decision like that can cause family strife. Perhaps it's merely all the upheaval of their relocation. At least *we* had a final destination when we moved. They seem to be going from town to town, searching for a place to settle as they travel."

While Harvey waited for their guests, Macia hurried inside the house to alert her parents of the imminent visit. Relieved to find her mother up and dressed, Macia delightedly regaled her parents with all the information that she could pass on before the Faradays entered the house.

The moment their guests arrived, her mother rang the small brass bell and directed Fern to prepare tea. "Why don't you assist her, Macia? I'm sure Fern would appreciate your assistance."

The idea of spending time alone with Fern was the last thing Macia sought, but she didn't want to cause a scene. So while the Faradays settled themselves and began to talk with her parents, Macia hastened to help in the kitchen. She spied a pot of boiling water on the stove. Thankfully, it wouldn't take long to prepare the tea. After setting the tea to brew, she cut pieces of lemon pound cake and carefully arranged them on her mother's best cake plate. Skirting the outer perimeter of the room in order to avoid Fern's path, Macia gathered cups and saucers and poured cream into the china pitcher. Though Fern muttered several complaints, Macia completed the tasks without comment.

"Thank you, my dear," her mother said as Macia put the tray

down on the table beside her chair. "You sit down and visit. I'll pour." Apparently her mother had taken a liking to Mrs. Faraday. Otherwise, she wouldn't have considered assuming hostess duties.

While Harvey entertained Camille and Jonas with tales of life in Hill City, Mrs. Faraday offered flowery praise for the Boyles' house and willingly participated in discussions about decorating schemes and the latest fashions. However, her attention remained divided. At times, she even interrupted the men to interject a comment regarding the pharmacy business or their family's relocation. When Macia's father suggested a visit to a possible site for a pharmacy, Mrs. Faraday jumped to her feet, prepared to accompany the men.

It was Macia's mother who waved the visitor back into her chair. "I believe we should permit the men to make the visit into town. You said you'd like an opportunity to view our previous home. I would be delighted to accompany you for a tour—provided you promise not to expect too much."

Mrs. Faraday assured her mother that she'd seen the soddies and dugouts as they'd traveled from Ellis and she would be pleased to live in any house so long as it wasn't made of dirt. The visitor gasped when Mrs. Boyle revealed that theirs had been the only wood house in Hill City when they'd arrived in 1877. While her mother went upstairs to fetch her hat, Mrs. Faraday pulled her husband aside for a private conversation. Macia couldn't hear what was said, but on several occasions Mrs. Faraday pointed her index finger and seemed more like a scolding parent than a wife.

Macia would have preferred to accompany the men because she assumed Mr. Faraday would be more forthcoming than his wife.

However, she had no choice in the matter, for her mother insisted she and Camille join the women while Harvey entertained Jonas. Without much difficulty, Harvey convinced Jonas he would enjoy seeing the old house, too. Macia grinned. There was no doubt Harvey wanted to remain near Camille.

Macia found her mother's transformation amazing. The two women discussed the challenges of living in a small town without the proper accoutrements. "I do miss my ladies' group," her mother commented as they walked up the steps of the house the Boyles had lived in when they first arrived in Hill City. "We enjoyed discussing books while we did our needlework each week."

"You know, Margaret, we could begin a group in Hill City—do our part to help civilize these folks. Between the two of us, I'm certain we'd have an excellent choice of books, and we could enrich the lives of the other residents."

When their mother readily agreed to the plan, Macia looked at Harvey, her mouth agape. She'd not seen their mother express this much fervor since their arrival in Hill City. The thought of the two women organizing the women of Hill City for a discussion of William Shakespeare or Sir Walter Raleigh was more than a little amusing. Betsy Turnbull, who couldn't even read, would probably be one of the first to attend. Macia wondered how enthusiastic Mrs. Faraday would remain after she encountered some of these unschooled women.

Tired of constantly having to be aware of proper manners around Mrs. Faraday and Camille, Macia was glad when the tour of their old home was complete and they'd returned to the Boyle residence, meeting up with her father and Mr. Faraday along the way. Mr. Faraday informed his wife that he'd signed the paperwork to purchase a limestone building that would more than adequately serve as a pharmacy. Macia had heard stories of Richard Martin, the building's former occupant, leaving to pursue his fortune in Colorado, and Mr. Faraday said the building's owner, W. R. Hill, had offered him an excellent price. Though Mr. Martin had operated a tailor shop and lived in the rear of the building, Mr. Faraday assured his wife the building would need few modifications.

While Mr. Faraday excitedly described all the attributes of the building, his wife's shoulders squared and her features tightened until they resembled a granite carving. "You've purchased the building? Without my being present?" A foreboding silence hung in the air as the woman directed an icy glare at her husband.

Macia's mother stepped forward and clasped Mrs. Faraday's arm. "Isn't that the most wonderful news? I can't tell you how delighted I am." Margaret chirped on as though she hadn't noticed Mrs. Faraday's angry behavior.

Fortunately, her words served to lighten the mood. When Fern announced supper was served, the scowl disappeared from Mrs. Faraday's face. In fact, she became quite animated during the supper hour as she listened to details regarding the early settlement of Hill City and asked many questions.

After Dr. Boyle described the difficult circumstances encountered by the first settlers to Nicodemus—caused in large part by Mr. Hill's unconscionable behavior—Mrs. Faraday shook her head in disgust. "Unfortunately, there are all too many men willing to take advantage of others in order to serve their own selfish purposes."

Macia noted Mrs. Faraday's quick glance at her husband and once again wondered if there wasn't much more than met the eye with this family. If so, perhaps Camille would be more forthcoming in the future. The girl had certainly remained a closed book thus far. In fact, Camille's only revelation had been her intensifying interest in Harvey.

Jonas dipped a spoonful of creamed peas onto his plate and asked if Harvey needed any assistance at the newspaper. Mrs. Faraday motioned for her son's silence. "If we remain in Hill City, you'll be attending school."

Camille sighed as she passed the bowl of mashed potatoes to her brother. "What do you mean, Mother? You heard Father say he's already signed papers to purchase the pharmacy. Of course we're staying."

Mrs. Faraday leveled a warning look at her daughter. "I doubt any money has exchanged hands. I'm sure Mr. Hill won't hold your father to the contract if we decide this isn't where we want to settle."

Harvey laughed. "I wouldn't rely upon that notion. Mr. Hill may have softened a bit in the last year or two, but when it comes to business, he'll hold you to the contract."

Though Mrs. Faraday appeared unconvinced, she didn't argue. "In that case, I suppose we should finalize our living arrangements. I believe I saw a hotel in town."

Mrs. Boyle waved away the comment. "I see no reason you couldn't stay at our old house. It's been unoccupied since we moved into this home. Of course, if you find it comfortable, you may even want to purchase it in the future. I can send Fern over to remove the dustcovers from the furniture and tidy things up a bit. I know you're accustomed to much finer, but we'd be willing to rent it to you until you decide whether you prefer to purchase or build. Wouldn't we, Samuel?"

Macia's father gave a hearty nod. "You've seen the house, Mrs. Faraday, and your family is most welcome to rent the dwelling. In addition, you'd have time to make a proper assessment of the town before deciding to build a house."

Mrs. Faraday chased a single pea across her dinner plate and speared it with her fork. "Since my husband has already sealed our fate in Hill City, we will thankfully accept your proposal—and the offer of your housekeeper to set things aright."

Macia immediately turned her attention to Mrs. Faraday. "Will you be requiring a housekeeper on a permanent basis?"

The question appeared to cause the woman a moment of discomfort. "Not immediately, though we might after we're settled. I imagine it's somewhat difficult to find good help that you can trust."

Macia jumped to her feet, shrieking as cold liquid splashed down her back. Fern was holding a pitcher that had been filled with milk only moments earlier. "Oh, I'm terribly sorry. I tripped on the rug. I do hope I haven't ruined your gown, Miss Macia." Fern offered a napkin, but she was wearing a smile so unctuous it nearly slid off her face.

Holding her temper in check, Macia excused herself and headed toward the stairs. "You're absolutely correct, Mrs. Faraday. Finding capable help is virtually impossible."

Camille stood up and followed Macia. "I'll come along and help you out of your dress."

"Thank you, Camille. It's obvious Fern isn't going to offer her assistance—not that I'd trust her to help me. She'd likely tear this gown to shreds, also."

Fern returned Macia's icy stare with a look of pure hatred that sent a chill of fear coursing through Macia's being. She *must* convince her father to terminate Fern's employment before the woman did more than just destroy her gowns and pour milk down her back.

Once in Macia's room, Camille motioned for Macia to turn around and began to unbutton the soggy gown. "I didn't want to say anything downstairs, but I know your housekeeper didn't trip. I watched her intentionally pour that milk on you."

"I don't doubt you." As Macia slipped out of her gown, she explained the circumstances surrounding her return to Hill City and Fern's obvious fears about losing Jeb Malone's affection. "I've truly done nothing to warrant such outrageous behavior. I'm not competing for Jeb's attention, but she remains jealous of any contact I have with Jeb or his sister."

After she draped the gown over a chair, Camille blotted out the dampness with a towel. "So even though you were planning to marry Jeb, you no longer have any romantic feelings for him?"

Macia paused. She didn't want to admit she still cared for Jeb. "Time and circumstances have a way of changing our feelings. Besides, I've met someone new—Garrett Johnson. He's quite handsome and extremely kind." She didn't give Camille the opportunity to quiz her further. Instead, she talked—about Garrett, about the canning factory, about her trip abroad, about Mrs. Donlevy's illness and subsequent death, and about her own family's move to Hill City years earlier. By the time her narrative finally ended, she had sponged off and redressed.

"I feel like we've been friends for years," Camille said as they departed the bedroom.

Macia laughed. "You should. I've told you my entire life history. And next time we're alone, you must do the same. I want to hear all about your life before arriving in Hill City."

"I doubt you'd find it very interesting." Camille tugged on Macia's hand before they descended the steps. "Tell me, does Harvey have somebody special?"

Macia gave her a wink. "He doesn't seem to have time for anything or anyone other than his printing press. Perhaps you can change that."

Camille responded with a beaming smile.

CHAPTER

— 9 —

Nicodemus, Kansas

The unfolding events swirled around Truth like a prairie whirlwind. When had her life gotten so out of control?

When Moses mentioned his plan to visit Harvey Boyle in Hill City, Aunt Lilly jumped up from her chair. Truth listened in amazement as her aunt declared her desire to visit the Nelson children in Hill City. In fact, Truth nearly laughed aloud at the declaration. Aunt Lilly wanted to go visit the Nelson children? Had the woman lost her senses out in Colorado and forgotten she disliked children? Obviously, Lilly had no memory of the trials and tribulations she purportedly suffered at the hands of the Nelson children while in the employ of the Hill City banker and his wife a couple years ago. Or was this merely a masquerade? A ruse to conceal the genuine reason she wanted to accompany Moses to Hill City? One could never be sure with Aunt Lilly.

Lilly glanced across the table at Jarena. "I'm certain Truth won't feel up to making the journey in her condition, but perhaps you'd be willing to accompany me, Jarena. Thomas won't mind the fact that you want to spend time with me, will you, Thomas?"

Without waiting for a response, Lilly continued to formulate her plan. Truth waited and watched as Jarena and Lilly outlined their journey. Pained and somewhat confused about the fact that they'd just assumed she wouldn't want to join them for the trip, Truth motioned for Moses to join her in the kitchen.

"I believe I'll go with you to Hill City. I'd like to see the Boyles before we move to Topeka, and this may be my final opportunity."

Moses looked delighted, but Truth didn't fail to notice Aunt Lilly's frown when they returned to the dining room and she heard the news. Clearly, Lilly wanted to spend time alone with Jarena and likely surmised Truth would listen in on everything they said. And she would! Truth was curious to discover how and when Jarena and Lilly had developed this seemingly close relationship. So far as she knew, the two women hadn't even been corresponding.

After breakfast, the four of them loaded into the wagon, and Jarena held out her arms to take Jennie from Thomas's arms. With an air of authority, Lilly pushed Jarena's arms aside. "Surely the child would be more comfortable at home with Grace or her father."

Truth turned from her seat up front and gave her aunt a wry grin.

"Why, Aunt Lilly! I thought you enjoyed children. Isn't that why you're going to Hill City? To reunite with the Nelson youngsters?"

"I'm thinking of Jennie, not myself. It's chilly and she'll likely catch her death of cold if she's out in this weather."

"There are blankets, and Jennie would much prefer being with her mother," Truth pointed out. "Besides, the sun is out and it's going to warm considerably. Don't you agree, Jarena?"

"Yes. Besides, I wouldn't consider leaving her behind." Jarena settled the child onto her lap and leaned from the buggy to kiss Thomas good-bye. "You can help me if Jennie becomes fussy, Truth." Jarena giggled as she playfully tapped her sister's shoulder. "You'll need the experience more than Lilly."

When the baby was settled, Moses flicked the reins, and they headed out of town. Apart from the clopping of the horses' hooves on the hardened dirt road and Jennie's gurgling coos, silence permeated the buggy. The open plains soon spread before them like a painted canvas portraying the change of season. The prairie grass had turned to a dull shade of brown, and the curled, dry yellow leaves from an occasional cottonwood crunched beneath their wagon wheels. Rather than a full palette of autumnal colors, the canvas presented a stark, barren beauty all its own—one that Truth had grown to love. She leaned back against the seat and inhaled the prairie's grassy scent and the musky aroma of the fallen leaves.

While the buggy rolled along the well-worn path, bits of conversation drifted to her from the rear of the carriage. Truth shifted in her seat and strained to hear. The slight breeze carried the conversation directly to her ears, and she unashamedly eavesdropped as Jarena questioned Lilly about her life in Colorado. And Lilly, always so secretive in the past, seemed eager to tell of her escapades. Strange!

Truth managed to discern that Lilly had received word from a woman in New Orleans that Bentley Cummings had contracted a lung disease. Truth wondered if he was alive or dead, but Lilly hadn't said. It would be nice to know, for Mr. Cummings had placed a bounty on Lilly's head for the kidnapping and death of his child back in New Orleans.

Truth vividly recalled her first meeting with Mr. Cummings. They'd been on the same train when Truth and Silas had whisked Macia Boyle away from New York's Rutledge Academy. On the train, Mr. Cummings had revealed that he was traveling to Nicodemus in search of an old acquaintance—his former courtesan, Lilly Verdue. Though their father had long ago told Truth and her sisters that Lilly practiced voodoo and was a woman of ill repute, the actual arrival of Mr. Cummings proved disquieting—but not so startling as Lilly's revelation that she was Jarena's birth mother. That piece of information had threatened to shred the very fabric of their family. Slowly, with God's grace and much prayer, the emotional wounds had healed. However, with Lilly back in their lives, Truth wondered if those old wounds would be reopened.

As Truth and Jarena spread a blanket on the ground to partake of the noonday meal Jarena had packed for their journey, Truth considered asking if Mr. Cummings had died of his disease. She quickly decided the question injudicious and opted for a neutral topic. "You've obviously done well for yourself in Colorado." Truth lightly brushed her fingers across the skirt of Lilly's gown. "The very finest silk."

Lilly nodded. "God abundantly blessed me in Colorado."

Truth gaped at her aunt, thinking something or someone had muddled the woman's mind. Had Lilly actually mentioned God and blessings? Was this another ploy the woman was using for her own gain?

While the group dug into Jarena's sandwiches, Lilly told of how she'd come into her own financially while in Colorado—a story she seemed eager to share with all of them. They sat circled in front of her on the ground, Moses and Truth side-by-side and little Jennie on her mother's lap. Truth was mesmerized as Lilly told of the preacher she'd met on the train to Colorado.

"I explained to him that I'd been giving a lot of thought to my past life and thought I was overdue for a change." She gazed into the distance as if she could see images from that long-ago day. "He promised to help me stay on the straight and narrow. He had a fledgling church in Leadville and thought I'd be a good witness to the girls working in the brothels." She shrugged her shoulders. "I decided to go with him and see if he was correct."

Truth clasped a hand to her mouth. "So is that how you earned your money? Working in a brothel?"

Lilly laughed and shook her head. "I did what the preacher asked. I talked with the girls, telling them about my history and asking about theirs, and helped them in any way I could." She told about befriending Belle Hawkins, the owner of the place. "I can't say that I didn't slip from time to time. I still do, but I believe I did a lot of good, too."

And when Belle became ill, Lilly had cared for her. Tears began to well in Lilly's eyes and she laughed with a false bravado. "Why, I even learned to cook chicken soup. Not that my soup helped much. Belle died a few weeks later, but she accepted Jesus before she passed." Lilly dabbed her eyes with a lace handkerchief.

Jarena patted Lilly's arm consolingly as the older woman explained that she'd been shocked when Belle's lawyer came calling after the funeral and advised her of the fact that Belle had rewritten her will only days before she died. The terms of the will specified that half of her estate would go to the church and the other half to Lilly.

Truth's eyes widened. "And so you left town?"

"No. Belle's been dead for quite a while. I used some of the money to turn the brothel into a millinery shop and sunk part of it into a silver mine." She casually brushed several bread crumbs from the folds of her skirt. "I also helped a couple of the women leave Leadville so they could have a fresh start in a new town. They've begun reputable businesses of their own. A few of the girls have married. I'm proud of all of them."

Jarena gave a squeal of delight and wrapped Lilly in an embrace. "How wonderful! You provided those women with an alternative to the sad life they'd been living. You've done something truly astonishing for each of them."

Truth flinched at the show of affection between the two women. Although she found Lilly's story fascinating, she still didn't entirely trust her. After all, it wasn't as though Lilly had a stellar past—her former lies were innumerable. She could tell them anything. In fact, Truth hadn't even heard Lilly say she'd personally accepted Jesus—just that she'd promised that preacher to walk the straight and narrow.

Truth figured Lilly's interpretation of walking the straight and narrow involved a much wider road than the one Jesus walked. Plus, they had no way to verify the truth of her stories. Yet, despite all that had happened between them, Jarena appeared more than willing to forgive and forget Lilly's transgressions.

As Truth and Jarena repacked the picnic basket, Lilly picked up and folded the blanket they'd been sitting on. She spoke over her shoulder as she walked toward the buggy. "And now I must decide what I'd like to do with the rest of my life. Returning to the warmth of this family has meant more than any of you can imagine."

Truth shuddered. After all her lies, Aunt Lilly was trying to slide back into their lives like a snake slithering onto a rock to sun itself. Truth inhaled a deep breath before addressing her aunt. "And so you accepted Jesus and became a Christian while living in Colorado, Aunt Lilly?"

Lilly hesitated, but only for a moment. "Yes, I did, Truth, but I still have much to learn. Too often, I slip back into my old ways. Unfortunately, I find that happens to all Christians with greater frequency than many of us would like to admit."

Was that final remark intended as a jab at me? Truth couldn't be sure, but her own guilt forced her into silence for the remainder of the journey.

When they arrived in Hill City, Moses pulled the carriage to a halt in front of the newspaper office and then handed the reins to Truth. "You ladies take your time. I'll have no difficulty locating you when I finish my meeting with Harvey."

Truth glanced over her shoulder and announced her plans to visit at the Boyles'. Instead of requesting a ride to the Nelsons' home, Lilly stepped out of the carriage and held out her arms to Jarena's baby. "I believe I'd like to stop at the general store and walk about town before visiting the Nelsons." She waved a hand at Truth as though shooing away an annoying fly. "You go on to see the Boyles by yourself. Come along, Jarena."

Truth leaned back in the buggy and watched the two women saunter down the street. Lilly had dismissed her like an unwanted guest at a tea party. So much for Christian love! Turning away, she snapped the reins and encouraged the horse into a trot. Hopefully Macia would be pleased to have her come calling.

Beginning to shiver from the cold, Truth got out of the buggy and walked up the front steps of the Boyle house. She knocked and waited, clutching her wool cloak a bit more tightly. She hoped Macia would be at home, for she needed someone with whom to share her concerns about the future—someone other than family members. Even though she and Macia had shared a special bond during their time in New York, Truth could trust her to render an objective opinion.

Moments later, the front door opened and a surly-appearing housekeeper stood in the doorway, obviously not happy about being interrupted. The woman's expression could have soured milk. The housekeeper folded her arms across her chest. "Well? What is it *you* want?"

Truth took a step backward. "I've come to call on your mistress."

The housekeeper blew a strand of dark hair from her face. "Come on in. We're heating the outdoors."

For a moment, Truth considered telling the woman she considered her behavior rude and abrasive. Instead, she held her tongue. Perhaps Mrs. Boyle had taken ill and the housekeeper had been forced to endure a hectic morning. Removing her gloves, Truth waited a moment. When the housekeeper wasn't forthcoming, she inquired as to Macia's whereabouts. Without offering to take Truth's cloak, the woman pointed her thumb in the direction of the dining room and then strode off toward the kitchen.

Stunned by the woman's conduct, Truth hung her cloak near the entrance and walked down the hallway, where she discovered Macia seated at the table polishing the silver.

Macia jumped up from her chair and gathered Truth in a warm embrace. "It's difficult to believe we haven't seen each other for two years. You look wonderful."

"I didn't know if I'd find you at home. I assume you're not teaching this year?"

Macia shook her head as she explained the teaching contract had been offered to someone else shortly before her return from Europe. "Not that I blame the district supervisor, of course. He needed assurance he could count on having a teacher present, and unfortunately my parents couldn't confirm when I would arrive home."

"So you now occupy your days polishing the silver? And *who* is that housekeeper your family has employed? She isn't pleasant in the least."

Macia giggled and leaned closer. "She intensely dislikes me."

Truth listened attentively while Macia explained her situation in a hushed voice—the distressing story of Jeb's affection for the Boyles' housekeeper and Macia's concerns for young Lucy. When Macia finally grew silent, Truth patted her hand. "So Fern and Jeb are to be married?"

Macia shrugged. "If Fern has her way, I'm sure they will. Poor Lucy—I hope I can find some way to help her. In all fairness, my parents tell me Fern was an excellent housekeeper before my arrival. However, she considers me competition for Jeb's affection, and that fact has . . . well, drastically interfered with the performance of her duties."

Truth grinned. "Wouldn't it be best if she found employment somewhere else—before she ruins *all* of your gowns?" She hoped her attempt at levity would boost Macia's spirits.

Though Macia giggled at the remark, her somberness returned as she explained her father's stalwart position along with her unsuccessful attempts to find someone willing to employ Fern. "But that's enough about that. What's going on with you?"

Truth updated Macia on the recent upheaval in her life.

After a sigh, Macia took up the polishing cloth and rubbed one of the teaspoons. "I truly am amazed to hear Lilly is back. I never thought any of us would see her again. For your sake, I hope she'll decide against the move to Topeka. Surely your father or Moses can dissuade her."

"I doubt that will happen. Aunt Lilly has a mind of her own."

The mantel clock chimed the hour, and Truth pushed away from the table. As she stood up, the front door opened and the hallway soon overflowed with people. Harvey, Dr. Boyle, Jarena, Jennie, Lilly,

Moses, and a young woman Truth didn't know came into the parlor and sat down.

When Truth entered the parlor, Harvey hastened to introduce Camille Faraday. "I stopped and asked Camille to join us. Her father is setting up a new pharmacy here in town." He waved toward Dr. Boyle. "Needless to say, Father is delighted to have someone he can rely on to dispense medicine." Harvey rambled on until the obviously embarrassed Camille called a halt to his flattering account of her family.

After Harvey ceased his adulation, Lilly monopolized the conversation. She quizzed Camille with a surprising intensity, inquiring into Camille's family background as though she were digging for some of that gold she'd inherited back in Colorado. For some reason Lilly had developed an unmistakable interest in the young woman.

Truth watched her aunt with curiosity. When they'd finally loaded into the buggy and were headed back to Nicodemus, Truth quizzed Lilly with the same dogged determination she'd seen her use on Camille earlier. Lilly held up a gloved hand and feigned ignorance. However, Truth remained undeterred.

Finally, Lilly acquiesced. "I've seen and heard my share of stories, and there's more than meets the eye with the Faraday family, I can tell. I stopped to make a purchase at the general store, and after being introduced by Mrs. Johnson, I attempted to engage Mrs. Faraday in conversation. The woman is as tight-lipped as a corpse at a wake. Harvey Boyle had best be careful if he plans to marry into that family."

Moses glanced over his shoulder and grinned. "I'll be certain to offer Harvey that sage piece of advice."

— 10 —

U nwise! The doctor had wagged his head back and forth while uttering the warning. The physician's one-word pronouncement had further convinced Truth what she must do. Her decision wouldn't sit well at home. Moses and other members of the family would think her behavior childish and petulant. However, she didn't want anyone to know her occasional spotting had continued. *I can't tell anyone. Giving voice to the possibility of a miscarriage will make it seem too real. Maybe if I don't talk about it, everything will work out fine. No matter what, I'm not boarding a train for Topeka anytime soon.*

The doctor had advised all should go well if she took care for the next six weeks—proper rest, no heavy lifting or running up and down stairs, and *no* travel on bumpy roads or lurching trains.

He had shook his head again when he heard of her journey to Hill City only days earlier. "What were you thinking to do such a thing without checking with me?" he asked.

Truth quickly admitted her ignorance in such matters and promised to seek his approval in the future. Somewhat mollified, the doctor offered reassurance that the remainder of her pregnancy should pass without incident—*if* she followed his rules.

Moses was determined to locate adequate housing in Topeka as soon as possible. And though she understood his reasoning, Truth believed a letter to one of his acquaintances in Topeka could resolve the issue, and had said as much. With the proper paperwork in hand, couldn't one of those men act as a representative and make living arrangements on their behalf?

After Moses had provided a litany of reasons why he couldn't or shouldn't ask such a favor, Truth had ceased to argue. If she told Moses of her present medical condition, he'd willingly travel to Topeka without her. Undoubtedly, the revelation would ease the strain in their marriage. Deep down, she knew her reluctance was foolish. She also knew she would remain silent.

As if to challenge her resolve, when she entered her house after the doctor's appointment she found it filled with unexpected visitors. Mostly family, but she noted Silas was in attendance, also. *Why are they here? Did Moses invite them without telling me?*

After removing her bonnet, Truth joined the ominous-appearing group. "To what do I owe this surprise?"

Silas stepped forward. "I's thinking it's downright foolishness for Grace to come and live in Topeka when yo' aunt Lilly's gonna be right there to help you. Ain't no need for Grace to be there, too."

Truth's stomach flip-flopped wildly. She quickly scanned the room for an unoccupied chair and a possible ally. Unfortunately, only the chair next to Lilly remained available. As for any ally, it appeared there were none. In fact, most of the family seemed to concur with Silas.

Folding her arms around her swelling waistline, Truth focused a steady gaze upon her twin sister. "I understand you'd prefer Grace remain in Nicodemus, Silas. However, she has already agreed to accompany me. Where Lilly lives has no bearing upon my request that Grace act as my companion until after the baby is born."

"Don't make no sense," Silas countered. "You's being downright selfish, Truth. All you's thinking about is yerself."

Silas stormed out of the house and Grace retreated upstairs while the others stared at Truth as if she'd grown a second head. When no one spoke, Truth finally broke the silence. "Is there something else you gathered to decide in my absence?"

Moses nodded. "As a matter of fact, I was telling the family that we'd be traveling to Topeka the first of the week to secure housing."

Truth gathered her courage before speaking. "As I mentioned previously, I don't plan on making the journey—I don't think it's wise. I won't object if you decide to go, but I hope you'll plan to return before Thanksgiving."

Lilly lifted a hand to her lips and chortled. "Sounds like Truth's got a tight hold on the reins in this family."

Truth frowned. *Why don't you keep your opinions to yourself, Aunt Lilly? This matter doesn't concern you. Why does everyone think they should give me advice about my own life?*

Moses tilted his head and gave a slight shrug. "If you don't want a say in where you'll be living, then I suppose the matter is settled, Truth."

The hint of a smile played upon Lilly's lips as she waved her handkerchief in the air. "I believe I will accompany you, Moses. I think this might prove an excellent opportunity to explore my possibilities for a business venture. In fact, I'd even be willing to assist you with your house search."

Truth swallowed the cry of refusal that threatened to erupt. She didn't want Lilly choosing anything for her—especially a house she'd be living in for the next four years. Between Moses's election and Lilly's arrival in Kansas, her life had gone from serene to chaotic in a matter of days.

Even the arrangement with Grace now remained unresolved. She couldn't believe Silas would consider Aunt Lilly a substitute for Grace. *Outlandish!* And to make matters worse, he'd rushed from the house, leaving Grace in tears.

Perhaps I should tell them the truth. She opened her mouth, but the words stuck in her throat like a piece of dry bread. *No.* She couldn't. She wouldn't. Instead, she remained in her chair while the group disbanded. Moses and Lilly departed for the train station to purchase tickets, while her father and Thomas mumbled something about going to the livery. Jarena remained in one corner of the parlor quietly rocking Jennie.

Once everyone had disappeared and quiet had returned, Truth detected the sound of Grace's footsteps on the stairs. Head bowed and shoulders slumped, her sister trudged across the room and dropped onto the divan.

Bending forward, Grace cupped her hands over her face. "I don't think I'm goin' to go with you, Truth."

Jarena rose to her feet and scurried toward the stairs, carrying Jennie. "I'll put the baby down and then go to the kitchen and make tea."

Truth moved to her twin sister's side. She gently grasped one of Grace's hands and attempted to lower it away from her face. "You promised, Grace. We don't break promises, especially to each other."

Grace moved her hands from her face and folded them in her lap. Pain shone in her swollen eyes, but Truth remained steadfast. She couldn't permit her sister's emotion to sway her. There was too much at stake; her fear was too great; too much could go wrong. She couldn't have this baby without one of her sisters at hand.

While Grace tearfully expressed her growing anxiety over losing Silas, Truth fidgeted with the lace edging of her burgundy dress.

"Besides, I've been wondering how all those white folks in Topeka are gonna accept us, anyway. I keep remembering how they treated the Exodusters when they arrived in town. I don't reckon they're gonna be too happy to see even more coloreds coming to live there."

Finally, Grace had expressed concern over an issue Truth could address with a degree of authority. "There's no need to worry on that account. I've already discussed that very issue with Moses and he says we will be accepted with open arms."

Grace narrowed her eyes. "How's he know for sure? Folks might be willing to welcome *him*, but that doesn't mean they won't treat us like Exodusters."

"No, they won't. Moses said the problem with the Exodusters was that so many arrived at one time without any means of support. The city didn't have enough resources to help all of them." Truth tilted her head to one side and met her sister's intense stare. "This is completely different. You may push aside any cares over being welcome in Topeka. Silas remains the only obstacle."

At the mention of Silas's name, Grace looked away. "I can't blame him for being upset with me, Truth. You know he's been talking of marriage for over a year now. He thinks this is just another way to delay setting the date. He's a good man, and I love him. I don't plan on losing him to someone else."

"Maybe you could set a definite date—sometime in summer. After harvest. He's not going to look for anyone else. Silas will wait as long as he has to. After all, it's *you* he wants to marry."

Jarena walked into the room, carrying a tea tray. "That's easy enough for you to say, Truth," Jarena commented. "Love or not, men don't always wait. Jeb Malone didn't wait for Macia Boyle."

Truth wished her older sister had remained in the kitchen. Grace's decision didn't involve Jarena, and no one had asked for her opinion— especially Truth. While Jarena poured the hot brew into the three delicate cups, Truth reminded herself she should remain calm.

"I believe we've already had our discussion, Jarena. My life is changing, and I need help. Grace agreed to come with me until after the baby is born, and you agreed to move in and take care of the house. Suddenly matters have changed. I'm attempting to reach a res-olution. I don't need you to interfere."

Grace toyed with the handle of her teacup until she nearly spilled the liquid on her dress. "Please don't argue. It's just that I think Silas is right. If Aunt Lilly is going to be in Topeka, you truly don't need me, too."

Jarena added her agreement, and soon her sisters were engrossed in a conversation of mutual accord that totally undermined all of Truth's plans.

Truth clanked her spoon on the edge of her saucer. "Whether Lilly is in Topeka is of little consequence. She is *not* the person I want with me during my confinement. I don't think that fact should be difficult for either of you to understand."

Jarena shook her head. "I think you're being selfish, Truth."

Truth's heart pounded like a military drum roll, sabotaging her earlier thoughts to remain calm. "Do you? Well, if it weren't for *you*, this argument wouldn't be taking place."

"*Me?*" Jarena arched her eyebrows. "How is any of this *my* doing?"

Truth scooted forward on the divan and pointed her finger like an angry schoolmarm. "You're the one who took it upon herself to write Lilly and tell her Moses had been nominated for statewide office. *That's* why she came back here—she said so herself. She sees this as an opportunity to advance herself."

Jarena jumped up from her chair and began to pace in front of the fireplace. "You're blaming me because I wrote to Lilly?"

"Moses's election wasn't any of her business." Truth narrowed her eyes. "Everything was settled until Lilly arrived. Who else is to blame, Jarena?"

Anger sparked in Jarena's eyes as she swirled around to face her sister. "Your husband's candidacy wasn't a secret. It was in all the newspapers. You're merely angry because not everything is going your way. It's time you grew up and acted like an adult. You need to support your husband in his decision, but that doesn't mean the entire family must be disrupted to make your life easier."

"Truly? Then why don't you have Lilly step in and disrupt your life—ask her to move in with you and Thomas. Why should she move to Topeka? After all, she's *your* mother."

Truth longed to snatch back the words, but they'd already hit the mark. The damage had been done. Jarena looked angrier than Truth had ever seen her. She knew she should tell her sisters of the doctor's orders and her own unbridled fear. She needed to speak. Yet she remained silent.

"You're right, Truth," Jarena stormed. "Lilly gave birth to me, but my loyalties have never changed. However, since you find me and my behavior distasteful, I suggest you find someone else to move in and take care of your house when you move to Topeka." Jarena gathered the fullness of her skirt in one hand and hurried from the room.

Grace gasped. "Go after her, Truth."

Her twin's tearful plea rang in her ears, but Truth couldn't move. Though she wanted to heed Grace's advice, she remained frozen. When the front door slammed, Truth continued to stare into the fireplace. "If you want to leave, I understand, Grace. And I'll try my best not to be angry with you."

Grace turned to look woefully at her sister. "You must admit you've not been yourself of late."

Suddenly the floodgates opened and Truth's tears flowed. She wept, softly at first. But as her tears continued, the crying became more soulful until it swelled to fill the room with a crescendo of snorts and sniffles. As she supplied Truth first with a handkerchief and then with several linen tea napkins, Grace begged her sister to stop weeping. Finally, a severe bout of hiccoughs brought an end to the tears.

When she'd recovered, Truth wiped her eyes and took a sip of cold tea. "I know I haven't been myself. I'm frightened and . . ." She dabbed a tear from her cheek. "And one day I'll explain in more detail. But trust me when I say that I *need* you to come with me to Topeka."

Grace sighed. "Then I will come. But I can't make the journey until after Christmas, and I want to tell Silas I'll come home two weeks after the baby is born."

Truth hugged her sister. "Oh, Grace, I can't thank you enough."

One problem solved. She would attempt to find someone else to care for the house while they were in Topeka. Though she disliked the idea of placing her home under the supervision of a stranger, she doubted Jarena would look favorably upon any further plea for help. With any luck, she might be able to find someone with good references. She cleared away the tea tray and with a final hug, bid Grace good-bye.

Lilly and Moses departed for Topeka the following Monday. Though Truth knew her husband was less than pleased by her decision to stay in Nicodemus, he hadn't asked many questions and he'd promised to return home by Thanksgiving. For those things, she'd been most grateful.

Much to Truth's surprise, Macia Boyle appeared at her front door only a few days after Moses's departure. Her heavy woolen coat was pulled tight around her neck, and her teeth chattered. Truth waved her unexpected visitor into the hallway. She hurried Macia into the parlor and excused herself to set a kettle of water to boil.

When she returned, Truth offered an apologetic smile. "Normally I keep hot water on the back of the stove, but with Moses off to Topeka looking for living accommodations, I wasn't expecting—"

"No need for an explanation. You had no way of knowing I'd appear on your doorstep. When Harvey told me he was coming to Nicodemus to pick up some things Moses left for him at the newspaper office, I asked if I could accompany him." Macia rubbed her hands together. "Your house is lovely. Not quite as large as the Rutledge Academy, but very nice indeed."

Truth giggled, but the reference to the Rutledge Academy and the harrowing experience the two girls had shared in New York had a disquieting effect upon them. Finally, Truth asked Macia if she'd like to see the rest of the house.

Macia bobbed her head, and as Truth led her on a tour, Macia praised the well-appointed rooms and the impressive furnishings. These were all of the things Truth had grown to love and enjoy. *All the things I'll soon have to leave behind.* She had worked feverishly as they'd built this house, intent upon shaping it into a comfortable home where she and Moses would raise their family, entertain their friends, and grow old. She had pictured all of it in her mind, even rocking her grandchildren on the front porch.

Now her dream was being pushed aside to be replaced by another—Moses's dream. This time of happiness in their new home and the anticipation of their first child had been relegated to a place of lesser importance, at least in Moses's plans.

A beautiful music box of rich rosewood sat atop Truth's dressing table, and Macia absentmindedly lifted the lid before returning her attention to Truth. "I'm surprised you didn't accompany Moses—especially since you say he's planning to choose a new home. Were you not feeling well enough to make the journey?"

Truth sidestepped the question. "There were other matters needing my attention here at home. I must find someone to look after the house during our absence. I can't bear to walk off and leave it unattended." Truth traced a finger along an ornate picture frame in the hallway before descending the stairs. "We'll be required to leave many of the household goods behind."

Macia hurried behind her like a chick following a mother hen. She hovered while Truth brewed the tea and then insisted they sit down at the kitchen table. Leaning forward, she clasped Truth's hand. "I think I have a solution to your problem. And one of mine, as well." When she'd finished laying out her plan, Macia cupped her chin in one hand, expectancy in her pale blue eyes.

Truth sipped her tea and thought for a moment. "I should like to discuss your idea with Moses, but I don't know when he'll return from Topeka."

"He won't object. Why would he? Right now he'd agree to most anything if it would make you happy." Macia giggled. "You know I'm right."

"But I'm not certain Fern is a good choice to move into our house. I had hoped for a family member—or at least a husband and wife to look after the place." Truth stared out the window. "And Fern is *white*."

Macia shrugged. "So are the Greens and the Wilsons."

"And the Oxfords and Slapes," Truth added. "Your solution isn't without its share of problems, however."

"And merits. Fern is an excellent housekeeper. It's just me she doesn't like. Promise me you'll at least think about the possibility."

Truth nodded. She would think about the prospect, and if all else failed, she'd likely have no other choice. She didn't want the house to remain empty. Yet she hadn't planned to hire a live-in housekeeper. With no one to cook and clean for, what would Fern do all day?

The clank of Macia's teacup stirred Truth from her private thoughts. "I'm sorry. I didn't mean to ignore you. How would Fern possibly keep busy if I hired her?"

"Do you think one of the stores in town might need some help? Surely there's someplace where she could work part of the time." Macia tapped her fingertip to her pursed lips. "I know! What about the newspaper? Perhaps Harvey could have her do something for the newspaper here in Nicodemus since he's going to be operating both papers now."

Truth sighed. "I doubt Fern has a talent for newspaper work. I don't think we should worry overmuch about finding additional work for her until we know if she's willing to move away from Hill City— and if your father will agree to the idea."

Truth's cautionary words didn't seem to deter Macia. The moment Harvey arrived to pick her up, Macia drew him into her snare. And although Harvey agreed help might be needed with the newspaper, he wasn't nearly as convinced Fern was the one to perform such duties. He needed someone who would gather information and write stories for the paper—preferably a person who knew the township and its residents. And that wouldn't be Fern Kingston.

Macia forged on with her arguments. In her earlier years back in Kentucky, she had been declared an outstanding debate student by her instructor of oratory skills. Truth now understood why.

Finally Harvey said, "Should everyone agree to this arrangement—and *if* Fern is qualified to perform the duties, I'll consider her."

Macia lunged at her brother and wrapped her arms around his neck. "Thank you, Harvey. Even if she merely gathers the information, I'll write the articles for you."

Her brother grinned and shook his head. "I know how anxious you are to be rid of Fern. I understand you no longer have feelings for Jeb—especially now that Garrett has begun calling on you in earnest. However, have you given any thought to Jeb's reaction when he hears of this plan?"

"Jeb? What difference will any of this make to him?"

Harvey chuckled. "The woman he cares for is going to be moving out of town. Have you considered the fact that this scheme may cause Jeb and Fern to actually set a wedding date? They may decide to wed before the end of the year."

Macia visibly wilted. Truth patted her hand and consoled, "There's more than sufficient time to explore your plan. We can't decide anything this minute. You continue to think about the possibility, but if Jarena should change her mind . . ."

"I know you'd much prefer to have family living in the house."

———

After Macia and Harvey had departed, Truth considered Macia's idea while she cleared away the teacups. Macia's plan was self-serving—no denying that fact—yet it contained a nugget of merit. As she dipped the cups and saucers into the hot dishwater, Truth's thoughts slowly steeped like the tea she'd brewed only a short time earlier. Having Fern move into the house would alleviate any need to beg Jarena to reconsider, an option that held little appeal. Truth picked up the dish towel and methodically dried the few items. She owed Jarena an apology, but her heart wasn't prepared to take that step just yet.

CHAPTER

—11—

Hill City, Kansas

Macia shivered as she adjusted the basket on her arm. A damp chill saturated the gust of north wind. The billowing blue skies of summer had given way to the shorter days of fall, and a dull gray ceiling of clouds had settled across the horizon to forecast a long, hard winter—at least that's what the older folks in Hill City were saying. *"Gonna be a hard winter. Just look at those skies."*

The tinny jingle of the bell positioned above the mercantile's front door announced Macia's arrival. A number of Saturday shoppers were in the store, the women going over their lists while the men took up their posts at the table near the window to visit and play checkers.

Just as they had each previous Saturday, the men intermittently helped themselves to the coffee boiling on the stove in the northeast corner of the store while pointing to the heavens to affirm their weather predictions. Their wives mostly ignored them, for they were too busy examining the newly arrived fabric or cooking utensils. Macia could hear the women *ooh* and *ah* while inspecting the goods. However, she had learned that in the end, the women would purchase only the necessities. They had to be frugal. A farmer couldn't count on decent yields every year.

Macia skirted around two men who were sucking on their pipes while they contemplated their next checker move. She'd offered to make the trip to the Johnsons' store because she wanted to get away from the house, not because she wanted to help Fern with her duties. Upon her return from Nicodemus, Macia had been prepared to discuss the possibility of Fern being employed by the Wymans. Before she'd had an opportunity to pull her father aside for a private chat, though, her mother informed the family she had extended Thanksgiving dinner invitations to a host of Hill City residents. Stunned, Macia had immediately excused herself from the table.

On the one day she'd gone out of town, her mother had taken it upon herself to actually *do* something—in this case, plan a dinner party that would force Macia to interact with Fern. The bevy of guests invited for the holiday would require a sumptuous offering of food preceded by days of preparation. And Mrs. Boyle would expect Macia to assist Fern wherever needed. The idea was unsettling.

Mrs. Johnson beamed as she approached Macia with an armload of newly arrived fabric. She chattered delightedly as she extolled the kindness of Macia's mother and arranged the bolts of material. "Why, who else but your mother would realize how difficult it is to work in this store every day and then be expected to prepare a large Thanksgiving supper? It's difficult enough serving up plain fare after being on my feet all day long."

"Who else indeed," Macia agreed halfheartedly. She wanted to explain that her mother had absolutely no concept of life as a storekeeper's wife. For most of her life, Margaret Boyle had employed someone else to perform her cooking and housekeeping duties.

Mrs. Johnson surveyed her fabric display. Apparently the arrangement suited her, for she gave a quick nod and then drew closer to Macia. "This will give me an opportunity to get to know the Faraday family a little better. They seem a bit standoffish, don't you think?"

Macia shrugged. She hadn't considered the Faradays standoffish. In fact, she hadn't given them much thought at all. Her brother, on the other hand, had been making every effort to better acquaint himself with the family—or at least Camille. Once Harvey had made his intentions known, Macia had decided against pursuing a friendship with the girl. If Camille and Harvey's relationship didn't work out, could she still be friends with Camille? Harvey's continuing friendship with Jeb caused strain enough!

Mrs. Johnson perused Macia's list and then accompanied her through the store, helping her find each of the items written on the paper. Though Macia would have chosen to stroll through the store unaccompanied, Mrs. Johnson hadn't asked about her preference.

Lifting a tin of crackers from the shelf, Mrs. Johnson nodded toward the side window, the one facing Faraday Pharmacy. "They haven't been open long, but I notice that all the salesmen coming through spend a lot of time over there."

Uncertain what kind of response Mrs. Johnson expected, Macia looked out the window. "I imagine they want Mr. Faraday to carry their products."

"*Hmmph!* Mr. Faraday doesn't sell frying pans or teakettles or jewelry or books, so I see no reason for those peddlers to be making stops at his pharmacy. And sometimes they remain the entire afternoon. Makes a body wonder how he gets any work done."

While the two of them stared out the window, Macia reflected upon Mrs. Faraday's stern qualities. So long as the matriarch of the Faraday family had a hand in the business, nothing would escape her scrutiny. And from what Macia had observed when the Faradays arrived in town, she remained convinced Mrs. Faraday was quite familiar with everything that occurred within the walls of her home and the pharmacy.

Mrs. Johnson poked Macia's arm. "See! There comes one of them now," she said as a man emerged from the pharmacy. "That fellow's in town because he delivered supplies to Jeb Malone over at the livery. Now why would he go to the pharmacy? He was in there for nearly two hours."

"Perhaps he's not feeling well and remained in the store to recuperate before departing."

Mrs. Johnson's sigh of disgust sent her unruly wisps of hair fluttering above her forehead. "That man's as healthy as the rest of us."

Everyone had learned that Mrs. Johnson enjoyed peering out the windows to spy on her neighbors and their businesses. Then she would share her findings as "prayer needs." She prefaced each morsel of tittle-tattle with "We should pray for . . ." That said, she'd be off and running, spreading rumors as though they were verified facts. Frankly, Macia wondered how the gossiping woman found time to stock shelves and wait on customers.

Apparently the Faraday family was Mrs. Johnson's latest target. Unfortunately for them, the pharmacy was in plain view of the mercantile's proprietress—from two different vantage points.

"See those three fellows leaving the pharmacy?" The woman didn't wait for Macia to answer her question. Instead, she pointed to her Seth Thomas regulator clock that hung on the wall, high above the marble counter. "Mrs. Faraday will arrive in exactly fifteen minutes. She'll remain no longer than half an hour. Those men will return shortly after she departs. You mark my word. I know what I'm talking about. We need to pray that nothing terrible goes amiss in that store."

"Who are you praying for now, Aunt Ada?" Garrett Johnson strode toward them with a confident gait. Though the question had been directed to his aunt, Garrett's gaze settled upon Macia.

Mrs. Johnson poked a loose strand of hair behind one ear and mumbled an incoherent reply before scuttling off to the front window, where the men were playing checkers.

"This is a pleasant surprise. I planned to call on you when I left here."

"You did? Why?"

Garrett laughed. "Because I enjoy your company. And also because I thought you might ride along with me to look at some land I want to survey as a possible site for the cannery."

Macia wondered exactly where he was headed. Her hope had been to speak to the German girl Mrs. Johnson had mentioned, the one who might be interested in a housekeeping position. "I'm eager to meet the new German family that moved here while I was in Europe. I had thought to introduce myself at one of the community church gatherings, but I've not seen them."

"They attend the Lutheran church out in the country. It's closer to their farm. I hadn't planned to go quite that far, but we can go out there if you like."

The hem of Macia's skirt swished across the wood floor as she and Garrett proceeded to the marble-topped counter. Garrett discussed the ongoing checker game with the two remaining players while his aunt tallied Macia's purchases, placing them in her basket, and Macia signed the store's credit ledger. Taking the basket from Macia, Garrett escorted her out the door and, with a wave, bid his aunt good-bye. At least Mrs. Johnson hadn't called after them to inquire about their plans.

Macia looked about as they stepped outside. "Your buggy?" She glanced up at Garrett, and he nodded toward the combined livery and blacksmith shop. Gently grasping her by the elbow, he guided her across the street to Jeb Malone's business establishment. A knot formed in the pit of her stomach as Garrett pulled open the heavy wood door and escorted her inside. The sweet scent of hay floated on the breeze to vaguely remind her of the past and memories she didn't want to recall—memories that made her wish she could race home. But running off would call for an explanation. And how could Macia explain what she herself didn't understand?

Hard as she'd tried, Macia's heart hadn't yet released Jeb Malone. Being around him forced her to keep her unwelcome emotions deep inside. Ultimately, avoidance had proven to be her best tactic. After all, she couldn't take to her bed like a lovesick pup. Folks expected her to get on with the business of life. There were people dealing with *real* problems. Besides, now that she and Garrett had attended one or two social gatherings, people assumed they were a couple. They wouldn't expect her to continue harboring any feelings for Jeb.

Glancing over his shoulder, Jeb greeted them and then resumed shoeing the chestnut gelding. Garrett's horse and buggy waited in readiness. Perhaps she wouldn't be required to exchange pleasantries as she had feared. Garrett offered his hand, and Macia moved toward the buggy. Suddenly, only the sounds of snorting horses and the shifting of hooves echoed in the livery. The hammering of shoe nails had ceased, and she instinctively looked down the length of the building. Jeb seemed to be moving forward in slow motion, his boots dropping onto the straw scattered on the floor, forcing a flurry of dust motes into the air.

"I didn't know you were going to be escorting one of the prettiest gals in town." Jeb grinned wryly at Macia.

Though his voice emanated warmth, his steel blue eyes bore the same iciness she'd seen on the day she met him—back when she'd offered to befriend his sister and he'd warned her not to make any false promises because he didn't want to see his sister hurt. She wondered if he'd given Fern that same admonishment.

Garrett pushed his hat back on his head and winked. "Afraid I can't agree with you on that account, Jeb. As far as I'm concerned, Macia *is* the prettiest girl in town."

Jeb ran his hand down the horse's thick, sleek neck. "You're likely right, Garrett." He stroked the horse one final time. "Pretty day to go on a picnic."

A flush rose in Macia's cheeks, and she silently chided herself, annoyed he still had an effect on her. When he asked where they were going, Macia wondered if he still had feelings for her or was merely being talkative with a customer. After all, he'd been the first to mention she was pretty.

"It is a pretty day and we had best be going before we lose light coming home," Garrett said.

Jeb started to turn back. If she didn't say something, he'd walk away. But there was something she wanted to ask him. "I-I wondered if you'd permit Lucy to join us for Thanksgiving dinner. Mother has invited a number of people and we . . . I'd like it if Lucy could be there, too."

"I s'pose that would be all right. What with Fern cooking over at your place, we weren't planning anything special for Thanksgiving." He rubbed his jaw. "Sure, that's fine."

"In that case, why don't both you and Lucy come?"

Macia swiveled her head so quickly she thought she heard the bones in her neck crack. What in the world was Garrett thinking? He had no business extending an invitation to dinner at *her* home.

Her fingers dug into the flesh of Garrett's arm, and she focused upon a broken board. She didn't want to look into Jeb's eyes and be greeted with a cold stare. "Don't feel obligated to come," she said. "I realize there are other things . . ."

He shook his head. "Nope. I've got nothing else to do. I'd enjoy a fine Thanksgiving meal. You can count on Lucy and me." He tucked a piece of straw between his teeth and started for the other side of the barn. "Thanks for the invite."

"You're welcome." Her voice was no more than a whisper.

CHAPTER

— 12 —

When Macia and Garrett arrived at her house to drop off her purchases, he carried the basket into the kitchen and Macia began to unpack it. She glanced up as Fern walked into the room. "Oh good. Would you finish putting these items away, please? I need to speak with my mother before I depart."

Fern glared as she grabbed the basket and yanked it across the worktable. Macia opened her mouth to condemn the rude behavior but stopped short when the housekeeper's features softened as Garrett entered the room. "I didn't know you had come calling, Mr. Johnson. You and Macia going somewhere together?"

Garrett nodded and greeted her warmly. The thought of leaving Garrett and Fern alone was distressing. Not that Macia didn't trust him—but she certainly didn't trust Fern! The minute Macia walked upstairs, Fern would likely ply Garrett with questions. Worse yet, she would exaggerate the facts and declare Jeb had broken Macia's heart. Unfortunately, Macia had no choice but to leave them together. Her mother would accuse her of thoughtlessness should she leave for the afternoon without a word—and she couldn't trust Fern to deliver a message.

She hurried up the back stairway and down the hall. Soft snores greeted Macia when she entered her mother's room. Though her mother refuted the very idea, she always snored when she slept on her back. Macia gently cleared her throat—though not so lightly as to leave her mother's sleep uninterrupted.

Wisps of Margaret Boyle's graying hair fanned around her head as she rolled over and her eyes snapped open. "Who's there?"

Macia approached, took her mother's hand, and hastily explained she was going on an afternoon outing. Shifting on the pillow, her mother gave her approval. "I'm pleased you've found someone to take Jeb's place. Garrett is a fine young man. He's going to have a future."

"We're *all* are going to have a future, even after we die, Mother."

"You know exactly what I mean, young lady. Garrett intends—"

"You're right. I do know. He has aspirations that will take him beyond Hill City. He will be financially secure—all the things *you* desire for my future." Macia released her mother's hand. "If I don't go downstairs, he'll wonder what's keeping me."

"Give Garrett my regards, and hurry along, now."

Macia closed the door and flew down the stairs like a bird that had escaped its cage. She stopped short, though, her wings suddenly clipped by the sight that greeted her in the kitchen. Garrett's large hand cupped Fern's chin as they stared into each other's eyes, Fern's lips puckered into a tight knot. Macia gasped, unable to speak as the horror of the sight constricted her throat. Taking a step back, she leaned against the doorjamb for support.

Garrett tilted his head to one side and grinned. "Excellent try, Fern. You keep practicing." The room seemed to swirl, and Macia felt as though she would faint. Her fingers dug into the cool, hard wood supporting her limp body as Garrett drew closer.

"Are you ill, Macia? You look quite pale."

Crooking her index finger, Macia beckoned him forward. She raised onto her toes and hissed into his ear, "We need to speak— alone."

Garrett grasped her elbow and escorted her into the parlor. "You haven't answered me. Are you ill?"

She glowered. "How *dare* you stand in my house, kissing my housekeeper and acting as though nothing is amiss? Did you think I wouldn't see you? I've never been so humiliated in my life. I think you should leave."

Garrett's jaw dropped. He glanced back and forth between the kitchen and Macia's angry scowl. "You think . . . I? Kissing? You think . . . ? Never!" While he sputtered, his head wagged back and forth like a puppy's tail. His chest heaved as he gulped a swallow of air and took hold of her arm. "I was teaching her how to *whistle*." He pursed his lips and blew a few high-pitched notes.

"Ha! You think I believe that?" Macia yanked loose of his hold and strutted away, but he leaned forward and grabbed her shoulders, his large hands holding her in place. "I don't know why you think I would even want to kiss Fern, but you're going to listen to what happened."

He explained while she looked straight ahead, staring at the turned down collar of his white cotton shirt. Several times he attempted to tip her chin upward, but she swiped his hand away as if it were a pesky fly. He might compel her to stand before him while he talked, but he couldn't force her to look at him.

Her shoulders slowly relaxed as he explained he'd been whistling a tune when Fern commented she'd never been able to accomplish such a feat. "So I explained that whistling is quite simple if you purse your lips properly." He lightened his grip on her shoulders as she finally looked up at him. "If I had wanted to kiss Fern, I would have merely bent forward and done this."

Before Macia could withdraw, he captured her lips in a gentle kiss. She pushed against his chest and stepped back. "My mother would judge you harshly for such behavior."

A twinkle danced in his eyes. "And *you?*"

"Forward and brash."

He laughed. "In that case, consider my kiss the administration of medical aid." He traced his finger along her cheek. "You've regained your rosy complexion. I believe my kiss has healed you. Shall we be going?"

If she weren't so anxious to meet the German family, she'd tell him to go by himself. "If I can trust that you will behave in a gentlemanly fashion."

"So long as you don't falsely accuse me of kissing Fern—or anyone else, for that matter."

"Agreed." She gave a curt nod and took his arm. "Then let's be on our way."

A short, plump woman with a knot of graying hair perched atop her head greeted them by waving her rug beater high in the air. She gave a final *whump* and then cast an irritated frown at the red-and-gold-patterned carpet that drooped heavily across the sagging rope clothesline. Before approaching them, she dropped the weaponlike cleaning device to the ground.

Garrett grinned at Macia. "Glad to see she put down that rug beater. I think she could knock me to the ground with one blow."

Macia giggled, imagining Garrett's assessment was correct. The sight of a young woman rounding the side of the house captured Macia's attention. She bore her mother's fair coloring and a mane of thick blond hair that she'd gathered at the nape of her neck. The young woman hastened to her mother's side.

"Hello, Mrs. Schmidt. I don't know if you remember me. Garrett Johnson—from the general store."

The older woman swiped a loose strand of hair from her forehead as she looked at her daughter. The two women conversed in German; then the younger one nodded her head. "She remembers you. Please come inside and sit down."

After they'd settled themselves in the neat but sparsely furnished parlor, Garrett made the appropriate introductions. However, conversation proved difficult, with each word requiring translation. Macia soon wondered if Mr. and Mrs. Schmidt could get along without their daughter acting as an interpreter.

Gerta Schmidt explained that her mother wished to be excused so the three of them could converse with less effort. Soon after they'd voiced their agreement, the echoing thump of the rug beater against the carpet started again outside. Macia decided Mrs. Schmidt's arms would ache come morning. If the woman's daughter had the same work ethic and could cook, she would prove invaluable to Macia's family.

Garrett glanced about the room, clearly bored as Macia and Gerta started talking. "Your father—is he out in the fields?" Garrett asked.

"*Nein*—no," she quickly corrected. "He's in the barn. Would you like to go out and speak with him, Mr. Johnson? See if he would like to stop working for a short time and come meet Miss Boyle?"

Garrett jumped up from the settee. "Yes, of course. But we'll need to be on our way before long."

Macia was thankful she would have this time alone with Gerta. The moment Garrett was out the door, she continued to question the young woman.

She pulled a chair close to Gerta's side—as though they were old friends preparing to share a secret. "Garrett's aunt, Mrs. Johnson, mentioned you might be looking for work. Is that true?"

"Ya. Do you know somewhere I can work?"

"I may. Not right away, but possibly before year's end." Macia hesitated, trying to form her question as delicately as possible. "How would your parents get along without you to help them with the language?"

Gerta leaned her head closer, her eyes as blue as a cloudless summer sky. "Papa's speech is not always so good, but he understands the

English. Besides, *Mutter* would try harder if she didn't have me to depend upon."

"Then they would agree to your leaving home—perhaps to work as a live-in housekeeper and cook? You do cook, don't you?"

"Ya, I am good cook. Papa would agree. We need the extra money for the farm—to get another cow and some better tools." She rubbed her fingers across a small stain on her skirt. "Could I come home to be with my family on Sundays?"

Macia didn't know what her parents might say to that particular request, but she didn't want to discourage Gerta. Besides, once her father talked to Gerta at length, Macia was confident he'd quickly agree to employ her. "I think that would likely be acceptable."

Gerta beamed. "Is this position of housekeeper for you? Are you and Mr. Johnson to be wed?"

Macia shook her head vigorously. "No, we're merely friends. My parents may need a new housekeeper. For the time being, however, I'd prefer you not mention this to anyone."

"It's a secret?" Her eyebrows furrowed into two thin question marks.

They heard men's voices nearing the house.

"Yes," Macia said quickly, "but I'll send word to you as soon as possible. Promise you won't say anything?"

Though her eyes were filled with confusion, Gerta agreed before the men entered the house. Macia nodded briefly in return, while what she wanted to do was squeal with excitement and skip to the buggy. Now to convince her father . . .

CHAPTER

— 13 —

Nicodemus, Kansas • Thanksgiving Day, 1882

Truth's feet hit the carpet on the bedroom floor early on Thanksgiving. Padding across the room, she glanced over her shoulder at Moses. He was sleeping soundly. The sight of him provided her with the extra layer of security she had longed for during his recent trip to Topeka. Rubbing her arms to ward off the chill, she peeked through the heavy bedroom drapes. A dull sliver of daylight danced upon the frosty ground and winked at her before she released the curtain and let it swing back into place. It was the dawning hour: that time of day when it seemed neither the moon nor the sun was in charge of the heavens. She sighed. Thankfully, yesterday's gray skies and gusty winds had failed to produce the snowstorm

Moses had predicted. Today must be a special Thanksgiving, for who knew when the entire family would be together again. Truth wanted to believe they would be together for Christmas, but given all the recent surprises and changes in her life, she had quit surmising what the future would bring. Especially with Lilly's persuasive nature added to the mix.

Lilly's talk of walking the straight and narrow hadn't fooled Truth. Lilly was still at her best when meddling in the lives of others. Hadn't she already done so by flitting off to Topeka with Moses?

No. Stop thinking that way. This is to be a day filled with joy and laughter. Truth had invited her entire family to her home to celebrate the holiday, and she'd promised herself this day would not contain animosity or argument. Now she prayed she could keep her vow.

She slipped into an old navy blue skirt and cotton waist. Pappy and Grace had come into town yesterday and spent the night, and her father would be anxious for his breakfast. There would be sufficient time to change into her holiday finery once she and Grace had completed their cooking chores. While Moses and Lilly were in Topeka, she'd purchased fabric and made a new dress to accommodate her expanding waistline. Though it wasn't particularly fancy, she'd added a fashionable standing collar and placed matching scarlet ribbons at the neck and down the sleeves. For a woman who had disliked sewing as a girl, she'd amazed herself with the final product. She doubted that even Jarena could fault her stitching.

The smell of coffee wafted down the hallway to greet her and she hastened her step. What kind of hostess remained abed and allowed her guests to prepare the morning coffee?

"Wondered when someone was gonna get up an' fix some breakfast. I done set the coffee to boilin'."

Truth startled at the sound of her father's voice. He sat in the shadows on the far side of the kitchen, apparently ready for the day to begin. She lifted an iron skillet with one hand and waved it toward her father. "Bacon and eggs?"

"Um-hmm. Wouldn't mind havin' me some nice warm biscuits, too."

Truth nibbled her bottom lip as she slid the skillet onto the stove. She'd have to move at top speed if she was going to make biscuits and prepare the pies before the kitchen filled with guests. Perhaps she should have baked the pies yesterday, but Moses liked his pies fresh and she wanted to please him. Especially since she'd not yet told him of her disagreement with Jarena.

Truth mixed the biscuit ingredients and then dropped the dough onto the pastry table. "While I'm rolling out the biscuits, would you knock on Grace's bedroom door and see if she's out of bed, Pappy? Tell her I could use her help."

Her father nodded and shuffled toward the stairs while she cut several slices of bacon. Although Truth had invited her father and Grace to stay with them for a few nights surrounding the Thanksgiving holiday, she'd excluded Jarena and her family. She knew Jarena wouldn't accept; too much animosity remained between them. Besides, with Lilly in one of the guest rooms, the bedrooms were full.

The scent of the frying bacon made her stomach roil, and she swallowed hard as she stepped back. For some reason, the smell of meat continued to bring on bouts of nausea. The undulating bacon sizzled and popped, and the fatty edges slowly rippled and curled. They reminded her of the ruffled edging she'd sewn along the hem of her dress only days earlier.

Her father soon returned and helped himself to a cup of the strong-smelling coffee. Keeping a vigilant eye, he watched as Truth cut the dough into even rounds and dropped them into a square baking tin.

"Is Grace coming down soon?" Truth asked.

"Soon as she finishes her Bible readin'. That sho' is one restful bed you got in that room I used last night. Slept like a baby." He took a swallow of the coffee. "I woke Lilly up, too. Ain't no reason she needs to be layin' in bed. Tol' her to get down here to the kitchen an' lend a hand."

Truth shuddered. She didn't want Aunt Lilly parading around the kitchen and getting underfoot. Besides, she knew that the woman wouldn't want to cream peas or peel potatoes, even if she did know how. Although Lilly knew how to stir up trouble, Truth doubted whether she'd stir up much of anything else this day. Maybe her aunt would roll over and go back to sleep.

Truth turned at the sound of footfalls on the stairs and smiled when she saw her twin. Not needing instruction, Grace immediately came alongside to assist her. The two of them worked in concert, knowing instinctively where the other would be. They moved about the kitchen with the precision of two synchronized timepieces—until Lilly entered the room. Then all activity shifted to chaos.

When she could take it no longer, Truth said, "Why don't you sit down over there with Pappy. When I need some additional help, I'll let you know, Aunt Lilly."

Looking as if this was what she'd been planning all along, Lilly poured herself a cup of coffee and plopped into the chair opposite Ezekiel. She sliced a piece of the bread and smeared it with a dollop of apple butter. When she'd finished her breakfast, Lilly wiped the corner of her mouth and tapped one of her freshly painted fingernails on the table. "I assume you all want to hear the news from Topeka."

Grace bobbed her head like an overwound bedspring, and Pappy pulled his chair a bit closer. Though Truth would have preferred hearing the news from Moses, she realized her father and Grace would be disappointed if they had to wait any longer.

Moses and Lilly hadn't returned until late last evening, and though she'd asked her husband to tell her about their trip, he'd promised a full report in the morning. Now she wished she hadn't agreed to the delay.

Lilly didn't wait for any response from Truth before launching into the details of their journey. She announced the first order of business had been finding a house for Moses and Truth. "I must say that it's good I was along, for I don't even want to think what Moses would have chosen without me." She proceeded to vividly describe each of the houses they'd inspected. When she finished the litany, she filled her coffee cup and declared herself ready to tell them about the house *she'd* finally chosen for Truth. With a sultry chuckle, she mentioned there were sufficient bedrooms in case *she* decided to live with them.

A knock sounded at the front door, interrupting Lilly's story.

"Don' bother runnin' out here to the door. We's already let our-
selves in." Miss Hattie's loud voice echoed down the hallway.

Though Truth had hoped none of her dinner guests would arrive
this early, she was pleased for any interruption—even Miss Hattie.
And where was Moses? Surely he couldn't be sleeping through all of
this noise and activity. Moments later, Miss Hattie trundled into the
room, ordering Calvin to put her several pies and cakes in the pie safe.

Hattie lifted the rolling pin lying atop Truth's worktable. "You
ain't gonna be needin' to make no pies, gal. I done brought enough
dessert to feed all of us for days."

"She's speaking the truth," Calvin said as he began to unload the
pies, "and she wouldn't even let me have one piece with my supper
last night."

"Is Nellie with you?" Truth asked.

"Course she is, gal," Miss Hattie answered. "She's helpin' the
young'uns out of the wagon."

Miss Hattie shooed Calvin from the kitchen, telling him to go
help his wife, and then watched Grace work, hands on her hips.
"You's chopping them onions way too big. Move over and lemme
show you how. What you doin' sittin' over there like you's somethin'
special, Lilly? Plenty of work needin' to be done." She pointed to the
pile of potatoes and a knife.

Miss Hattie had taken control of the kitchen. Truth and Grace
exchanged a look of disgruntlement, for they knew there was nothing
to be done except heed the old woman's orders. Even Lilly picked up
the knife and did as she'd been told. When Nellie joined them, Miss
Hattie put her to work immediately, as well.

Truth wiped her hands on her apron and patted Miss Hattie on the shoulder. "I'll leave you in charge, Miss Hattie. I'm going to check on Moses."

The old woman raised her brows. "He ain' here. We passed him in the hallway. He said to tell you he was going down to the office for an hour." She chuckled loudly. "I tol' him that was a good idea, 'cause he wasn't comin' in the kitchen and gettin' in the way."

Truth longed to take Miss Hattie to task for failing to deliver Moses's message earlier, as well as for banning her husband from the kitchen. But she returned to peeling the yams without a word.

Miss Hattie glanced at Lilly while breaking up pieces of stale corn bread for the dressing. "I hear you's movin' to Topekee, Lilly. What kinda mischief you plannin' to stir up there?"

Lilly slammed a lid on the pot of potatoes and skewered the old woman with a piercing glare. However, Miss Hattie was concentrating on her chopping and dicing, circumventing the effect of Lilly's intended wrath.

"I'm going to open a new business, Miss Hattie." The words hissed from between Lilly's teeth.

Hattie swiped the back of one hand across her forehead. "I's almost afeared to ask what kinda business."

"A millinery shop that will also offer jewelry and other ladies' accessories."

Miss Hattie looked heavenward. "You'd know 'bout them fancy things, so I s'pose you done made a good choice."

"Why thank you! I was concerned you wouldn't approve." Sarcasm dripped from Lilly's words like honey sliding off a hot biscuit. The words were directed at Miss Hattie, but Lilly's attention was focused on the kitchen door. Her scowl disappeared when Jarena and young Jennie arrived at the kitchen doorway. "Jarena and Jennie! How wonderful to see you." Her green-striped dress swished softly across the floor as she hastened to embrace them.

Lilly led Jarena to the kitchen table, where she delightedly boasted of the brilliant contract she'd negotiated for her shop while in Topeka. Truth was sure if the woman puffed up any more, the green and white buttons would burst from her dress.

"And are your rooms above the shop?" Truth asked. Knowing where Lilly planned to live was far more important to Truth than the bargain her aunt had struck for the purchase of the building.

Lilly arched her brows ever so slightly. "There's an unfinished second floor. I'll stay with you and Moses until I can have it made into a suitable living space."

Truth gave her a hard stare. Lilly hadn't *asked* if she could live with them. Instead, she'd made the pronouncement as though her presence would be welcomed.

Jarena placed Jennie on Lilly's lap and crossed the kitchen at a hurried pace. She lightly grasped Truth's arm. "There's a matter I'd like to discuss with you in private if you have a moment."

What Truth really wanted to do was to tell Aunt Lilly she couldn't live with them in Topeka, but instead Truth motioned for her sister to follow and led her upstairs to the master bedroom.

After closing the door behind them, Truth turned on her heel. "We'd better talk fast. I have a meal to prepare."

Jarena loosened the ribbon that circled the neckline of her dress.

"I realize we aren't in agreement regarding several issues right now, some of them influenced by Lilly's return."

"*All* of them influenced by Lilly's return would be a more correct statement. What is it you want to discuss?"

Sitting down on a chair near the window, Jarena glanced outdoors. "Since Lilly is going to be living in Topeka, I had hoped to stop you from saying something you might later regret. There is no doubt you'll be living in close proximity, and it would be best if you started out in good stead rather than with anger between you."

"It's good of you to show your concern, Jarena. But perhaps you should direct your advice to Lilly—you two appear to have established a solidarity that no longer exists between us."

"I know you're angry, Truth, but it's not my fault you're being forced to move away from Nicodemus. Moses—"

Truth halted her by putting her arm out straight, palm facing her sister. "I don't need you to explain what has happened or who has caused my difficulties. Suffice it to say that you've contributed your share, though I doubt I'll ever hear such an admission from you. However, the last thing I want is your advice regarding Aunt Lilly. I don't want her living in Topeka, and I certainly don't want her living in my house."

"But Truth, she can be a help to you, if you'll only give her a chance. I believe she's made great changes since we last saw her. And she's found you what sounds like a very lovely house. It wasn't even for rent, yet she convinced the owner to sign a year-long contract renting it to Moses."

"Apparently you know more about where I'm going to live than I do. I suppose you already know the number of rooms and amount of furniture needed to fill them." Truth strode across the room and gripped the doorknob. "And for your information, I would guess the rental agreement had more to do with Moses and his position in state government than with anything Aunt Lilly did or said."

"Please, Truth—just give her a chance. I don't know why you're so angry. You could have gone along to Topeka, but you chose to remain at home."

Slamming the door behind her, Truth hurried downstairs, with her sister's comments following her like a bloodhound on the trail of a strong scent. *I don't care how angry they make me, I'm not telling them why I chose to stay home.*

As she descended the final stair, the front door opened. Truth heaved a sigh of relief when she saw her husband walk in. Before Moses could say a word, she took her cloak from a carved hook in the entryway and steered him back outdoors.

"Trying to take me captive or merely attempting to escape the Thanksgiving preparations?" His soft brown eyes twinkled.

Truth quelled his grin with a chiseled scowl. "Move over here, away from the windows." She pulled him along to a spot on the far side of the porch. "I don't want anyone listening to our conversation."

His forehead creased with narrow wrinkles. "The windows are closed, Truth. No one can hear us."

"You'd be surprised what people can accomplish when they're determined. Aunt Lilly is proof of that. I understand she's secured quite a bargain for our living quarters, made an excellent deal on the purchase of a building for her new business, and will be living with us." Truth folded her arms across her chest and jutted her chin—fair warning that she'd heard all that had occurred in Topeka and wasn't happy about it.

"I don't believe standing out here in the cold on Thanksgiving Day is the time or place to discuss any of these matters. Let's—"

"When *is* the proper time, Moses? You asked me to wait until morning to hear about your trip, and so I waited. Then this morning you departed without even telling me farewell, and now I find that Jarena knows more about my future than I do."

"I can't change what's already happened. If it will salve your disappointment, we can go into my library and I'll tell you all that occurred." He gently held her chin between his index finger and thumb and leaned toward her. "You could have gone with me; then you would have been able to tell all the news instead of Lilly."

As they gathered around the table and bowed their heads in prayer, Truth felt her shoulders droop. She had vowed this would be a day without harsh words or petty arguments. She had failed. Instead of harmony, discord abounded with both her sister and her husband. And though Moses's soothing words of encouragement in the library had temporarily eased her pain, she remained unhappy. News of the house-hunting journey should have come to her first—not Jarena. Jarena, who now favored Lilly above her sisters. Jarena, who wanted her to give Lilly a chance. Jarena, who now refused to care for their house in Nicodemus. Truth had failed to mention that particular fact to Moses during their private conversation. He would find out soon enough.

CHAPTER

— 14 —

Hill City, Kansas • Thanksgiving Day, 1882

Macia pivoted in front of her bedroom mirror, hoping to view her new dress to full advantage. Convinced Fern would delight in damaging the gown, Macia had been careful to keep it hidden away until today. The dress boasted a green velvet-trimmed cuirass bodice and skirt that tightly hugged the front of her body, while the huge bustle at the back amplified her hidden backside. She hadn't decided if she liked this most recent style. Instead of her legs being demurely hidden beneath hoops, a strong wind would reveal the contours of her body. The populace of Hill City would likely think the dress unseemly, and her father would undoubtedly agree. However, she'd probably gain Garrett's approval.

161

She tucked her watch into the pocket of the dress and wondered what Jeb would think. Would he find the dress beguiling or think her attire too worldly? In any case, his attention would be devoted to Fern as she scurried about serving the meal. Macia grimaced at the thought: how could he possibly find someone like Fern appealing?

She took one final look in the mirror as a knock sounded at the front door. Lucy! She'd told her to come early and they'd set the table together. After Fern's complaints regarding her busy schedule with the meal preparation, her father had offered Macia's services for answering the door. Although Macia had quickly agreed and had also offered to set the table, Fern remained disgruntled. Nothing seemed to please her, and Macia wondered if Jeb would find her difficult to live with once they wed. But then, why should she care if Fern made Jeb's life difficult? Even more disturbing, why did she continue to think about Jeb?

She opened the front door. Lucy stood before her in her Sunday dress, her blond hair perfectly curled and held in place with the dazzling combs that had belonged to her now deceased mother.

Pulling the girl into a warm embrace, Macia complimented Lucy on her lovely appearance. She lightly touched one of the combs. "I see you've learned to manage these combs in excellent fashion. Your hair is perfect."

"Only because you taught me how to use the combs." Lucy beamed as she reached to finger one of the jeweled adornments. "I don't wear them except for very special occasions."

After hanging her coat, Macia took Lucy by the hand and led her to the dining room. "Come sit and talk to me. I promised to set the dining table."

The two of them chatted while Macia removed her mother's French dinnerware from the glass-fronted china cabinet. While Lucy arranged the plates, Macia retrieved crystal goblets from the shelf and began to position one at each place. They'd not yet arranged the silverware when Fern burst through the doorway. With her hands on her hips and elbows jutted outward like arrows, she loomed more than a little unfriendly. In fact, she looked downright hostile.

Lucy's smile faded at the sight. "Hello, Fern. We're setting the table."

"I'm not blind. I can see what you're doing. Amazing that it takes two of you to set the table, but I have no help preparing the entire meal." Her disdain hung in the air like a blanket of dense fog.

Macia noted the pained expression on Lucy's face. Why did Fern take such pleasure in hurting the girl? "You are paid a handsome sum to prepare meals and perform household chores," Macia stated. "Perhaps you should complete your duties with the same enthusiasm you demonstrate when you receive your pay envelope."

Fern didn't seem to hear the retort—she was staring directly at Lucy's flawlessly styled hair. "What are you doing wearing my combs?" she demanded, reaching for one of the shimmering combs tucked into the girl's hair. Lucy quickly tilted her head to one side and took a backward step.

Stunned by Fern's shameful behavior, Macia grabbed her wrist before she could get the comb. "What are you doing? Those aren't your combs."

Fern wrested her arm away and glared at Macia. "They will be on the day I marry Jeb. Until then, I want them secured at the house, not in Lucy's hair."

"They will *not* be yours. After Mama died, Jeb said they were mine. I'm not giving them to you, and Jeb won't make me." Lucy ran from the room, her blond curls waving back and forth as though bidding a sad farewell.

Macia angrily inhaled and exhaled and then followed after the girl, easily finding her by the woeful cries that emanated from the hallway linen closet. Opening the door, she sat on the floor and beckoned Lucy into her outstretched arms. "Come here, Lucy." She folded the girl into an embrace and lovingly held her close. "There's no need to worry. Jeb would never go back on his word to you about the combs."

Lucy's chest heaved in an attempt to hold back further tears. "I'm going to tell Jeb what she said as soon as he gets here." She hiccoughed several times in rapid succession.

After tucking a curl behind Lucy's ear, Macia cupped the girl's face and looked deep into her teary blue eyes. "I don't think that's a wise decision, Lucy. Usually, I find it's best to wait a while before I discuss something that has hurt or upset me. If you want to talk to Jeb, why don't you wait until you go home after Thanksgiving dinner? I think it would be more judicious if you talked to him in private."

"Where Fern can't possibly overhear our conversation." Lucy folded her arms and momentarily contemplated the suggestion. "You're probably right. I don't want to cause a scene and ruin your wonderful Thanksgiving plans." Her shoulders rose and fell in a nonchalant shrug. "I'll do as you ask, but Fern can finish setting the table herself."

While they awaited the dinner guests, Macia showed Lucy various picture postcards of the European cities she had visited and regaled the girl with more stories of her travels, hoping to erase the earlier encounter with Fern.

When a knock sounded at the front door, Macia commenced gathering up the postcards and waved Lucy toward the doorway. "Why don't you take over duties at the front door? I'm certain Fern won't leave the kitchen. I'll join you as soon as I've put these away."

Lucy jumped up, and Macia could hear her footfalls as the girl hurried downstairs. Macia hoped she'd been correct in assuming Fern would expect someone else to answer the door. The thought gave her pause. Scooping up the remaining cards, she tossed them onto her bed. Better to follow Lucy and make sure all remained calm downstairs.

Once she saw that her father was back home after an unexpected house call on one of his ailing patients, Macia heaved a sigh of relief. In addition, her mother's voice drifted from the kitchen as she issued final instructions to Fern. With others in the house and the last-minute preparations in full swing, Macia could finally relax. Fern wouldn't dare create an incident in front of the family and their guests. Jeb had arrived and was seated in the parlor beside Lucy. Macia strained to listen as Lucy told Jeb about Europe and the postcards, pleased when she heard no mention of their earlier encounter with Fern.

Before she could offer Jeb a cup of cider, Garrett arrived at the front door, cradling a pumpkin pie in his palm. His aunt and uncle followed close behind, each one carrying a substantial food offering for the Thanksgiving meal.

Lucy hung their wraps in the hallway, and Mr. and Mrs. Johnson quickly settled in the parlor while Macia and Garrett delivered the food to the kitchen. They entered the parlor in time to hear Macia's mother explain the Faradays had sent word they wouldn't be in attendance.

"Not illness, I hope," Mrs. Johnson ventured.

Macia sat down on the arm of her father's chair. "Mrs. Faraday sent her regrets with her son. I didn't question him."

"Rather rude, I'd say. Sending word at the last minute without any explanation." Mrs. Johnson adjusted the ruffles that surrounded her collar.

Mrs. Boyle entwined her fingers in her lap. "I find that a few more or less guests at a holiday meal doesn't change matters much."

"True. I suppose I'm somewhat disappointed," Mrs. Johnson said. "I had hoped I might get to know the family a bit more intimately. They do act a bit standoffish."

Macia decided that the Faradays were fortunate they hadn't arrived for dinner. It sounded as though Mrs. Johnson had been prepared to interrogate the lot of them.

Soon the conversation grew lively, and Macia marveled at the transformation in her mother. Her cheeks took on a rosy glow, and she seemed years younger as she played the perfect hostess to their visitors.

Although her mother had placed carefully scripted place cards at each setting, she still directed her guests to their seats like a conductor preparing his orchestra. Macia nearly gasped aloud when she realized her mother had placed her between Garrett and Jeb. And although she briefly attempted to switch Lucy and Jeb, her mother's cautionary frown warned against any such change in her plans. Her mother insisted upon her guests being seated man-woman-man-woman in order to maintain harmonious conversation.

As the guests circled the table, Fern moved forward and stepped down hard atop Macia's right foot. Macia yelped and danced on her left foot as she struggled to maintain her balance. Fern's features immediately tightened into a mask of concern. "I'm so sorry, Miss Macia. I forgot something in the kitchen and didn't watch where I was going."

Macia did not fail to notice the satisfied gleam that filled the girl's dark eyes. But Macia would not ruin her mother's party by confronting Fern now.

Garrett assisted her into her chair. Though her foot ached, Macia forced a brave facade and waved aside her father's offer to see if any bones were broken. "Let's proceed," Macia encouraged. "After all of Fern's hard work, I wouldn't want to be the cause of a cold Thanksgiving dinner."

"How kind of you." Though Fern's reply dripped with sarcasm, the others appeared oblivious.

Macia noted the servant didn't leave the room in order to retrieve the mysterious forgotten item from the kitchen. When they were finally seated, her father offered thanks for the many blessings bestowed upon all of them throughout the past year and then nodded to Fern. She moved to the end of the table and began passing dish after dish to Mrs. Boyle. As each of the bowls and platters circled the table in succession, they were handed back to Fern, who methodically set them on the heavily laden sideboard.

As Garrett prepared to pass the gravy boat to Macia, Fern swooped between them and took the dish. "This needs to be refilled. I'll be back in only a moment."

Though Macia didn't argue, she thought the contents of the bowl were more than sufficient to serve the few remaining guests. Everyone at the table continued to serve themselves, and soon Fern returned to the room. As Fern reached between Garrett and Macia, her wrist gave way and hot turkey gravy streamed down the front and side of Macia's gown in thick rivulets. Macia yelped as she grabbed her napkin and began to daub the mess. Her gown was ruined!

Righting the bowl, Fern gasped in mock horror. "Oh, I am terribly sorry. I should have used my right hand. I have a weakness in my left wrist."

Macia seethed. The apology was an outrageous lie to cover this latest occurrence of inexcusable behavior. She slapped the napkin onto the table and jumped up from her chair. "Don't you *dare* attempt to excuse your shoddy behavior as due to a weak wrist. Where was that weak wrist when you were lifting the mashed potatoes or the turkey platter? Why don't you tell the truth for once? You're angry because I'm sitting beside Jeb, and you're angry because I defended Lucy earlier in the day. However, nearly breaking my foot and ruining my dress is as much as I'm willing to withstand. You need to find employment elsewhere!"

Fern moved several steps nearer to Dr. Boyle. "I believe you are the one who hired me. Is your daughter in charge of this household?"

Without giving her father opportunity to reply, Macia took charge. "Lest you think me unfeeling, I have located an excellent position for you. Mr. and Mrs. Wyman will be departing for Topeka and are in need of a housekeeper to look after their home in Nicodemus while they're away."

"Nicodemus?" Jeb and Fern uttered the question in unison.

Macia glanced about the table. Her mother's rosy cheeks had turned ashen; Mr. and Mrs. Johnson stared at their plates as though they'd not seen or heard a thing; Jeb was leveling an icy glare upon her; Garrett appeared baffled; Lucy beamed with delight; and Harvey grinned as he looked around the table.

"Please be seated, Macia," her father instructed. "We will continue this discussion after we've finished our meal."

There was no use arguing. Her father's tone made it clear he would brook no argument. So while the gravy seeped into the fabric of Macia's gown, she forced down her dinner. The table was quiet, with everyone attempting to act as though nothing had occurred. A peek at the faces of their guests made it abundantly clear they longed to have any number of questions answered. Desserts were either refused or left half eaten on plates, and as tension mounted, Dr. Boyle asked Macia, the Johnsons, and the Malones to join him in the parlor. Harvey excused himself, and Mrs. Boyle told the group she was going upstairs to rest.

Jeb immediately disagreed with Dr. Boyle's decision to exclude the housekeeper. "If we're going to talk about her future, she should be present and able to defend herself."

"I'm attempting to keep matters from escalating into an argument, Jeb. I believe it would be best to handle the matter this way. I do plan to listen carefully to Fern's explanations later." He cast a disappointed look at Jeb. "I'm surprised you think I would do any less." He focused on Jeb's sister. "Lucy, I'd like to know what occurred earlier today—between you and Fern."

Lucy detailed the event in a clear and concise manner, though her voice warbled at the mention of Fern's angry attempt to remove the jeweled combs from her hair and claim them as her own. Jeb's brow creased and his lips tightened into a thin line as his sister related the story. He glanced at Macia as though seeking affirmation. She nodded in agreement, and he quickly looked away, obviously distressed by what had been revealed.

When she finished, Lucy gulped a trembling breath. "I don't have to give Fern the combs, do I, Jeb?"

"No, Lucy. Those belong to you. I never told Fern she could have them."

Lucy beamed in response, though Macia noted Jeb's features had creased to resemble the same heavy folds that defined Mr. Johnson's old hound, Lazybones. Though unkind, it was the most amusing thing she'd witnessed in quite a while. She folded her hands tightly and swallowed down a giggle.

Her father turned his attention to her and began his questioning. He requested an affirmation of Lucy's earlier account and then immediately moved on and asked that she recount any additional confrontations with Fern. As Macia detailed the incident relating to her ripped gown, she included Fern's accusation of Lucy. Jeb inched closer to his sister.

"Of course, I knew her accusation was preposterous," Macia added. "Lucy would never do such a thing."

Jeb's shoulders relaxed at Macia's unequivocal show of support for his sister. While her father continued to interrogate her, Macia noted both Mrs. Johnson and Garrett had moved forward on their chairs. They seemed to cling to her every word.

Her father tugged at his waistcoat. "Perhaps spoiling your gowns was Fern's way of warning you to stay away from Jeb?"

"Oh forevermore, Father! She needn't ruin my entire wardrobe to make her point. At any rate, I've given her no reason to believe I have any desire to resurrect my wedding plans with Jeb."

"I believe I'll go and visit privately with Fern; then we can reassemble." Her father caught Garrett's eye. "I think Harvey is in the library if you'd care to join him there—or you may remain here in the parlor if you prefer."

Garrett now eyed Jeb with open hostility. When he looked at Macia, his expression became a confused stare. Mrs. Johnson rubbed her hands together, obviously enjoying everything unfolding in front of her. Her husband seemed prepared to bolt from the room at any moment.

Garrett stood and moved to her chair. "Is there someplace we could talk privately?"

Macia led him to her father's office, which adjoined the library. Careful to close both doors, Macia sat down opposite Garrett. There was little doubt he expected a lengthy explanation. Though he knew Jeb had acted as her escort on several occasions, she'd never mentioned the fact that they had discussed marriage. If that bit of information had ever made its way to Mrs. Johnson's ears, she'd either forgotten or failed to tell Garrett.

While Garrett was entitled to know of her past, the actual telling felt as though she'd opened an old wound. Garrett listened and asked few questions, for which she was most grateful. She worried, though, that the topic would be revisited in the future if he intended to continue calling on her.

Her father's announcement that they should all reunite in the parlor brought their chat to an abrupt end, and the two of them hastened to join the others in the parlor.

Macia's father sighed wearily. "I find I'm not endowed with the wisdom of Solomon. However, one thing has become crystal clear to me." Lowering himself into the overstuffed chair he'd vacated only a short time earlier, Dr. Boyle loosened his tie. "Issues between Fern and Macia have escalated to a point that I believe it best if Fern seeks employment elsewhere. Fortunately, she agrees with my assessment. I've agreed to assume the costs of her room and board for two weeks at the hotel while she decides upon her future. Of course, I'm willing to listen if any of you have other ideas or suggestions."

Mrs. Johnson enthusiastically waved a hand. "I wish to say that you truly are a kind man, Dr. Boyle. Why, after the way that woman treated young Lucy and destroyed Macia's gowns, I'd be tempted to withhold her pay. Instead, you are offering to pay for her room and board."

Dr. Boyle's ruddy complexion deepened a shade as he scanned the room. "If there's nothing more to discuss, why don't we gather in the library? I believe Harvey is hoping to engage some of you in a game of whist."

As Garrett and the Johnsons left the room, Jeb motioned to Dr. Boyle and Macia. "I want to thank you for a fine Thanksgiving meal. Since I don't play cards, I believe Lucy and I will proceed home. Please extend my thanks to Mrs. Boyle."

Though Lucy whispered to her that she wished to remain, Macia determined she'd not interfere with Jeb's decision to depart. The situation had become uncomfortable for all of them, and Fern would soon be packing her trunk and moving to the hotel. Jeb could visit with her there if he so desired.

Dr. Boyle escorted them to the front door and handed Lucy her coat. "I know my wife was delighted to have both of you join us. And Fern asked me to tell you she plans to come and visit with you later this evening." Though her father lowered his voice a notch, Macia heard his final comment quite clearly. A pang of annoyance jabbed her—or was it jealousy?

Lucy peeked around her brother's lanky frame and waved at Macia. "May I come and see you tomorrow or the next day?"

She wasn't inclined to find herself in Jeb Malone's crosshairs again. "If your brother gives you permission, you may come for a visit."

While Lucy peered expectantly at her brother, Jeb acknowledged Macia's request with a slight nod. Macia wondered what he privately thought about all that had occurred this day. Likely he wished he had remained at home, eating his fill of bacon and eggs or butter beans. But then he wouldn't have learned the truth about Fern.

Macia didn't know if he believed all he'd heard, and Fern could be most convincing, but Jeb certainly had some things to think about. For Lucy's sake, Macia hoped he'd consider his next move carefully.

CHAPTER

— 15 —

Macia lifted aside the curtain covering her bedroom window and surveyed the sky. The low-hanging clouds and coating of lacy frost that lined her windowpanes served as a reminder that her journey to the Schmidt farm would require warm clothing and an extra blanket in the carriage. She had hoped Harvey would agree to accompany her on the trip, but he had quickly declined, citing deadlines with the newspaper. Then, without her knowledge or consent, he'd enlisted Garrett to act as her carriage driver. Even worse, Garrett had accepted. After yesterday's Thanksgiving fiasco there was little doubt the ride to the Schmidts' would be filled with more questions. When her father had summoned them back into the parlor, she knew Garrett hadn't finished his inquiry.

She shivered, uncertain if the thought of Garrett's queries or the cold air seeping through the bedroom window caused the sudden chill. She let the draperies fall back into place. Perhaps Garrett would honor her privacy in this one matter of the heart. After all, she would be more than willing to grant him reciprocity. She'd promise to never inquire into his previous relationships with other women. However, she doubted he'd accept such a pact.

After donning a pink and gray tartan dress of soft flannel, Macia fashioned her hair and slipped on a pair of black kid shoes. She hoped her choices would provide extra warmth. Hastening down the stairs, she tied an apron around her neck and hurried to prepare breakfast. Fern's sudden departure had created a gaping hole in the household, one that Macia would be expected to fill, at least to some extent. Her mother was not an early riser and would likely never change her ways, yet breakfast must be prepared for Harvey and her father. Macia could only hope her mother's health would remain stable. If so, her mother would cook dinner and at least begin preparations for the evening meal. With a modicum of good fortune, Gerta Schmidt would return home with her today and the housekeeping dilemma would be resolved.

A short time later, after downing their breakfast and wishing her well on the journey, her father and brother departed and left her to the dirty dishes. Though the breakfast fare had been tasty, no one would have considered the meal fine dining. But the men hadn't complained, and for that she was thankful. Yet she imagined they were more than a little anxious to have their meals prepared by someone with culinary skills beyond her own.

The final dishes had been dried and she'd removed her apron when a knock sounded at the front door. She was thankful she'd decided against preparing anything other than oatmeal and fresh biscuits for breakfast, for Garrett was half an hour early. She lifted her heavy coat from the ornate hall rack and checked her hair in the mirror before opening the door.

"Lucy!" She motioned the girl inside. "I wasn't expecting you."

"Were you leaving?"

Macia quickly explained her plans for the day. "However, there's time for a cup of tea, if you'd like. The water's still hot."

Lucy bobbed her head. "I have *lots* to tell you."

Macia took the girl's coat and hung it alongside her own before heading off to the kitchen, with Lucy following close on her heels. "Does Jeb know you're here?"

"Yes. He said I could spend the day with you, but . . ." Her voice faded like the rising vapor from the teakettle.

Macia moved about the kitchen, pouring the girl a cup of weak tea. After she'd tasted it, Lucy spooned a dollop of cream into the steaming brew and stirred.

"I suppose you could come along with us, though I'm not sure your brother would approve. As I said, Garrett is driving me out to the Schmidt farm. I'm going to see if their daughter is willing to begin work as our housekeeper." Macia fidgeted with the teapot as she watched Lucy. "Furthermore, we wouldn't be able to talk—what with Garrett along."

The girl's mournful look was nearly more than Macia could bear. She'd not yet decided whether it would be proper to take Lucy when a knock sounded. "Finish your tea while I answer the door."

Macia pasted on a pleasant expression before she opened the door. "Mr. Johnson! I was expecting—"

"Garrett. Yes, I know." He rubbed his hands together. "May I come in?"

Macia jumped aside. "Where *are* my manners? I do hope nothing is amiss. Has something happened to Garrett?"

Doffing his hat, Mr. Johnson came inside but shook his head when Macia offered to take his coat. "I must get back to the store. Garrett is ill. He asked me to stop by and tell you he won't be able to accompany you today."

Macia clasped a hand to her chest. "I do pray it's nothing serious. He appeared to be feeling quite well yesterday."

Mr. Johnson's frost-laden mustache drooped over his upper lip like a sodden plume. He raked his thick fingers through his damp facial hair. "He was fine yesterday—wife says he's running a bit of a fever and has a stomach ailment. He plans to check with your father if he's not improved by this afternoon."

Macia thanked Mr. Johnson as he prepared to depart. "Do extend my sympathy to Garrett."

Mr. Johnson pulled his collar up high around his neck. "I'll do that. He said he'd come by and make other arrangements once he's up and about."

In truth, Macia wanted to stomp her foot and tell Mr. Johnson she must travel to the Schmidt farm this morning. However, Mr. Johnson would care no more than Harvey or her father had. They each had their own work to attend to, and locating a housekeeper wasn't part of it. She leaned heavily against the door to gather her thoughts. There was no reason she couldn't go by herself. She could handle the buggy well enough to make it to the Schmidt farm—at least she thought she could.

Lucy looked up as Macia entered the kitchen. "I've finished my tea." Her words held a note of expectancy.

"Garrett has taken ill. I'm going to the Schmidts' farm by myself. I'm not the best carriage driver, Lucy. It's likely best if you stayed at home this time."

Lucy squared her shoulders. "I'm very good at handling horses— and carriages, too. Jeb says I have a way with the horses. *Please* let me go with you."

Macia frowned, uncertain what to do. She'd love to have the girl's company, yet would Jeb approve? "Only if Jeb gives his permission."

Jumping up from her chair, Lucy nodded her head enthusiastically. "I'll have Jeb hitch up the carriage, and I'll even drive it over here. I should return within the hour. You'll be pleased to have me along."

The girl's bright expression warmed Macia. The journey would be more enjoyable with Lucy by her side. She'd not be required to answer Garrett's expected questions, and Lucy would have ample time to relate her news. Macia was eager to hear all the girl had to tell. She hoped Jeb would agree to the arrangement.

Macia was waiting at the front door with extra carriage blankets when Lucy returned a short time later. She waited while Lucy tied the horse to the iron post at the front of their house and then bounded up the front steps. Macia opened the door. "What did Jeb have to say?"

Lucy gasped for breath. "I'm ready to go and so is the carriage."

Lucy bounced from foot to foot, and Macia wondered if the girl's haste was due to the excitement of the anticipated journey or if the weather was colder than she suspected. "May I drive the carriage?"

"Yes, if you prefer. I'm sure you'll do a much better job than I would." Macia marveled at the girl. With only a few words of praise, she beamed like the Kansas sunshine on a July afternoon.

They were soon on their way. Macia offered the directions while Lucy took command of the reins. They'd traveled only as far as the outskirts of town when Lucy relaxed and turned her attention to Macia. "Fern came over to our house last night. She and Jeb talked for a long time. I don't think I'll need to worry about Fern anymore. She and Jeb ended up in quite an argument."

Macia clenched her jaw. She ought not be listening to a report of the couple's private conversation, yet she longed to hear every detail.

Lucy's cornflower blue eyes sparkled with enthusiasm. "Guess what Jeb said?"

Instead of cautioning the girl to remain silent regarding her brother and Fern, Macia eagerly awaited the information. "I have no idea."

Lucy flicked the reins, encouraging the horse to move along. "Jeb told Fern he would never marry anyone who treated me badly. He said he now was convinced Fern wouldn't be nice to me. On top of that, he told her he thought she had a mean streak." Lucy giggled. "I think Fern's just like a skunk. She looks kinda pretty and seems nice enough, but when you get close, look out." Lucy pinched her nose between her thumb and index finger. "Phew. Not so nice!"

Macia laughed at the girl's antics. How could she chastise Lucy when what she'd said was absolutely true? "Did Fern mention what she might do now?" The question slipped out in spite of Macia's determination to remain silent on the subject of Fern and Jeb.

"She told Jeb she was going to talk to Mr. and Mrs. Wyman about that job you mentioned over in Nicodemus. She also said she doubted anyone in Hill City would hire her after you got through besmirching her name."

"Me?" Macia held onto her bonnet against a rush of brisk wind. "How dare she say such a thing!"

"Don't worry. Jeb came to your defense and told Fern you'd never do anything to prevent her from earning a living."

"That's true." Macia pointed at the fork in the road. "We go to the right. It won't be much farther now."

Calling on the Schmidts hadn't yielded exactly the response Macia had hoped for, though she couldn't complain. Mr. Schmidt had agreed he and his wife would drive Gerta to Hill City after their church services on Sunday in order to meet Macia's parents. Providing all went according to plan, Gerta would remain with the Boyle family and begin her duties the following morning. After Mr. Schmidt set forth the plan, his wife insisted Macia and Lucy join them for the noonday meal. Pointing insistently at the kitchen chairs, it became abundantly clear she'd not be refused.

The older woman obviously approved as the two visitors feasted upon her German fare of *Gulaschsuppe* and hard rolls. Lucy giggled when Mrs. Schmidt insisted she dip her *Brochen* into the hearty beef soup. "To soften the bread," Gerta explained. Mrs. Schmidt bobbed her head in agreement as she lifted a roll and dipped the thick crust into her own soup.

When she was satisfied the girls had eaten their fill of the substantial repast, Mrs. Schmidt pulled a heavy baking pan filled with apple dumplings from the warming oven. The mouth-watering aroma of cinnamon and apples drifted through the room and further whetted their appetites. No matter how much her stomach might protest, Macia knew she would have to have at least a spoonful of the dessert. Before serving, Mrs. Schmidt drizzled each dumpling with a warm, thick sauce of butter, burnt sugar, cream, and an added pinch of nutmeg to enhance the flavor.

The dumplings tasted as delicious as they smelled, and Macia ate more than one spoonful. After they had finished the meal, Macia offered to assist with the dishes—the offer was declined—and thanked the Schmidts for their kind hospitality. With the days continuing to grow shorter, she wanted to ensure their return well before dark. With a final wave and farewells, Lucy took hold of the reins and urged the horse down the lane.

"I like Gerta," Lucy said. "She's much nicer than Fern. Maybe she'll cook some of that *Suppe* for your family." Lucy giggled softly. "And you can invite me to eat with you when she does."

Macia joined her laughter and agreed. "I didn't believe I could eat so much, but Mrs. Schmidt changed my mind in short order."

Lucy turned her head and peeked from beneath the brim of her woolen bonnet. "Do you think Jeb will want to court Gerta?"

Macia shrugged. She had no idea what Jeb might prefer in women. She would have never guessed he would be taken by the likes of Fern. The idea that Lucy would think of Gerta as a possible love interest for Jeb astounded Macia. Truth be told, a pang of jealousy stabbed at her heart. She wondered if Gerta would soon replace her in the girl's affections. There was no denying the German woman was likeable and pretty enough, too. Her rosy cheeks, quick smile, and rounded figure made Gerta appear younger than her years, especially when her blond hair fell around her shoulders in two long braids as it had today. There was little doubt Lucy would be drawn to the young woman—not to mention the thought of having Gerta as a substitute mother who would prepare delicious meals each evening.

A stiff breeze assaulted their carriage, and Lucy offered the reins to Macia. "Would you take over for a while? Even with gloves, my fingers are growing numb. If I can use my muff for a while, they'll warm up and then I'll take over again."

Before taking the reins, Macia offered the girl her own fur muff. The warmth would surely help thaw Lucy's cold fingers. "Would you like another blanket?" Macia reached behind her and grabbed one of the additional quilts she'd placed in the buggy.

Lucy pulled it around her and shoved her hands into the muff. "This is much better."

Apparently the blanket and warm muff achieved their goal, for shortly Lucy's eyelids grew heavy and finally closed. Lucy's rhythmic breathing, mingled with the rocking motion of the buggy, lulled Macia into a state of drowsiness. The horse plodded along at a steady pace without encouragement, and the reins eventually fell lax in Macia's hands.

———

Macia didn't know what had awakened her. Perhaps it was the horse's frightened whinny or the abrupt tug of the reins in her hands. It may have been the changing motion of the carriage or the coyote's alarming howl. In any case, by the time she was fully alert, the horse's nostrils were flared and, with ears laid back, shoulders thrust forward, and head bowed low, the animal careened down the roadway at break-neck speed.

Lucy jarred to attention, her eyes wide with fear. "Give me the reins!" Her high-pitched command could barely be heard above the rumbling wheels beating upon the snow-packed road.

In spite of the wintry weather, the pounding hooves and rotating wagon wheels churned the ground at lightning speed and forced a flurry of snow to billow upward, surrounding them in a powdery whirlwind. Without thought, Macia tugged back hard on one of the reins when she handed them to Lucy. The horse turned abruptly to the right, pulling them off the roadway and onto the uneven, rutted prairie. Lucy struggled to gain control, using her best efforts to slow and reassure the animal.

For a brief moment, it appeared her tactics would work. Instead, the horse made one final surge and stepped into a hole. It attempted to right itself but then went down. The buggy jarred and twisted before it flipped onto its side. Macia hollered for Lucy to jump free, but the girl held tight to the reins until she hit the ground. She spilled out of the wagon and landed with a heavy thud.

Macia stared in horror as an axle broke and one of the wheels dropped with unyielding force upon the girl's leg. Lucy's shrill scream pierced the serene quietude of the isolated prairie. While the horse struggled to free itself from the twisted carriage, Macia raced to Lucy's side. Mustering her strength, she lifted the wheel and muttered thanks that they'd chosen a buggy rather than one of the lumbering wagons with massive wheels she couldn't possibly have lifted.

The girl grimaced as Macia rushed back to her side. "Let me check your leg."

"You best unhitch the animal from the buggy and tie him to that far tree before he hurts himself." Lucy gritted her teeth as she offered the instructions.

Macia did as the girl bid. After she'd managed to secure the animal, Macia returned with another blanket. She knelt at Lucy's side. "I fear the horse injured himself when he stepped into that hole. He seemed to be limping a bit."

Stooping down beside the girl, Macia grasped Lucy around the waist while Lucy encircled Macia's neck with one arm. "Do you think you're able to stand?"

Lucy nodded, but once she came to an upright position, she yelped in pain and immediately lifted her injured leg off the ground. Leaning her weight against Macia, Lucy shook her head. "I think it's broken. How are we going to get back home? Even if the horse would let us ride, I can't possibly mount him with this injured leg, and the buggy is of no use to us now."

After quickly surveying their surroundings, Macia squared her shoulders and forced her features into what she hoped was a brave expression. For Lucy's sake, she must remain calm. They were miles from home. If she had to make a guess, she'd gauge they were approximately halfway between the Schmidts' farm and Hill City. To add to her fear, Macia didn't know of any nearby farms where she could seek help. Should she leave the girl alone while she walked for help? What if a coyote attacked Lucy or the horse in her absence? They had no weapon she could leave with the girl.

Oh, why had she decided to come without Garrett? And why had Jeb granted permission for Lucy to accompany her? She wanted nothing more at this moment than for her and Lucy to be safe at home enjoying the warmth of a blazing fire.

— 16 —

A smattering of snowflakes dampened Macia's face as she scoured the low-hanging clouds. The steely skies continued to grow more ominous with each passing moment and warned of more snow this night. She uttered yet another prayer that Jeb would be stirred to action. With the increasing threat of a massive snowstorm, surely Jeb had anticipated their return before now. She could only pray he wasn't hard at work mucking stalls or grooming horses inside the barn. What if he hadn't bothered to look outdoors all afternoon? Would he hear the wind howling and sense the gloomy snow-laden skies? Or would he merely attribute the darkening heavens to the shortened days of winter? She had no way of knowing, but she prayed God would direct him to this place.

She knew little daylight remained, and Macia did not want to spend the night inside the makeshift tent she'd constructed out of the overturned buggy and blankets. The protection it provided would be scant on this cold night. And who could know what damage would be done to Lucy's leg if they didn't get medical help before tomorrow?

Sunset was upon them when Macia heard a shrill whistle—at least she hoped it had been a whistle and not an animal of some kind. "Did you hear that?" She hissed the question at Lucy. "Listen!" Another whistle sounded in the distance.

Excitement radiated from Lucy's blue eyes when she heard the sound. "That's Jeb. It's our signal. Go outside and whistle back at him."

Macia stared wide-eyed at the girl. "I can't whistle."

Lucy appeared flummoxed. "You can't whistle? Everyone can whistle."

"Not me," Macia said with a slight shrug.

"Then let's hope he can hear me from inside this tent you've made." Sticking her fingers into the recesses of her mouth, Lucy blew a long, squealing whistle.

Macia crawled from the makeshift shelter, rose on tiptoe, and studied the area as she strained to listen. *There!* Raised up in his saddle and scanning both sides of the road, she spotted Jeb riding toward them in the falling snow. She hollered and waved her handkerchief overhead. If her feet hadn't been so cold, she would have danced as the horse approached. Damp tendrils of hair poked out from beneath her bonnet.

His gaze rested on the overturned buggy, and he appeared less than impressed with her attempt to create a shelter. Macia pretended not to notice. She was too happy to care about anything except securing medical attention for Lucy's injured leg and getting out of this cold. "Jeb! We've been praying you would come after us."

"Where's Lucy? Is she all right?"

Macia pointed at the carriage. He swung down from the horse while surveying the situation. Taking long strides, he knelt down and poked his head under the blankets and immediately hollered from within the tent of blankets. "Care to tell me what happened, Macia?"

She removed the blankets covering Jeb's back and attempted to explain their plight. "I considered walking for help, but with coyotes nearby, I didn't want to leave Lucy alone."

"I reckon that's thoughtful, but I don't see how you planned to lend her much protection against wild animals." He jutted his chin forward. "Doesn't look like you've got any weapons with you."

"Well, no, but it's more frightening if you're alone."

He raised his brows. "So your solution was to sit out here and freeze to death? What about the horse? Did you consider riding him?"

Lucy quickly came to Macia's defense. "The horse stumbled in a hole. He may be lame."

Jeb stood and brushed the snow from his knees as he approached the horse. After a quick examination, he declared, "That horse is fine. He's probably hurt himself more stepping on a sharp rock than falling in that hole."

Macia swiped at the snowflakes accumulating on her eyelashes. "But he was limping. I thought his leg might be broken."

"No need to cry."

"I'm *not* crying." She dabbed her gloved hand across one cheek. "I was wiping snow from my face."

He shrugged. "Whatever you say." He moved toward the carriage and then stooped down to reexamine Lucy's leg. She squealed in pain when he attempted to straighten the leg. "Do you think you'd be able to ride Blue if I remove the saddle and you sit sideways in front of me?"

Lucy lightly touched her injured leg as she haltingly bobbed her head. "I th-th-think I can do it."

Jeb patted her shoulder. "That's the spirit. You keep thinking about getting home to a warm fire and you'll do fine."

Unfortunately, Macia wasn't certain what Jeb had told his sister was true. For if the leg was truly broken, and she believed it was, Lucy would be in considerable pain throughout the trip.

When Macia asked about fixing the buggy, Jeb laughed. "Ain't no tools out here, Macia. Besides, riding for help means leaving you and Lucy out in the cold even longer. I can come back with Harvey tomorrow and we'll bring it in. It's best we ride out of here on the two horses."

Macia held Lucy's hand as Jeb pondered their predicament. "Maybe if we stabilize her leg with a splint to hold it steady."

After Jeb located a couple of fairly straight branches, Macia ripped several strips of cloth from her petticoat, and while Jeb held the makeshift splints on either side of Lucy's leg, she carefully tied them in place. Lucy bit her lip and grimaced as Jeb situated her atop Blue. How Macia wished she could relieve the girl's pain. And how she wished just this once Jeb had told his sister no.

Jeb was silent throughout the journey back to town. He acted as if it were all Macia's fault. Maybe he was just angry with himself for allowing Lucy to come along, but he seemed awfully abrupt.

As they neared Hill City, Jeb motioned Macia forward. "You ride on ahead and fetch your father. Ask him to meet us at his office."

She did as he asked, thankful the snowfall had diminished shortly after their departure. Had it continued, their progress would have been markedly impeded. Fortunately, Jeb had been correct about the horse. It had made the journey without any evidence of discomfort. *Perhaps that's why Jeb was so sullen,* Macia mused as she entered town. *He thinks I should have examined the horse more carefully.* Still, she couldn't have physically managed Lucy on her own. She dismounted the horse and hurried into the house. There would be enough time to argue with herself—or with Jeb—after Lucy had received medical attention.

"Father! Father! Come quickly." Her shouts echoed in the empty foyer. She called out again as she hurried into the parlor and made her way to the warmth of the fireplace. Extending her cupped hands toward the fire, Macia immediately stepped back as the heat radiated upward to sting her freezing cheeks.

"Macia! I was beginning to worry. We expected you and Garrett to be back in time for supper." Her father stopped short when he walked into the parlor. With his mouth agape and eyes wide, he stared at her. "What has happened?"

"Lucy's injured. I think her leg may be broken. We need—"

His brows furrowed. "Lucy? I thought you were with Garrett."

"There's no time for explanations right now, Father. They'll be arriving at your office any minute. Please hurry."

Dr. Boyle grabbed his coat and hat from the hallway. As they made their way to the office, Macia hastily explained how Lucy had happened to accompany her to the Schmidts' farm. However, her father appeared even more confused when he saw Jeb's horse drawing near.

There would be little time to start a fire, but at least the office would be warmer than the bitter cold they'd endured while they had waited beneath the buggy and during their return home.

As Dr. Boyle placed his key in the lock, he glanced over his shoulder. "How did Jeb get involved in all of this?" The lock clicked; he turned the doorknob and pushed open the door. "And where is Garrett?"

While she watched out the window and her father prepared his instruments, she detailed the day's events. She'd barely completed the story when Jeb's horse came to a halt outside the office. "They're here."

Macia waited in the doorway while her father rushed outside to assist Jeb. With Lucy secure in his arms, he carried her inside. Jeb soon followed, brushing past Macia as though she were invisible and causing her to feel vulnerable and guilty.

Dr. Boyle soon shooed Jeb back to the waiting room, where Macia had to endure his sullen presence while her father examined Lucy's leg. Jeb paced back and forth, directing a menacing glare at her each time he passed by. Eventually, she could no longer bear his unseemly behavior in silence, and she jumped up as he neared her chair.

Folding her arms across her chest, she glared into his steely eyes. "Why are you acting as though this is my fault? You gave Lucy permission to accompany me. The overturned carriage was an accident that could have happened to anyone."

He dodged around her and continued pacing. "But it didn't happen to anyone—it happened to *you*." Suddenly he stopped and faced her. "And Lucy *didn't* have my consent to travel alone with you. She told me Garrett would be along. How is it that you failed to find it unimportant to notify me of that particular fact?"

"I didn't—I mean, Lucy said . . ." She hesitated. What *had* Lucy said when she returned with the carriage? She distinctly recalled asking the girl if Jeb had given permission, yet she couldn't remember Lucy's response. Absent Jeb's approval, Macia wouldn't have consented to take Lucy along. He should know that! And she told him so in no uncertain terms.

While she defended herself, Jeb bristled, squaring his shoulders and gazing down at her in an aloof manner. She clenched her fists, digging her fingernails into her palm. Who did he think he was, treating her as though she'd committed a crime! She'd only begun to tell him what she thought of his attitude when her father emerged from the examining room.

"If the two of you can cease your quarreling long enough, you can come in and see Lucy."

Without comment, Jeb stepped around Macia and entered the room. Macia followed closely behind. She grasped her father's hand. "Is she going to heal without any problem?"

Her father smoothed his hand over her hair. "Her leg is broken, but she's young and it was a clean break. There shouldn't be any problem, though she'll be slowed down until the leg heals." He put his hand on Jeb's shoulder. "Might be good for Lucy to come and stay at our place for a while so there's somebody to look after her while you're working."

Jeb glowered. "She needed someone looking after her today, but that didn't happen."

Lucy reached for her brother's hand. "It's my fault, Jeb. Macia thought you had given me permission. She told me to make sure you knew Garrett wasn't coming along." She blinked back the tears that had pooled in her eyes. "Please don't blame Macia. I knew you would say no but I wanted to go. I'm sorry."

Macia sighed, thankful the truth had finally come to light. Jeb would likely go easy on Lucy since she was already suffering from an injury. And though Jeb's apology to Macia was less than effusive, he at least admitted he'd misjudged her. She wouldn't press for anything more.

A tear rolled down Lucy's cheek. "I'm sorry, Macia. I was untruthful to you and got us both in trouble."

"Apology accepted, Lucy." Macia wiped the girl's tears with her handkerchief. "What do you think, Jeb? May we take Lucy home with us? You'd be welcome to stop by anytime to see her."

Dr. Boyle slapped Jeb on the shoulder and grinned. "Why don't you plan to join us for supper each evening? That way you'll be more involved with Lucy. The two of you can share news of what's happened throughout the day and play some checkers or a game of dominoes."

Jeb fidgeted nervously before finally agreeing. "Sounds like that might be an acceptable arrangement."

Macia gulped. She hadn't intended for Jeb to spend every evening at their house. Most likely he'd plan on being present the entire day on Sundays, too. She would talk to Harvey. Perhaps he could discourage Jeb from visiting every evening. Harvey could more easily convey the discomfort it would cause for Macia and Garrett. Besides, Macia doubted whether Lucy would want her brother spending every evening at the house.

Lucy responded before Jeb could. "It's a perfect solution. You will agree to come see me *every* evening, won't you, Jeb? And we can be together on Sundays, too!" Though Lucy's voice sounded groggy, she maintained a surprising command of the situation. "This is going to be grand."

Grand wasn't *quite* the word that Macia would have chosen.

CHAPTER

— 17 —

Truth wasn't expecting company this afternoon. She wiped her handkerchief across her forehead, tilted her head, and listened, hoping she'd misheard. She wasn't at all prepared to receive guests. Her hair was in complete disarray, and her old dress was frayed around the collar. However, the attire served well enough for cleaning house or packing her belongings. Preparing to move seemed to consume at least part of each day lately, though she was careful not to lift the boxes or move any of the heavy furniture. Attempting to decide which items she wanted to take with her, which items she would leave in the house, and which items she wanted to take but couldn't yet pack was proving to be a monumental task.

She was leaning down to pick up a porcelain music box when the tapping resumed. This time the knocking persisted until she finally relented and answered the door.

Patting her hair into what she hoped was some semblance of order, she met the surprised stare of her unknown caller. The woman appeared deflated as she looked Truth up and down. "Looks like I've arrived too late for the housekeeping position. I thought Mrs. Wyman didn't plan to fill the job until after the Christmas holidays."

Truth frowned as she studied the woman. Obviously Fern didn't recognize her. Of course, Truth had been dressed in her finery the day she called on Macia in Hill City. And Fern hadn't given her any more than a fleeting glance before rushing off and leaving Truth to hang up her own cloak.

"I *am* Mrs. Wyman. Macia Boyle mentioned you might be seeking employment sometime in the future, Miss Kingston." The woman's cheeks suddenly turned rosy. Truth didn't know if the occurrence was due to the cold weather or Fern's recent blunder. Of course, what could Truth expect when she gave so little care to her clothing and hair? Any stranger would assume she was the housekeeper rather than the mistress of the house.

Rubbing her arms, Fern apologized and then peered into the hallway. "I hope she also mentioned I'm an excellent housekeeper. Could I step inside? It's mighty cold standing in this wind and my coat's not doing much in the way of keeping me warm in this bitter weather."

Truth bid the woman come in and took her coat. Fern's dress was more comely than her own. Little wonder the woman had thought she was the hired help. Leading her unexpected visitor into the parlor, Truth explained she and Moses would depart for Topeka after the Christmas holidays.

Fern arched her brows. "Then why do you want a housekeeper? Why not close the house?"

The question was valid—everyone else wondered the same thing. Although Moses had conceded to her wishes, even he thought the idea of a housekeeper rather preposterous. It was possible that her need to have a housekeeper during their absence would eventually subside, though she doubted whether such a time would ever arrive. Miss Hattie had accused her of turning the house into an idol, but Truth knew better. She viewed her position as that of a good steward charged to protect and care for the gift she'd received. Needless to say, Miss Hattie had brushed aside her argument as foolishness. *"This here's a house, not a flock of sheep needin' to be tended."* The old woman's words echoed in Truth's thoughts as she continued to discuss the position with Fern.

"Although this is a large house, I realize time may grow heavy on your hands. I wouldn't object if you wanted to work part time—perhaps take in seamstress work or the like."

Fern wrinkled her nose. "I don't think anyone would pay for my limited abilities with a needle. Since you're granting permission to find additional work, am I to assume you would pay me less than the Boyles did?"

The woman was certainly forthright. Well, Truth could be forthright, also. "I have no idea what the Boyles paid for your services, Miss Kingston. Before we discuss wages, let me explain exactly what the job entails."

When they'd finally completed their tour of the house and agreed upon a satisfactory wage, Fern folded her hands in her lap. "I know you hadn't planned to hire a housekeeper until the end of December. But if you like, I could begin work today. I have my belongings with me, and surely you could use some assistance with all the packing. And I'd be happy to take over the cooking duties."

Truth briefly considered waiting to discuss the idea with Moses. In fact, she wondered if she should visit further with Macia before hiring the woman. Fern had been somewhat vague when questioned about leaving the Boyles. And although Truth knew difficulties existed between Fern and Macia, she had expected Fern to be more forthcoming now.

She wondered if something more had gone amiss at the Boyle home. Macia knew Truth hadn't planned to hire a housekeeper until the end of December. Nevertheless, she pushed aside her concerns and agreed to Fern's offer. The entire concept seemed strange—a white woman cleaning and cooking for her. Yet Fern seemed not to care so long as she had a place to live and an income. In fact, she appeared quite pleased with the arrangement.

———

Scarcely able to believe her good fortune, Fern carried her bags upstairs and placed them in front of the oak wardrobe. This room was considerably larger than the one she'd occupied at the Boyles', and the furnishings were lovely, also. As she hung her dresses in the large wardrobe, Fern decided Macia had actually done her a favor. Living in Nicodemus was going to prove financially beneficial—much more so than marrying Jeb Malone would have. Furthermore, she hadn't loved him—he'd merely been a means to what she had hoped would be a better life, although she knew the marriage wouldn't have lasted. Jeb's sniveling little sister had been more than she could bear when they were courting. If they had wed, Lucy would have come between them—of that she was convinced. Lucy had been patently clear: she wanted Jeb to marry Macia Boyle. Well, Macia could have him. Fern would have no trouble beginning anew.

Closing the wardrobe doors, she walked to the window and pulled aside the curtain. The possibilities were endless. She considered taking in several boarders after the Wymans departed. Likely Mrs. Wyman wouldn't be pleased with such an idea, but if she rented to peddlers who were in and out of town, her idea might be successful. After all, the house was out of the way, and perhaps this town wasn't filled with as many gossips as she'd encountered in Hill City. She dropped the curtain back in place. No need for an immediate decision. There would be ample time to consider her options prior to the end of the month. For the time being, she would act the perfect employee.

Truth met her at the bottom of the staircase. "Would you care to go to the general store and purchase some items I need? It would give you an opportunity to become acquainted with some of the folks in town."

Fern hastily agreed. She'd enjoy nothing more. Yes indeed! As far as she was concerned, life had taken a turn in the proper direction. She embraced the feeling of self-satisfaction as she donned her coat. Her future appeared bright.

Lucy Malone's presence had instilled new life in the Boyle household. Her liveliness and cheery personality infused all of them with renewed vigor. She regaled them with stories throughout the evening meal, and even Macia's mother encouraged Lucy's antics. Except for being faced with Jeb's daily visits, Macia delighted in having Lucy nearby. The girl seemed to fill the void of the younger sister she'd always longed for. She'd nearly settled Lucy in the library with a book when Gerta announced Camille Faraday had come calling and she'd asked her to wait in the parlor.

Lucy closed the book, her eyes bright with anticipation. "Bring her in the library so we can all have a nice chat."

"Let me ascertain the reason for Camille's visit. She doesn't normally arrive unexpectedly." Macia patted the girl's shoulder. "She may want to speak privately. Why don't you begin reading?"

Though she appeared downcast by the idea of being left out, Lucy nodded. "Just don't forget I'm in here by myself."

Macia laughed. "How could *any* of us ever forget when you're around, Lucy? You're the one who keeps us smiling."

Lucy beamed at the remark before turning her attention back to the pages of *Little Women*.

Macia couldn't deny her own curiosity. Though she had attempted to develop a friendship with Camille, the girl had never appeared interested. Not that she'd been rude. But like the rest of her family, she appeared withdrawn and unwilling to develop any close relationships.

Although Mrs. Faraday had mentioned forming a ladies' literary guild when the family first arrived, there'd been no further talk of the idea. Still, they'd not been in town for long. Perhaps she planned to wait until spring to embark upon the endeavor—not that Macia thought the idea held much merit. Mrs. Faraday would have more success hosting a quilting bee or Bible class.

Macia also hoped to find out exactly why the family hadn't appeared for Thanksgiving dinner. Even her father hadn't been able to elicit further information from Mr. Faraday.

"Camille! What a pleasant surprise. I see that Gerta has taken your coat. May I serve you a cup of tea?"

Camille wrung her hands. "No. But thank you for the kind offer. I do hope I'm not intruding, but I'm in need of advice. I'm ever so worried about my family and I don't know where to turn. Promise you'll not tell my family I've spoken to you."

Macia sat in a chair next to Camille's and placed her hand atop the girl's. Camille's hand trembled beneath her own, and she wondered what could cause her such distress. "You have my word. How can I help?"

A faraway look glazed Camille's eyes. "My family has been beset by difficulties for as long as I can remember, most of them due to my father's behavior. He is the reason we moved to Hill City."

Macia settled into her chair and listened as Camille related the secret tales of the Faraday family and their ongoing problems— accounts of how her family had faced financial ruin due to her father and his troublesome ways.

Camille pressed her hand down the pleat in her skirt. "Hoping she could frighten Father into changing his ways, my mother even threatened to divorce him. This move to Hill City was to be his final chance. Unfortunately, I believe he's fallen back into his old habits.

Soon mother will discover his wayward activities, and I truly do not know what will happen."

Macia didn't know what *wayward activities* consumed Mr. Faraday's life and would not inquire. Right now, she wished she had insisted upon serving tea. With a cup of warm liquid to calm her, Macia might not feel so utterly confused. Obviously Camille expected something of her, but she didn't know what. Camille stared at her with a look of unwavering anticipation that demanded a reaction.

Uncertain how to proceed, Macia decided she must forge ahead before Lucy came and interrupted their conversation. "I'm willing to help you, Camille, but I have no idea what I can do."

Camille drew in a deep breath and then related the remainder of her story, which was far from pretty. She said her father had become addicted to gambling—much the way other men become addicted to alcohol. Unfortunately, none of them had realized what was happening until it was too late. Without her mother's knowledge, her father had gambled away the family fortune and left them destitute. When they arrived in Hill City, the only money they'd had to begin their new life was an inheritance Mrs. Faraday had received only weeks earlier. When she had received the inheritance, Mrs. Faraday issued her husband an ultimatum and soon thereafter the family was on their way west.

Camille's eyes brimmed with tears. "We were sworn to secrecy regarding our past. Mother feared if anyone knew we wouldn't be accepted." She wiped away a tear that had escaped and rolled down her cheek. "You likely wondered why I was unsociable toward you— and withdrew from Harvey's affections. I longed to form a friendship with you, but I was afraid I'd slip and say something about my past."

"Is that why your family didn't attend Thanksgiving dinner?"

Hurt flashed in Camille's eyes. "I was so much looking forward to Thanksgiving dinner with your family. However, my parents had a terrible argument regarding money that was missing from the pharmacy receipts. Mother believes the funds were gambled away by Father. Accusations flew back and forth between my parents until Father left the house. Rather than attempt to explain the circumstances, Mother penned the note saying we were dealing with an emergency." Camille shrugged her narrow shoulders. "I didn't understand why we all had to remain at home. In retrospect, I suppose Mother was correct. Father's absence would have been difficult to explain, and one of us might have slipped up."

Now Macia understood why Camille had turned down Harvey's numerous social invitations. The young woman's fear of divulging family confidences appeared to circumscribe her entire life. In fact, fear probably governed the lives of the entire Faraday clan. Certainly it explained Mrs. Faraday's controlling behavior toward her husband.

With all she'd divulged, though, Camille still hadn't answered Macia's question. As she once again made inquiry as to how she could assist, Macia fleetingly recalled her visit to the general store and Mrs. Johnson's declaration that something was amiss at the pharmacy.

"I fear my father may have gambled away our house. I know Mother's name was on the deed for the pharmacy, but I don't know about the house. Since your parents owned the property, would you consider asking your father if he recalls?"

Fear engulfed Macia like a summer freshet flooding the banks of a creek. *Surely* Mr. Faraday wouldn't jeopardize his family's home. Or would he? She'd heard Harvey tell stories about the men he had gambled with back in Kentucky—how they'd lose all sense of reason when they were drinking and playing cards.

"I'll ask him when we're alone later today. Then I'll plan to stop by the pharmacy tomorrow morning." Macia leaned in closer and whispered, "Has your father done something that makes you believe he's deeded away the house?"

Camille lowered her head and fidgeted, obviously uncomfortable. Just as Macia decided she should withdraw her question, Camille said she'd overheard her father and a skinny pock-faced peddler talking the previous afternoon. "He asked my father if *I* came with the house. Why else would he ask such a thing?"

In an attempt to assuage Camille's fears, Macia replied the comment could mean any number of things. However, when pressed, she couldn't name even one alternative. "Let's wait until we know there's something to worry about. I know my father will do anything he can to help." With a tilt of her head, Macia motioned toward the library. "If you don't at least greet Lucy, I'll never be forgiven. I hope you have a few moments to say hello."

Camille nodded. "I'll peek in, but I must return before I'm missed. I told Father I was going for a short walk. I'm sure he thought me daft, what with the cold weather, but he waved me off when his card-playing friends arrived." She grasped Macia's hand. "You won't mention this to anyone except your father, will you? I'd rather no one else knows just yet."

Macia gently embraced the young woman. "You needn't worry. I'll not breathe a word."

— 18 —

Hill City, Kansas

Macia donned her heavy blue woolen coat and hat and tucked her hands into her white fur muff as she descended the front porch steps. She'd gotten Lucy settled with a supply of art paper, paintbrushes, and oil paints that had been packed away since their move to Hill City. Though Macia doubted the quality of the paints was the same after several years in storage, Lucy had doggedly insisted they would be fine. And so Macia had set up an easel of sorts near one of the tall library windows. Shortly before Macia departed, Lucy had secured her place as the Boyles' artist in residence.

As far as Macia was concerned, the best possible painting would be one that captured Lucy's likeness as she sat at her easel attempting to paint. Macia wondered if she could possibly create a decent likeness of Lucy. Though she'd once had artistic talent, it had been years since she'd taken up a paintbrush.

Her fanciful idea disappeared as she neared the pharmacy. She hoped Camille would be in the store. Otherwise, she'd be forced to make a purchase and return at a later time. As she approached the front door, she spied Camille standing at the counter; she didn't catch sight of Mr. Faraday anywhere nearby.

The moment she entered the door, Camille rounded the counter and neared her side. "My father is in the back room."

Before she could say another word, Mr. Faraday entered the room. "Macia! What brings you out on this cold morning? I hope your mother isn't ill."

Macia shook her head. "No, but thank you for your concern. I was going over to the general store and stopped to see if Camille would like to join me for a cup of tea—if you can do without her help for a short time." Mr. Faraday's shoulders tightened, straining the buttons on his cassimere vest. He cast a wary glance in his daughter's direction. Macia feared he sensed something might be amiss as she'd never before stopped by the store to invite Camille to join her for tea.

Hoping to ease any suspicion, Macia shrugged her shoulders and grinned. "I've been cooped up with Lucy Malone, and I long to talk to someone my own age for a short time. You *did* know Lucy had moved in with us until she recuperates, didn't you?"

Mr. Faraday nodded. "Yes. Your father told me." His shoulders remained rigid, but he said, "Don't be gone too long."

"I won't." Camille grabbed her coat, and the two of them headed for the door. Moving side by side, they bowed their heads against the stinging wind and crossed the street. Macia sensed that if she turned and looked back, she'd see Mr. Faraday watching after them.

The table near the front of the store was unoccupied, a propitious happenstance. Garrett walked from the rear of the store and greeted Macia with a broad smile. "I fear you ladies will have only me to assist you with your shopping today. My aunt and uncle departed for Ellis before sunup." He waved toward the merchandise-laden shelves and tables with a worried look in his eyes. "Believe me, I'm going to need your help locating anything that isn't easily within view."

Macia couldn't help but commiserate. He looked like a forlorn child on the first day of school. She quickly explained he'd have no trouble with them since they wanted only a cup of tea and she'd be happy to take care of that particular chore. Leaving Camille to secure the small table, she walked alongside Garrett to the heating stove, where a pot of coffee and a pot of tea simmered during the winter months. She was thrilled with their good fortune: they wouldn't have to contend with Mrs. Johnson's attempts to overhear their conversation.

Garrett handed her two empty cups. "I was wondering if you'd like to join me for supper tonight. If there's enough moonlight, we could even go ice skating."

The expectancy in his eyes made the offer difficult to refuse. "Thank you for the kind invitation, Garrett. However, Lucy Malone is staying with us until—"

"I don't think Lucy would mind if you went out for one evening. Surely you're not going to refuse all invitations until her broken leg has mended."

"No, but we've begun a new project. She's trying her hand at painting, and—"

"I understand Jeb is joining you each evening, also."

Did she detect a hint of irritation in his words? Well, she would set the record straight here and now. "*I* didn't extend the invitation to Jeb. My father did so as a kindness to Lucy."

Garrett looked heavenward.

Now certain he didn't believe her, Macia forged onward. "My father realized Lucy would miss seeing her brother each day. Jeb spends his time visiting with Lucy, *not* with me."

Macia glanced over her shoulder. Camille was staring at the grandfather clock in a nearby corner. Though Garrett didn't seem convinced, Macia hadn't come to the store to argue with him. In fact, she hadn't come to see him at all! She needed to get back to the table. Accordingly, she placed the cups on one of the small trays Mrs. Johnson used for serving coffee to her customers.

"Camille doesn't have much time. She's needed back at the pharmacy soon." Lifting the tray, she stepped around him.

"Since you won't go out with me, perhaps you could set an extra place at your dining table this evening?"

Knowing he hoped to detain her, Macia merely smiled. "We'll talk before I depart for home."

After a quick apology for her delay, Macia seated herself across from Camille. With their heads close together, the young ladies talked in hushed tones as customers entered and departed the store. Two of the regular checker players arrived and stood nearby until Macia waved them off with a promise she and Camille would be leaving in only a few more minutes.

She disliked delivering her father's message about the deed, for she knew it would only compound Camille's fears. Only Mr. Faraday's name had been placed on the deed to the house. Although Dr. Boyle related he had questioned Mr. Faraday's decision, the man had been insistent. On the day they'd made the transfer, he'd declared his wife had taken ill and couldn't possibly be in attendance. Mr. Faraday had stated his wife was in total agreement. In addition, the purchase money had already exchanged hands—so how could Macia's parents argue against signing the deed?

As they prepared to leave, Macia clasped Camille's hand. "My father said he will help in any way possible. He frequently talks to your father regarding medication for his patients and thought he might broach the subject without arousing suspicion."

"I need time to think before doing anything further. Give your father my thanks, but tell him not to do anything until he hears from me."

"You had best hurry back to the store. I told Garrett I'd speak to him before I departed for home."

The girls bid each other good-bye, and Macia gathered up the cups. She'd barely removed them from the table when the two men rushed over, collapsed into the chairs, and began to set up their checkerboard.

She replaced the tray and surveyed the room, finally locating

Garrett, who was now surrounded by several customers. Two more women entered the store, and she decided the remainder of their conversation could wait until another day. Besides, she had made it clear that Jeb's nightly presence in her home was due solely to Lucy's condition.

Macia's father had barely finished saying grace when Gerta hurried back into the dining room. She clasped one hand to her chest and breathlessly announced Mr. Garrett Johnson was in the foyer insisting he had received a supper invitation—for this evening. The housekeeper's eyes darted around the table. "Who invited a guest without telling me to prepare more food?" Her voice warbled by nearly a full octave as she spoke.

All eyes immediately focused on Macia, and Jeb appeared particularly amused by her predicament. Ignoring his obvious enjoyment of the situation, Macia excused herself and motioned to Gerta. Drawing the girl aside, she hastened to explain and offered her apologies. She didn't want Gerta overly upset, for her family would not soon forgive her if Gerta quit her employment. With the woman's excellent cooking skills and pleasant personality, she'd quickly developed into an essential member of the Boyle household. Macia volunteered to be served last; thus she would be the only one shorted if there was insufficient food. Gerta agreed to hurriedly set another place at the table while Macia greeted Garrett.

He smiled broadly as she approached. "When you didn't stop to visit any further, I assumed you were expecting me for supper."

Macia didn't respond. Instead, she motioned Garrett forward. She suspected he didn't actually believe he had been expected for supper, and she surmised he was taking an aggressive stand to prove his point. Surely he realized this encounter would cause her discomfort. She didn't chide him for his rude behavior, but he'd not win her favor if he continued down this path.

Supper proved to be exactly what Macia had expected—a disaster. Knowing Gerta had prepared for one less guest than the current company, Jeb cheerfully and consistently helped himself to heaping portions from every bowl and plate that circled the table. When Macia scowled in his direction, he merely winked and increased the size of his helpings even more.

And then there was Lucy. She announced how happy she was living in the same house with Macia. Obviously feeling optimistic by the encouragement she received in return, she continued, telling the entire group that she wished Macia and Jeb would reconsider marriage so the three of them could be together all of the time. An uncomfortable silence followed, and Macia wondered if Jeb had encouraged Lucy's remark.

Although Jeb had been cordial during his daily visits, he and Macia had engaged in only one private discussion—and that talk had consisted of matters related to Fern's departure and Lucy's medical care. There had definitely not been any mention of renewing their old relationship.

When supper was finally over, Macia suggested Lucy take Jeb into the library and show him the painting she'd begun earlier in the day.

Lucy leaned forward to peek around Garrett. "Do come with us, Macia. You can show Jeb some of your paintings, too."

Macia winced as Garrett clasped his water goblet with an intensity that threatened to shatter the piece of glassware. "You and Jeb go along," she said. "I believe I'll visit with Garrett in the parlor." She sighed with relief when the twosome finally heeded her suggestion.

Regrettably, the respite was brief. When she once again refused Garrett's invitation to go ice skating, he grew unusually quiet, with his few answers to her questions pithy and his mood sullen. "I believe you're still in love with him." He folded his arms tightly across his broad chest. "If that's the case, I'd rather know right now."

How could she truthfully answer Garrett's question when even she didn't know the depth of her persistent feelings for Jeb Malone? On the one hand, she detested what Jeb had done. He should have waited for her to return from Europe. On the other hand, had the situation been reversed, she wasn't sure she would have acted any differently. And, truth be told, she *had* given thought to a future with Jeb— especially since Fern's recent departure. Lucy's presence in the house kept Jeb at the forefront of Macia's thoughts.

"I can see you're having difficulty answering my question. Unfortunately, that tells me I'm correct in my assumption." Garrett brushed a lock of hair from his forehead as he stood to leave.

Macia grasped his hand. "Please, Garrett. Let me explain. Try to understand that at this moment, I'm not certain how I feel about either of you."

She released his hand as he stepped away. "I'm surprised you would give Jeb a second thought after the way he treated you. However, I'll not make a fool of myself by fighting for your attentions. When you come to a decision, you let me know." He glanced over his shoulder as he walked from the room. "Like Jeb, I won't wait forever. I don't intend to play second fiddle to the man who jilted you, either."

Macia hugged herself against the stinging pain of Garrett's final words. She wanted to stop him before he walked out. Instead, she remained silent and motionless as he left the house without another word.

Nicodemus, Kansas

Fern shivered inside her heavy winter coat as the frigid December air wrapped around her body. She hunched her shoulders against a gust of the icy wind, warming herself with thoughts of her accomplishments since arriving in Nicodemus two weeks earlier. Even Mr. and Mrs. Wyman had been surprised by her rapid integration into community life. Thus far, she'd arranged for work at Mr. Wilson's general store beginning the first of the year. Soon thereafter, she'd convinced the Wilsons' son, Arthur, he would be a fool if he didn't begin courting her. At the Wilsons' invitation, she had attended church services at their home with a few other white members of the community. The population of Nicodemus might all join together for their parades, picnics, and other celebrations, but folks didn't gather under the same roof to worship God. Oh no, that was one place where they all agreed to separate.

Never having thought much about church, or even God for that matter—Fern had naïvely inquired if it wouldn't be more convenient for everyone to attend one of the churches in town. By the horrified look on Mrs. Wilson's face, Fern would have thought she'd suggested robbing a bank. The older woman had finally sputtered something about combined worship being a foolish suggestion. But Fern still didn't understand why the color of a person's skin determined where one attended church in Nicodemus. After all, nothing else in the town was decided on that basis. Nonetheless, she followed the rules and attended church at the Wilsons' house. Not because she was interested in hearing a sermon or was afraid to break the church rule, but because it afforded her one more opportunity to see Arthur Wilson and spend time away from her household duties.

As she entered the general store, Fern scanned the room until she located Arthur stocking shelves near the west wall. Setting her sights upon the young man, she edged around several customers and moved toward him. In spite of her best efforts to avoid Arthur's mother, the older woman came out from behind a counter where she'd been arranging a new shipment of glassware.

Fern greeted Mrs. Wilson and took a moment to admire the arrangement of berry dishes, cut-glass cruets, and hot chocolate sets. "Any of these items would make lovely Christmas gifts. And you've arranged them in a delightful fashion." Hoping Mrs. Wilson considered her words of praise sufficient conversation to meet the standard of proper etiquette, Fern attempted to move along. But Mrs. Wilson didn't budge.

Instead, she held out her hand. "I can help you with your list, Fern. No need bothering Arthur. He has more than enough to keep him busy for the remainder of the day." Mrs. Wilson snapped the list from between Fern's fingers and waved her forward. "Follow me."

What had previously been no more than a vague suspicion had now become abundantly clear. Mrs. Wilson didn't approve of her, at least not as a prospective bride for her son. Though Fern obligingly followed along behind the woman, she quickly decided she'd not depart the store without accomplishing her mission. When Arthur glanced her way, she crooked her index finger in a comely manner, and when he immediately pushed aside the crate of canned goods and came rushing in her direction, she basked in a moment of self-satisfaction.

Keeping her back to Mrs. Wilson, Fern raised up on tiptoe and whispered in Arthur's ear. He nodded, though he turned somber the moment his mother looked away from the shelf. It took only a dour look from the woman to send him darting back to his work. Fern cared little, however, for Arthur had shown interest in her. Therefore, she could bear Mrs. Wilson's taciturn conduct. After all, this wasn't the first time she'd been forced to handle a disagreeable woman.

Cloaked against the blustery cold that seemed a few degrees warmer than Mrs. Wilson's manner, Fern walked home. The basket of groceries weighed heavily on her arm as she considered Mrs. Wilson's behavior. It might have been better to have set her sights on John Green instead of Arthur.

She immediately shuddered, more from the thought of Mr. Green than from the cold. Dire circumstances would be required before she ever considered taking the widower as a suitor. When she'd asked him for a job, the man had appeared more interested in having her become his wife and the stepmother of his two children than hiring her as a clerk in his store. He explained that Mrs. Green had *gone to meet her maker*. Before Fern could express her condolences, he offered to discuss her employment over supper, preferably one that she prepared. With his rotund body, beefy hands, and bald pate, Fern had no desire to share a meal with him. The fact that he would suggest she cook for him had been the final straw, underscoring the man's utter lack of charm. She'd refused, departed his establishment, and hastened across the street to the Wilsons' mercantile, where Arthur had become her marital objective.

Yes, winning over Mrs. Wilson would be easier than spending even a few hours alone with Mr. Green. She needed only to develop a strategy for convincing the woman she would be the proper wife for her son. But she doubted she'd won much favor with Mrs. Wilson this day. On the other hand, if she could help Arthur develop a measure of courage, he could do some of the work for her.

She entered the Wymans' house using the back door and went into the kitchen to empty her shopping basket. Fern had nearly completed the task when Truth entered the kitchen.

"When you have a free moment, I'd like to discuss the menus and entertaining schedule for the Christmas holiday."

Entertaining schedule? It sounded as though Mrs. Wyman had already begun to take on the attitude of big city living. However, how could Fern expect any less? Ever since Mrs. Wyman's aunt Lilly had returned from her brief visit with Jarena and her family, she'd been encouraging such nonsensical talk. With all her tips on etiquette and entertaining, Lilly Verdue seemed obsessed with Truth's duty to bolster her husband's image in Topeka. Fern could only assume that Truth had taken the message to heart and now desired to practice her skills with friends and family. Fern would accommodate the young woman in any way possible—she didn't want to do anything to jeopardize her position with the Wymans. She'd be alone in this house soon enough.

"No reason why we can't work on that right now. What events are you planning?"

Before Truth could respond, Lilly sauntered into the kitchen, her hair perfectly coiffed and her nose held a notch higher than necessary. "Did I hear someone mention planning an event?"

Truth folded the piece of paper she'd carried into the kitchen and tucked it into the pocket of her dress. "I'm merely going over the menu for our Christmas Eve supper. I thought you agreed to help finalize details for the church Christmas program. Aren't the ladies meeting this afternoon?"

"Jarena said they've postponed it until tomorrow afternoon. Hannah Thatcher said she can't finish writing the program until tomorrow." Lilly shrugged. "We can't do much until we have a program."

Fern raised an eyebrow. Lilly wasn't the type of woman she expected would be working on a church program. She was more worldly than most of the folks living in Nicodemus. Perhaps she could lend some insight regarding the matter of race and church attendance. . . .

Easing herself onto one of the heavy kitchen chairs, Fern rested an elbow on the table and cupped her chin. "May I ask you a question, Mrs. Verdue?"

The older woman squared her shoulders and looked down her nose at Fern. "Of course."

Fern decided the woman looked regal—all she needed to complete the illusion was a crown and scepter. She tilted her head upward and looked directly into Lilly's eyes. "I've been wondering how come the coloreds and whites don't worship together. Can you tell me why it's that way?"

Lilly's perfectly tinted lips curved. "That's what you wanted to ask? Why would you ask *me*? I'm no preacher. I don't even live in this town."

"Exactly. That's why I asked you. I overheard someone mention you had lived in New Orleans and out in Colorado, also. I thought you would know if this is the way of things everywhere. Or is it unique to Nicodemus?"

Lilly eased into a chair across from Fern. "Where you been living all your life, gal? *Course* it's the way of things." She paused. "Everywhere!"

"But why? I don't know much about God, and I never did go to church when I was growing up, but I figured there must be a rule or something."

Heaving a sigh, Lilly leaned back in her chair. "There's no rule. Nobody would stop you from going into one of the churches in town.

And I doubt whether anyone would stop one of us from going to hear Mr. Wilson preach on Sunday morning—but no one will try it. It's just the way of things."

Fern shrugged. "Seems odd." She didn't inquire any further. Her question seemed to make everyone uncomfortable—even Truth.

After clearing away and washing the breakfast dishes, Fern removed her apron. The others had departed for church. With a final glance in the hallway mirror, she donned her coat and headed out. Walking briskly to help ward off the cold, she hastened toward the Wilsons'. It mattered little how early or late she arrived; Mrs. Wilson would ensure that the chairs near her son were already occupied. As Fern strode by the newspaper office, she wondered if Mrs. Wilson had exhibited the same dislike for other women who'd shown an interest in Arthur. She fleetingly wondered if Macia Boyle had sent a warning about her to Mrs. Wilson. *Silly!* Macia wouldn't even know of her recent interest in Arthur Wilson.

As she approached the Baptist church, the sounds emanating from inside the building interrupted her thoughts. Even with the doors and windows closed tight against the cold, she could hear the joyful sounds of singing and clapping. She slowed her pace and finally stopped outside the door, listening, wondering.

Contemplating the idea of going inside, she hesitated and listened a few moments longer. She didn't want to miss her opportunity to be with Arthur. On the other hand, the sounds of a jubilant celebration beckoned her. Maybe she could go in for just a few moments. . . . As she moved into the back of the church, she was greeted by several wide-eyed stares from the surrounding pews.

Mrs. Verdue had been correct—no one told her to get out. She watched the other worshipers and followed their lead: she clapped, she swayed, and she tried to sing. But she didn't know the words. And there were no songbooks like the ones she had used at the Wilsons'. Anyway, there was no way to hold a songbook if you were clapping and dancing. So she moved her mouth as if she were singing the words.

When the music ended, she couldn't imagine what would happen next. They'd barely taken their seats when the reverend stood before the crowd. Unlike Mr. Wilson's monotone teachings that had nearly put her to sleep the past two Sundays, this man's voice boomed from the front of the church. He paced back and forth, perspiration beading on his dark brow as he held an open Bible in one of his large hands. He jabbed the index finger of his other hand toward the ground and shouted claims of God's wrath and the fires of hell that awaited those who rejected Jesus. Fern lost all track of time as she listened to the frightening words of the fiery afterlife the man proclaimed.

Finally, she was able to breathe a bit easier, for the preacher said they could all leave church today and never again worry about spending eternity in the flaming pit of hell. He raised his Bible high and proclaimed God had provided a way for sinners to avoid the blazing flames. Fern scooted to the edge of her seat. She didn't want to miss hearing about her means of escape from eternal damnation.

"Jesus! Jesus is the answer. All you must do is accept Jesus into your heart and ask Him to forgive your sins. Repent and ask Jesus to be your Savior!"

Fern jumped a good two inches when the folks around her began to shout "hallelujah" and "amen." The man across the aisle sprang to his feet and hollered, "Praise God!" The interruptions didn't seem to bother the preacher. In fact, he appeared to relish the disruption. Each time someone called out, he would raise his Bible a little higher and bob his head up and down. And when the church got quiet, the reverend would wave his free hand in the air and shout, "Can I hear an amen?" Then any number of folks would shout amen and the reverend would give a toothy smile, which Fern figured meant he was pleased with the reaction.

She couldn't muster up enough courage to say anything, although she truly wanted to give it a try and see how it would feel to shout in church. At the few churches she'd attended as a girl, the meetings were like the ones at the Wilsons' house—solemn and quiet. But not this. This was more like a celebration—a party in which she could participate. She liked it. Except for that part about hell. She wasn't so sure the preacher had everything correct on that account. She figured there must be something more to avoiding hell than simply asking Jesus to take care of things on her behalf. That sounded too easy.

She startled when she noted the time as she departed the church. Services would likely be over at the Wilsons', and Arthur would wonder about her whereabouts. At least she hoped he had been concerned, for she hoped to convince him to spend the afternoon with her. Unfortunately, the bitter temperatures weren't as conducive to courting as the warmer seasons of the year. Still, she planned to persuade Arthur that an afternoon sitting near a warm fire and watching the ice skaters at the Wymans' pond would be most delightful. And so long as Mrs. Wilson didn't interfere, Fern thought Arthur would seize the opportunity.

Fern climbed the outer stairway that led to the upstairs living quarters of the Wilson family. She didn't think she'd enjoy such a housing arrangement, but Mrs. Wilson had said she found it wonderfully convenient. Well, she could have it. When Fern and Arthur married, they would build a lovely house of their own. Not so fine as the Wymans', but one where she would be proud to invite their guests. Of course, if they continued to live in Nicodemus, her opportunities to entertain would be limited. She would have to find out if Arthur would be willing to leave Nicodemus and start his own mercantile in another city. *Yes!* She'd introduce the topic when they were alone this afternoon.

Her stomach growled noisily, and she clutched her waist. Perhaps the Wilsons hadn't yet eaten their noonday meal. If not, she hoped Mrs. Wilson would invite her to join them.

"Fern! When you didn't arrive for church services, I thought you might be ill." Arthur held open the door, and the luscious aroma of roasting chicken drew her forward. "I was going to come to the Wymans' and check on you, but Mother insisted I wait until after dinner. Would you care to join us?" His smile warmed her nearly as much as the heat radiating from the Sunshine stove.

Fern followed him into the kitchen. Mrs. Wilson didn't appear nearly as pleased to see her—or to hear that Arthur had invited her to join them for the noonday meal.

The woman lifted an apron from the hook near the door. "You can mash the potatoes." Too much remained at stake where Arthur was concerned—Fern couldn't object. As Arthur's mother handed her the potato masher, Fern determined that Mrs. Wilson realized that very fact and would use it to her advantage.

Though the Wilsons' furnishings were nice enough, Mrs. Wilson didn't appear to have much knack for decorating. Although there was no dining room, the kitchen was quite large and well-appointed. While the women finalized preparations, Mr. Wilson and Arthur sat at the large oak dining table.

Mr. Wilson folded a copy of the weekly newspaper and removed his glasses. "We missed you in church this morning, Fern. Did the Wymans not permit you time off from your duties this morning?"

Fern ceased mashing the potatoes long enough to drop a lump of butter into the bowl. "I attended over at First Baptist this morning."

Mrs. Wilson's carving knife plummeted to the floor and lodged into one of the wood planks in a perfect handle-up position adjacent to Fern's right foot. Quickly taking a step to the side, Fern looked at the knife and then at Mrs. Wilson. The woman appeared dumbstruck. Not certain what else to do, Fern leaned down, pulled the knife from the floorboard, and placed it on the worktable.

Mrs. Wilson continued to watch Fern's every movement. At last she said, "You didn't."

"Yes, I did."

Neither of the men showed much reaction to her revelation, so she told them about her Sunday morning, detailing the singing, the clapping, the shouts of praise, and of course, the dancing. By the time she completed her discourse, Mrs. Wilson was as pale as the heaping bowl of mashed potatoes.

With trembling hands, Mrs. Wilson placed the remaining dish of vegetables on the table and sat down between her husband and son. They joined hands while Mr. Wilson blessed the food, a concept Fern had first observed at the Boyles' and then the Wymans' house. She decided both coloreds and whites found this particular religious practice acceptable.

After dropping a spoonful of potatoes onto her plate, she passed the bowl to Arthur. "Mr. Wilson, I was wondering if you could tell me what the Bible says about eternal damnation." She lowered her voice to a near whisper. "About hell."

A whistling gasp sounded from Mrs. Wilson's throat and then she started anxiously fanning herself with her linen napkin. "I do believe I am going to faint."

Fern looked across the table at Arthur, who grinned before touching his index finger to his pursed lips. Forcing a solemn expression, Fern dampened her napkin and passed it to Mrs. Wilson. "Perhaps if you'd place this on the back of your neck, it would help."

Eyes glistening, Mrs. Wilson shoved the napkin away. "If you want to help, you'll cease this talk of . . . of . . ."

Fern raised an eyebrow. "Hell?"

Fire exploded in Mrs. Wilson's eyes. "Yes!" The reply hissed through the woman's teeth.

Fern remained in her chair for two reasons: she was exceedingly hungry and she didn't want to forfeit her time alone with Arthur—especially now. Her behavior had obviously offended Mrs. Wilson, and she would need the afternoon hours with Arthur to help seal his affections, for his mother would surely use this incident to convince Arthur she was an unsuitable choice for him.

For the remainder of the meal, the only sound was an occasional piece of silverware clanking against a plate or bowl. Surprisingly, once coffee had been served, Mrs. Wilson suggested her husband take Fern into the parlor and thoroughly explain the ramifications of living an unholy life. "I will see to the dishes while you answer Fern's questions. After all, I don't want her eternal soul on my conscience."

Fern didn't know how her soul could be on Mrs. Wilson's conscience, but she didn't question the woman. Instead, she followed Arthur's father into the parlor and listened to what he had to say about Jesus. It was just as she'd suspected: being a part of the group going to heaven wasn't quite so easy as that free gift the preacher over at First Baptist had talked about. Mr. Wilson said there were lots of laws to be followed if she was going to avoid God's wrath and spend eternity in heaven. As he began to list a few of these rules, she realized she could never be good enough to receive the gift. He never did say anything about Jesus coming to live in your heart.

When he offered to tell her a few more of the laws, she declined. How could she follow all those rules when she couldn't even remember them? There was a lot more to this religion thing than she had imagined.

She thanked him for his help and sighed with relief when he ambled off to the kitchen. She'd best turn her thoughts back to winning Arthur's affections. *That* was something she easily understood!

CHAPTER

— 20 —

Although Truth and Fern had packed many of the items selected for shipment to Topeka, the Wymans' clothing and personal items remained. Of course, most of the furnishings were being left behind, which was more to assure Truth that they would come back to this house than for any other reason. Quite frankly, she believed Moses would willingly sell the house and furnishings and settle permanently in the capital city. Given the time and love they'd invested in building their home, Truth found the idea most disconcerting. Aunt Lilly had patted her on the head and explained that men were less likely to place sentimental value on houses and the like. Perhaps Lilly was right, but Truth loved this house and wanted to return to it as soon as possible.

Fern pulled a small package from her basket and held it out to her. "There was a delivery for you at the post office." She winked and put her finger on the return address in the corner. "Christmas gifts?"

Fern's fingers lingered on the box as she handed it to Truth.

Truth accepted the package without comment. She knew what was inside. She caressed the parcel, relieved it had finally arrived, and then tucked it into her skirt pocket. She didn't plan to tell Fern, or anyone else, what she had purchased for Moses. She didn't want to risk the possibility of his Christmas surprise being ruined. Not that he seemed particularly interested in the Christmas festivities—in fact she wondered if he would even think to purchase a present for her. His attention was focused on getting them moved to Topeka.

Since the dusting of snow they'd received early in the week, her husband's greatest concern and constant topic of conversation was the weather. His desire to be settled in Topeka by January 8, ensuring his presence at the swearing-in ceremonies, had become an obsession. Moses fretted daily that a massive snowstorm would arrive and force them to remain in Nicodemus. *Sad.* Moses's greatest fear had become her deepest desire.

The preparations for the holiday celebration would be her responsibility, for Moses seemed to care not one whit about what was happening at home. Truth glanced at the clock as she helped Fern unload the basket of groceries. Stopping in front of the stove, she gave the soup a quick stir. The aroma of the simmering chicken stock drifted up and tantalized her.

Early this morning, Fern had made noodles and spread them to dry on the worktable. She'd soon need to bring the stock to a boil and add them to the pot. "I'll finish up here if you'd like to complete preparations for dinner," Truth offered. "Moses should be home soon."

Fern rested her hand atop the basket. "I forgot to mention I saw

Mr. Wyman at the mercantile. He said to tell you he wouldn't be home for dinner today."

Truth stopped short. "Did he say why?"

"No, ma'am, just that he wouldn't be home. Shall I plan on using the noodles for supper, or would you prefer the soup for your noonday meal?"

Shoving a tin of raisins onto the shelf, Truth quickly shook her head. "No need to prepare a noonday meal. Since Moses isn't coming home, I believe I'll go upstairs and rest." She hurried from the room, unwilling to have Fern see her tears. *It's silly to cry over something so inconsequential.* These days most anything could reduce her to tears. Miss Hattie said such behavior was common with women in her condition, but she didn't recall Jarena having crying spells.

The comfort of her room wasn't nearly as inviting as she'd hoped, but she lay down on the bed, planning to rest for only a few minutes.

Several hours later, she awakened with a start and looked out the bedroom windows. Cobwebs clouded her mind, but a glimpse of the late-afternoon sun dipping toward the horizon moved her to action. She opened her small pocket watch and gasped. She'd slept for most of the afternoon!

Glancing in the mirror, she pressed her hands to her head and finger-combed her hair into place. The mirror revealed a small bulge in her right pocket and she reached inside to remove the box. She'd completely forgotten about Moses's gift. Placing the package on the dresser, she carefully unwrapped the paper and opened the lid of the box. Lifting the sterling silver charm she'd had specially fashioned for his pocket watch, she placed it gently in her palm to admire it. Yes, this would be the perfect gift.

———

After assuring herself no one was watching, Macia unfolded the paper Camille had slipped into her hand as they'd departed church this morning. She looked at the porcelain clock before she hurried to the foyer and donned her coat and bonnet. Moving at a lively pace, she silently chastised herself for waiting so long to read the missive.

She was breathless when she finally neared the Faradays' pharmacy. After quickly scouring the vicinity for anyone who might see her, she tapped lightly on the door and entered. Camille stood in the doorway that led to the backroom. She frantically motioned Macia toward her.

"Did anyone see you?" Camille asked in a hushed whisper as Macia approached. Camille quickly peeked out each of the four pharmacy windows.

"No. Why are we whispering and hiding in the back of the store?"

Camille collapsed into one of the heavy wooden chairs that surrounded a circular table. Macia followed her lead and waited for her friend's response.

With a nervous laugh, Camille placed a key on the table. "I took my father's key to the pharmacy so we could meet here, but Mother has a key, also. If we speak quietly, we should be able to hear if she comes looking for me." Camille picked up the key and flipped it back and forth in her palm. "I fear my father has indeed lost our house to the man I told you about. We may have to move within the week— and with Christmas almost here . . ."

Startled, Macia leaned across the table and took Camille's hand in her own. The door key clattered to the table and lay between them. "What? I thought you were going to come and speak to me or my father if that issue hadn't been favorably resolved. Why didn't you talk to one of us before now?"

Tears formed in Camille's eyes. "Like you, I thought I'd misunderstood or that Father had managed to win back the deed." She pulled a scallop-edged handkerchief from her pocket and dabbed her eyes. "Yesterday when I arrived at the pharmacy, that man was in this very room with Father. I overheard them talking. It seems the salesman had traveled back east on business. He had agreed that if Father could pay him his winnings upon his return to Hill City, he would freely give back the deed. Unfortunately, Father doesn't have that much money." Camille slumped in the chair.

Macia's head ached, but she forced herself to ignore the pain. How could a man place his family in jeopardy over a card game? There had to be help for the Faradays, but their redemption was well beyond her meager capabilities. "If you truly want help, we must involve my father. Can you meet me at his office first thing in the morning?"

Camille's lips trembled. "Yes. But please don't tell anyone else."

"Agreed." Macia stood and slipped into her coat. "Please don't worry. Father will find a solution." The words were spoken with as much confidence as she could muster. In truth, she had no idea how her father could resolve this matter. On the other hand, she knew he would help in any way possible.

The women parted, and Macia made her way home. The house

was silent when she went inside. Obviously, she'd not been missed in her absence. Lucy had begged to spend the afternoon at home with Jeb. Harvey, who had generously offered to go to the Schmidt farm and collect Gerta from her weekend visit, was not yet back. And her parents were exactly where they'd been when she departed: her mother remained upstairs napping while her father leafed through his medical books in the library.

She lightly tapped on the library door before entering and then closed the door behind her before sitting down across from her father. Once she'd revealed the reason for her interruption, her father tented his fingers beneath his chin and pursed his lips. Neither of them spoke. Macia had learned long ago that her father preferred to mull over his ideas before speaking. And interpreting his thoughts was nearly impossible. Until prepared to speak, he maintained a thought-ful posture.

He'd remained quiet for so long that Macia quietly rose from her chair. If he was going to cogitate on this matter for the remainder of the afternoon, she need not sit and watch him. Her hand had barely touched the doorknob when her father called her name.

"I can arrive at only one resolution. I believe Faraday will agree—especially if he doesn't want his wife to discover what he's done."

Macia scooted forward and leaned on her father's desk. "Can you tell me?"

He outlined the simple plan. Her father would pay off the debt and hold the deed until Mr. Faraday repaid him.

Macia tilted her head. "But what's to prevent him from doing the same thing in the future?"

"I plan to insist upon drafting a new deed in both Mr. and Mrs. Faraday's names. I'm guessing that's the only thing that has stopped him from gambling away the pharmacy." He stood up and walked to the window to look out at the frozen patch of flower garden. "You realize this is a matter of privacy. We don't want the family to suffer embarrassment."

"Yes, of course, Father. I know Camille will be most grateful."

"Tell her I will speak to her father tomorrow." He strode from the window and stopped in front of the fireplace. "In the event Mr. Faraday is reluctant to take the loan, I'll explain my motives aren't completely altruistic. After all, having a pharmacist nearby has been particularly helpful to me."

Macia went to him and kissed his cheek. "You are a fine man. I'm proud to call you my father."

"Off with you, now," he commanded with a grin.

She laughed and offered a mock salute, knowing her praise had embarrassed him and that she need not worry. By this time tomorrow, all would be resolved for Camille and her family.

————

There was no snow on the ground when Christmas Eve arrived, and for that Moses was grateful. Though a nip remained in the air, the frigid cold of the previous week had passed and temperatures now hovered in the thirties. Moses sighed with relief as he headed toward home with Truth's Christmas presents tucked into a leather satchel. His wife enjoyed the holidays, and though she said she enjoyed being surprised on her birthday and Christmas Eve, he wasn't completely convinced. He'd discovered her snooping for her gifts on several occasions. In fact, he was certain she'd discovered and peeked at the birthday gift he'd purchased for her last year. Though he'd never received an absolute admission from his wife, she'd not denied his accusation, either. Consequently, he'd been particularly careful this year. And he'd sworn all of the family members to secrecy, also—even though Jarena and Grace hadn't been visiting as frequently as in the past. Moses did hold himself somewhat accountable for the obvious breach in the sisters' relationship. Each one of them believed she'd been wronged. Unfortunately, all of it related back to his election and their impending move to Topeka. Perhaps as the family came together to celebrate Christ's birth, healing would take place.

They didn't have a large fir Christmas tree like some folks in the East now decorated in celebration of the holiday, but Moses had purchased a small cedar from a farmer who had passed through town. He'd paid one of the local boys to break through the ice near the riverbank and fill a bucket with wet sand to hold the tree upright and keep it fresh for a few days. Last night, Truth had directed him as he set the tree on a table she had bedecked with a white linen tablecloth embroidered with an edging of dark green.

After arranging a piece of white muslin to cover the bucket, they'd popped corn over the fire in the hearth. She'd laughed at his efforts to string the corn and soon decided he was intentionally breaking the pieces as an excuse to eat them. He grinned as he recalled her mock indignation. The tree looked lovely with the candleholders clipped in place. After the church service this evening, their family and friends would gather and they would light the candles and sing carols around the tree.

Entering the house quietly, he tiptoed into the parlor and hid the packages beneath the festive overlay that covered the table. His satchel now empty, Moses stepped back to admire the tree.

"I didn't hear you come in."

He startled and swung around, his heart racing like a Thoroughbred nearing the finish line. Patting his chest, he managed a feeble smile. "You all but scared me to death."

She drew near, craning her neck at the leather satchel. "What have you got there?"

He paused, wondering if she'd seen him place the packages under the tablecloth. Lifting the bag ever so slightly, he shrugged. "I thought it might be useful for items we want to take on the train with us." It wasn't completely a lie—the bag *would* be useful for such a purpose.

She raised an eyebrow but didn't question him further. Instead, she waited patiently while he hung his coat in the foyer. He reentered the parlor, looking expectantly toward the dining room. The table hadn't been set for supper, and his stomach rumbled as if in protest.

"I thought we could eat a light supper in the kitchen," Truth said. "Fern wants to begin preparing the dining room for our guests' arrival later this evening." She grasped his hand. "Would you like a small bowl of stew?"

Moses laughed. "No, I'd like a *large* bowl of stew." He squeezed her hand. "And I promise to be ravenous when we come home from church. Is Lilly here?"

"She's spending the day with Jarena. I've grown weary of her overbearing nature, Moses. She's nearly as bossy as Miss Hattie. Quite honestly, I don't know how I'm going to stand her constant presence once we move to Topeka."

He winked at her. "I promise to immediately find capable workmen who will have her living quarters above the store finished in no time."

She tugged on his hand as he put his bowl on the table. "Instead of opening our gifts to each other in front of the family, I'd prefer to wait until we're alone. I know that in the past—"

He pulled her close, not caring that Fern might come in unexpectedly. Leaning down, he covered her lips with a gentle kiss full of yearning and love. When they finally parted, he gazed into her eyes. "If that pleases you, I have no objection. Now, let's eat!"

Truth lightly slapped his chest. "You sure know how to spoil a romantic moment, Mr. Wyman."

Her eyes twinkled with delight, and Moses wondered why his wife suddenly desired privacy while they opened their gifts. She'd mentioned Christmas presents on more than one occasion in the past two weeks. If she'd been snooping for her present, this request was probably a cunning way to discover if he'd actually purchased a gift. He'd be certain she didn't spend any time alone in the parlor before they departed for church.

CHAPTER

— 21 —

Fern completed preparations for the evening repast shortly
before Truth's family and friends arrived home from the
Christmas Eve church services. She'd worked hard to satisfy
Mrs. Wyman and hoped her attempts would meet with approval.
Although her initial efforts to please had been based upon selfish
motives, recollections of the message at First Baptist now pricked her
conscience from time to time. In fact, having convinced Arthur to
stand up to his parents and attend with her last Sunday, she'd actually
now heard two sermons at the church. In some respects, she regretted
having convinced Arthur to attend, for she later discovered he'd lied
to his parents in order to accompany her. As if to compound matters,
the preacher had taken to his pulpit and bellowed a demand that his
congregation emulate Jesus. No more stealing, no more cheating, no
more lusting, no more gossiping, and no more evil thoughts. Each

warning was spoken with increasing intensity until he finally thundered, "And no more lying!"

Later that afternoon, a wide-eyed Arthur had avowed the preacher must possess some kind of abnormal powers. Fern laughed at him, saying that likely everyone in the church believed the preacher's message had been directed at him or her. Fern's words seemed to calm him; he went home and immediately confessed his sin to his parents, though she didn't know if he'd asked God's forgiveness. Of one thing she was very certain: Mrs. Wilson's dislike for her had intensified since Arthur's confession. Although his mother had gained Arthur's promise to avoid the Baptist church in the future, he'd adamantly refused the request to cease courting Fern. For that act of bravery, Fern was most grateful; it took little to remind her of old Mr. Green and his offer of a future as his wife.

While the guests removed their wraps, Fern ladled corn chowder into a large china tureen and carried it to the buffet in the dining room. The remainder of the feast waited in readiness. Once the entire group had gathered, Mr. Harban led them in prayer.

From a distance, Fern maintained a watch over the table, refilling plates and bowls as needed. When she returned to the kitchen with the soup tureen, she was surprised to see Miss Hattie sitting at the kitchen table. "Is there something you need?"

"I likes sittin' in the kitchen. Too crowded in there," she said, pointing her spoon handle toward the dining room. Miss Hattie swallowed a spoonful of soup. "Good soup—must be my recipe." She grinned and took another bite before wiping her mouth with a linen square. "I hear tell you been over to the Baptist church the past couple Sundays. How come?"

Fern drew closer and explained her curiosity.

The old woman cackled. "So has you figured out why the coloreds and whites go to different churches?"

Fern shook her head.

"Me, neither. And I don' reckon no one's gonna figure that one out in my lifetime." The older woman held out her bowl. "Now, why don' you fetch me a little mo' soup."

Folks in Nicodemus frequently talked about Miss Hattie's wisdom. Even Miss Hattie acted like she was an authority on everything from boiling water to raising children. If Miss Hattie didn't know the answer, no one did. Like everyone else, Fern decided she would just accept that separation in church was the way of things.

Truth tried to hide her disappointment that none of her family planned to spend the night as in past years. Her father wanted to sleep in his own bed and pointed to the clear skies and lack of snow as sound reasons for departing. And the remainder of the family had followed his lead. Truth wondered if the matter had been predetermined, for it didn't appear any of them had come prepared to remain beyond the evening visit. Truth had questioned Grace, but her sister assured her nothing was amiss. However, Truth remained uncertain, especially since her father had previously lauded the comfort of the bed in their spare room.

When the hour grew late, she had no choice but to bid her family farewell. Uneasiness plagued her as she climbed the stairs to fetch Moses's gifts. When she returned a short time later, several packages had been placed in front of the tree. He grinned, obviously pleased that he'd been able to keep the gifts away from her curious eyes. She wondered if she should tell him that he hadn't fooled her when he'd come in earlier in the evening. No. Best to let him think she hadn't guessed the packages had been hidden under the table all evening.

Moses patted the cushion of the divan. "Shall we take turns opening?"

She took her seat beside him and agreed as she handed him his first gift—a leather journal she'd had engraved with his initials. He thanked her profusely and then gave her a small package. He watched closely as she opened the box. Nestled inside was the most beautiful pair of diamond eardrops she'd ever seen. "Oh, Moses, these were *much* too expensive. Where I am going to wear anything so fine?"

"To my swearing in. And to the social gatherings we'll attend in Topeka."

Was his primary concern that they impress folks in the capital city? Is that what had guided his choice of her gift? She waited in anticipation as he opened her final gift. He lifted the sterling silver watch charm from the box and held it in his hand.

"A fine miniature of a printer's stick. Thank you, my dear." He removed his pocket watch from his jacket, attached the charm, and held it up for her to see.

She nodded. "It's a perfect reminder of what we had once planned for our future in Nicodemus."

He winced at the remark but tucked the watch into his pocket without comment and then handed her a final gift. Now she wished she'd let him draw his own conclusions, or at least waited until he asked why she'd made that choice.

She avoided his eyes as she pulled away the wrapping paper to reveal a beautiful velvet photograph album. She traced her finger along the intricate pattern on the cover and whispered her thanks.

"Open it." He clicked the gold clasp.

She lifted the cover and gasped. The first page revealed a perfect picture of their house. Moses's horse and buggy sat in front as if waiting for him to depart for his office. He reached forward and turned the page. She was totally unprepared for what she saw. Tears welled in the corners of her eyes, and she attempted to focus upon the pictures of her family. Her father in front of his house waving, with Grace standing beside him laughing; Jarena, Thomas, and baby Jennie outside their barn; Grace gathering eggs; and even a family photograph of Miss Hattie, Calvin and Nellie, and their children. As Truth flipped through the pages, tears rolled down her cheeks.

Moses lifted her chin until their eyes met. "Please don't be filled with regret or sadness. I'm not upset about your gift or the words you spoke. I know you're wounded by this change in our lives. All I can do is attempt to make our time in Topeka much happier than you anticipate." He traced his fingertips down her cheek as he gently kissed her lips. "Merry Christmas, my love."

Truth hugged the album to her chest. "Thank you for these photographs. I will treasure them always." She tapped the velvet cover. "All that is missing is one of you."

He kissed her hand. "I wanted one of us together. I'm sure we can arrange a sitting . . ."

"In Topeka." She smiled as she completed the sentence. He pulled her close, his embrace radiating the warmth and affection that endeared him to her. Both his words and his actions throughout the evening reflected only his love. Without a doubt, he desired to ease her fears of loneliness. And for that, she was most thankful.

She'd gone to the doctor earlier in the week, and he'd declared all seemed to be fine with her pregnancy. The weather had been clear, and there were no signs of a snowstorm on the way. Everything was falling into place for their move. But Truth still had the disquieting feeling that she was about to leave her very existence in Nicodemus. Even if they returned one day, nothing would be the same.

CHAPTER

— 22 —

Topeka, Kansas • January 1883

Since Truth, Moses, and Lilly had arrived in Topeka, the days
had passed in rapid succession, each one appearing and vanish-
ing as rapidly as snow during a spring thaw. Setting up housekeeping in a new home had proved more demanding than Truth had
imagined. Not that she was actually settled. Numerous unpacked
crates lined the walls, and she remained perplexed about how to re-
arrange the house with its narrow rooms and unseemly design. She
now understood Moses's admonition to leave most of their belongings
in Nicodemus. The house he had rented was smaller than their own.
And though the landlord had boasted that the furnishings were mag-
nificent, Truth strongly disagreed. Upon their arrival, she had declared

the house both sparsely and shabbily furnished and the landlord's claims fallacious, and she hadn't changed her mind. *Then again, I doubt any house in Topeka would suit me. I want to go home.*

Aunt Lilly had reminded Truth of her humble beginnings in Kentucky and the sod house the Harban family had lived in during their early years in Nicodemus, reminding her to be thankful for what they had. After all, rentals were at a premium in Topeka. Truth wondered if Lilly's time in Colorado had lowered her expectations regarding proper living quarters.

Grace had asked to stay in Nicodemus a few more days. Although she'd said her delayed departure was at Silas's request, Truth wondered if she hoped a blizzard would arrive and prohibit her departure entirely. As long as the weather held, Grace was expected to arrive in Topeka today.

The snowfalls in Topeka this year had consisted of no more than numerous smatterings of light flurries or the unexpected appearance of several inches that melted as quickly as it had arrived. At Truth's insistence, Moses had visited the railroad depot the previous day to ask if any tracks had been closed due to weather conditions. Truth had breathed more easily when her husband reported the tracks were clear throughout the state. Truth could only pray her sister's wagon journey from Nicodemus to the train station in Ellis had been without mishap.

The mantel clock chimed three times, and Truth hastened up the stairs. There was insufficient time to make the house more presentable—not that any amount of effort would have elevated the house to the status of acceptable as far as Truth was concerned. However, she intended to look her best when Moses arrived to escort her to the train station.

After changing her dress, Truth arranged her hair, pinned a brooch to the neckline of her dress, and descended the steps as Moses entered the front door. She hoped the train wouldn't arrive early. If so, Grace would surely wonder if they'd forgotten her.

Moses helped Truth into her coat. Unfortunately, it no longer closed across her ever-increasing girth, and her cloak wasn't nearly warm enough. Though she was excited for the baby, growing big with child made things awfully inconvenient. Moses had engaged a local dressmaker to stitch a lovely warm cloak to wear to his swearing-in ceremony, but the woman had not yet completed the task.

Moses assisted her into the carriage, and she draped the wool carriage blanket across her lap. He grinned and pulled the blanket higher, tucking it tightly in place before taking up the reins. The horse clopped along at a lumbering pace. Had Truth been driving, she would have given the animal a flick of the reins for encouragement. When she muttered in complaint, Moses assured her they had more than sufficient time before the train arrived. But when she heard a train whistle, she nudged Moses hard with her elbow. He gently reminded her there were two train depots located in close proximity and the whistle could have been signaling a train arriving from most anywhere.

She hurried into the depot and scanned the crowd for any sign of her sister. Pushing through the throng of arriving and departing passengers, she soon spied Grace entering a far door. Truth's cheeks burned with joy. Waving her handkerchief overhead, she called out

Grace's name while she made her way to her sister. A hurrying pas-
senger jostled Truth with his large suitcases, and Moses stepped forward to command the lead.

Grace beamed when she finally spotted Truth and Moses in the
crowd. Jumping up and down she waved her handkerchief in
response.

The twins embraced with a ferocity that belied the fact that they'd
been separated for less than ten days. While Moses edged his way to
the platform, Truth and Grace followed along, laughing and chattering as they went. Though Moses had assured them he could locate
the proper trunk, Grace looked doubtful.

On the ride home, Truth and Grace reminisced about the first
time they'd arrived in Topeka, giggling as they remembered Miss
Hattie's remarks about the growing city, and the first time they had
met Thomas Grayson.

"And now Thomas is Jarena's husband!" Grace exclaimed. "I never
imagined he'd end up marrying into the family when we met him."
Grace snuggled closer to share the blanket with Truth. "You and Aunt
Lilly managing to get along?"

Truth chuckled. "We are now. She moved into a boardinghouse
yesterday." Truth pointed to a building on Kansas Avenue. "That's
Aunt Lilly's shop. She'll be living in the upstairs rooms after the work
is completed."

Grace's jaw went slack as she leaned back and looked into Truth's
eyes. "Why did she move to the boardinghouse?"

"I told her I was going to hire a housekeeper, so Lilly would have
to share her room with you."

Grace's eyes widened at the remark, and Truth put her arm around her twin's shoulders. "Don't worry. It's the best thing that could have happened. Aunt Lilly and I weren't getting along anyway, and now we have *two* spare bedrooms."

Moses glanced over his shoulder. "Only until you hire a house-keeper."

"This is a big city, Moses. I should be able to hire a housekeeper who lives in Topeka and doesn't require sleeping quarters." Truth winked at her sister. "Our first task is to try and locate Dovie Tuttle. Moses told me he would, but with all of his meetings prior to taking office, he hasn't had time."

Moses informed them he did not want them wandering about town unescorted. Though Truth was confident she and Grace would have no difficulty finding their way to the Tuttles' home—after all, at one time she had navigated the streets of New York on her own—she agreed to Moses's request. For now.

The following afternoon Grace and Truth were sitting side-by-side unwrapping china from one of several crates when Moses un-expectedly arrived home in the middle of the afternoon. They looked up in unison when they heard a young woman's voice. In a flash, Grace was on her feet, shouting Dovie's name and pulling her into an embrace. Soon Truth joined them, and the three formed a laughing, chattering huddle, each attempting to be heard above the other—just like when they'd been best friends back in Kentucky. Truth turned as Moses tapped her shoulder and waved good-bye. She quickly kissed her husband's cheek and thanked him.

Not wanting to miss out on any portion of the conversation, Truth motioned for the pair to follow her to the kitchen while she prepared tea. After setting the water to boil, she cut three large slices of lemon pound cake.

Dovie cupped her chin in one hand as she sat at the table. "When yo' husband come knockin' at our door, I couldn' believe my eyes. He looks *white*, Truth." She hunched forward and continued to speak in a hushed voice. "And when I ask 'im where he worked, he said he was the auditor fer the state. I don' know what the auditor does, but my mama figured from the way he was dressed, it must be somethin' special. I sure hope so, 'cause she's telling ever'one in the neighborhood that we know someone important."

Truth placed the tea and cake on a tray. "Let's have our tea in the parlor. No sense sitting out here in this dismal kitchen."

"Dismal?" Dovie scanned the room. "This is almost as nice as Senator Johnson's house—you know, the folks I worked for 'til last year." Dovie cast another look around the house as they walked into the parlor. "He lost the election. Did I tell you 'bout that?"

"No." Truth placed the tray on a small table. "I didn't receive any letters after you wrote saying he was running for reelection. I wondered what had happened."

"Ain't been an easy time since then. I packed up and went back home after the new senator took office. Times been hard, and there weren't no extra money for postage. We been needin' every cent to keep a roof over our heads and food in our mouths."

Grace edged forward. "Didn't the new senator need a housekeeper?"

"Huh-uh. They brung their housekeeper with 'em." She ran her finger around the edge of the teacup. "Since all the Exodusters come here, there's plenty of folks looking for work and lots who ain't finding it."

"*Aren't*. Lots who *aren't* finding it." Truth automatically corrected her friend and then noted Dovie's surprised stare. "I'm sorry. I sound just like Jarena—busy correcting everyone's grammar."

"Ain't no need to . . ." Dovie slapped her palm across her lips. "I mean, you don't need to apologize. What kind of life you got back there in Nicodemus that you's thinkin' the kitchen in this house ain't truly fine?"

Truth bit her lip. No matter how hard Dovie might try, she soon slipped back into her old speech patterns. Of course, she hadn't had years of Jarena's correction and discipline. And though Truth hadn't told her older sister, she now appreciated the effort she'd made to educate them. Otherwise, Truth would now be even more frightened to mingle with the politicians and their wives.

Grace poured tea into each of the three china cups. "Moses built Truth a lovely new home in Nicodemus—much nicer than this. Of course, I plan to live on a farm when Silas and I jump the broom."

"You seeing someone special, Dovie?" Truth asked as she handed the girl a cup of tea.

"Ain't found no one I want to marry. Most all the single men living in Tennessee Town is poor, and I'm looking to find me a rich man—like you, Truth." She took a sip of her tea. "Most of the men living nearby is part of the Exodusters that come from Tennessee. Ain't *really* a town—jest called that 'cause all the folks from Tennessee moved into the same area." She held her cup at eye level and examined the thin, finely painted porcelain.

Truth watched as Dovie once again traced her finger around the rim of the cup. The envy she saw in her friend's eyes was disconcerting. Dovie fingered the engraved initials on the silver spoon as if they were the most beautiful thing she'd seen in her life.

Truth placed her cup and saucer on a nearby table. "Like the house, most of the furniture belongs to Mr. Epps. But I'll be certain to tell him you approve of his choices."

"I wish I could live in a house like this again." Dovie reached out for Truth's hand. "Your husband said you's looking for a cook and housekeeper. Would you consider hiring me, Truth?"

"Well, I . . ."

Before Truth could complete her reply, Dovie clenched her hand more tightly. "I promise I'll do a good job, and I won't let our friendship get in the way. You can correct me when I do things wrong or if you ain't happy with my work. Mr. Johnson never did have much complaint 'bout me."

Truth had hoped to speak with Moses before she officially hired someone, but she doubted he would voice an objection considering Dovie was one of Truth's best friends. With Dovie waiting in wide-eyed anticipation, Truth nodded. Dovie immediately jumped up from the settee with a promise to be moved in before nightfall.

Moved in? "There's no need for you to leave your home, Dovie. Moses will make arrangements for transportation back and forth."

But her words fell on deaf ears, for unlike Truth, Dovie proclaimed that she was anxious to leave home, especially if it meant the opportunity to once again live in a fine house.

Though Truth didn't understand Dovie's decision, she didn't voice an objection. "You be sure and tell your mama that I was willing for you to live at home. I don't want her thinking I forced you to leave home again."

Dovie giggled and waved. "You don't need to be worrying none 'bout Mama. She's gonna be even happier than me. Only thing that would please her more is iffen I brought home some well-to-do fella like what you got." Removing her cloak from the ornate hall tree, Dovie wrapped it around her shoulders and fastened the frayed collar before she departed.

Truth sighed and leaned against the door. At least Lilly couldn't accuse her of deceit, for it now appeared all of the bedrooms *would* be occupied.

Dovie returned much earlier than expected. In fact, when Truth saw her at the door only two hours later, she thought Dovie had decided the idea of working for her friend was preposterous or that her mother had disapproved of the situation. However, when she noticed the satchel Dovie held in one hand and Dovie's father lumbering toward her carrying a large trunk, she knew she was mistaken.

She held open the door and waved Mr. Tuttle up the stairs to what was now Dovie's room. He looked older than she remembered, but she supposed that was to be expected. She hadn't seen him for more than five years. Mr. Tuttle situated the trunk along one wall and quickly exited the room. Making a rapid descent down the stairs, he placed a fleeting kiss on his daughter's cheek.

Truth said she had hoped he would remain long enough to meet Moses, but Mr. Tuttle declined, citing work that awaited him at the livery. With a wave, Dovie bid her father farewell, seemingly undaunted by his departure. Truth mentioned that Dovie was free to go home on Saturday evenings and spend Sundays with her family, but Dovie quickly refused the offer. Perhaps she'd grown accustomed to separation from her family when she worked for the Johnsons, but something about the whole matter nagged at Truth. Before Truth could inquire further, Dovie hastened to the kitchen to help Grace prepare the evening meal.

Truth had little time to dwell upon the matter of Dovie's apathy toward her family and home when Moses returned for the evening. There was a spring to his step and a twinkle in his eyes. Apparently things had gone well at his office. His predecessor had generously agreed that Moses could observe the practices and procedures of the state auditor's office prior to taking office.

He wrapped Truth in a welcoming hug, and she shivered and yelped as he placed his icy cheek alongside her own. Pushing her hands against his broad chest, she backed away and scolded him.

Chuckling, Moses removed his coat and hung it in the hallway. "Did you and Grace have a nice visit with Dovie?"

She motioned for him to follow her upstairs. "Dovie is now our housekeeper. Our *live-in* housekeeper." She nibbled her lower lip as she awaited his reaction.

Moses stared at her for a moment, his eyebrows raised. "Is that a bad thing? I thought you planned to have her come and work for us if she was available."

"It will be fine—at least I hope it will. I do worry about what will happen when I have to assign her duties or correct her work."

"I doubt there will be problems. The two of you haven't been around one another for several years. You'll soon slip into a natural pattern that's comfortable for both of you."

He took her hands and pulled her close. "I believe I've warmed up enough for a proper welcome-home kiss."

She placed her palm along his jaw. "I do believe you have." She tilted her head and raised up on her toes. His lips covered hers with a long, ardent kiss, and several moments passed before he released her. She gave him a half smile as she looked at him from beneath hooded eyelids. "There's absolutely no doubt you've warmed up, Mr. Wyman."

He laughed and wagged his finger. "Careful or you'll miss your supper, and that would be extremely difficult to explain to the new housekeeper."

Truth giggled at the thought as she grabbed her husband by the hand and led him back down the stairs. "You certainly came home in a cheerful mood," she said as they reached the landing.

"I'm *always* cheerful—just a bit more so today. I'll tell you why at supper."

Grace emerged from the kitchen and joined them. "Dovie says she wants to finish up on her own and serve the meal. I hope she's able to find everything."

"You two worry far too much. I believe she's bright enough to come and ask for assistance whenever she needs it."

The three of them walked into the dining room, with Grace on one side of Moses and Truth on the other. They chatted for several minutes, but soon they were all expectantly watching for the door between the kitchen and dining room to open. When Dovie didn't appear after several minutes, Truth excused herself and hurried to the kitchen. She was stunned to find Dovie sitting near the worktable with the dishes and bowls of food piled high.

"Why are you sitting here, Dovie? The food is growing cold."

"I never heard you ring the bell. Mrs. Johnson always rang a bell when it was time to bring in the food."

Truth giggled. "Oh, Dovie. I don't even own a bell." Truth picked up a bowl in one hand and a platter in the other. "Let's get this food on the table." Hesitating for only a moment, she instructed Dovie to bring the remainder of the dishes.

While they filled their plates, Moses revealed he'd met a young lawyer earlier in the day—a fine black man who had begun a law practice in Topeka, a man Moses believed could become a friend. An idea struck her, and Truth stole a look across the table. This man sounded perfect for Grace! Or was he already married?

"We should invite him and his wife to supper next week," Truth hedged.

"He's not married," Moses said, "but you'll meet him at the swearing-in ceremonies. His name is John Rockley."

Perfect! If Grace developed a relationship with John Rockley, maybe she'd forget about Silas and decide to stay in Topeka rather than return to Nicodemus. Nothing would make Truth happier than to have her sister nearby, and she'd never considered Silas and Grace to be particularly well suited anyway.

"Do you think he'd like to attend the ceremonies with us?" Truth asked. "Perhaps he could act as Grace's escort at the gala."

She didn't know who looked more surprised by the suggestion— her husband or Grace. Before either of them could reject her proposal, she hastily explained it would make for better seating arrangements. She'd heard few people attended these functions unescorted. And those who did . . . well, Grace could end up seated beside some pretentious old man who would bore her to tears with tales of his past accomplishments. It would save her sister from myriad uncomfortable circumstances if she had a trustworthy escort.

"If Grace don't want that fella, I'd be right pleased to meet him."

All three of them turned their attention to Dovie, who had taken a seat at the far end of the dining room table. Truth couldn't believe her eyes. Forevermore! What did Dovie think she was doing sitting at the table and entering into their conversation as though she were a guest? Apparently she viewed this new position differently than her employment with the Johnson family. Trying to avoid a reprimand, Truth merely shook her head and frowned. Dovie remained undeterred. She didn't budge from the chair. Gaining Moses's attention, Truth frowned and signaled toward Dovie with a slight dip of her head. Moses held up his water glass and Dovie promptly fetched the pitcher. When she drew near his side, Moses crooked his finger to beckon her closer. As Dovie leaned forward, Moses whispered into her ear.

After filling his glass, Dovie scampered from the room without a word. Truth mouthed a silent *thank-you* to her husband. She didn't know what he'd said, but his words had been effective.

"Since I plan to marry Silas, do you believe it would be appropriate to have Mr. Rockley escort me to the gala?" Grace asked, staring at her plate. "I'm not certain what Silas would think."

Truth sighed and raised her eyebrows. "It's not as though Mr. Rockley would be *courting* you, Grace. I'm only suggesting he act as your escort. You'd be with *us* the entire time."

"What do you think, Moses? If Truth had attended a function with someone else, would you have been troubled by her actions?"

Moses laughed and reminded Grace that her sister had traveled to New York City without his complete approval and he'd still married her.

Grace took a sip of water. "What about Aunt Lilly? Won't she be attending with us? If the two of us could sit together at the events, the seating wouldn't be a problem."

"Aunt Lilly isn't attending. Moses was entitled to only one additional ticket for the event, and I wanted you to be there with me." Truth stabbed several green beans onto her fork.

"Truly?" She looked to Moses for affirmation, and when he nodded, she said, "I'm honored that I was the one selected to attend. Thank you."

"You are most welcome, Grace. And you may rest assured that we will respect your wishes regarding Mr. Rockley." Moses gave Truth a pointed look. "Won't we, my dear?"

Grace spoke before Truth could respond. "I don't suppose having Mr. Rockley act as my escort would be improper. Silas and I aren't married yet."

Truth wanted to giggle with delight, but she forced herself to give only a solemn nod while she mentally considered details for the upcoming event. Fortunately she and Grace wore the same size dress. Her blue-and-white silk dress, one she'd purchased during a trip to Boston with Moses, would be perfect for Grace. If Mr. Rockley and Grace agreed to see each other for future social engagements, her sister would have an entire wardrobe of suitable attire at her disposal since none of Truth's gowns fit her increasing figure. And if Truth had her way, they *would* be seeing each other frequently.

CHAPTER

— 23 —

Truth was filled with pride when Moses raised his right hand and took the oath of office on January 8. The first black official in the state! Although this whole move to Topeka still wasn't sitting well with her, she felt her chest puff up a little as she beamed at her husband.

The swearing-in ceremony was followed by a reception to greet and honor the new officials and their wives and special guests. John Rockley joined Truth, Grace, and Moses in the east wing of the capital. Mr. Rockley had remained by Grace's side throughout all the formalities, and Truth soon discovered what a powerful member of the community he was. He had already been involved in several well-publicized cases. He had acted as special counsel to the Republican Party on several occasions, and his presence was desired at all political functions. With his knowledge of protocol, he'd been able to answer all of Truth and Grace's questions with ease.

They discovered there was little time between each of the events, but Truth suspected a woman may have been consulted regarding the actual schedule. Though there wouldn't be time to tarry, they would have sufficient time to return home and change into their gowns for the supper and dance that would follow.

As the foursome prepared to depart, Moses pulled John aside. "Why don't we all attend in one carriage? Could you come by the house at five-thirty?"

"Excellent idea. There are always far too many carriages at these events." John gave Grace a slight bow. "I shall look forward to joining you for the evening."

After they had piled into the carriage, Truth quizzed her sister. Though Grace occasionally appeared to object to the questions, Truth persisted; she must discover her sister's thoughts if her plan was going to work. If only Grace were more open about her opinions . . .

Grace exhaled an audible sigh when they finally arrived home, and Moses grinned as he assisted her down from the carriage. "You must be pleased to be home, where you can avoid your sister's probing questions—at least for a time."

Truth playfully slapped at his arm. She was certain Mr. Rockley thought Grace attractive. He'd said as much to Moses. Now if she could only convince Grace to relax and enjoy the evening, her sister's natural charm and intelligence would captivate Mr. Rockley even further. Coupled with the blue-and-white silk gown, how could he possibly resist?

After changing into her evening dress, Truth headed down to the parlor to await Mr. Rockley's arrival. She could barely believe her eyes when she entered the parlor. Dovie was sitting on the settee entertaining Mr. Rockley as though she were the mistress of the house!

Truth hastened into the room and tapped the servant on her shoulder. "Would you please go upstairs and advise Grace we're preparing to depart, Dovie?"

Dovie's guilty expression showed that she was aware she'd overstepped her boundaries and was taking unacceptable liberties. Anger caused Truth's cheeks to burn. After her earlier blunder at the supper table, why would Dovie behave in such a bold manner? She had to realize Truth would disapprove. Apparently the desire to find a prosperous husband was of greater import to Dovie than her job.

Truth sighed. Now there was little doubt Dovie's employment was going to prove awkward. If she dismissed the girl after only a few days on the job and word trickled back to Nicodemus, folks would doubtless think Truth's behavior rash and inappropriate. Perhaps she should have more carefully considered the possibility of such problems before hiring her old friend.

As Grace descended the steps, Truth noted John's appreciative look. Obviously, Mr. Rockley found Grace quite enchanting—not that Truth was surprised. Her sister looked particularly lovely this evening.

As the foursome prepared to depart, Dovie reappeared in the hallway. Circling around Moses, she moved near John's side. "It was truly a pleasure to meet you, Mr. Rockley. You have a fine time this evening." Without a word to the rest of them, Dovie disappeared from the foyer as quickly as she'd entered.

Truth was rendered speechless by her friend's flirtatious behavior. Dovie had even batted her lashes as she beamed up at John Rockley. She and Dovie must talk!

After they'd all climbed into the carriage, John leaned slightly forward in his seat. "Miss Tuttle mentioned the three of you ladies were friends back in Kentucky and came west at the same time."

Truth nodded, wondering what else Dovie had disclosed about their past. Not that she was ashamed of her humble beginnings. However, the fact that Dovie would discuss her employer's personal history or business with a total stranger was even more disconcerting than her rude behavior. She and Moses must decide upon a plan of action; she would speak to him when they arrived home.

Though the trouble with Dovie had stolen her earlier excitement, Truth's mood lightened as they entered the gaily decorated banquet hall. A bunting of golden yellow and navy blue hung from the speaker's platform, and each of the dining tables was covered with a dark blue cloth. The pristine white dishes were rimmed in gold, and the delicate crystal water goblets shimmered in the candlelight, giving the entire room a formal yet festive appearance.

Each table held a placard bearing the name of the distinguished guest being honored. Truth's pride resurfaced when she noted the signage centered on their table. The card was engraved with the words *Kansas State Auditor* in bold dark letters and her husband's name in a beautiful script directly below. An engraved place card was situated by the water goblet at each setting.

Truth tugged at Moses's arm. "Shall we peek at the cards and see who else will be sitting at our table?"

"No need."

Truth spun around at the sound of her aunt's voice. "Aunt Lilly! How did you . . . What are you . . ."

Her aunt's right hand rested on the arm of a distinguished-looking gentleman Truth had never before seen. However, Moses clapped him on the shoulder while he enthusiastically shook the stranger's other hand. "Mr. Rockley, I'd like to introduce you to my wife, Truth, and her sister, Grace."

Truth glanced back and forth between John and the stranger. The older gentleman smiled and nodded at John. "I'm John's uncle—Charles Rockley. It's a pleasure to meet you. And I believe you have all met my lovely guest for the evening."

Truth noted that even Moses appeared taken aback by Lilly's presence. She wondered how and when John and Charles Rockley had met her aunt. Lilly grinned like a Cheshire cat as she and the elder Mr. Rockley circled the table and then claimed the remaining two places.

John reached to assist Grace with her chair. "Your aunt insisted upon surprising the three of you. I was sworn to secrecy."

After seating Truth, Moses eased into his chair. "Well, I'd say you succeeded. I didn't even realize you'd met Truth's aunt."

Lilly squared her shoulders. "I've hired Mr. Rockley as my lawyer. He handled the purchase of my business here in Topeka." She tapped her folded fan on Moses's arm. "Surely you realize I'm an astute businesswoman who wouldn't enter into a contract without a lawyer's advice."

Truth stifled a guffaw. The entire family knew Lilly's prowess as a businesswoman. Of all people, Lilly didn't need a lawyer to point out any possible flaws in a real estate contract. In all probability, Lilly had sought Mr. Rockley's counsel after learning he was an eligible man of distinction. Using her business contract as an effective tool, Lilly obviously planned to snare him into her web. Knowing Lilly's history, Truth decided that if Mr. Rockley proved to be a man of considerable financial means, Lilly would be Mrs. Charles Rockley by winter's end.

By the time dessert was served, Truth was convinced Lilly had set her cap for Mr. Rockley. Her coquettish behavior was obvious and embarrassing—at least in Truth's opinion—though none of the others seemed to notice. In fact, Truth was pleased to observe that her sister appeared more interested in conversing with John than in observing Aunt Lilly's flirtations.

Their tables had been cleared and the musicians had taken to the platform in preparation for the ball when Lilly tapped her fan on the table to get Grace's attention. "Grace, I was surprised when John told me he was your escort this evening. Whatever will Silas think?"

Without waiting for Grace's response, Lilly accepted Charles's invitation to dance. Taking his arm, Lilly rose from the table and strolled to the dance floor. Glancing over her shoulder, she winked at Truth. To say Lilly was infuriating would be an understatement. Grace shot a look of panic in Truth's direction.

John raised an eyebrow. "May I assume that Silas is someone who lives in Nicodemus? Your fiancé, perhaps?"

"No!" Truth said before Grace could answer. "They're not engaged, Mr. Rockley. Merely close friends. Silas and I are friends, also. Silas was employed at the boarding school Macia Boyle attended in New York City. When we learned he was anxious to begin life anew outside of the city and subsequently agreed to help us escape Macia's boarding school, I told him he could come west with us."

"Escape?" John asked.

Truth told him the whole story, and John seemed captivated. When she'd finished the tale, she glanced at the dance floor. "The musicians will want to go home before we have even one dance." She looked at her husband, knowing he'd get the hint.

Moses laughed and took his wife's hand. "You two may as well join us, John. No need to sit at the table by yourselves."

John stood and offered his hand to Grace.

"Besides," Moses said over his shoulder to John, "I don't want to be the only one stumbling over my feet."

Truth followed her husband's lead as the other couples swirled around them, pleased when John and Grace came into view. She wondered if her matchmaking efforts were destined for failure. Between Dovie's unconcealed attraction to Mr. Rockley and Lilly's reminder of Silas, she doubted whether Grace would be comfortable seeing the dashing young lawyer again. Still, they danced together with an ease that belied the fact they'd met only recently. Surely they were intended for each other.

Truth had already put Silas out of her mind. The young man had come to Kansas thinking he might marry *her*. His interest in Grace hadn't taken seed until after Truth and Moses married. Even then, both Jarena and Truth had questioned Silas's intent. Did he truly care for Grace or had he chosen her because she resembled Truth? Grace deserved a man who cared for her solely because of who she was, not because she looked like someone else.

Much to Truth's frustration, Grace would say little regarding her feelings about the day of the swearing-in. On several occasions since the ball, Grace had confirmed her enjoyment of the various celebratory events, but the perfunctory responses were all Truth could get out of her. She would say nothing about her feelings toward John Rockley.

Truth concluded that Grace thought others would consider her disloyal to Silas. Although it seemed Silas need not worry. At least two times a week Truth saw a letter addressed to Silas on the table near the front door. Moses dutifully took each letter and posted it for Grace. No, Silas need not worry about Grace's loyalty—at least not yet.

In the last week, Truth and Moses had taken Dovie aside and outlined the behavior they expected of their servant. Moses had at first said he thought Truth needed to handle the training and discipline of household servants, but after a bit of cajoling, Truth convinced him that she needed his moral support when dealing with her friend. After their discussion with Dovie, Moses said he'd felt unnecessary. But Truth knew that was not the case. It was his presence and not Truth's words that had caused Dovie's meek demeanor and quick acquiescence to the household rules. Thus far, Dovie had taken the admonitions to heart. However, she would soon be put to the test, for Truth had invited John Rockley to be their supper guest.

After Moses had agreed that a gathering any night the following week would suit, Truth had forwarded an invitation to Mr. Rockley. She now looked forward to his affirmative reply. And although Moses had suggested she also invite John's uncle and Aunt Lilly, Truth quickly vetoed the idea. Aunt Lilly's reminders of Silas weren't the table conversation she desired at her dinner party. But she did invite Mr. and Mrs. Ditmore, a friendly middle-aged couple John had introduced them to at the inaugural party. Truth was well aware that without the addition of at least one or two guests, Grace would become suspicious and accuse Truth of interfering—or worse, matchmaking.

Moses came home a little before noon and entered the parlor still rubbing his hands together. "Even wearing thick gloves isn't enough protection against this weather. I hope Dovie has prepared a good hot soup for our noonday meal." He leaned down and kissed Truth's cheek, but when he attempted to nuzzle her neck, she playfully pushed him away.

"You'll not warm your cold face in my neck." She laughed as she shook a warning finger in his face. When he continued to try, she laid her hands upon his chest. "I'll tell Dovie not to serve dinner if you keep up your antics."

Moses plopped down beside her looking like a recalcitrant child. "In that case, I suppose I had best behave."

A short time later, Truth set aside her stitching and took Moses's hand as they walked to the dining room. While Dovie hastened upstairs to fetch Grace, the two of them took their seats at the table.

Moses stood as Grace entered the dining room a short time later. After saying a quick prayer, he unfolded his napkin and placed it on his lap. "I nearly forgot. Your invitations have been accepted, so you best begin preparing your menu."

"Menu for what?" Grace looked back and forth between her sister and brother-in-law.

"We've invited a few guests for supper on Friday night. Nothing elaborate—just supper and visiting. My condition will soon prevent entertaining until after the baby's birth. I hoped to squeeze in one or two supper parties before then." Truth snapped open her napkin and placed it on her lap.

Nodding, Grace spread a dollop of butter on a thick piece of crusty bread. "Who have you invited?"

"Mr. and Mrs. Ditmore—you remember them from the dance, don't you? The older couple who sat at our table and visited toward the end of the evening?"

Grace bobbed her head. "Oh yes. They were nice. Mr. Ditmore said he was involved with the railroads. Who else?"

Truth dipped a ladle of stew into her bowl. "John."

"John Rockley? That's all? The Ditmores and John Rockley?"

Truth passed the steaming bowl of stew to her sister. "I didn't want to invite eight or ten guests the first time I hosted a supper party. It would be rather unfair to Dovie, don't you think?" She raised an eyebrow and met her sister's inquiring stare. "She hasn't been required to prepare and serve a large dinner for over a year. In addition, there are only a few days to organize a menu and shop."

"Oh. I wasn't thinking of the trouble it might create for Dovie." Grace gave her sister a sidelong glance. "I thought you were . . . well, trying to bring John and me . . . well . . ." She ate a spoonful of stew as she collected her thoughts. "I should quit thinking everything that occurs has something to do with me. Pappy would say I need to get my mind off myself and start thinking about others."

Guilt pricked Truth's conscience, but she remained silent. Even her husband's raised eyebrows weren't enough to force an admission that Grace's assumption had been correct. Instead, she suggested she and Grace sit down and plan the menu later in the afternoon—a meal that would be elegant yet simple.

Grace giggled. "I don't know how much help I'll be 'cause I'm not sure what 'elegant but simple' means. Between your spending time in New York and living with a cultured husband, you know more about elegant meals than I do." Grace finished her final bite of stew. "As far as I'm concerned, this stew is simply elegant."

Moses pushed his chair away from the table and smiled at his sister-in-law. "I believe the Ditmores may expect something a little more lavish. John, on the other hand, probably won't care what we serve for supper, as long as you're seated next to him."

Grace swiveled around to face her sister. Truth forced herself to remain a model of control as she carefully masked her surprise. Why had Moses stirred things up? Grace had already stated her suspicions. Surely he knew such a comment would only fuel her concern.

Truth forced a laugh. "That's a relief. I would be alarmed if he desired to sit next to one of the married women."

Grace's frown disappeared and her shoulders relaxed. "Yes, I suppose that would cause quite a stir."

Whether Truth had completely convinced Grace remained to be seen, but she looked as though she believed the dinner party was not just a ploy to force her to spend more time with John.

As her husband leaned down to kiss her good-bye, Truth turned to whisper in his ear. "We need to have a talk about your unnecessary comments to my sister."

Moses's breath tickled her ear as he replied, "You need to stop meddling, my dear." With that, he kissed her lips soundly, donned his coat, and bid the two women good-day.

— 24 —

Plans for the supper party progressed more smoothly than Truth had imagined they would, and thus far, Dovie had followed through on all of her instructions. Hopefully, she would also remember to keep her interactions with John to a minimum—Truth planned to admonish her shortly before the guests arrived. If Dovie followed all of the protocol and etiquette she'd been taught by her former employer's wife and by Truth and Moses, the evening should prove a success.

Grace seemed a bit despondent the night of the party, and Truth wondered if it was because she had received no letters from Silas. Secretly, Truth celebrated each day that passed without an envelope bearing Grace's name, for it might work to give John the advantage. Truth still wondered how much Silas actually cared for her sister. Why didn't he answer at least one of her frequent letters?

As Grace assisted her with the fawn velvet dress and carefully arranged the silk overlay, Truth considered the cost of the gown. It was an extravagance Moses had insisted upon, stating he expected she would have future use for the gown as their family increased.

"This is truly a lovely dress." Grace drew a circle in the air with her index finger. "Turn around and let me see that the back of the gown is in order."

Once Grace gave her approval, Truth held out a necklace. After her sister clasped it around her neck, she retrieved the matching ear-bobs. "You can borrow the gown when you're expecting a child of your own."

Grace smiled into the mirror and locked eyes with her sister in the oval glass. "I think I best have a husband before we speak of children."

Truth chuckled and gave her sister a hug. "I suppose you're correct. I'm going downstairs to give Dovie her last-minute instructions and inspect the dining room. Please join me downstairs as soon as you've dressed." She glanced at the porcelain clock sitting on her dresser. "I do hope Moses comes home soon."

"We have plenty of time until the guests are scheduled to arrive," Grace reminded her.

Truth assumed she would need the time to ensure everything was prepared according to her exacting requirements. And to be certain Dovie understood she must avoid interacting with any of the guests, especially John Rockley. Descending the stairway, she made a brief stop in the dining room. The table had been set with the best china, and large gold candelabra flanked both ends of the table. A third ornate candelabrum had been centered on the buffet. A large mirror hanging above the buffet would reflect light from all three, providing a luminescent glow—at least that was Truth's plan. She would remind Dovie to light the candles before announcing supper.

Setting off toward the kitchen, she did her best to walk with a refined sashay. She feared her endeavor more closely resembled the lumbering gait of an old workhorse. She had never realized the difficulties expectant mothers were required to overcome each day. It was still hard to believe she'd be holding her own child in such a short time.

"The dining room looks marvelous, Dovie," she said as a greeting. "Are the meal preparations going smoothly?"

Dovie was concentrating on her work at the chopping table, where she was pressing potatoes through a sieve. "I think so. I hope this soufflé turns out like the one I made fer supper las' week. If it don't, it's gonna look more like a potato pancake." She looked up long enough to grin at Truth.

"It will be wonderful." Truth didn't want to interrupt Dovie's duties, but she needed to make sure they had reached a clear understanding. "You do remember what I said about conversing with the guests?"

"I understand." She added salt, pepper, and a dollop of cream to the potatoes before she stirred the mixture. "What you want is clear as a sun-filled Kansas sky, Truth."

The tone of Dovie's voice belied the innocuous response. Choosing to ignore the remark, Truth started to leave. When her curiosity overruled her better judgment, she turned back into the kitchen. "Just what is it you think I want, Dovie?"

"You think you's hiding it real good, but you're not." Dovie carefully separated six eggs and added the yolks to the potato mixture. Then she added a pinch of salt to the egg whites and whipped them into a stiff froth with more vehemence than Truth thought necessary. "You want yer sister to marry John Rockley." As she folded the beaten egg whites into the potato mixture, she gave a mirthless chuckle. "I always did know when you was scheming, Truth."

Truth silently chastised herself. She should have left before getting ensnared in this conversation. Well, she would leave now. Without a word, she lifted her chin and walked toward the parlor. Her stomach lurched when she realized talkative Dovie might tell someone else what Truth was up to. *Please don't let Dovie share her suspicions with Grace.*

"Not feeling well?"

She startled at Moses's question. Where had he come from and what had he heard from the kitchen? "No, I'm fine. Why do you ask?"

He shrugged. "You seem a bit tired, although you certainly look beautiful in that gown. I'm glad I insisted upon having it made."

She touched a palm to his cheek. "So am I." She glanced at his suit and gave her approval. "I didn't realize you'd been home long enough to change clothes."

He chuckled. "I didn't want to give you cause for concern. However, it looks as if all is in order and there's nothing for me to do except await our guests."

When she heard a carriage pull up outside, Truth fingered one of the combs she'd tucked into her hair and gave it a firm shove. She hoped it would remain secure throughout the evening. "I told Dovie you would see to the door," she told Moses. "Running back and forth while she's attempting to finalize the meal would be asking far too much of her."

"And would increase her opportunities to speak with John?" There was a teasing lilt to his voice.

Truth took his hand as they walked to the door. "You wouldn't believe me if I denied your claim, so I may as well agree."

His laughter echoed in the hallway as Moses opened the front door. "Good evening, John. Do come in."

As Truth hung up John's coat, Grace joined them in the foyer. Her honey-brown skin glowed against the pale yellow of the cashmere gown, and Truth marveled at her sister's transformation. Grace had blossomed since her arrival in Topeka. However, it was John's undeniable look of approval that delighted Truth. The man was obviously smitten with Grace.

The foursome hadn't yet moved from the foyer when Mr. and Mrs. Ditmore arrived. They had little time to visit before Dovie announced supper. As the group dined on thin slices of succulent beef roast and the potato soufflé, Mr. Ditmore quizzed each of them about Nicodemus. Truth let her sister take the lead. She wanted Grace to gain John's attention, and what better way than conversing about the town they'd grown to love?

Grace took a sip of water from her crystal goblet. After regaling their guests with tales of their arrival and the settling of Nicodemus, Grace grew more somber. "Now the greatest concern in Nicodemus is that the railroad will pass us by. We've heard such an occurrence can mean death for a small community."

Nodding his head, Mr. Ditmore helped himself to the creamed spinach. "You are absolutely correct, my dear."

"Surely you could help them, Edward." Mrs. Ditmore's eyes sparkled with excitement. She looked across the table at Grace. "My husband has a degree of influence with some of the railroads, don't you, dear?"

Picking up his napkin, Mr. Ditmore wiped his lips. His lengthy pause caused Truth to wonder if their guest hoped to avoid the question or perhaps thought his wife had placed him in an embarrassing situation. Finally his wife nudged him and he sparked to attention.

"I'm sorry. I was attempting to decide who might be of greatest assistance." He glanced at John. "John has handled many legal issues regarding the railroads, so he could lend some insight. I prefer to visit a location before I promote it to my colleagues. We're all heavily invested in the railroads, along with mining and several other ventures. Capital is needed for all of these new business enterprises. Money represents power to these companies. And because my group of investors has money, I can sometimes influence decisions. Of course, there's never a guarantee of success, right, John?"

John agreed and then explained that a while back both of them had strongly suggested a railroad route pass through a particular town that they thought held much promise. "We thought the matter had been settled and suddenly one of the railroad officials pushed for another route. Of course, he won and the town was bypassed. To this day, I still believe our suggestion was the better, more cost-effective solution, but someone likely received a more lucrative monetary enticement."

Mr. Ditmore eyed the piece of applesauce cake Dovie set before him. "Exactly. And I fear that greedy attitude will be the ruination of many a good business—railroads included."

Truth didn't see how Mr. Ditmore's attitude differed from that of the other wealthy investors he'd vilified, but she remained silent.

Mrs. Ditmore patted her husband's arm. "Now, now, my dear. No need for talk of gloom and doom—especially during such a fine meal." Mrs. Ditmore leaned forward and good-humoredly shook her finger at Truth. "If you're not careful, I'll attempt to steal your cook away from you. This applesauce cake is divine. I especially like the burnt sugar glaze. Do tell me you'll share the recipe."

Truth swelled with pride at the compliment. "I would be delighted. It's one of our family's favorites, isn't it, Grace?"

"Indeed." Without further comment on the recipe, Grace turned her attention back to Mr. Ditmore. "Do you think you might be willing to travel to Nicodemus, Mr. Ditmore—to help folks learn what will make the town more appealing to the railroads and to take a look at the town to see if you might recommend us for a route?"

The older gentleman thoughtfully tugged on his vest before speaking. Truth decided that if he ate one more bite of food, his buttons would pop off and go sailing in all directions. She could picture the ornate silver studs flying about the room like a scatter of buckshot.

He leaned back in his chair. "I'd be willing to consider making the journey so long as the weather cooperates and both Grace and John are willing to accompany me." He tilted his head toward Moses. "In addition, there's the possibility that your brother-in-law's political power may aid in the cause, also."

"I doubt my position will be of much help in this matter," Moses said, "though I will do all in my power to see Nicodemus is on the route of one of the railroad companies."

"Then you'll join us when we visit the town?" Grace inquired.

Wait! Truth didn't like the turn the conversation had taken. She didn't want Moses traveling to Nicodemus before the baby's birth—especially if she couldn't go along. Who could say when a snowstorm would strike and keep him stranded for longer than anticipated? What was Grace thinking? Surely she realized the unpredictable weather meant travel would be unwise for several months. Perhaps she longed to visit Silas and determine why he hadn't yet written to her. . . . *Uh-oh.*

"Certainly you aren't planning to go until spring," Truth put in.

Grace's shoulders collapsed in exasperation. "There's more than sufficient time before the baby is due."

Truth drew in a deep breath and focused her attention on Mr. Ditmore. "You *do* realize that a portion of the journey to Nicodemus must be traveled by horse and wagon."

Mrs. Ditmore looked surprised, then she tapped a finger on the table. "Truth is correct. No sense taking undue risks, my dear. Imagine trying to survive a snowstorm with nothing more than a horse and wagon. And it isn't as if this matter can't wait until spring."

Mr. Ditmore reached out and patted his wife's hand. "I suppose you're correct on that account. I'll talk to some of my acquaintances. If all goes well, we can plan to make the journey at winter's end."

Grace avoided the frown Truth directed her way, but she dutifully agreed they should wait until the weather was better. Pushing away from the table, Moses beckoned the guests into the parlor, where they could continue their conversation in comfort.

Mrs. Ditmore clung to her husband's arm as though she planned to walk several miles rather than a few steps into the adjoining room. She settled beside him and waved her fan in rapid fashion.

Her husband frowned at the accessory and his wife snapped the fan together with a flourish. "Edward surprised me with tickets to the theater for next Saturday night. I understand an excellent new play is opening. What was the name, my dear?"

Her husband shrugged and directed a bemused look at his wife. "I have no idea, Ruth. I merely know that when a new play comes to town, I'm expected to purchase tickets."

Mrs. Ditmore laughed but she didn't dispute her husband's statement. Instead, she shook a finger at Moses and instructed him he should learn to do the same.

When the older woman turned toward John, he reached into his pocket and held up two tickets. "Before you set your sights upon me, let me assure you that I've already purchased mine." He settled into a chair beside Grace. "And if I can convince Grace to accompany me, all the better."

A heavy, uncomfortable silence cloaked the room as they awaited Grace's reply. The aroma of Mrs. Ditmore's too-sweet perfume hung in the air like a cloying accompaniment to the unnerving quiet.

Unable to bear the silence any longer, Truth tapped Moses on the arm. "We could attend the performance with Grace and John. Perhaps you could purchase tickets tomorrow."

Though the others twittered, one look at Grace's frown revealed she was unhappy with Truth and her hastily proposed solution. No need discussing the matter further, Truth decided. There would be time enough to argue about the theater tomorrow. But for now, she ignored her sister's scowl.

Truth smiled to herself, pleased that this evening of entertaining had gone so well. She'd managed to postpone any possible journey to Nicodemus until spring, and if all went according to plan, Grace and John would be attending the theater together next week.

A small pang of guilt struck; she didn't want to impede the possibility of a rail line passing through Nicodemus. She wanted progress for the town, for she and Moses planned to return to their grand Nicodemus home once his term as state auditor had been completed. However, sending a delegation in the middle of winter made no sense, especially if Grace planned to accompany the group. Truth had nearly assuaged any feelings of guilt by the time their guests departed.

As they waved good-bye to their guests, Grace clutched her arm and tugged her into the parlor. "We need to talk before you retire for the night."

As she had feared, the *talk* was much more a speech than a conversation. In fact, Grace didn't pause long enough for Truth to interject one word. Truth half listened while her sister rambled on about the impropriety of attending the theater with John, as well as John's obvious interest in courting her. Then she took Truth to task for what she considered Truth's blatant disregard for the residents of Nicodemus.

Those particular comments stirred Truth to defend herself, but only briefly. Finally, she raised her hand and signaled her sister to stop. "I'm tired and I'm going to bed. Moses is already upstairs, and Dovie has likely been asleep for at least half an hour. You may feel free to continue your lecture tomorrow." That said, Truth rose from her chair. She longed to glide swiftly across the room with an air of decorum. Instead, she swayed back and forth in an ungainly fashion, feeling more like a waddling duck than a regal woman.

She could feel her sister's glare follow her as she departed the room. Relief washed over her as she ascended the stairs, for at least Grace had finally terminated her lecture.

CHAPTER

— 25 —

Nicodemus, Kansas • March 1883

It was only March, but thoughts of spring loomed in Ezekiel Harban's mind, and he'd noticed recently that most of the Nicodemus residents seemed to be suffering from cabin fever. Though the weather remained unusually cold and snow covered the ground, it wouldn't be long until the crocuses poked through the frozen soil of the small flower gardens in the township and announced spring's arrival. Ezekiel had no complaints about the snow—it provided a blanket of protection to his crop of winter wheat—but he sure was looking forward to warmer weather.

He wrapped his large hands around a cup of coffee and eyed the letter lying on the table. He figured Grace had saved postage and sent his letter along with one to Silas. No one could deny that Grace had been faithful in her letter writing, though he didn't think Silas had been keeping up on his end. The young man struggled with both his reading and writing, and Ezekiel was of no help to him. Silas had gone to Jarena on a couple of occasions to ask her assistance, but Jarena had told Ezekiel that Silas hadn't been to see her recently. He understood that—what young man wanted someone else scrutinizing his words of endearment?—but he wondered if Silas had managed to send even one letter. And what was Grace thinking about the lack of correspondence?

Since Grace's departure, Silas had continued to help Ezekiel with his farm even though the young man had more than enough to keep him busy on his own acreage. Ezekiel was thankful for both the help and the young man's company. Accordingly, he didn't alienate him with prying questions about letter writing.

Silas came into the kitchen, poured himself a cup of coffee, and sat down opposite Ezekiel. Silas tapped the folded piece of paper on the tabletop. "Guess you already figured that there letter's fer you. I picked up the mail when I was in town. It's from Grace."

Ezekiel grunted in the affirmative. "I figured that myself. Ain' no one else gonna send us letters in one envelope." He straightened in his chair. "Mebbe she's writin' to tell me Truth's had her young'un. Can you read it for me?"

"Truth ain't had the baby yet. I read my letter afore I come inside." He held up the sheet of paper. "You still want me to try an' read this?"

Ezekiel nodded before downing another mouthful of coffee. Silas read slowly, stumbling over several words, but at the first mention of the railroad, Ezekiel waved his hand and slowed him to a snail's pace. He listened carefully, wanting to understand every word Grace had to say about the Ditmores. The railroad coming to Nicodemus was his greatest wish, and he didn't want to build false hope by misunderstanding. This letter sounded very encouraging: Grace and a couple of influential men might visit Nicodemus in the spring.

Ezekiel slapped his beefy hand on the table, and his coffee cup skipped across the wooden surface. He grabbed hold of the cup and gulped the final drops of coffee. "That there is some good news. Folks is gonna be mighty excited to hear 'bout this."

"We'll see if she keeps her promise this time." Silas folded the letter and handed it back to Ezekiel.

"What's that s'posed to mean? Grace ain' broke no promises."

"Mebbe not to you, but she told me she'd be home for a visit afore the baby was born. I sure ain't seen her darkening any doorways in Nicodemus. Have you?"

"Nope, I ain' seen her. But you's smart enough to know folks ain' gonna be making extra trips back and forth across this here state during the dead of winter. I don' care what Grace tol' ya." Ezekiel touched his index finger to the side of his head. "I think you's got enough up there to a knowed better, now ain't ya?"

Ezekiel reached across the table and gave the young man a jovial slap on the shoulder. Instead of being pleased Grace would soon be paying him a visit, the young man was busy feeling sorry for himself. Pushing aside his intention to remain aloof, Ezekiel decided to jolt Silas out of his pitiful self-righteous mood. "I s'pose you posted a letter to Grace when you went into town to pick up this here mail."

Ezekiel waved the piece of paper back and forth.

Silas folded his muscular arms and met Ezekiel's piercing stare. "Naw. I ain' been able to find the right words to put in a letter. I know what I wanna say, but it never seems to sound right when I get it on the paper."

"Iffen you ain' even written one letter, I'd say you got no complaint. Fer all that gal knows, you found someone else to take her place. You ever think 'bout that?" he said, pointed a warning finger in Silas's direction.

"Grace knows better. Ain't no one could turn my head when I'm hopin' to marry her. 'Sides, she knows Jarena or someone else would write and tell her if I was looking at another gal."

Ezekiel shrugged his broad shoulders. "Womenfolk don' think the same as us. Iffen you's smart and want to hold onto her, you best set a pen to paper and tell her so."

Silas shoved his long arms into his heavy wool coat as he headed toward the door. He pushed a floppy-brimmed felt hat onto his head and waved as he opened the door. "I'll stop back over in a couple days."

"You mind what I tol' ya, Silas."

The door closed with a heavy thud. Ezekiel had said more than he'd intended, and now he wondered if he should have remained silent. He would have except for Jarena's comment last week. *"Sounds to me like Grace might be developing more than a mere friendship with John Rockley,"* she'd said. He figured Jarena knew exactly what was going on between Grace and Mr. Rockley, but she didn't reveal any specifics, and Ezekiel wouldn't inquire. Right now, he was more interested in finding out about the town's chances of wooing one of the railroad companies to run a line through Nicodemus.

The town had gathered and discussed the issue at length. In fact, some of the residents had written letters to several of the railroad lines pledging support and requesting a commitment. Thus far, they'd been unsuccessful in receiving any promises. But if these men Grace had mentioned would lend their assistance, perhaps they'd stand a better chance. Possibly one of the roads would push farther west with a northern route across Kansas even sooner than anticipated . . . maybe even this summer!

———

Truth stared at the envelope. The handwriting was neat, the letters well formed—superior to what she would have expected from Fern. Though she had never asked, Truth assumed the housekeeper had received little in the way of education.

Moses dropped down beside her on the settee and tapped his finger on the envelope. "Aren't you going to open that? I made a special trip home. I thought you'd be anxious to hear how Fern was faring in Nicodemus."

"Yes, of course." Truth slipped the point of her letter opener beneath the flap and neatly slit open the thick envelope. She removed the folded pages from the envelope and glanced at her husband. "Appears she's written us a lengthy letter. What could be going on in our empty house that would take up so many pages of explanation?"

Truth pressed open the pages and silently began to read.

Dear Mrs. Wyman,

I hope this letter finds you well and happy in Topeka. All remains fine with your home. I have not had any problems caring for it as you requested.

Truth sighed and met her husband's steady gaze. "She says all is fine with the house."

"Well, that much is good news. What else does she say?"

Truth returned to reading.

I would very much like to continue my position as your house-keeper, but first I must tell you of a change in circumstances. I considered keeping this matter a secret. However, I have had a long talk with Pastor James from over at the First Baptist Church, and he said I should tell you the truth. He says honesty is always repaid with kindness and I hope that will remain true in this cir-cumstance. You will recall that prior to your departure Arthur Wilson had expressed an interest in me. Our devotion to one another flourished, and although Arthur's parents aren't particu-larly fond of me (particularly his mother), we were secretly mar-ried. As of this writing, we have not told anyone except Pastor James. And now you, of course. Arthur doesn't know how his par-ents will react to this news. In addition, there isn't adequate space in their rooms above the store to accommodate two families. Would you heartily object if Arthur moved into your house with me?

I pray you will be accepting of this idea as we have nowhere else to go. We would not take advantage and you could forego payment of my wages as payment for Arthur's lodging. I give you my word, I will continue to look after the house with due diligence. I anxiously await your response.

Your servant, Fern Kingston

The pages fluttered to Truth's lap. "Fern has secretly married Arthur Wilson!"

Moses retrieved the letter and quickly scanned the contents. He laughed and slapped his leg. "I thought she'd have him at the altar before six months had passed."

"But what of her request, Moses? Do we permit them to live in our house? I'm not certain I like the idea."

"Why? Arthur is a fine young man, and what Fern has said is true. Living with his parents would be difficult. Arthur's days working at the store will be misery enough. You know his mother's tongue will wag against Fern and their marriage from morning until evening. The young man will need some form of escape." Moses folded the letter and handed it to his wife. "In addition, you want someone living at the house. There is no one else readily available. Fern has shown herself to be trustworthy by sending this letter. I say we let her and Arthur remain."

"I suppose you're correct. I'll write a letter to her this afternoon, and you can post it in the morning." Truth tucked the letter into the envelope and shook her head.

"What is it that befuddles you, my dear?"

"The fact that Fern has chosen Pastor James as her advisor. Knowing him, he'll lead her to Jesus, and Arthur and Fern will become the first white members of First Baptist."

Moses grinned. "Not such a bad thing. Not such a bad thing at all."

———————

Macia hesitated outside her father's office, contemplating whether she should go in. Her father had willingly come to Mr. Faraday's assistance once. She doubted he'd take kindly to helping the man again, especially since Mr. Faraday hadn't learned from his earlier near catastrophe. At least it *appeared* he hadn't learned anything. Yet how could Macia help Camille on her own? Her father was the only one Mr. Faraday listened to.

Macia peeked through the office door. Seeing no one in the waiting room, she drew in a deep breath and opened the door. "Father?"

"In here, Macia."

She followed the sound of his voice. She guessed he was reading one of the many medical books that filled his office bookcases. Her father was leaning back in his large, cushioned chair, his shoes resting atop one corner of the desk. His reading spectacles were perched on the tip of his nose. Her father placed the book on his desk and lowered his feet to the floor as he met her worried look.

The robust scent of the tobacco blend her father tamped into his pipe several times a day wafted through the room as if to greet her. Though her mother wouldn't permit him to smoke his pipe in the house, her father had never completely given up the habit. "What brings you to the office? Not feeling well?"

Macia plopped into one of the chairs across the desk from him. "I'm fine, Father. Well, at least physically." She glanced toward the waiting room. "Are you expecting any patients?"

"No. Mrs. Cafferty was my final patient for today. Unless an emergency should arise." Leaning forward, he rested his arms atop his shiny mahogany desk. "Now, tell me what brings you to the office on this blustery March day—nothing better to do than walk about in a cold, gusty wind?"

Macia cleared her throat and told him of her recent meeting with Camille Faraday. Her father's face tightened as she relayed what Camille had told her, and Macia feared his anger would outweigh his willingness to once again be drawn into the pharmacist's familial difficulties.

Leaning back in his chair, Dr. Boyle pulled the intricately carved pipe from his pocket and cupped the bowl in his right hand. "I truly don't know what I can do in this instance, Macia. Even if what Camille tells you is true, how can I approach him? He'd wonder how I came by this information, don't you think?"

Macia absently tapped his desk with her fingers as she gave the matter thought. The fact that Mr. Faraday was illegally selling medicines that contained high levels of alcohol and opiates to finance his gambling habit wouldn't be public knowledge. Yet those who gambled with Mr. Faraday knew how he came by his gambling money. In addition, Mrs. Faraday had become suspicious when her husband's sales and the diminishing pharmacy stock didn't balance. And now, Mrs. Faraday had charged Camille with the task of acting as her father's overseer—an unseemly arrangement for their daughter.

Macia fidgeted with her handbag for a moment and then perked to attention when she got an idea. "Why don't you state your case and if he should ask, tell him you promised you'd not break a confidence?" Macia bobbed her head excitedly. "Should he ask, you can honestly tell him the information didn't come from any member of his family."

Her father packed a pinch of tobacco into his pipe and tamped it tightly into the bowl. "I don't like meddling into—"

"Please, Father. If you won't do it for Camille, please say you'll do it for me. I can't imagine how difficult this is for her. If you could have seen her when she was telling me—"

"Oh, I suppose it won't hurt to have a talk with Faraday. However, if the man didn't learn his lesson when he nearly lost his house, I doubt another visit with him is going to have much impact." He held a match to the bowl of his pipe and sucked on the amber stem. Once the fire took hold, he took a deep draw on his pipe. "I'll give it a try if it will make you happy."

Quickly circling her father's desk, Macia leaned down and kissed his lightly stubbled cheek. "Thank you. I'm very happy *you're* my father. I can't imagine having someone like Mr. Faraday as a parent."

Her father chuckled softly, holding the pipe stem between his teeth. Macia knew what he was thinking; at least she thought she knew. He was likely remembering the many times when she'd objected to his fatherly decisions—particularly his decision to move west. She knew now his judgment had been sound. She shuddered to think what her life would have been like had she married Jackson Kincaid, the beau she'd had back in Kentucky.

Macia tied the black satin ribbons that edged the collar of her dark gray cape. "You'll talk to Mr. Faraday this afternoon—before you come home for supper?"

"As long as you and Camille realize this may prove to be a futile effort."

Macia retrieved her reticule from atop the desk. "I have faith in your ability, Father. I'll look forward to hearing what Mr. Faraday has to say for himself."

CHAPTER

— 26 —

Macia shifted in her chair. She'd thought supper would never end. Then, to make matters worse, her mother hadn't gone directly to bed after supper as she usually did; she'd decided to remain downstairs and stitch on her latest piece of needlepoint. Macia had attempted to lure her father into his library for a private conversation, but he hadn't seemed to get the hint. If she was to hear her father's report about his conversation with Mr. Faraday, she'd be forced to wait until her mother retired for the night. She'd tried to read, but lacked the ability to concentrate. The few times she'd been able to catch her father's eye, he had merely smiled and continued reading his paper.

When she could bear the waiting no longer, she asked to be excused. "I believe I'll go upstairs and prepare for bed."

Her mother folded her needlepoint and placed it in her sewing basket. "Excellent idea, my dear. I believe I'll go upstairs, too." Mrs.

Boyle kissed her husband and then took Macia by the hand.

"Macia," Mr. Boyle said, "would you consider fetching me a glass of buttermilk before you go upstairs?"

"Buttermilk?" she asked.

He nodded and winked. Evidently he was going to tell her about his meeting with Mr. Faraday. She kissed her mother good-night and hurried off to the kitchen. Stretching, she reached to retrieve a glass from the upper shelf of the cupboard as her father entered the room.

He replaced the glass. "Merely a ruse, my dear. I do not want a glass of buttermilk." He put his hand on her shoulder. "Let's go into my library and talk."

Macia settled into one of the comfortable overstuffed chairs and wrapped a wool throw around her shoulders. No fire had been started in the room, and the March winds seeped through the windows, leaving the library very chilly.

Dr. Boyle rubbed his hands together. "A bit cold in here this evening." He eased into a nearby chair.

Without fanfare, he told her what she'd been waiting to hear. He'd met with Mr. Faraday. As her father had expected, the pharmacist denied misusing any medicine and stated he understood the liquor laws. Mr. Faraday had said he couldn't imagine who was passing along erroneous information.

"Mr. Faraday appeared genuinely affronted by the accusations." Her father rested his elbows on his knees as he leaned toward her. "I'd like to believe I've wrongly accused him, but I fear he's a man who has lost control over his life. Like those who have need of alcohol coursing through their bloodstream, Mr. Faraday is obsessed with his gambling. And until he admits he has a problem, there is little anyone can do to help him."

Macia's shoulders collapsed as she listened to her father's verdict. She knew he was correct, yet she longed to carry some words of encouragement to Camille. Drawing the wool throw close around her neck, Macia wondered what it would take before Mr. Faraday changed his ways.

Her teeth chattered as she slowly rose from the chair. There was nothing more to discuss. She would talk to Camille in the morning.

"Thank you for trying, Father."

He took her hands and held them between his own. "Pray for him, Macia. That's all we can do at this juncture."

She knew her father was correct, yet she wondered if Mrs. Faraday, Camille, and Jonas didn't deserve her prayers more than Mr. Faraday!

"I'll answer the door." Macia tucked a blond curl behind one ear and waved to Gerta.

Gerta's rosy cheeks rounded into the shape of two ripe apples as she thanked Macia. She realized how peaceful their home had become since Fern's departure. With her sweet disposition and constant smile, Gerta made a pleasant addition to their family.

A lace curtain covered the door's oval window, obscuring Macia's view. Although she couldn't clearly distinguish who stood on the other side, she knew the caller was a woman—unless men had taken to wearing skirts. Her wandering thoughts immediately dissipated when she pulled open the door. "Camille! Whatever is the matter?"

Startled by her friend's ashen complexion and solemn countenance, Macia tugged her forward. "Come in. We're having breakfast—come join us."

Camille touched her right hand to her stomach. "I couldn't bear to eat right now, but if your father is here, may I speak with him?"

Macia reached to remove Camille's cape from her shoulders, but her friend shook her head. "I can't stay. I must get back home to Mother."

Macia led the way into the dining room, thankful her own mother had decided to take breakfast upstairs this morning. There would be fewer questions. Her father's eyes widened as the two young women entered the room. He pushed his chair away from the table, but Camille waved for him to remain seated.

Macia nodded to Gerta and the servant immediately scurried from the room. Taking Camille by the arm, Macia seated their visitor to her father's left. While Macia sat down across the table, Camille perched on the edge of a tapestry-covered chair as though ready to take flight.

Dr. Boyle looked back and forth between the two young ladies. "Is someone going to tell me what this is about or am I supposed to guess?"

Camille traced her finger across the edge of the linen tablecloth. "My father has disappeared. He's gone—for good, I fear."

"What's that? Someone's disappeared? A kidnapping or runaway?" Harvey burst into the room, his eyes alight with excitement. When he noticed Camille, his features grew somber. "Sorry, Camille. I didn't realize . . ." Harvey dropped into the chair beside Camille.

"We're discussing a confidential matter, Harvey." Macia motioned for him to leave.

But her brother didn't budge from the table. Instead, he took Camille's hand and patted it as though he'd been soothing distraught damsels all of his life. "How can we help you, Camille? Who has gone missing?"

She hesitated, but Harvey nodded his encouragement.

"This must remain confidential." Her words were no more than a whisper. "Nothing in the newspaper."

Harvey's features remained solemn as he pledged his agreement.

Camille fished a handkerchief from her pocket as she began the story. "Father came home for supper in a foul mood last evening. He ate in silence. Soon after, he departed, saying he'd be late and my mother should go on to bed." Her voice grew softer, and she dabbed her eyes with the handkerchief. "I never heard him return, but he must have come home sometime during the night, for all of his clothing and personal items are missing from the house."

"Are you absolutely certain?" When Camille stated that she was, Dr. Boyle massaged his forehead. "I shouldn't have gone and talked to him. Perhaps none of this would have occurred."

"No. I'm the one who asked for your assistance, Dr. Boyle. You wouldn't have spoken to Father had it not been at my urging." Camille didn't linger over the news of her father's absence for long. "If we're unable to continue operating the pharmacy, we'll lose everything. I've learned a great deal working alongside my father, and if you will lend me assistance as needed, I believe we can eventually turn a profit."

"You'll be willing to help, won't you?" Macia looked pleadingly at her father.

"I believe it would be best if I spoke directly with your mother, Camille. I wouldn't want to undermine any plans she might have for the future."

Camille's shoulders drooped. "I suppose I have no choice. Thank you, Dr. Boyle. And I'm sorry to have interrupted your breakfast."

Macia pushed away from the table as her friend prepared to depart, but Harvey shooed his sister aside. "I'll see Camille to the door. You and Father can proceed with your breakfast."

Her father chased a forkful of scrambled eggs across his plate. "Hmm, cold." His lip curled after he'd swallowed the eggs. "I think I'll settle for bread and jam instead."

Macia passed the bread plate to her father. "I didn't realize Harvey and Camille had become more than friends. Did you know?"

Her father took a thick slice of crusty bread from the plate. He shrugged as he liberally spread the bread with layers of butter and strawberry jam. "I knew Harvey was interested in her; I didn't know if Camille had feelings for him. From the looks they exchanged just now, it would seem that she does."

Macia picked up a piece of limp bacon but then put it back on her plate. Likely it would be no more appetizing than the cold eggs. "Seems I'm always the last to know what's going on."

Her father chuckled. "Now, I doubt—"

"Father! Come quick!" Harvey's shout echoed down the hallway. Dr. Boyle jumped to his feet and raced toward the front door. Harvey and Camille stood on the front porch, anxiously pointing in the direction of the river. "Mr. Johnson says for you to hurry. And bring your bag! There's been an accident down at the river."

Without stopping to put on her coat, Macia rushed outdoors. She folded her arms across her chest and hastily rubbed them to ward off the icy chill in the air. She had hoped for more information, but when she could gain nothing further from her brother, she returned indoors. Her father had already shrugged into his heavy coat. Macia handed him his fleece-lined leather gloves as he grabbed his medical bag from the table and then hurried out of the house.

Could one of the children have skipped school and gone ice fishing or skating at the river? Though the weather remained cold, the ice had probably begun to melt near the middle, where the men and boys tried their luck at catching the big ones and the skaters attempted their pirouettes. She shivered at the thought of someone falling through the ice and sent a fleeting prayer heavenward. Perhaps her father would find nothing more than a stranded animal that had fallen through the ice. Folks didn't hesitate to call on her father to tend their sick farm animals when no one else was available.

Macia walked down the hallway and then turned back. She donned her heavy coat and a pair of woolen mittens. "I'm going down to the river, Gerta." Before the housekeeper could reply, Macia hastened outdoors.

The stinging air was cold on her cheeks and she panted for breath. As the cold air seared her aching lungs, she slowed her pace. Rounding the corner of her house, she spied one of the Morris children outside the general store.

She waved to him and then rubbed her hands together, hoping to warm her fingers. "Why aren't you in school today, Melvin?"

The towheaded boy's grin revealed two missing front teeth. "Mrs. Markley's sick, so there's no school the rest of the week." He hopped from foot to foot. "I'm waiting to see if they got Lucy outta the river. My ma said I couldn't go no closer than the general store."

Lucy! Macia nearly swooned at the revelation. "Lucy *Malone?*" She grasped the boy by the lapels of his checkered wool coat. "Are you sure?"

The boy's ruddy cheeks paled. "Yes, ma'am. That's what Mr. Johnson said, and Lucy Malone is the only Lucy in town."

She let go of his jacket. A brisk north wind catapulted tiny shards of sleet, and Macia bowed low against the onslaught. Fear gripped her heart as she hurried onward, her leather soles slipping on the patches of ice and snow along the way. Macia now wished she had taken time to change into her boots. The men's voices drifted toward her as she neared the riverbank. A sense of urgency tinged the men's shouted commands, and dread enfolded Macia like a burial shroud.

When she finally caught sight of the men, they were clustered along the river's edge. Her father was on his knees, bending over someone—most likely Lucy. Macia's heart hammered in her chest as she continued down the path. The packed snow had been worn into an icy path, and she felt herself slip-slide forward, her arms flailing at her sides as she attempted to remain upright. Jeb turned as she approached the group of men. He pulled her close, and she saw the fear in his eyes.

"Lucy?"

He nodded. "Your father says she's going to make it."

The chill wind tried to freeze the stream of tears that now flowed down her cheeks, and she buried her face in Jeb's wool jacket. He held her, his arms strong and reassuring as he whispered into her ear. "She's going to be fine, Macia. Your father said she would recover."

Macia knew her father wouldn't give Jeb unfounded hope, yet that thought didn't totally eradicate her fear. She needed to see Lucy for herself. "Has she spoken at all?" She lifted her head from his chest.

"Not yet."

Macia pushed her way forward, where Lucy lay wrapped in blankets while her father diligently checked her breathing.

"Jeb!" Dr. Boyle called. "Her breathing is regular. Let's get her in the wagon and back to my office."

"Please come with me," Jeb implored Macia.

"Of course."

Jeb carried Lucy to the wagon and climbed in, folding his legs under himself so he could sit and hold Lucy close. Harvey helped Macia into the back of the wagon and she settled in beside Jeb, leaning over Lucy and whispering to her as tears welled in her eyes. When the wagon lurched forward, she looked out upon the gathered group of men. Garrett was staring at her. When their eyes met, she turned away, unable to discern if what she had observed was condemnation, anger, or jealousy. However, there was no doubt Garrett was unhappy. But surely he could understand her concern was for Lucy's welfare and not for Jeb. Or was it for both of them? As she watched Jeb lovingly hold his sister in his arms, she couldn't be certain.

Lucy's first words were an apology to her brother, immediately followed by a plea for Macia to remain with her.

"I'm not planning on going anywhere." Macia grinned at the girl. "It seems you've become my father's primary patient. No sooner does he get your leg healed than you heave yourself into the icy river water." She brushed a kiss upon the girl's cheek. "I don't know what we're going to do with you."

"Nor do I." Jeb's voice cracked.

"Don't cry, Jeb. I'm going to be fine. I feel plenty good already—just a little cold." Lucy began to lift the blanket away. "See? I can—"

"I'll have none of that, young lady." Dr. Boyle immediately stepped forward and tucked the blanket around his young patient. "You remain where you are and keep those blankets in place until I say you can get up." He tucked the corner in under her feet and winked. "I expect full cooperation."

"You'll have no problem on that account. I doubt I'll be letting her out of my sight until the day she marries." Jeb's attempt at levity was overshadowed by the somber look in his eyes.

Lucy held out a hand to her brother. "I didn't mean to fall in. It was an accident."

Jeb clutched her hand, but his features didn't soften. "You didn't even ask for permission before going ice skating, Lucy. Had you asked—"

"You would have said no."

"Exactly! Because I would have told you the ice is unstable at this time of year. There have been too many warm days in between these cold ones. You can't trust the ice in this kind of weather, Lucy." Jeb rubbed his palm across his forehead. "You could have died."

"I said I'm sorry. It's over and I can't change it, Jeb. All I can do is promise to never do it again."

"You're right. A lecture isn't going to do either of us any good. How soon do you think I can take her home, Dr. Boyle?"

"Let me check her over one more time. If her heart and lungs sound good, she can go with you, provided she stays warm. It would be best to have her remain in bed at least the remainder of the day."

"I'll keep her in bed the rest of the week," Jeb said. "School's not in session, and she can get all the rest she'll need."

After a final examination, Dr. Boyle declared his young patient fit to go home. "And you do as your brother tells you."

"I promise." Lucy looked expectantly at Macia. "You're coming with us, aren't you?"

"Oh, I don't think—"

"Please say you will. Please."

Macia hesitated, unwilling to interfere with Jeb's wishes.

"Yes, please come along. I doubt she'll forgive me unless you do."

"Very well. I'll help Father clean up here; then I'll stop by your place before I go home. But only for a brief visit."

From Lucy's pout, Macia knew her answer wasn't what the girl had hoped for. However, she didn't want Jeb to feel as though she were interfering. She decided it would be best for him to get Lucy settled before she arrived.

She remained in the office while her father assisted Jeb during the brief journey to his little house behind the livery. By the time he returned, she had cleaned and organized everything for the following day.

"Thank you, Macia. I appreciate your help, but I do think you should go and visit with Lucy. She doesn't believe you're going to come and see her."

Macia laughed. "Oh, Father. That's Lucy's way of getting me to hurry down there. You've played right into her hand."

Her father laughed as he hugged her around the shoulder. "Well, it worked. Even if your presence isn't needed to aid in her healing process, it will make her significantly more content."

Macia shoved her hands deep into her coat pockets and hurried off in the direction of the livery. If she was going to make it home in time for supper, there'd not be time for an extended visit with Lucy. Long shadows stretched across the snowy street, and she shivered beneath her woolen coat. Although she sought to hasten her pace, the icy streets forced Macia to take slow and deliberate steps. She passed Mr. Hill's real estate office, and she heard the faint jingle of the bell over the front door of Mr. Johnson's General Store—the bell used to signal the comings and goings of the mercantile's customers.

"Macia!"

Startled, she twisted, her feet sliding in haphazard fashion as she attempted to gain a foothold.

Garrett's strong hands circled her waist, and she clutched his forearms to steady herself.

"I'm truly sorry. I didn't mean to frighten you. I'm relieved you didn't actually take a fall on the ice." He abruptly released his hold when she glanced at his hands. "I happened by the front window and saw you heading this way. Guess that's what folks call happenstance."

She raised her eyebrows. "Happenstance?"

He held her elbow and directed her toward the door. "Happenstance. Coincidence. Whatever you want to call it. Anyway, I was wanting to talk to you, and now here you are." He opened the door and ushered her inside.

"To be honest, a stop at the store wasn't a part of my plans." She hesitated, uncertain how he would react to the truth.

"It's mighty cold to be out for a walk, and there's nothing farther down the street except . . ." Realization shone in his eyes. "You were going to see Jeb down at the livery."

"No, I'm going to see Lucy at their house." Even to her own ears, the correction seemed childishly absurd. She was, after all, going to the Malone house, and Jeb would be there. She realized the import of Garrett's insinuation.

"Why don't we sit down for a few moments?" He guided her inside and to the small table at the front of the store. She glanced at the clock as he pulled out a chair for her. "I promise not to keep you away from your visit with the Malones for long."

His tone was congenial, and the tightness eased from her shoulders. Thankful for the warmth of the heating stove, she pulled off her gloves and rubbed her hands together.

Pulling another chair close, Garrett sat down, their knees all but touching. "I don't want my aunt to overhear our discussion. She's already somewhat distressed."

Immediately the tension seized her shoulders again. She remembered the look in Garrett's eyes when he'd watched her climb into the wagon with Jeb and Lucy, and she hoped he hadn't discussed his displeasure with Mrs. Johnson. Her apprehension escalated when

Garrett reached into his pocket. What if he planned to present her with an engagement ring and propose marriage? If so, she would be compelled to refuse, and he would expect an explanation. A sigh escaped her lips when he removed an envelope and placed it atop the table.

"This is a letter from a friend of mine. He's in California." Garrett tapped the edge of the envelope on the table. "I don't know if Harvey mentioned that the deal on the land outside of town fell through." He raised his eyebrows expectantly, and she shook her head. "Well, it did. Seems as though things aren't going to work out quite the way I anticipated, either with the cannery . . . or with you." He held up the envelope. "Which brings me to this letter and my friend out in California."

"Yes?"

"He's gone into the cannery business there—fish." Garrett tucked the letter back into his pocket. "Fishing is big business out along the coast. Anyway, he wants me to go out and look things over. Maybe throw in with him if I like the look of things once I get out there." He lowered his eyes for a moment. "I don't think there's much future between you and me, Macia. Appears as if Jeb Malone still has the advantage where your heart's concerned, and like I told you before— I'm not willing to wait around and play second fiddle to another man."

"Jeb and I aren't—"

He held a finger to her lips. "I don't want to hear your denials, Macia. If there were any hope of a future between us, you would have stopped me before now." He leaned forward and rested his arms on the table. "Course, Aunt Ada isn't happy with my decision. You might want to prepare yourself for a possible tongue-lashing. She blames you for my plan to depart. I've tried to convince her otherwise, but once she's made up her mind . . ."

"I understand. Having you here is important to her—and to your uncle, too. I'm sure they've come to rely upon having you close at hand. And if it's easier for her to place the blame on my shoulders, so be it." She cupped her hand on top of his. "In some respects, I suppose it is."

He pulled his hand from beneath hers and chuckled. "Don't give yourself too much credit. Even if things had worked out between us, I would have attempted to move you to California and give this a try. I believe this is going to prove quite profitable. I may even see if Harvey wants to invest."

"How soon will you depart?"

He pushed his chair away from the table and stood. "I told Uncle Walt I'd wait until the first of April. He has several spring shipments due in, and I know he can use the help. It's the least I can do."

The clock chimed the hour. Macia picked up her gloves. "I do hope the business will prove to be everything you want, Garrett."

He stood and laughed softly. "It won't be everything, Macia. In fact, a fish cannery won't even begin to fulfill what I truly want." He leaned down and softly kissed her cheek. "I wish you well, Macia. I hope your future with Jeb will prove to be everything *you* want."

She opened her mouth to object, to tell him that she and Jeb weren't planning a future—at least not together—not yet. But before she could speak, he turned on his heel and strode off toward the rear of the store.

CHAPTER

— 27 —

Topeka, Kansas • April 1883

After plumping several pillows behind her, Truth scooted into a sitting position. Her bed had become most uncomfortable, and she was certain she had located every lump in the mattress during the past four hours. Her labor pains had begun—at least Truth thought they were contractions—and Grace had immediately insisted her sister take to her bed.

After much cajoling, Truth had convinced Grace they need not send for the doctor just yet. Truth didn't want to be poked and probed for hours on end, but Grace didn't want the baby arriving before she had time to fetch the doctor. Grace had insisted Truth maintain a careful record of each contraction. And Truth had readily agreed. The compromise suited both of them.

Truth didn't plan to tell Grace, but she was beginning to doubt the twinges were actual contractions, and she had grown weary of her sister's frequent forays into the bedroom. The moment Truth began to fall asleep, the door would burst open and Grace would enter. While she paced the floor, Grace asked the same tiresome questions over and over until Truth wanted to utter a protest. The moment Truth reported a pain, Grace would check the clock, wait until the pain subsided, and then depart. Clearly her sister was attempting to help, but her ministrations reminded Truth of an agitated prairie dog popping in and out of its burrow to check the lay of the land.

When she heard a carriage pulling up outside, she pushed herself to the edge of the bed and slid her feet into the slippers sitting nearby. Pressing her palm against her lower spine, she arched her back and lumbered toward the window. Her yellow nightgown protruded in front of her like a huge harvest moon, and she wondered how much time must pass after the baby's birth before she would once again fit into her old gowns. Glancing in the mirror as she passed by, Truth rested her arm atop the well-defined protrusion. Moses had teased and predicted she would give him twins, though the doctor had nullified that idea. For all the aches and pains of pregnancy, she had enjoyed this time carrying her child. However, she was looking forward to having the baby out and holding him in her arms. As if in response to her thoughts, another slight twinge came and went. Truth rubbed her stomach. *Not much longer, little one.*

She pulled aside the curtain and peeked down at the street below. Aunt Lilly! And John Rockley was with her! What were *they* doing together? And why had they come calling unannounced? Her mind whirred as several scenarios came to mind. She released the curtain, shuffled back across the room, and opened her bedroom door a crack. Walking into the hallway was out of the question, for the floorboards would surely creak and Grace would scold her for getting out of bed. She listened as Lilly and John exchanged greetings with Grace, but the sound of their conversation diminished as they entered the parlor. Though she strained to hear, the most she could distinguish was an occasional word or two.

When she heard rapid footsteps ascending the stairway, Truth hurriedly shuffled back to her bed. She'd not yet pulled the covers over her legs when Lilly pushed open the door and quickly surveyed the room. She pointed at the bedcovers. "Were you out of bed and eavesdropping, my dear?"

Truth yanked the sheet over her legs. She wanted to make a denial, but instead she pasted on a winsome smile. "I merely wanted to know who had come calling since Grace hadn't mentioned she was expecting visitors."

"Of course. A sweet girl like you would never consider such unbecoming behavior as eavesdropping." With an exaggerated wink, Lilly spread a quilt across Truth's protruding abdomen. "Grace tells me we can expect this baby to make its way into the world today."

"I'm not as convinced as Grace. My contractions are sporadic, and they've lessened over the past hour. I had gotten out of bed thinking a bit of activity might cause them to resume." There! That response should prevent any further accusations from her aunt.

Lilly pulled a chair near Truth's bed and sat down. After placing her purse atop the bedside table, she turned her full attention upon

Truth. "John and I have been visiting a good deal of late—what with his uncle's undeniable interest in me, John and I have formed quite a friendship. In fact, he's taken me into his confidence on several occasions. Now that his Uncle Charles and I are spending more time together, I've grown to think of John as . . . well, almost family."

Truth mashed her lips together. Lilly was up to something, and she undoubtedly held Truth at a disadvantage. In any case, she would play along and see where this discussion might lead. Long ago, Truth had discovered that her aunt didn't participate in idle chatter. Lilly's seemingly casual conversations always bore some hidden agenda, and Truth wondered what Lilly might be scheming this day.

"Now, you let me know if your pains begin anew; I'll have John fetch the doctor." Lilly leaned forward and glanced about. She lowered her voice as though she and Truth were conspiring to commit a crime. "I'm pleased to know we agree John is an excellent choice for Grace. His attributes outshine Silas by . . . well . . ." She hesitated as though seeking the proper description. "Actually there's no way to even compare the two of them, is there? They are worlds apart in all respects."

Hearing Lilly's enthusiastic approval of John and Grace as a couple was nearly enough for Truth to decide maybe she didn't want to continue her matchmaking campaign. However, her desire for Grace to take up permanent residence in Topeka outweighed her need to defy any decision made by Aunt Lilly.

"And what brought you and John calling this afternoon?"

Lilly explained that she'd coerced John into assisting her with several business matters before requesting he drive her to the house. "How could he refuse when I told him I wanted to check on your condition?" Rising from the chair, Lilly sauntered across the room and looked out the window at the perfect April day. "Of course, I couldn't tell him the *complete* reason."

Truth raised an eyebrow. "And that would be?"

Lilly returned to her chair. "To discuss what you've told John about your sister and Silas."

Truth clenched her jaw. Exactly what had John related to Lilly? She'd made any number of remarks to him when he'd come seeking advice about courting Grace. Though Moses had cautioned her against interfering, Truth had forged ahead, certain John would be a perfect husband for her sister. She'd provided glowing accounts of her sister, and though she'd managed to skirt several of John's questions, she'd not been completely truthful with him. Now she wondered precisely what information Lilly hoped to exact from her. Well, she'd not offer up any details. Lilly would have to take the lead.

Of course, Lilly was accustomed to taking the offensive. When Truth maintained a quizzical face, Lilly didn't hesitate. "John tells me you assured him Grace and Silas are merely friends. I was stunned to hear you'd made such an assertion. We both know that what you've told John is a complete and utter falsehood."

"Did you tell John I had lied? Because what you've related is not exactly what I told him." Truth shifted forward in the bed, her heart now fluttering at a rapid pace.

Lilly folded her arms across her waist and leaned back in the chair. "What *exactly* did you tell him, Truth?"

She contemplated her answer, attempting to recall the precise words she'd spoken. "I mentioned Silas had come calling on several occasions, and I said that I didn't think their relationship was of a serious nature."

"When two people have spoken about marriage, you don't think it's serious?" Lilly drummed her fingers atop the bedside table.

Truth flinched as a twinge of pain struck her lower back and then eased as quickly as it had arrived. She sighed. "I think their entire relationship is based upon convenience rather than love. Back when Silas accompanied Macia and me from New York, he thought he was in love with me. I believe he substituted Grace after Moses and I wed." Truth shifted onto her side and tucked the pillow beneath her head. "Theirs is more of a friendship than the love between a man and woman who intend to marry."

Lilly's rippling laughter filled the room. "Why, Truth. I do believe you've learned a lesson or two from your aunt Lilly."

Truth flashed an angry look at her aunt. "And just what are you implying?"

"Seems you've become quite accomplished at twisting words in order to manipulate people and circumstances to suit your own desires." Lilly edged closer. "Be careful with your meddling, Truth. My past has taught me that scheming plans can lead to much heart-ache. You are dabbling in a risky business, young lady."

Truth eyed her aunt suspiciously. "But you said you didn't approve of Silas and that Grace was an excellent choice for John. I thought we were of the same mind in this matter."

With a sly grin, Lilly wagged her index finger back and forth. "Don't you see, Truth? By making you think I was your ally, you've divulged what I wanted to know. You're attempting to match wits with me, and you failed."

Truth was utterly puzzled. She had been certain Lilly thought John and Grace a good match. "So you think Grace should return to Silas?"

"I think we should both permit Grace to decide for herself. I've given up my matchmaking attempts. You married the man of your choice; permit your sister the same pleasure."

Before Truth could offer a retort, a searing pain coursed down her back and circled her hips. She scooted deeper into the bed, gasping for breath. Lilly sympathetically recommended she remain calm, but to no avail. How could she relax with this unspeakable pain taking control of her body?

When she could finally catch her breath, Truth clutched Lilly's arm. "Tell Grace to fetch the doctor." She turned Lilly loose as another surge of pain assaulted her body. *"Now!"*

She didn't want to scream, but the contractions had taken control and were not easing in the slightest. She no longer was able to restrain herself.

Grace ran pell-mell into the room and knelt beside the bed. She wiped Truth's perspiring forehead with her handkerchief. "John has gone for the doctor. When he knows the doctor is on his way here, he'll go and fetch Moses. Everything is going to be fine, Truth." Grace continued to wipe her sister's brow. "By this time tomorrow, all this pain will be nothing but a distant memory. Just think—you'll be holding a little son or daughter in your arms."

Truth tried to be brave, but as the hours wore on and the pain continued to ravage her body, she weakened and wondered if she could sustain the assaults. She wanted the pain to end. In fact, right now she believed she would prefer death to childbirth. Something was wrong: the birth was taking much too long. Though the doctor continued to encourage her, she could see the look of concern on her husband's face the few times he came into the room. The sound of hushed whispers drifted to her from the hallway. Although Grace and Lilly spoke cheerfully as they took turns near her bedside, she could see the fear and worry in their eyes.

Without warning, another bolt of burning pain ripped through her. She howled like an injured animal and then felt herself falling into a dark abyss.

Moses was hovering over her when her eyes fluttered open again. He kissed her hand. "Truth? Can you hear me?"

She tried to speak, but her lips wouldn't move. Instead, she blinked her eyes. Moses gently lifted her head and held a cup of water to her lips. She managed a small sip before he placed her head back on the pillow.

"You gave me quite a scare." He motioned the doctor forward. "Dr. Rafferty says you're going to be fine. Right, Doctor?"

The doctor nodded as he stepped forward. "You'll need to get some rest, but you're young and healthy—and there's plenty of time."

Truth grasped Moses's hand. "Time for what? Where's the baby?" She turned her head on the pillow, looking toward the cradle they'd had specially made for their child.

Moses stroked her cheek. "The baby didn't live, Truth."

Once again, the shadowy abyss rose up to snatch her, and Truth welcomed the comfort of dark oblivion.

CHAPTER

— 28 —

Hill City, Kansas

Macia tightly clasped Camille's hand while Dr. Boyle pointed Mrs. Faraday to a chair. Camille's brother, Jonas, hadn't been at the pharmacy when they'd arrived, and for that Macia was grateful. They had awful news to deliver.

Not wanting to deal with weeping women, Erik Peterson had delivered the telegram to Dr. Boyle with the request that Macia's father be the one who talked to Mrs. Faraday. Hoping to lend Camille some support, Macia had volunteered to come along, though she now wondered if she'd made a wise decision. There was no way to know how the two women would react to the tragic news.

Strands of Mrs. Faraday's graying hair had come loose from the pins and now flew about like thin, waving fingers. Dr. Boyle removed the telegram from the pocket of his jacket. Mrs. Faraday immediately frowned as though she knew nothing good would come from their visit.

"Erik Peterson delivered this to me a short time ago. It's from the sheriff down in Abilene. Seems your husband was involved in a card game at one of the local saloons. One of the men accused him of cheating."

"He's been killed."

She knew?

"I'm sorry to tell you that he died of a gunshot wound, Mrs. Faraday." Dr. Boyle held out the telegram. "This says a letter will follow with additional details."

"His body?"

"The telegram doesn't say. The undertaker may have buried him down in Abilene. Perhaps when you receive the letter . . ."

"Yes, of course." She drew a cleansing breath and reached for Camille. "We must decide what we're to do."

Camille jutted her chin and knelt down beside her mother. "We'll continue on as we have since he vanished. We're getting by, Mother. With Dr. Boyle's help, we can continue to operate the pharmacy here in Hill City, don't you think, Dr. Boyle?"

"Yes, of course. You've been doing an admirable job, Camille, and there's no reason to think of leaving. After all, you've established the business, and you own a home here."

Macia nodded to affirm the statement. She hoped they would

stay; Camille had become a good friend in recent months.

After a glance at Macia and Dr. Boyle, Mrs. Faraday looked back to her daughter. "We also have a great deal of debt. I worry whether the pharmacy can turn enough profit to keep us afloat."

"Don't fret over the future, Mrs. Faraday," Macia's father said. "I'll do everything in my power to help you maintain the business. In addition, young Jonas may want to plan his future around operating the pharmacy."

"I think he's more interested in the newspaper business than the pharmacy," Camille said. "That's where his free time is occupied nowadays."

As she and her father prepared to depart, Macia took Camille's hands in her own. "Do let me know if there's anything I can do, Camille. If you'd like to stop by the house, please feel free to do so without an invitation."

Mrs. Faraday suddenly smiled. "That's an excellent idea. In fact, you could go over and visit this evening. Perhaps a game of whist? It will take your mind off of our family problems. Moreover, you need to be around people your own age. You spend far too much time alone in this pharmacy."

Camille stared wide-eyed at her mother. "I truly don't believe this is an appropriate time for me to go about town visiting, Mother. We've received word of Father's death only minutes ago, and you're now sending me off for a game of cards?"

Mrs. Faraday rested her hands on her hips, her elbows projecting like two chicken wings. "Your father has been detached from this family for years. In addition, he chose to completely disappear from our lives without so much as a farewell. I don't plan to spend time mourning over a man who cared nothing for me or the welfare of this family, and I'll not permit you or Jonas to do so, either."

Macia bowed her head close to Camille's ear. "It might be best if you agreed to come visit this evening. Your mother is likely in shock, and further disagreement will only make matters worse."

Camille nodded and then accompanied Macia and Dr. Boyle outside. After Dr. Boyle departed for his office, Camille tugged Macia away from the front door of the pharmacy. Keeping her voice low, Camille hastened to explain that her mother's behavior wasn't due to grief over her father's death. "She's not suffering from shock. My parents ceased caring about each other long ago. My mother is pushing me to visit at your home because she holds out hope that Harvey will propose marriage."

Macia grinned and squeezed Camille's hand. "I'd be most pleased to have you as a member of the family. I've always wanted a sister. From the way Harvey was looking at you just the other day, I don't think he needs your mother's assistance. He appears more than a little interested in you, but you no doubt already know that."

"We've been seeing each other on occasion—secretly, because I didn't want my mother interfering. She's pushed me toward Harvey from the day we arrived. I truly like him, but I would never want him to believe I pursued him because I was seeking a husband to provide for my future security." The wind whipped at Camille's skirt, and she gripped the folds between her fingers. "You do understand my dilemma, don't you?"

"Of course. But Harvey isn't a child who can easily be deceived.

I'm certain he already realizes that your mother would like to see a match. Believe me, my brother won't propose unless he truly loves you, Camille." She looped arms with Camille as they walked back to the front door of the pharmacy. "I do hope you'll come to the house this evening."

"In that case, I'll see you tonight." Camille waved good-bye as she entered the small business establishment.

Macia contemplated stopping by the newspaper office before heading back home but just as quickly decided against the idea. Camille and Harvey didn't need another person meddling in their lives. The weather had warmed considerably, though a strong southerly wind yanked at her cloak and then whipped the bonnet from her head. Thankful she'd knotted the ribbons, she attempted to pull the hat back into place.

The sound of Lucy's voice carried on the breeze. Macia turned to see the girl racing headlong toward her. Lucy's books hung in a leather strap that bounced at her side, and Macia wondered that they didn't go scattering onto the street. Macia couldn't resist grinning at the sight. "School out for the day?"

Lucy came to a screeching halt and pulled Macia into a forceful embrace. "Yep. Where have you been? Down to see Harvey at the newspaper office?"

"No, I was at the pharmacy. How were your lessons today?"

"I'm having a bit of trouble. Could you come over this evening and help me?"

Macia doubted Lucy was having any difficulty with her schoolwork. More likely, she was once again up to her matchmaking. The girl was determined that nothing would stand in the way of Jeb and Macia resuming their relationship. So far as Lucy was concerned, now that Fern and Garrett were no longer contenders for Jeb's and Macia's affections, there was nothing impeding their marriage.

"I'm sorry, but I'm expecting company this evening, Lucy. I'm sure Jeb can help you with your lessons."

Lucy's smile crumpled like an ill-prepared soufflé. Macia knew her reply wasn't the answer Jeb's sister wanted to hear. However, the girl wasn't easily deterred. "Why don't you stop in now? You could help me before you go home."

"I suppose I could help you for a half hour, but then I must return home."

"We can cut through the livery."

Macia walked along behind, knowing Lucy thought herself quite clever. There was little doubt what she was up to.

Lucy waved at her brother as they walked across the hay-strewn floor of the barn. "Look who I brought home with me."

Jeb waved in greeting and walked toward her with a currycomb in one hand. "Erik told me the news about Mr. Faraday. He said you went down to see the family with your father. How are they doing?"

Lucy came closer and took hold of her brother's arm. "What happened? Did they find Mr. Faraday?"

After explaining the circumstances of Mr. Faraday's death to his sister, Jeb turned his attention back to Macia. "Is Mrs. Faraday going to pull up stakes and leave town?"

"No. Seems they plan to remain and try to make a go of the pharmacy. At least I hope so."

"I'm sure your brother hopes for the same. I reckon he and Camille have taken a liking to one another." Jeb grinned as they walked through the barn.

Macia merely shrugged, though she surmised the clandestine visits between Camille and her brother hadn't been nearly as private as they thought. "Lucy and I had best get to that schoolwork as I'll need to return home before long."

Jeb stepped aside and then headed back toward the horse he'd been grooming. When Lucy didn't move, Macia tugged at her hand. "Come on."

After they'd entered the house, Lucy placed her hands on her hips. "He wanted to talk some more. How are you two ever gonna get back together if you won't talk to him?"

Macia couldn't fault the girl. If nothing else, she had determination! Unfortunately for Lucy, Macia was not prepared to give her heart to Jeb Malone again—at least not yet.

———

Ezekiel cupped his hands over his face in despair. He'd expected to hear he had another grandchild to welcome into the fold. Instead, Jarena's voice quivered as she read the letter telling him of the stillborn infant. Somehow he couldn't wrap his mind around the idea. Not once had he envisioned such a thing. And from the gist of Moses's letter, it didn't sound as though Truth was recuperating like the doctor had predicted.

In fact, the only good news in the entire letter was Grace's note saying she would accompany representatives of the railroad on a visit to Nicodemus in a few weeks. She didn't mention whether she would return to Topeka after her visit, and he wondered who would win— Truth or Silas. Ezekiel didn't doubt that Truth would want her sister's company during this time of loss. On the other hand, Silas wouldn't easily let Grace leave him again.

From what Ezekiel had seen, Silas still hadn't sent any letters to Grace while she was off in Topeka. Ezekiel massaged his forehead with his fingertips. If Silas lost this battle, he'd have only himself to blame.

CHAPTER

— 29 —

Topeka, Kansas • May 1883

Truth stared listlessly at the beige-and-claret bedroom carpet. Sunlight splashed into the room and reflected a crisscross pattern on the rug, but Truth cared little if the sun shone. She wanted only to have this day pass by without interruption—to wrap in a blanket of quietude until she no longer felt the pain and grief of losing her infant son. However, she knew that would not happen, for each day she fought the same battle. Today would be no different.

At the sound of footsteps in the hallway, Truth scooted down and pulled the sheet over her head. She had no plan to get out of bed. Moreover, she was weary of Moses and Grace, as well as Aunt Lilly and the doctor, telling her she'd feel much better if she'd just get up and dressed for the day. Well, she'd tried that yesterday and the day before—it hadn't worked. In fact, she'd felt worse. Being forced to sit and listen to idle chatter or answer Dovie's questions about meal preparation was the worst thing she could imagine right now. Why must she force herself to paste on a smile and act as though life had returned to normal when it hadn't? First she'd been dragged against her will to Topeka and then she'd lost her baby—no, life would never be normal again.

Forcing herself to breathe deeply, she remained still as she heard the familiar click of the turning doorknob and then the soft clinking of china. Good! Someone had brought her a breakfast tray. Perhaps there were no plans to force her out of bed today. Waiting until she heard the sound of retreating footsteps and the recognizable snap of the closing door, she tossed back the sheet. Her eyes opened wide at the sight of her sister standing at the end of the bed.

"Just as I thought. You're playing possum." Grace folded her arms across her waist, obviously waiting for an apology.

Truth simply pointed at the breakfast tray. "I believe I'll take my tray in bed."

"I think *not*! If you want breakfast, you'll come downstairs to the dining room. You'll find the tray I brought to you is filled with nothing more than empty dishes. I refuse to serve any more meals to you in this room, Truth."

Grace moved to the dresser and brought the tray close enough for Truth to examine. Anger swelled in Truth's chest. She didn't want to play these silly games! Could none of them understand her pain or need for gentle sympathy? She had lost her child—the baby she'd carried for nine months—and yet they expected her to carry on as though nothing had happened.

Grace put the silver tray back on the dresser. "Please get out of this bed, Truth. It has been over a month since your loss, and you must move on with your life. The doctor declared you fit as a fiddle weeks ago. You'll not conquer your feelings of loss and sadness by remaining in this bedroom. In addition, I have matters of importance to discuss with you."

"*What* matters?" A prickle of fear raced down Truth's spine.

Grace gathered up the tray of empty dishes. "Get dressed and come downstairs. We'll talk."

Truth tossed back the coverlet and padded across the room. Caring little for her appearance, she yanked an old gown from the wardrobe. She might go downstairs, but she certainly didn't plan to spend any time on her toilette. After wrapping an old scarf about her head, she slipped into a pair of shoes. Without so much as a glance in the mirror, she plodded down the stairs and into the dining room.

Dovie covered her mouth and let out a slight gasp as she walked into the room, but Grace remained unusually quiet while Truth ate breakfast and then poured a second cup of coffee.

"I've dressed, come downstairs, and eaten breakfast. Now, what is this important matter you must discuss with me?"

Grace scooted forward on her chair. "I plan to travel back to Nicodemus with the Ditmores and John Rockley. We'll depart the day after tomorrow."

Truth sent her teaspoon clanking to the floor as she lurched forward. "*What?* Why haven't you told me of this before now?"

"You knew of these plans. They were made back when you convinced Mrs. Ditmore the weather would prohibit such a journey in January or February. Surely you recall that discussion?"

"Yes, I recall the discussion, but I don't remember hearing of these recent plans. You haven't spoken of making the trip—at least not to me." Truth frowned and waited for her sister's response.

"You've not made yourself available to discuss anything, Truth. I've spoken to Moses, and he knows of the plans. He voiced no objection."

An unbidden anger swelled in Truth's chest. "So you're going to run off and leave me when I need you the most?" She folded her arms and glared across the table. "How long will you be gone?"

Grace fidgeted with the edge of the tablecloth. "I don't plan to return."

"*Not return!* How can you even *think* such a thing? I need you, Grace!" Truth leaned across the table and grasped her sister's hand. "Please don't do this, Grace. Promise me you'll come back. Stay several weeks, if you like, but then promise you'll return. I don't think I could bear it here alone."

"You're not alone, Truth. You have a wonderful husband, you've got Dovie, and Aunt Lilly has agreed to look in on you every day."

Truth yanked the napkin from her lap and tossed it on the table. "And that's supposed to make me feel better? Aunt Lilly is the last person I want coming around here poking her nose into my business."

Grace poured herself a cup of coffee and settled back in her chair. "Then I suggest you begin getting out of bed and taking up your normal routine. When Aunt Lilly realizes you're on the road to recovery, she'll likely visit less often."

"I'm starting to think I should go with you."

Grace's eyebrows arched in surprise. "To Nicodemus?"

"Yes. Do you think I would have sufficient time to prepare for the journey?"

"I don't think Moses would agree. Furthermore, you've spent little time out of bed in the past month, and I daresay the journey would be overtaxing for you in your . . . weakened condition."

Truth frowned at her sister. "Only a short time ago, you said the doctor had declared me fit as a fiddle. Now you say I'm in a weakened condition. Which is it, Grace?" Her features tightened into a scowl. "Or is it that you don't want me to come along?"

Grace pushed her chair away from the table and jumped to her feet. "I'm not going to continue this discussion. We'll both end up saying things we'll regret."

Before Truth could stop her, Grace vanished from the room like a fleeting mist, leaving her to contemplate her actions over a cold cup of coffee. Since giving birth she had evolved into an angry shrew, yet she felt unable to control her ugly temperament.

A knock at the front door forced Truth to move. A visitor was not what she wanted. Using the back stairway, she trudged upstairs, but she stopped in the hallway at the sound of Aunt Lilly's voice drifting up from the foyer. Grace had greeted her, and the two of them were engaged in conversation. Truth edged along the wall and positioned herself out of sight near the top of the stairway, listening as the two women talked.

They were discussing her! She marched back downstairs and stopped in the center of the parlor entryway.

Lilly appeared dismayed when Truth entered the room. "Wherever did you find that awful dress? The color reminds me of muddy water, and it hangs on you like a nightgown." Lilly pointed to Truth's head. "And why do you have that rag wrapped around your head?"

Truth gave her a cool stare. "You do have a way of spreading cheer, Aunt Lilly. I'm so pleased to know I'll have your pleasantries to brighten my days after Grace departs for Nicodemus." After a long look at her sister, Truth crossed the room and sat down. "I had thought to travel with her, but it seems she doesn't want my company."

"Could I have a moment alone with your sister, Grace?" Lilly waited until Grace left the room. "Once again, you are attempting to manipulate your sister, Truth." Lilly shook her head when Truth attempted to interrupt. "Please don't insult me by objecting. I'm an authority on this topic. Your place is here in Topeka with your husband. We both know that. As for your sarcastic remark regarding my spreading of cheer, I will brighten your day with kind remarks once you quit wallowing in self-pity. Perhaps you should search your Bible for some words of comfort."

Truth's jaw dropped at the suggestion. "Who would have thought *you* would ever suggest reading the Bible."

Lilly's shrugged her narrow shoulders. "You see? That proves there is hope for every person and circumstance—even yours, Truth." She waved her hand. "Now go and tell your sister to come back into the room."

Truth wanted to argue that this was her house and she was the one who should be giving the orders. However, she knew she'd have little success arguing with her aunt. After doing Lilly's bidding, Truth retreated to her bedroom. She no longer cared what her aunt and sister might discuss. Let them talk about her. She didn't plan to listen, and she certainly didn't plan to read the Bible. All she wanted to do was bury her head under the bedcovers and try to forget everything that had happened in the last six months.

———————

When Moses entered their bedroom that evening, Truth was in her nightgown—as she'd been since they'd lost the baby—and in bed. Though the covers weren't pulled over her head, her eyes reflected the same listlessness he'd seen since the day she'd given birth. He wondered if he would ever again see the spirited woman he had married.

"I understand you're in agreement with Grace returning to Nicodemus."

There was venom in his wife's words; he forced himself to speak calmly in response. "We have no right to infringe upon Grace's plans. She shouldn't be made to feel guilty simply because she wants to go home." He shook his head. "She told you she wouldn't stay in Topeka any more than two weeks after the baby's birth. She's remained longer than she originally agreed."

"But I need her. It would be different if—"

Moses sat down on the edge of the bed. "No, Truth, it wouldn't be different. Had the baby lived, you still would have attempted to keep Grace here with us. You would have insisted you needed her help with the baby. The fact is you don't really need Grace. It gives you pleasure to have her close at hand. And there's nothing wrong with having your sister nearby—if that's what she wants, too." He patted his wife's hand. "Unfortunately, it isn't."

He stood up, removed his jacket, and hung it in the oak wardrobe. He longed to share his own grief with Truth, but right now his wife's condition made a discussion of what had happened impossible. She couldn't seem to pull herself from the depths of sadness to which she'd succumbed. He'd given much thought to helping her recover from this bout of melancholy. He had to do something before she permanently embraced this way of life, and he prayed daily for guidance. Today he'd received an answer. He knew it would take much convincing to get Truth out of the house, but he planned to use Grace's departure to advantage.

If he could persuade Truth she should go to the train station and bid her sister farewell, he'd succeed with his plan. He'd already enlisted Grace's assistance, and they'd reached an agreement: if necessary, they would inflict Truth with a healthy dose of the guilt she so readily imposed upon others. If all went well, though, they'd not be required to resort to dire action.

———

Truth stared into the mirror for several long minutes. She barely recognized her own reflection. Deep, dark hollows underscored her dull brown eyes and had transformed the face of the lively young woman who used to greet her in the looking glass. Instead of the snug fit she'd been warned to expect after the birth of a child, her dress hung in loose pleats. She had eaten little during the past month, and she still had no appetite.

She dropped to the edge of the bed, drained of all energy. Even simply dressing to accompany her sister to the train station had sapped her strength. She'd remained in her room all morning, knowing that she'd likely burst into tears at the sight of Grace preparing to depart. Moses had given her strict orders to be dressed by one o'clock. Although she'd objected to going, he'd chided her and told her he would not allow such behavior. It was the least she could do for her twin, who had foregone her own plans to come and live in Topeka for several months. Giving her a proper good-bye was, he had said, the least she could do.

Moments later, the bedroom door burst open and Moses greeted her with a broad smile, obviously pleased she'd heeded his request. He held out his hand and accompanied her down the stairs. "Your sister is waiting in the carriage. The others are meeting her at the train station."

Truth tightened her hold on his arm. "It would be much easier if I remained behind. Accompanying Grace to the train station is going to make saying good-bye much more difficult."

"Think of the good it will do for your sister," he encouraged. "Sometimes we absolutely must put others first, don't you think?"

Truth didn't respond, knowing her husband didn't expect an answer. She managed to force a smile as she settled onto the seat across from her sister. The only benefit that would come from Grace's departure would be knowing all was well within their home back in Nicodemus. Since sending Fern their approval about her living situation, Fern had written to offer her thanks and they'd had two additional notes saying all was well. However, Grace's appraisal would ease Truth's mind.

The Ditmores and John Rockley would be staying in the Wymans' house while in Nicodemus, and Truth hoped Grace had written to advise Fern of the guests' arrival. If not, Truth couldn't be blamed for that predicament.

"You look lovely, Truth. I'm so pleased you've agreed to see me off. And it won't be long until we see each other again," Grace said.

Truth looked up. "You've decided to return to Topeka?"

Grace and Moses exchanged a quick look before Grace replied. "No, but Moses tells me that the two of you will visit us in Nicodemus the moment you've regained your strength and want to make the journey."

Truth wilted like a damp dishcloth—she should have known. While Grace and Moses amicably chatted, she drifted into a quiet solitude, staring out the carriage window as they passed the familiar sights leading to the railroad depot. Though she begged to remain in the carriage, Moses and Grace insisted she come inside the depot, if for only a few minutes. The shrill sound of a train whistle drowned out her negative response. Moses took hold of her arm and gently urged her out of the coach. They were pushed along with the crowd until they finally located the Ditmores and John Rockley on the far side of the depot.

John shook Moses's hand and then greeted the two women. "We were beginning to worry. The train has arrived. We should get your baggage on board, Grace."

Moses strode across the depot toward the ticket window while John took charge of Grace's luggage. Although they were surrounded by the hubbub inside the depot, a strained silence descended upon their small group. They stared at one another as if they'd all been struck dumb.

Finally, Mrs. Ditmore retrieved a fan from her handbag and began waving it back and forth. "Do wish us well, Truth. I'm a bit fearful of traveling through the unsettled portions of the state. We still hear stories of Indians and such."

Grace winked at her sister. "No need to worry, Mrs. Ditmore. All of the Indians who live near Nicodemus are friendly—there are few renegades."

The older woman clutched her bodice and paled. "Renegades? Perhaps I should rethink my decision to accompany you, my dear."

"Too late now," her husband said. "Your baggage is already on the train, and they're beginning to board. Come along, now."

Moses waved a ticket high in the air; Truth and Grace followed along behind the Ditmores. Truth leaned toward her sister. "That wasn't very kind of you, Grace. In fact, now that you've mentioned Indians, you'll likely have to listen to Mrs. Ditmore's worries through-out the journey."

Grace shrugged and grinned. "It was worth it just to see you smile again."

Although she wanted to cling to Grace, Truth hugged her quickly and then bid her sister good-bye. Moses maintained a firm hold around Truth's waist as they departed the depot, and Truth wondered if he thought she might turn and run after Grace—or perhaps he thought she might faint.

Moses helped her into the carriage, and she leaned back. The leather seat enveloped her like a warm blanket. They would be home shortly, and she could return to the security of her bedroom.

The horses' hooves clopped a drumming cadence as they crossed the bridge and then turned to the east. Truth looked out the window and then signaled to Moses. "We've turned in the wrong direction."

"I have one stop to make before we go home."

Sighing, she folded her hands in her lap. She hoped this wouldn't take long.

A short time later, the carriage came to a halt in front of an unfamiliar stone building. Carved into a small limestone arch were the words *St. Vincent's Orphanage*.

She stared at Moses as he held out his hand. "Why are we here?"

"I thought you might want to grace some of these young children with a loving embrace and a gentle word." He drew near. "They are in need, Truth."

She hesitated, but he remained steadfast until she finally took his hand and stepped down from the carriage. "I don't . . . I don't think this is a good idea."

Moses pulled her close as they walked toward the front door. "Trust me."

— 30 —

While Truth rolled a cloth ball across the floor to the tot, Aunt Lilly pulled back the lace curtains and stared out the front window. Turning around when the little boy giggled and clutched the toy to his chest, Lilly dropped the curtain back into place.

She stepped close to the child and tapped her toe in front of him. "I do believe you've taken this orphanage work to the extreme, Truth. It's one thing to go down there and volunteer a few hours of your time. However, I find it disturbing that you've begun bringing them home with you—especially this one."

"This one? You speak as though he's less than human, Aunt Lilly. His name is Jacob." Truth grinned at the child. "Isn't that your name? You're our little Jake, aren't you?" She cooed the words at the little boy, who gurgled and crawled toward her in helter-skelter fashion.

"Oh, forevermore, Truth. He isn't *your* little anything. That child is an orphan. I fear you've decided to replace your own child with one of these homeless ragamuffins." Lilly grimaced and shook her head. "Don't you see the problem in all of this? You're a bright young woman. It's highly probable you can have another child. And even if you don't, you and Moses can lead a fulfilling life without children. In fact, if you aren't tied down with a child, you'll be able to devote more time to helping Moses achieve his political goals."

Truth scooped the child onto her lap and bounced him up and down. "Don't you pay any attention to that heartless woman." She purred the words at the little boy and nuzzled his neck before looking at her aunt. "Helping at the orphanage was Moses's idea. He is delighted to have me bring the children home."

Lilly drew near and dropped down beside Truth. Jake held out his arms to the older woman. She ignored his chubby outstretched arms and instead directed her attention at Truth. "He wanted you to get out of bed; he wanted to have his wife back. Drastic measures were required to entice you back into some sort of normalcy. Now that you've seen life goes on, though, I think you could find opportunities to further Moses's career rather than whiling away your time wiping drippy noses and playing games. It's time you matured and proved you're worthy of a man such as Moses."

Truth hugged Jake close and then set him back on the carpeted floor. She tossed the ball and watched as his arms and legs propelled him forward in perfect synchronization. Rolling onto his hip, he looked over his shoulder and grinned at her when he arrived at the colorful plaything.

"Seems your Bible knowledge doesn't include the part about loving and caring for widows and orphans."

Lilly groaned. "Please, Truth. Don't drape yourself with a cloak of self-righteousness. After all, since my return from Colorado, I've observed your selfish behavior. You've manipulated and attempted to coerce both your husband and your sister. So please don't embarrass yourself by using the Bible in an effort to prove your point."

Truth winced at the retort. Although her aunt was correct, and Truth had admitted such behavior and asked God for His forgiveness, she wouldn't confess her sins to Aunt Lilly. In fact, she wished her aunt would leave so she could enjoy her time with Jake.

Instead, her aunt called Dovie from the kitchen and requested the maid prepare tea. Truth sighed. Tea meant her aunt would be here for at least another hour. She'd have little time alone with Jake, for she needed to have him back to the orphanage before suppertime. The little boy had become one of her favorites, and she'd even spoken to Moses about the possibility of adoption. Although he'd not yet met Jake, Moses had lovingly agreed to consider the idea. Truth had hoped he might be home in time to meet the child today. However, with Aunt Lilly standing watch, it mattered little if Moses arrived. She didn't want to discuss Jake's possible adoption in front of her aunt, especially after Lilly's earlier remarks.

Lilly went back to the window and peered outdoors. This time she immediately dropped the sheer curtain back into place and peeked through a tiny slit. Truth watched as the scene unfolded and wondered if her aunt would soon press her nose to the glass. "Has something interesting captured your attention?"

Lilly immediately jumped away from the window. "I believe I see someone I know. I do dislike rushing off, but please offer my apologies to Dovie. I won't be staying for tea."

Truth couldn't imagine who or what had sparked Lilly's early departure. Nevertheless, she was thankful for the reprieve. Assuring her aunt the tea preparations were of little consequence, she bid the woman good-bye and lifted Jake into her arms before going into the kitchen to deliver the news.

Dovie grinned as she removed the kettle from the stove. "Good! Yer aunt Lilly makes me as nervous as a long-tailed cat in a roomful of rockers."

Truth chuckled, and both women spun in unison as the front door opened.

"Oh no. She's back." Dovie leaned close and whispered the words into Jake's ear.

Thinking the entire matter a game, Jake chortled as he reached out and clutched a fistful of Dovie's hair. Truth clasped his chubby hand and gently pried his fingers loose. "Sorry, Dovie. Young Jake thinks everything is a game."

"Does he now?"

Truth looked up to see her husband walking down the hall, a sack in his hand.

"So this is the young man who has captured my wife's heart." Moses reached out for the boy, who immediately lunged into his arms.

Truth laughed as Jake clung to Moses. "Seems as though he's now bent upon winning *your* heart, also."

She followed her husband into the parlor, where he settled the child on his lap and then handed Jake the package he had carried in with him. "See what you think of this, young man."

Jake chortled as he slapped at the paper wrapping and finally discovered a shiny, multicolored top. Moses carried him off the carpeted portion of the room. "Now, watch this." Moses sat down with Jake and pumped the top's handle up and down rapidly. Jake watched the toy whirl around as it traveled across the wood floor. Flipping his chubby body into a crawling position, Jake chased after the toy. He slapped his hand against the outer rim and giggled in wild abandon when the top flew and clanked across the foyer and came to an abrupt halt against the far wall.

"He's a fine little fellow, isn't he?" Moses commented while Jake crawled after the top.

"You're quite right," she agreed. "He's not the ragamuffin Aunt Lilly labeled him."

Moses rocked back on his heels. "She called him a ragamuffin? What a terrible thing to say." Moses looked about the room as if he expected Lilly to appear from behind the divan. "I didn't realize Lilly had been here today."

"She stopped by unexpectedly and departed the same way. Something or someone attracted her attention when she was looking out the front window. She hastily excused herself." Truth held her hand atop Jake's and helped him pump the handle.

"Strange behavior for your aunt. Perhaps she remembered something that required her attention at the store."

Truth shrugged. She didn't want to discuss her aunt. Right now, she wanted to enjoy their time with Jake.

———

Lilly lifted her parasol the moment she departed Truth's house. Careful to keep her face concealed, she walked slowly down the street, intently watching the man walking twenty feet in front of her. His shoulders were stooped, and he leaned heavily upon a cane as he proceeded forward at a snail's pace. Without warning, he stopped. Lilly crossed the street and looked into the window of the jewelry shop, occasionally peering from beneath the ruffled parasol.

She peered in the shop window, pretending to be perusing the array of brooches and rings. When the man finally rounded the corner onto Kansas Avenue, she hurried after him. Reaching the turn, she stepped out only far enough to keep the man in view and then silently chastised herself for waiting until he was out of sight. The stranger was nowhere to be seen.

Closing her parasol, Lilly sashayed past the row of stores that lined the avenue until she reached her millinery. Two fashionably dressed women acknowledged her as they departed the store, obviously completely unaware she owned the shop. Though she lived in exquisitely furnished rooms above the store, Lilly employed a manager to operate the shop. Lilly enjoyed creating the hats, and Mildred worked well with the customers. Only when Mildred was in need of a day off did she take over operations.

Lilly tried to act nonchalant as she entered the store and waved at Mildred. "Any new orders?"

Mildred held up several pieces of paper. "These should keep you busy." The woman bent down and retrieved her satchel from beneath the counter. "I didn't think you were going to return before closing time. Shall I lock the door on my way out?"

"No need. I'll go over the orders and then lock up."

Mildred hung the key on the hook by the front door. "I'll see you in the morning." Mildred's gloves bowed in a limp salute as she brandished them overhead to wave good-bye.

Lilly absently bid the woman good-night as she pored over the sheets of paper. Several of the orders would take no time at all, but this one—she tapped her finger atop the paper—this one presented an exciting challenge.

With a renewed spring in her step, she strode off toward the back room. After a mindful look at the shelves, she pulled down several boxes of feathers and artificial flowers, as well as the bolt of net veiling with chenille dots that had arrived only yesterday. If properly ruffled, the veiling would create a lovely effect when fastened beneath the outer edge of the straw hat. Lilly carefully began to gather the netting, startled when the bell over the front door jingled. With a sigh, she dropped the veiling atop her worktable, irritated she'd forgotten to lock the door.

Reaching the doorway of her workroom, she called out, "The store is closed, but we'll reopen in the—" She stopped and gasped. "Bentley! So it *is* you."

He leaned on his cane and casually surveyed the shelves lined with perfume bottles and flower-bedecked hats before facing her. "Yes, Lilly. It's me."

Scenes from the early years of her life flashed before her. Notwithstanding his grayish pallor, Bentley Cummings conveyed the frightening and undeniable strength she remembered. She tried to swallow but couldn't. Her throat felt as though it had been packed with cotton. She leaned slightly to the side and glanced at the front door.

Bentley shook his head and dangled the key from his finger. "Careless of you to leave your key hanging by the door."

Lilly nibbled her lip. He'd barred any escape out the front, and the back door always remained locked. The only key lay beneath her worktable. Her mind raced as she attempted to form a plan. Above all, she must remain calm. Bentley could smell fear.

She walked forward a few paces and then stopped. She forced a sardonic smile. "You don't look particularly well, Bentley. I can't say that the years have been good to you."

"Ah, but *you*, my dear Lilly, don't look a day older than when I last set eyes upon you." He tucked the key into his waistcoat and nodded toward the rear doorway. "Why don't we go back there. Passersby may assume your shop is still open if they see us standing here in the aisle, and I've already locked the door."

No good would come from arguing, so she led the way to the back room and took her place behind the worktable. She picked up the piece of veiling and worked her threaded needle through the edge, pulling it tight to enhance the ruffling. Ignoring Bentley's amused grin, she continued to work.

"If you prefer to sit . . ." she said, indicating a chair on the far side of the room.

He maintained a watchful eye while he pulled the chair to the opposite side of the worktable. "Aren't you going to ask how I found you, Lilly?" He propped his weight on the cane as he eased onto the chair.

She looked up from the table and obligingly inquired, "How did you find me, Bentley?"

His smile was as thinly veiled as the netting she held between her fingers. While she continued to fashion the ruffle, she listened to his tale. Lilly lifted the hat to eye level and gave a satisfied nod. Placing her creation on the counter, Lilly stooped behind the workbench. Moments later she bobbed up and dropped an artificial spray of lilacs in front of her.

Bentley pointed at an artificial magnolia. "I prefer that one. The clump of lilacs is rather gaudy, don't you think?"

As he spoke of reading a New Orleans newspaper that lauded Moses's election as state auditor, she sensed he was toying with her, playing a game of cat and mouse. "I knew you'd follow him. You never could stay away from powerful or wealthy men—preferably both." His rasping laugh rang hollow. "Did Jarena send you the bounty notice and my letter?"

"Yes. I received them." Her fingers trembled as she sewed the net ruffle to the hat brim. She prayed he wouldn't notice.

"Then you know why I'm here."

"I can't give you what I don't have, Bentley."

He shifted his weight on the chair and ran his fingers through his thinning gray hair. "Surely you can see that my health has failed. I'm dying, Lilly. I want to find my son before that occurs. Is it so much to ask that you tell me if he's alive or dead?"

His words were compelling, yet she must not forget this was

Bentley Cummings sitting before her, the man who had placed a bounty on her head. She steeled herself before looking directly into his eyes. His body convulsed in a spasm as a wracking cough besieged him. The powerful man whom she had long feared was replaced by a weakened old man. Her fingers wrapped tightly around the key she'd retrieved from beneath the worktable. If she moved quickly, there would be sufficient time to unlock the back door and race down the alley before he could catch his breath and pursue her. Yet she remained fixed, watching as he pulled a handkerchief from his pocket and held it to his lips. A deep red streak stained the crisp white linen square.

She couldn't deny his request, so she told him what she knew. "Only a few months ago I received information from New Orleans that your son is alive. However, I was sworn to secrecy, and I'll not tell you his whereabouts. He is safe, being well educated, and receives excellent care. Your interference in his life is not welcome."

He shoved the tainted handkerchief back into his pocket. "And my money? Would it be welcomed?"

Lilly shrugged. "I have no idea."

"It's my desire to leave my estate to my son, if he's truly alive. My will has been drawn to reflect my wishes, and it is in safekeeping at the First National Bank of New Orleans. All I ask is that you send word to my son so that he can file a proper claim upon my death." Supporting himself with the cane, Bentley lifted himself up from the chair. "Will you agree?"

"I'll post a letter once you've boarded a train for New Orleans."

"Agreed." He reached into his pocket and withdrew the front door key. "You look content, Lilly. Perhaps the West suits you."

She came around the workbench and accepted the key. "I've discovered it's not where I live that's given me contentment. I spent far too many years seeking peace and happiness from the wrong things—and so did you, Bentley."

He made no attempt to stop her as she walked past him and hurried upstairs, speaking to him over her shoulder. "Wait just a moment."

When she returned, she handed him a small leather-bound Bible. "Read this on your way home. It's where I found my answers. I hope you'll find yours before it's too late."

CHAPTER

— 31 —

Nicodemus, Kansas

Though Fern had looked surprised when Grace arrived, along with the Ditmores and John Rockley, on the doorstep of Truth's home, she'd welcomed the group with aplomb that surprised Grace. Fern quickly set Arthur to work carrying baggage upstairs while she hastened to remove the dust covers from the furniture.

Fern glanced over her shoulder. "I'm glad Arthur was home for his noonday meal. Your guests have a good deal of luggage." She opened the pocket doors into the dining room. "We don't use the parlor, so I thought it best to cover the furniture and keep the doors closed. I do apologize."

Grace folded one of the sheets and shook her head. "No need for an apology, Fern. You had no way of knowing we would arrive. What else can I do to assist you?"

"Will they be expecting tea right away? I can set a kettle to boil, and I'll make a grocery list for Arthur. He can stop at the store on his way home from work this evening." She stopped long enough to catch her breath.

"I'll help you prepare the tea, and we can plan the meals together, Fern." Grace silently chastised herself. She should have written to Fern. Even if the letter had arrived only a few days in advance, the housekeeper would have at least had some warning.

Fern raked her hand through her hair and virtually raced to the kitchen. "How long will you folks be staying—so I know how much to purchase?" She asked the question while bolting through the kitchen door. "With just Arthur and me to feed, I don't keep a large quantity of food on hand. I hope they won't want fancy food—my cooking is plain. I did a few fancy dishes for Mrs. Boyle, but not much."

"Please don't fret." Grace tried to reassure her. "You can be sure they'll be pleased with whatever is served. Why don't you begin making the tea and I'll jot down a few items Arthur can purchase for us."

The words appeared to have a calming effect. At least Fern had slowed her frantic pace.

Fern set the kettle on the stove and met Grace's gaze. "How's Mrs. Wyman getting on? I was sorry to hear the news about the baby. I should have written to her, but I didn't know what to say."

"Thank you for your concern. Her progress has been slow, but she is doing somewhat better. When I write, I'll tell Truth you asked about her health."

"That would be kind of you." Fern pointed at a worktable on the far side of the kitchen. "I baked a gingerbread cake this morning. I could make a lemon sauce for on top if you think folks might want that with their tea."

Fern certainly wasn't the same person Grace remembered. She hadn't had a great deal of contact with Truth's housekeeper, but from the accounts she'd heard from Macia Boyle, a remarkable change had occurred in Fern's life. Perhaps it was her marriage to Arthur. Then again, Truth had mentioned that Fern was attending First Baptist— listening to Pastor James on Sunday mornings might have had some effect.

As she prepared for the dinner party she'd planned with Fern, Grace thought about Silas and his cool reception since her return. If she didn't know better, she'd think he was avoiding her. It seemed as if each time she attempted to pull him aside for a moment alone, he found some excuse to sidestep her invitation. Grace decided to take special care with her appearance this evening. Silas would be coming to the party.

After selecting the yellow gown—one of several Truth had insisted upon giving her—Grace prepared for the evening. She tucked a small spray of yellow and white silk blossoms into her hair and pir- ouetted in front of the large oval mirror. She hoped her efforts would not be in vain.

There was little time to worry if Silas would find her appearance captivating, for the sound of her father's voice boomed up the stairway only moments later. "Grace! Hello! Ain' nobody 'round this here place?"

By the time Grace reached the bottom of the stairs, her father was peering into the dining room and Silas was standing in the parlor. Though she embraced her father, it was Silas she watched. Instead of beaming approval, he stiffly acknowledged her and then immediately ignored her. *Why is he acting so aloof?*

Grace glanced at the mantel clock. None of the other guests had come downstairs yet, and a half hour remained before the appointed supper hour. Forcing herself to act boldly, she stepped forward and slipped her hand through the crook of Silas's arm. "I'd like to talk to you in the garden."

His forehead wrinkled. "Now?"

"Yes, now. There's plenty of time before supper. When our guests come down, my father can entertain Mr. and Mrs. Ditmore and Mr. Rockley for a short time." With a gentle tug, she pulled him toward the door, stopping only long enough to pick up her shawl. Once they neared the garden, she turned to face him. "I want to know why you're acting so cold when I'm the one who should be angry with you."

His head jerked back as though she'd slapped him. "You bring that Rockley fella to town and he's looking at you like the two of you is all but ready to jump the broom, and you say *I* ain't got no right to be angry?" He kicked a clod of loose dirt and watched it land in the rose garden. "I'm trying to figure out 'zackly what's going on with you, Grace."

"If you won't talk to me, I don't know how you plan to figure it out." She clutched his arm and they wandered toward a wooden bench near one of the small budding oak trees Moses had planted in the backyard. "I won't deny John has shown an interest in me. However, I told him about you—about us. I can't control how he looks at me or even what he says, but surely you know . . . Didn't you read my letters? You're the one I care about." Grace eased onto the bench but he remained standing. "What about you, Silas? I didn't receive even one letter from you while I was in Topeka. Many's the night I wondered if you had found someone to replace me in your heart. *I* had no letters to reassure me all was well at home." When she looked up at him again, a shaft of light fell across his face and she saw sorrow in his eyes.

Silas retrieved a folded piece of paper from his front pocket and then sat down beside her. "This here is what I got to show for tryin' to write you." He carefully opened the paper and placed it between them on the bench. Using his palm, he pressed out the folds. The edges were tattered and smudges of dirt lined the creases of the letter. "I been carrying this here piece of paper with me, trying to put on paper how much I care for you and that I wanted you to come home and marry me. I ain't no good reading and writing—you know that, Grace. I tried. But every time I'd get a few words on the page, I didn't like 'em. I'd scratch 'em out and put the page back in my pocket. Same thing would happen the next time. This here paper shows that I tried. But it never did come out the way I wanted." He leaned forward with his forearms on his thighs.

Grace slid closer to him. "Did you think I would be critical of your handwriting? You knew better than that, Silas." She touched a corner of the smudged letter. "More than anything, I wanted to know that you were thinking of me and that you missed me. You could have scribbled only a few words on a sheet of paper and I would have been happy." She picked up the page. It was clear that he'd tried to write her many times. Both sides of the page were covered with his attempted correspondence that was scratched out with either ink or pencil. How she wished he had posted his attempts. For to her, each line was beautiful.

He lightly touched her cheek. "Will you forgive me?" There was a tremor in his voice.

"Yes, I forgive you, Silas." She folded the piece of paper and tucked it into her pocket.

"You ain't planning on keeping that ol' piece of paper, are you?"

She patted the pocket of her dress and nodded. "This is more precious to me than you can imagine. I plan to keep it always. She took his hand and stood up. "We best go inside. The others will be expecting supper soon."

As the waning sunlight cast a luminescent pattern across the rose garden, he pulled her close and enveloped her in his arms. "They can wait a little longer." He covered her mouth in a gentle kiss. When their lips pulled apart, he softly touched her cheek. "When we gonna get married, Grace?"

"I think July sounds like a fine time for a wedding."

"I s'pose I could wait that long if you got your heart set on July."

There was little talk of anything except the railroad at the dinner party and during the next several days. Grace spent most of her time showing the Ditmores and Mr. Rockley around Nicodemus and introducing them to the shop owners. She noticed Mrs. Ditmore always looked worried, as if she thought a group of renegade Indians or wild animals would attack at any moment. Grace attempted to reassure the woman, but to no avail.

An early morning fog shrouded the town as John and Mr. and Mrs. Ditmore prepared for their return to Topeka. They had deposited their luggage on the front porch and were now gathered near the street, all of them straining to see through the foggy vapor that covered the town like a bridal veil. The clopping of the horses' hooves and groans of the shifting wagon announced Silas's arrival before any of them could actually see him. He sat tall on the wagon seat and held the reins firmly as he brought the horses about.

While Silas maneuvered the wagon to a halt in front of the house, Grace removed a letter from her pocket and held it out for John. "I'd be most appreciative if you would deliver this to my sister." As Grace handed him the envelope, John gently squeezed her fingers. She looked into his eyes and saw sadness. With a soft tug, she pulled her hand from his grasp. "If you wouldn't find it inconvenient."

He shook his head. "No. I'll be pleased to deliver your letter."

She wanted to tell him she was sorry if he'd misunderstood anything she'd said or done, but before she could speak of such matters, Silas drew near. He embraced Grace around the waist and cheerily requested John's help with the baggage. Grace bid their guests farewell and received Silas's good-bye kiss on her cheek. She watched until the wagon rolled out of sight.

The sun peeked over the horizon, and Grace took a moment to

enjoy the morning. She was glad to be home where she could once again tend her garden and help her father in the fields.

Like everyone in Nicodemus, she wanted the town to survive, but the Ditmores' visit hadn't produced the hope she'd wished it would. Mr. Ditmore had often said he was just a small cog in the wheel of progress. He'd promised he would carry a banner for Nicodemus, recommend to his many acquaintances at the various railroads a route that would pass through their town, and ask for the support of his group of investors. However, he cautioned that he could only do so much and that there were many towns that wanted the railroad. The railroad officials were the ones who would make the final decisions about where the tracks would be laid.

There was also the issue of money. Mr. Ditmore repeatedly mentioned that Nicodemus had to raise money, for the railroads wanted public subsidies to help pay for their construction costs. The town had begun raising funds over a year ago—not that any of the citizens thought the idea of subsidies was right or proper; after all, the railroads were already making plenty of money. Still, they had little choice but to pay if they wanted tracks passing near their town. Without a railroad, small communities would likely shrivel up and die. And Nicodemus didn't want to die.

———

"Mr. Rockley is in the foyer, Truth. He says he has word from Grace. Would you like me to bring him in?"

Truth glanced up from the floor, where she sat playing with young Jake. "Yes, Dovie. Please do." Truth swooped the baby into her arms and stood to greet her visitor. "John. What a pleasant surprise. I didn't expect we would see you so soon. Do come in and sit down." Jacob stretched forward, his chubby arms and legs wiggling as though they would propel him out of Truth's arms and into the arms of their visitor.

John reached to tousle the toddler's hair, but gurgling with delight, Jake grabbed the man's finger and pulled it toward his mouth. With a chuckle, John pulled his hand away. "I don't think that's a good idea, young man." He raised his brows. "And who is this little fellow?"

"This is Jacob." Truth pressed her lips close to the child's ear. "Jacob, this is Mr. Rockley." Jacob bounced up and down then twisted around in her arms and began to pull the pins from her hair. Truth gave John an apologetic smile. "Let me see if Dovie will entertain him. Otherwise, I doubt we'll be able to visit."

Once Jake had been given over to Dovie's care, Truth returned to the parlor. "May I offer you refreshments, John?"

"No, but thank you." He leaned back and crossed one leg over the other. "The child? Does he belong to a friend?"

Truth shook her head. "He's a ward of St. Vincent's Orphanage." As she explained the side trip she and Moses had recently taken to the orphanage, Truth was struck by the changes that had occurred in her life during the past several days. Good changes. Changes made by reaching out and caring about the needs of someone other than herself. "There are so many children in need at the orphanage. I go each day and help, and usually I bring at least one of the children home with me for several hours."

"You must write and tell Grace. She will be much relieved to hear of your astonishing recovery." He tugged at his collar. "During the journey to Nicodemus, she spoke of little other than you." He laughed nervously. "And the railroad. She wanted to talk about the railroad, too."

"I'll write a letter to Grace this evening and tell her about the orphanage and the work I'm doing there." Truth settled back in her chair. "And Nicodemus? What did you think of our town?"

"With the exception of being primarily populated by our people, I found it quite similar to the other small communities that dot the prairie. All of them are dependent upon good weather and a decent yield on their crops. And all of them fear they'll shrivel up and die if the railroad bypasses them." He shrugged. "And they're probably correct."

"But that's not going to happen in Nicodemus, is it?"

"I have no idea. These matters take time and money. We told the residents of Nicodemus what things would be beneficial, but the decision remains in the hands of the railroad."

His answer wasn't what Truth had expected, nor was it what she had hoped to hear. John was supposed to be an advocate, argue on behalf of their town, help them. Instead, he seemed indifferent—as if he cared not at all whether the railroad passed through Nicodemus or some other prairie town. Something had changed since he'd departed Topeka.

Truth clasped her hands together and watched him closely. "I was expecting you or Mr. Ditmore would bring a much more encouraging report."

"I'm not one to build false hope. I find it too painful when things don't work out."

His cold words hit their mark. Truth tightened her clasped hands until her knuckles ached. There was no doubt John was referring to the false hope she'd given him about building a relationship with Grace. Her meddling ways were coming back to haunt her. Too bad Aunt Lilly wasn't here. She'd take great pleasure in seeing Truth receive her comeuppance.

Truth took a deep breath. "I owe you an apology, John. I behaved badly, thinking only of myself, and I hope you'll forgive me. I was consumed with the thought of keeping Grace in Topeka, and I didn't consider whom I might hurt in the process. Not Grace, not you, not Silas, not anyone." She sighed and forced her fingers apart. "But please say my selfish actions won't affect the possibility of the railroad passing through Nicodemus. I couldn't bear to think I might cause such a tragic event."

"Your apology is accepted, Truth. Believe me, I don't have enough influence to defeat any plans made by the railroad officials. I merely assist with negotiations and prepare the legal paperwork." A sad smile curved his lips as he met Truth's gaze. "Lilly warned me Grace and Silas had spoken of marriage. However, I did think I might have a chance with her. I held out hope even through Grace discouraged my attention."

At the sound of Jake's wail, Truth said, "I had best see to him. Will you excuse me for a moment?"

John jumped to his feet. "I have another appointment. Don't bother seeing me to the door. I can find my way out." He reached into his jacket pocket and removed the letter Grace had given him. "I promised your sister I would deliver this to you."

At the sight of Grace's familiar script, Truth clutched the letter close to her chest. "Thank you, John—for everything."

He nodded. "Please give Grace my regards when you write."

Before she could respond, Dovie hurried from the kitchen, the crying child now flailing as he reached for Truth. John hastily bid them both good-bye. Truth lifted Jake from Dovie's arms, cooing to him as she paced the length of the room, still clutching the letter in one hand. She would read it the moment the youngster ceased his crying.

Young Jake's body grew heavy in Truth's arms, and his soft baby snores signaled he had been in dire need of a nap. Truth gently laid him on the divan and pulled her chair close by. Though he'd likely sleep for at least half an hour, she dare not leave him where he might fall onto the floor. She had considered taking him upstairs and placing him in the bed they'd had specially made for their own child. But she couldn't do it—not yet. Perhaps one day soon.

For a moment, she stared down at the sleeping child. His tiny lips curved into a small bow, and his long lashes formed miniature fans across his cheeks. Such a beautiful child. Though she'd never know, she wondered what their own little Daniel might have looked like when he reached this age. She wiped away a tear that had formed in her eye and forced away her musings. No good would come from dwelling on such things. She was thankful to have young Jake in her life as well as a letter from Grace. This was a good day.

Her anticipation continued to build as she removed the multi-paged letter from the envelope, delighted Grace had written more than only a brief note. She pressed open the pages.

Dearest Sister,

It is my fervent prayer that by the time you receive this letter you will have come to terms with my departure and have forgiven me. Know that I am praying daily that you will soon recover from your grief over the loss of little Daniel. Though one child can never replace another, perhaps God will bless you with a baby before too very long.

Since you are reading this letter, I know that John has visited with you concerning the fact that I dashed his hopes for any future with me. I truly attempted to discourage his affections while still in Topeka, but I believe he preferred to think that once I compared him alongside Silas I would have a change of heart. Of course, John did not realize I am not a fickle woman!

Jacob shifted on the divan, raising his arm until his thumb met its mark. His eyelids fluttered and then tightly closed as he noisily sucked his thumb. Truth brushed a feathery kiss on his plump cheek. Settling back in her chair again with Grace's letter, she began the next page.

Now for my most important news. I wish you were here so you could share in my joy. Unfortunately, this letter must suffice. Silas and I plan to wed in July! We have set July 10 as our wedding date. It is my greatest desire that you and Moses will come home for the wedding. I am anxious to know if you will agree to stand with me at my wedding. Please send me your response at an early date. Silas is a good man and we are well suited. I believe he will make me a fine husband.

As for information regarding your housekeeper, Fern: I could write volumes, but time does not permit. Suffice it to say you are fortunate to have her in charge of your home. She took great care to treat all with the utmost care and kindness. She is, without doubt, a changed woman. She inquired into your health and sends her regards.

Truth read the remaining pages, each sheet filled with news of family and friends. She giggled when she read Miss Hattie had already begun to plan Grace's wedding. One thing in life remained constant: Miss Hattie would never change.

Please answer promptly and tell me if you will plan to be in Nicodemus for my wedding.

With loving affection,
Your sister Grace

Truth folded the letter and tucked it back into the envelope. She would talk to Moses this evening at supper and then write to Grace.

— 32 —

Hill City, Kansas

Macia lined the large woven basket with a checkered linen towel. Where could Lucy be? She'd said she would arrive no later than ten o'clock to help prepare for the picnic. Perhaps Macia should go ahead with the preparations. Otherwise they'd have little time for their outing. When Lucy had suggested the picnic, Macia had explained she must return home by two o'clock. She couldn't disappoint Gerta; the housekeeper had made plans to go home for an extended visit and would depart today. Macia had agreed to take over meal preparations during Gerta's absence, and if Macia wasn't back before the appointed time for Gerta's departure, the housekeeper would feel obligated to wait and ensure all was in order.

As if summoned by Macia's thoughts, the housekeeper entered the kitchen and surveyed the area. "I see young Lucy hasn't arrived to lend a hand." Retrieving a sharp knife from the counter, she picked up a loaf of crusty bread and began to slice it. "I'll spread these with some butter, and you can slice the ham. There's a jar of pickles you might want to take along. Oh, and slices of my apple cake."

Macia patted her stomach and groaned. "I don't think we need much more food. Otherwise, we'll fall asleep after eating and never get back home."

"*Ach.*" Gerta slapped her palm to her forehead. "Then maybe it would be better if we left the cake at home."

"It's me!" Lucy's shoes clattered as she stepped off the carpeted hallway and into the kitchen. "Sorry I'm late, but I had to help Jeb with some chores." She looking longingly at the uncut cake. "You're saving the cake for supper tonight, I s'pose."

Macia and Gerta looked at each other and burst into laughter.

"What's so funny?"

Macia shook her head. "I guess we'll take along *one* slice, Gerta. At least *I'll* be able to remain awake."

Lucy fidgeted as Gerta sliced a small wedge and placed it on a crisp cloth napkin. "Could we take two? I'm very hungry."

With a chuckle, Gerta expertly cut another portion and positioned it alongside the first. Drawing the four corners of the napkin upward, she tied them into a loose knot and deftly tucked the wrapped cake inside their basket.

Lucy grabbed the basket by both handles and beamed at the

housekeeper on their way out of the kitchen. "Thanks, Gerta. We'll be back before two o'clock."

Macia picked up her bonnet as they passed through the hallway. Head bowed, she pulled the flower-bedecked straw hat onto her head and was tying the ribbons when she looked up and saw Jeb sitting atop the wagon. Holding the reins in his hands, he grinned and tipped his floppy hat.

She stopped midstep and stared, wide-eyed. While he jumped down from the wagon, Lucy pulled Macia forward. "Jeb said if I helped with chores this morning, he'd go fishing with us. He's got the poles and bait in the back of the wagon." Lucy gave another gentle tug. "Come on."

Macia trailed behind the girl, wanting to yank her hand away and run back inside. She didn't want to be alone with Jeb. And if she knew Lucy, the girl would finagle some way to make certain they were alone—except perhaps when it came time to eat the apple cake. Apple cake! Now she realized why Lucy had wanted Gerta to pack two pieces. How long had Lucy been planning this scheme?

Jeb walked beside Macia as she rounded the wagon and then helped her up. His touch stirred unexpected pleasant memories of the past—memories she'd carefully tucked away. A part of her wanted to yank Lucy aside and chastise the girl for such impudent behavior. Lucy realized Macia had been avoiding her brother ever since Garrett's abrupt departure. She no longer trusted her judgment when it came to men. Back in Kentucky, she'd thought Jackson Kincaid was everything a woman could want in a husband, but she had discovered he was a fraud. Then she'd decided Jeb loved her enough to wait for her return from Europe, but Fern had come to town and turned his head. And then she'd thought Garrett might possibly be the man for whom she was intended. But when Macia couldn't hurry into a commitment, Garrett had taken off to pursue his dreams—much to Lucy's delight, of course.

Lucy had talked of nothing but wedding plans for Jeb and Macia until Macia finally had no choice but to set the issue of marriage to rest. She'd patiently explained that the entire matter was a closed book. When Macia had completed her talk, she'd been pleasantly surprised, for she believed Lucy had taken note and agreed. However, it now seemed she'd not listened at all.

Lucy chattered unceasingly until they arrived at the river. With a fishing pole in one hand, she jumped down from the wagon and scurried off before Macia had even descended. Jeb reached up and took her hand. After stepping down, she teetered on the uneven ground, and he put his arm around her to steady her.

He pulled her a little closer. "Please don't be angry with Lucy. This was my idea. In fact, she didn't want to agree to any of this. I forced her to let me come along."

Tilting her head to avoid the sun, Macia looked into his eyes. "I didn't know Lucy could be forced to do anything she didn't want to."

He chuckled, still holding her close. "All I had to do was say that if I didn't get to come along, she couldn't come, either." He shrugged his broad shoulders. "Not a very brotherly thing to do, I suppose. But desperate situations call for desperate actions."

She gave a slight twist, hoping to move farther away. His nearness was discomfiting and made it impossible to think straight. However, he only tightened his hold.

"You may as well relax. I'm not going to turn you loose until I say my piece."

"Then have your say and release me."

"First off, I want you to know I am genuinely sorry for what's happened between us. I'm not taking all the blame, because I don't think you should have let your mother send you off to Europe. But I took up with Fern for all the wrong reasons. I wanted to hurt you the way you hurt me. So I made up my mind that when you returned to Hill City, you wouldn't find me waiting for you. I wanted to prove I could move on with my life, too. That was a mistake, and for that, I'm truly sorry."

She could tell his words were heartfelt. His voice trembled with emotion as he struggled through the speech. "I accept your apology, Jeb. And I'm sorry, too—for all the pain I caused both of us."

He sighed. "Good. Because that leads me to this next part." Without warning, he tipped his head down and kissed her with a passion she'd never before experienced. When he finally pulled back and released his hold, she wobbled backwards. With a broad grin, he pulled her close again. "Maybe I'm going to have to hold you close to me the rest of the day." He winked. "And that would be just fine with me."

She placed her palms on his chest. The steady beat of his heart thumped against her fingertips and spread surprising warmth through her body. She flushed at the recognition of his effect upon her and quickly lifted her hands and moved away.

"I believe I'm quite steady on my feet now." She motioned toward the wagon. "Why don't you bring the blanket and picnic basket, and we'll see if we can locate Lucy."

He reached forward and grasped her hand. Macia's fingers tingled at his touch. She pulled away, wanting to shake off these feelings she thought she had buried months ago. He needed to let their apologies be enough. They'd made real progress today, and if nothing more occurred, maybe their wounds would heal.

Hoping to hold him at bay, Macia quietly explained her view. As she did, though, he shook his head while a slow, easy smile curved his lips.

"One day I want to marry you, Macia. Maybe we're not ready right now, but I need you to know my intentions. Even more, I need to know if you're willing to give me—give *us*—another chance. What do you say?"

Her cheeks smoldered. She knew they were likely as red as the apples Gerta had peeled for her cake earlier in the day. She couldn't tell him no; she didn't want to. "I say we should give it a try." She held him at arm's length, her palm once again pressing against his chest. "So long as we move slowly. No more mistakes."

He nodded and pulled her close. "No more mistakes," he whispered before capturing her lips with another tender kiss.

CHAPTER

— 33 —

Topeka, Kansas • July 1883

T ruth settled in beside Moses and peered out the train window. It seemed a lifetime had passed since they'd first come to Topeka. And yet it had been only six months. "Amazing how much life can change in such a short period of time," she said.

Moses folded his newspaper. "Indeed, it is." He tucked the paper on the seat beside him. "And would you say your life has changed for the better or the worse over these past months?"

"Some of both, of course. But right now, I am extremely happy."

"I know how difficult it's been for you to be away from your family. Grace's wedding will be a wonderful celebration, and I'm pleased you'll have time to help her prepare for the festivities."

"Only a few days. And if I know Grace, she'll have everything done before we arrive. If not, Miss Hattie will have taken command of the affair." Truth grinned.

The baby stirred, and Truth looked down at his cherubic face. How blessed they were to have this wondrous child. When she'd thought she couldn't survive the loss of her own baby, Jacob had wiggled his way into her life and wound his tiny fingers around her heart. And now he was theirs. The adoption had been completed only two days earlier, and the Sisters of Charity at St. Vincent's Orphanage had declared Jake a most fortunate little boy. But Truth knew better: she and Moses were the fortunate ones. God had blessed them with this little boy, who needed their love and affection at the time when they most needed him. She still didn't understand why her little Daniel had to die, and likely she never would. She could do nothing to change what had happened to Daniel, but she could change Jacob's life for the better.

Only Aunt Lilly had declared the idea foolhardy. But once they'd made their decision, Moses told her he wouldn't tolerate her disapproving attitude. In no uncertain terms, he'd said she had best accept Jacob as their child if she intended to spend any time in their home. And after Lilly had come to terms with the arrangement, Jacob managed to win her affection with his quick smile and wet kisses.

The baby whimpered, and Lilly immediately moved to the seat across from Truth. "Let me hold him." She took the child from Truth and hugged him close. "You just want your Aunt Lilly, don't you?"

Moses grinned and shook his head as Truth grasped his arm. She leaned close to her husband's ear. "Who would have ever believed

Aunt Lilly would make such a fool of herself over little Jake?"

"I know. Wonderful to see the hand of God at work, isn't it?"

She raised her brows and nodded. She hadn't thought of it that way, but Moses was right. God had been hard at work in all of their lives. And soon they would be home.

Truth peered out the window at the seemingly unending expanse of prairie grass that stretched along either side of the railroad tracks. Carving out a life in this harsh land had been a genuine testament to their perseverance, and Truth was thankful those days were behind them. Though she knew there would be hard days to come, they had learned they could survive. They'd broken through the tough prairie sod, and they'd made monumental strides. Indeed, daylight had come.

A MESSAGE TO MY READERS

aylight Comes is a novel based upon the settlement in the late-nineteenth century of two towns formed by a group of African-American and Caucasian men with a vision to settle western Kansas. Their plan called for one city, Nicodemus, to be predominately settled by Negroes and the other community, Hill City, to be predominately settled by Caucasians.

While grounded in fact, this book is a work of fiction and not a historical documentary. However, I have made every attempt to honestly portray the harsh circumstances these early settlers faced and the intense courage they displayed as they struggled to settle on the western plains.

As reflected in this novel, the residents of Nicodemus realized early on that the railroad would mean prosperity and growth for their community. By 1887, prospects seemed bright that the Missouri Pacific Railroad would include Nicodemus on its route. The railroad wanted $132,000 in public subsidy from the eight towns located along the Graham County section. Nicodemus's share would have been $16,000. Residents of Nicodemus voted to borrow the money by issuing bonds and believed that their future had been secured. However, the Missouri Pacific delayed and eventually terminated construction of the line at Stockton, Kansas (twenty miles east of Nicodemus).

Once again, hope swelled when surveyors from the Santa Fe Railroad visited the area. However, the Santa Fe, too, backed out. The town's final hope lay with the Union Pacific. Unfortunately, those hopes were dashed when the Union Pacific laid track six miles southwest of Nicodemus, adjacent to the temporary rail camp of Bogue. By the end of 1888, many of the merchants and residents had departed Nicodemus, but a core of faithful citizens remained in spite of their town having been snubbed by the railroad.

Nicodemus continues its crusade to survive with a current population of approximately thirty. Nicodemus is the only African-American frontier town in existence today.

For additional information about these communities, visit the Kansas State Historical Society Web site at *www.kshs.org* or the National Park Service Web site at *www.nps.gov/nico/*.

ACKNOWLEDGMENTS

Special thanks to:

The stalwart pioneers who willingly sacrificed to settle the Kansas prairie

The staff of the National Park Service, Nicodemus Historic Site

The staff of the Kansas State Historical Society

Mary Greb-Hall

Mary Kay Woodford

Angela Bates-Tompkins

Deletria Nash

Books by Judith Miller

FROM BETHANY HOUSE PUBLISHERS

BELLS OF LOWELL*

Daughter of the Loom

A Fragile Design

These Tangled Threads

LIGHTS OF LOWELL*

A Tapestry of Hope

A Love Woven True

The Pattern of Her Heart

FREEDOM'S PATH

First Dawn

Morning Sky

Daylight Comes

*with Tracie Peterson

Looking for More Good Books to Read?

You can find out what is new and exciting with previews, descriptions, and reviews by signing up for Bethany House newsletters at

www.bethanynewsletters.com

We will send you updates for as many authors or categories as you desire so you get only the information you really want.

Sign up today!